CAPTIVATION &
MAGGIE AND THE MASTER

by

SARAH FISHER

Published by **CHIMERA**
ISBN 9781780807355

I0630249

CAPTIVATION
CHAPTER 1

Peter Tourne ran his hand over the shaft of the whip, his handsome face closed and expressionless. Against the wall the blonde girl began to writhe, pulling frantically against the manacles that secured her. Her struggles raised a fine slick of sweat over her slim body.

He let the end of the whip drape across her narrow shoulders - just the lightest of caresses. He watched with pleasure as her breasts spread and pressed against the cold wall in an effort to avoid his attentions. The girl whimpered, closing her eyes to block out the images. They both knew what was to follow.

'Please, Peter,' she hissed, her words barely more than a sigh. It was difficult to decide whether she was begging him to stop or imploring him to begin.

He swung the whip, watching the tip flick back in a wide arc. As he brought it down the fine leather caught the girl squarely across the shoulders. Her cry came an instant later as the pain coursed through her. Her body bucked away from him, her instinctive movements exposing the soft pink crevices between her heavy buttocks. A thin red weal lifted on her flesh. Peter Tourne smiled, relishing the delicate flush that crept across her body.

She broke into a sob. 'No, Peter,' she shuddered, tears coursing down her face. 'Please! Don't hurt me. Please...!'

He swung the whip back again, concentrating on the satisfying hiss it made as it cut through the still afternoon air.

'It'll be all right,' he said softly, almost to himself, feeling the excitement building low in his belly. 'It'll be all right. Just trust me.'

The girl screamed again as the whip found its mark for the second time.

In her studio, Alex Sanderson heard the phone ring and then the tone of the answering machine as it cut in.

'*I know you're there, Alex. Pick the bloody phone up,*' snapped a familiar voice.

Alex grinned and climbed off the stool near her drawing board.

'Morning, Laurence,' she said, cradling the receiver on her shoulder as she wiped her hands on a rag. 'You sound as if you're in a good mood today. What can I do for you?

At the end of the line her agent snorted angrily. '*I had arranged for you to come in to see me first thing this morning. Remember?*'

Alex groaned and felt a sickening lurch in her stomach. She'd been on Laurence Russell's books for less than a year. He was an established agent with connections in all the right circles - as a virtual unknown she'd been lucky he'd taken her on. She grimaced - besides being a damned good agent he was also extremely good looking in an intimidating sort of way, and it didn't do to upset him.

'God, I'm so sorry Laurence, I'd completely forgotten about it.'

Laurence Russell sighed. *'You really must learn to take business commitments more seriously, Alex. You're not in college now, you know.'*

'I know, I really am sorry,' she said apologetically.

'Okay, enough said. Now, I've got a commission for you.'

'I'll get my notebook.' Alex stretched across the workbench on which the phone, the answering machine, and a thousand other things were piled with careless abandon.

'It's for a mural.'

Alex frowned. 'Oh God, not more *trompe l'oeil* for the rich and famous.'

'No. One of my existing clients saw the piece you painted at Vernis Restaurant and asked me if you could do something similar for him.'

Alex paused. Vernis had given her a free rein. She'd created a tableau of medieval images in rich golds and reds on a huge wall in their function room. It had been one of her most successful pieces of work so far.

'I'd be delighted,' she said enthusiastically. 'I've still got all the preliminary sketches. Who's the client? Have you got the address?' She teased a pen out of a pot on the bench and scribbled it into life.

Laurence laughed. *'Not so fast, not so fast, there is a slight problem with this one.'*

Alex groaned. 'I knew it. Go on, tell me.'

'That's why I wanted you to come in this morning, so we could discuss it. The site is in a place called KaRoche, D'arnos.'

Alex pouted. 'Run that by me again.'

'It's on a Greek island. My client lives there in his villa.'

'So, are you saying I've got to do it all on panels, and then we'll ship them out?'

'No, not exactly. The client, Mr Peter Tourne, has suggested you fly out there and work on site.'

Alex let out a low whistle. 'In Greece?'

'That's right, all expenses paid. Would that be a problem?'

Alex glanced around her tiny studio apartment. Rain lashed at the skylight above her drawing board. She grinned. 'No, I think I could manage that,' she said. 'Would you like me to come over right now?'

Less than a week later Alex found herself leaning against the handrail of a little Greek ferry, surrounded by local people making their way back from the mainland. Despite it being the beginning of the tourist season, hers was the only foreign face amongst the passengers on deck. She stretched, letting the warm fresh breeze tug and tumble through her long coppery coloured hair. Above her the sky was clear and cloudless. She closed her eyes, enjoying the sensation of the sun on her body.

This has to be the life, she thought, drinking in the heat. The sea was as blue as any of the brochure photos she'd ever seen. Ahead, a cluster of islands rose from the water like glistening white pebbles.

When the ferry chugged slowly into port, it looked as if the harbour was sleeping in the midday heat. At the far end of the jetty Alex could make out a motley collection of dusty cabs waiting for the passengers to disembark.

She glanced at the piece of paper in her hand and murmured under her breath, 'The Villa KaRoche, D'arnos.' She wondered if she would be able to make the local taxi-drivers understand her phrase book Greek.

White painted houses gleamed around the quay. Above the harbour the landscape was verdant green with dramatic outcrops of rock pressing up between the trees and foliage. Dotted here and there were villas, clinging precariously to the rocky hillsides. It was stunningly beautiful.

Must remember to send Laurence a postcard, Alex thought wryly, shouldering her bag and picking up her suitcases.

At the far end of the pier a man in peculiar mongrel uniform, made up of a smart military jacket worn with tattered cream cotton chinos and sandals, was holding a cardboard sign that read 'Alex Sanderson'. She pushed her way towards him, relieved that she wouldn't have to tussle with the language, and extended her hand.

'Alex Sanderson,' she said cheerfully.

The man's eyes roamed over her body, drinking in the details, lingering on the curve of her breasts where a thin cotton shirt clung to her warm skin. Alex shivered as he licked his lips and spoke.

'Not taxi,' he said in an accent so thick that she could barely make out what he was saying.

She pointed to his sign. 'Alex Sanderson,' she repeated more slowly, enunciating each syllable.

The man raised his eyebrows and muttered something she didn't understand, while his eyes continued to work across her travel-weary body. Feeling uneasy under his undisguised interest, she pointed to herself, repeating her name for a third time.

The man's reaction was to pull a face and then say very slowly, 'Alex Sanderson. I pick him up from ferry, today.'

Comprehension dawned: someone had assumed Alex was a man! She pulled her passport from her bag and showed the driver her photograph and name. 'It's me!' she said slowly and loudly as though speaking to an idiot. 'I'm Alex Sanderson, Alexandra! I've come to paint a mural for Mr Peter Tourne, at...' she showed him the piece of paper upon which was written her destination, '...KaRoche!'

The man barely glanced at her passport, but at the mention of his employer's name, rolled his eyes heavenward and snatched her suitcases. Reluctantly Alex fell into step behind him.

Parked a little way from the jetty, surrounded by village children, was a sleek black Mercedes. The driver opened the boot and slung her suitcases inside. Alex winced, obviously she was a great disappointment to him, and as if reading her mind, he glowered at her.

'You should be man,' he snorted disjointedly.

Alex shrugged philosophically and climbed into the car, which the man immediately gunned into life.

The main road meandered up around the island, taking in spectacular views of the coast and the sea below. Alex peered out from the cool confines of the car's luxurious interior, while in the front her driver turned up the radio and watched her face in the rear-view mirror.

Finally, as they rounded a steep bend, Alex saw a huge pair of wrought iron gates with the name 'KaRoche' set into them.

'Is this it?' she asked, hoping to finally break through the uneasy silence between them.

He nodded. 'You should be man,' he repeated.

Alex sighed with exasperation. 'Well, I'm not - I'm really very sorry.'

The drive through the island had not prepared her for KaRoche. The villa, built on a series of broad terraces, seemed to grow straight out of the hillside. Set amongst a tumble of vines, trees and fragrant shrubs, it was breathtaking. Alex gasped. The driver lifted an eyebrow at her reaction, but said nothing.

The car purred to a halt outside the front door. The driver unceremoniously dumped Alex's bags on the doorstep before disappearing inside. Alex, perturbed by the man's rudeness, picked up her luggage and followed him nervously into the villa.

The interior was cool and dark. It took Alex a few seconds before her eyes adjusted to the gloom. She glanced around the hallway. It had a red tiled floor and pale cream walls, set with a wealth of ferns and plants in huge urns. In the centre of the room a fountain and pool added a crystal babble of water to the cool and elegant interior.

Alex hesitated on the steps, uncertain what she should do next. Her thoughts were interrupted by a low melodious voice.

'Alex Sanderson?'

She turned towards the sound. Across the room, a tall slim man in his early forties stepped forward. He was dressed casually in a soft white shirt and cream slacks. His features were refined and aristocratic, the impression heightened by his dark hair, shot through with grey, which he wore in a ponytail.

Alex smiled and extended her hand politely. 'Mr Tourne?'

The man nodded, lightly pressing her fingers between his. His touch was cool and disturbing. Alex fought the urge to shiver as he lifted her hand to his lips.

'There seems to have been a misunderstanding,' he said, with the slightest trace of an accent. His dark eyes moved slowly and confidently across her face and body. 'You are Alex Sanderson, the artist?'

'Yes, and from the reaction of your driver, I assume you were expecting a man?'

Peter Tourne nodded, his eyes lingering on the curve of her breasts.

'Does this cause a problem?' she continued unsteadily. 'My agent said you'd seen my work at Vernis.'

He nodded. 'Indeed I have, and I was very impressed. But you're right - please forgive me, I had no idea you were a woman. Your agent - Mr Russell - is perhaps having a joke with me?' His eyes held hers. 'But I am forgetting my manners. I trust your journey was a good one? My housekeeper has already prepared the guest cabin for you.' He paused, and she detected the slightest flicker in his dark eyes. 'Or perhaps you might prefer to stay here, in the main villa?'

Alex shook her head, a peculiar feeling of unease growing in the pit of her belly. 'No, the guest cabin will be fine, thank you.'

The man pressed a bell set into the wall. Alex wasn't sure what kind of reception she had expected, but this certainly wasn't like anything she could have imagined.

'Please don't think me rude, but I am working at the moment. My housekeeper will ensure you have everything you need. We will discuss my plans for the mural when you have had a chance to recover from your journey. You will join me for dinner?'

Alex nodded. 'Of course, that would be very nice. Thank you.'

A small woman, dressed in a faded cotton smock, appeared from the far side of the fountain. She eyed Alex suspiciously and then murmured something to Peter Tourne in Greek. He glared at her, his icy look stifling the words in the old woman's mouth.

'This,' he said, with a hint of annoyance aimed at the elderly woman, 'is Alex Sanderson. Would you please show Miss Sanderson to the guest cabin.'

The woman snatched up Alex's cases and bustled across the tiled hall.

'I'll see you at dinner tonight,' said Peter Tourne.

Alex turned to thank him, but he'd already vanished into the shadows. With her sense of unease growing alarmingly, she followed the old woman out into the sun-drenched garden.

The cabin, almost completely obscured by creepers, stood away from the main house, up a steep flight of steps. The housekeeper hesitated at the open door of the little building, her face closed and stormy.

'You shouldn't have come here,' she said flatly. 'It's very bad place.'

Alex glanced back at her, uncertain that she'd heard the words correctly. 'I'm sorry?'

The woman lifted her hands in resignation. 'Mr Tourne, he very bad man,' she snapped. 'Better if you were man.'

Alex sighed and glanced around the sparse but comfortable interior of the little cabin. 'Well, I'm not, and I've come to paint - not to discuss the morals of my client. What time is dinner?'

The woman pulled a face. 'Eight. You find everything you want here; kettle, tea, bottled water.' She paused. 'He make you do terrible things, you know.'

Alex swung round, her degree of unease increasing her annoyance. 'I'm painting a mural, that's what he's paying me for!'

The woman stepped back out onto the sunlit steps. 'Mr Tourne, he a wizard, he make a magic on women. Much better you had been a man.' She closed the door behind her.

Alex wondered what on earth she had got herself into. She glanced anxiously back through the windows, watching the elderly woman bustle down the steps, and wondered why her agent, Laurence, hadn't let Peter Tourne know that she was a female. As for the housekeeper - what could she make of someone like that?

Grateful to be alone, Alex slipped off her sandals and turned her attention to the chore of unpacking.

Outside, the afternoon sunlight touched everything with a brilliant exotic hue. Creepers and flowering plants that had been trained around the windows and doors filled the air with an heady exotic scent. Alex yawned, suddenly feeling tired and dirty from the journey. Her arrival at KaRoche had not been exactly auspicious, but surely things could only get better from here on in? Once she had unpacked her things, Alex slipped off her clothes and headed for the shower.

Under the refreshing torrent of water Alex soaped her aching body and thoughtfully considered her host. Peter Tourne was an odd man, but it was difficult to define exactly why. She thought about the housekeeper, and smiled at the woman's melodramatic pronouncements.

Clean and rejuvenated Alex turned off the taps, wrapped herself in a towel, and lay down on the comfortable bed. She closed her eyes, and within seconds travel weariness led her gently into sleep.

In the villa Peter Tourne poured himself a drink and looked out into the garden below his office. Amongst the intricate tumble of foliage and heavily scented flowers he could make out the tiled roof of the guest cabin.

He was both surprised and delighted that his resident artist had turned out to be female - and Alex Sanderson was quite beautiful. He let his mind conjure up a picture of her slim muscular frame, her deliciously firm breasts, and the way her hair curled into the curve of her long white neck.

He had planned on a mural, something cool and green in the long gallery overlooking the swimming pool, but now - he smiled and sipped his aperitif - now perhaps the mural could wait awhile. He sat down by the desk and opened the top drawer. Inside, in a small box, were a set of ornate body rings. He stroked the cool silvery metal and let his mind picture a dozen erotic possibilities. He imagined Alex tied and subdued, completely at his mercy, bucking against her restraints as he taught her the lessons he loved so well. She would learn to be compliant and obedient, and she would learn to understand that his word was law, and that her body was his alone to command or give away as the fancy took him.

He imagined her nipples, puckered and dark, pierced by the silver rings. He could see them glittering in the gloom, and below them the subdued flash of the one that would nestle in the lips of her sex. The rings, and other sets like them, were reserved as a gift, as markers for members of his discreet and beautifully trained stable of girls. He lit a cigar and then picked up the phone.

7

He knew someone else who might enjoy the education of Miss Alex Sanderson.

Alex woke just after seven. Outside the light had subtly changed to a softer evening glow. Although the sun was lower it was still pleasantly warm. Alex pulled a thin cotton dress off its hanger and slipped it on. Glancing at her reflection in the bedroom mirror, she twisted her thick copper hair into a bun and secured it with a clip. The effect was soft and feminine. She stretched and smiled at herself. Recovered from the journey she felt relaxed and ready to face whatever Peter Tourne might have in mind. At least this time she would be ready for him. As she leant forward to add the lightest touch of lipstick there was a knock on the door. It was barely ten to eight, fleetingly she wondered if it was the housekeeper returning with another dire warning.

'Come in,' Alex called.

The door opened slowly to reveal a beautiful blonde girl, dressed in a cream evening dress. The girl hesitated in the doorway.

'Hi, can I help you?' said Alex, spraying on some cologne.

'I come to invite you to join Peter for drink before dinner,' she said slowly, struggling with the English words.

Alex turned and extended her hand. 'I'd love to, my name's Alex - Alex Sanderson.'

The girl smiled and blushed. 'I know. I'm Gena.'

'Right, and are you Mr Tourne's girlfriend?'

The girl's colour deepened and she shook her head. 'No.' She paused for a moment, considering her reply. 'I am his slave. He understand me.'

Alex turned to pick up her handbag. Gena's words must have lost something in translation; surely she really meant servant, or secretary.

In the hall of the villa Peter Tourne was sitting by the little fountain waiting for the two girls to arrive. Beside him stood another man, dressed in expensively casual clothes. As Alex and Gena came in through the French windows the other man stepped proprietarily towards Gena. Peter Tourne smiled a welcome towards Alex.

'Good evening,' he purred as he got to his feet. 'You look lovely.'

Alex smiled politely. 'Thank you,' and then glanced back at Gena and her companion.

'Forgive me. Let me introduce my friends,' he said, taking her arm. 'May I present Starn Fettico and Gena?'

Starn Fettico's smile was fixed as he stepped forward to shake her hand. His eyes moved slowly over her face, as if he could look inside her mind, whilst his other hand rested casually on Gena's hip. Alex sensed there was something wrong, something unsettling, but didn't resist as Peter Tourne led her up a sweeping flight of stairs into a sitting room.

'Would you like an aperitif?' he asked, indicating a tray on the side table. Alex nodded and accepted the glass he offered before turning back towards

Gena and Starn, who had followed them up.

What she saw made her gasp. Starn was standing close behind Gena, his hands reaching around and cradling her large breasts, his tongue lapping at her throat. Alex looked away quickly, feeling her colour rise. Peter Tourne lifted an eyebrow as Alex fought to compose herself. Behind her she heard Starn moan.

Alex coughed. 'Look, Mr Tourne,' she began uncomfortably, 'if I'm interrupting something...' her voice faded away.

He casually sipped his drink. 'They disturb you?'

Alex shook her head. 'No, but I'm employed to—'

Lifting his hand he silenced her. His eyes were dark and hypnotic and did not leave hers as he spoke. 'Gena, take off your dress.'

Alex blushed furiously. 'Please, this is hardly what I'm here for!' she blustered indignantly and turned to leave.

Behind her, framed in the doorway, Gena had already slipped off her evening dress. Alex swallowed hard, feeling the heat flooding through her body. The blonde girl was naked beneath the creamy silk sheath, her body as pale as snow, but what was more startling was that she was shaved, her sex as pale and vulnerable as the rest of her body. Alex froze, feeling a thread of panic bubbling up inside her. The girl's heavy breasts were pierced with silver rings and below her outer labia were similarly adorned.

'What is this all about?' Alex hissed, suddenly remembering the housekeeper's words to her earlier.

Peter Tourne laughed softly. 'Perhaps you would like to paint Gena for me?'

'Perhaps not! Usually I'm told before I get a life model!' She struggled to regain her poise. 'And they don't usually strip off just before dinner!' As she spoke she noticed the way Starn's eyes slithered over the ripe and vulnerable curves of Gena's body. She shivered and then swung back to face Peter Tourne. 'Is this some kind of test?'

He lifted his hands. 'No, not at all. Gena, come here.' The blonde moved closer, so close that Alex could smell her expensive perfume and feel her body heat.

'Closer,' he coaxed.

Alex stepped aside as Gena glided towards him, and then watched mesmerised as he stroked the girl's heavy breasts without her offering any form of resistance. His fingertips lingered over the puckered outline of her nipples and the glittering silver rings that hung from them. Gena, eyes downcast in submission, moaned softly as he caressed her.

Alex shivered, wondering why the exhibition excited her almost as much as it repulsed her. 'Please,' she murmured, uncomfortably aware of the fluttering sensation deep in her sex. 'I think I've seen quite enough of this.'

As she spoke, his fingers moved down over the soft swell of Gena's belly. He looked across at Alex, his eyes reduced to dark pinpricks.

'Don't tell me this doesn't move you, Miss Sanderson,' he said softly, his fingers tracing the plump outer lips of the other girl's quim.

Gena shuddered under his touch and to her horror Alex felt the flurry of excitement flare white hot deep in her belly.

She swallowed hard and took a deep breath, controlling her voice as she spoke. 'I'd have to be dead not to be moved by something so erotic, Mr Tourne, but I think you're making a grave mistake.'

Peter Tourne chuckled, his slim fingers parting the moist lips of Gena's sex, sliding unhindered past the heavy ring. Alex gasped, unable to look away as he caressed the girl's compliant body. It felt as if his fingers were on her own flesh.

He looked at her levelly. 'A mistake? I don't think so,' he said softly. 'Do you?'

Alex felt her colour draining. From the corner of her eye she could see Starn moving around to get a better view. He moved silently, like a predatory wolf.

Alex stared at Gena. 'Is this what you meant when you said Mr Tourne understood you? That you were his slave?' she asked. The blonde girl nodded, her excitement was obvious.

As Alex spoke, Tourne tipped his glass, trickling the wine over Gena's gorgeous body. She shivered as the sticky liquid trickled down over her breasts, leaving a slick glistening trail in its wake.

'Wouldn't you like to lick it off?' he said quietly, staring at Alex. 'Wouldn't you like to taste her sweat and her juices mingling with the bittersweet taste of the wine?'

Alex didn't move.

Tourne shrugged and then glanced at Starn who was now standing beside him. Starn grinned and stepped towards Gena, his tongue already protruding between thick red lips. Alex closed her eyes and looked away as Starn's lips closed around one of Gena's engorged nipples.

Tourne laughed. 'Open your eyes, Miss Sanderson, we'll leave them to play while we have our dinner.'

Alex flinched as his fingers closed around hers, but she did not protest as he led her away. As they moved across the room, she heard the soft little noises of pleasure as Starn sucked greedily at Gena's willing body.

Alex let her host guide her up another set of steps to a large airy dining room. From the windows she could see the garden below, and beyond that the rich blue waters of the sea. Her discomfort was rapidly turning to anger.

She swung round to face him. 'I think,' she said with great deliberation, 'that you would be better getting someone else to paint your mural, Mr Tourne. I am not particularly impressed with your behaviour so far, and I am not sure that I can give you whatever it is you want.'

Peter Tourne smiled. 'So spirited - I like that. Just tell me truthfully that Gena's activities didn't excite you?'

Alex swallowed. 'I'm really not into women or voyeurism,' she said flatly.

He laughed. 'Perhaps not. But her obedience, her compliance, tell me that didn't fascinate you.'

Alex slammed her glass down onto a side table. 'I'm really very sorry, I'm not sure what it is that you want from me, Mr Tourne. What do you want me to say? That you shocked me? Well, you did. That what I saw excited me? Well, as I said just now, you'd have to be made of clay not to find...' she hesitated, wondering why it was she didn't just walk out.

Why on earth was she arguing with him? All she had to do was collect her things and leave. What held her back? She realised with horror it was because there was something about this bizarre and stunning scenario that had electrified her. She could still feel the little frisson of excitement that Gena's performance had ignited in her belly. She couldn't define what it was, or perhaps she was afraid to admit that the blonde's unquestioning obedience to Peter Tourne had mesmerised her. Sex without responsibility, an unquestioning obedience to another's desires, wasn't that a dark dream she had always denied existed in her heart? Alex felt herself flush scarlet.

Tourne smiled warmly and guided her to the exquisitely arranged table.

'Don't worry about that now - let's eat,' he purred softly. His powerful self-confidence frustrated Alex. 'Let me tell you about my plans for the mural. Perhaps you and I can take a walk down to the gallery after dinner?' His tone was now matter of fact. Alex nodded dumbly and didn't resist as he poured her another glass of wine.

Dinner was exquisite, served by Peter Tourne's houseboy who moved like a ballet dancer between them. Despite the convivial surroundings Alex found it impossible to concentrate on the meal, her mind drawn again and again to thoughts of Gena and Starn in the room below. Peter Tourne reverted to the role of perfect host, spoiling her and asking questions about her trip, her life her art.

She willed herself to relax. The combination of wine, food, and conversation slowly eased away the tension. If it hadn't been for the recurring images of Gena's smooth excited body and Starn's glittering predatory eyes constantly bubbling up in Alex's mind, the meal would have been perfect.

The young servant served their coffee on the balcony outside the dining room. As Alex and Tourne stood side by side, looking out over the evening, watching the light changing on the sea and sky, he turned to her.

'You will stay.' It was a statement, not a question.

Alex bit her lip, not letting her eyes meet his.

'Yes,' she said, in a voice barely above a whisper. As she said it she knew that she'd agreed to more than just painting the mural - and the forbidden, unspoken possibilities excited her.

He nodded. 'Good, in that case I think we should go and look at the gallery,' he said, indicating she should follow him. When she finally caught his eye she could see the gleam of desire there. Alex swallowed hard as she allowed him to take her arm, her heart beating like a drum in her chest.

Below the terrace a winding stairway threaded a path around the outside of the villa. Alex tried to keep her eyes on the sea, resisting the temptation to look in through the windows in case she caught sight of Gena and Starn.

Finally Tourne led her under an archway and into a wide gallery overlooking a swimming pool below. She could immediately see why he'd commissioned the mural; the gallery was a superb site. She turned round, about to congratulate him, but something about the way he looked made her swallow the words. His eyes glistened, while the rest of his face seemed devoid of expression. She stared at him, all her previous fears returning.

'What do you want from me?' she stammered, backing away from him.

He smiled thinly, though she noticed the smile did not quite reach his eyes.

'Oh Alex, you disappoint me. Can't you guess? I want to instruct you, to teach you to obey, to let go—'

'Like Gena?' she whispered.

He watched her slow retreat along the gallery, the heady mix of emotions propelling her back towards the steps.

'You'll be better than Gena - far, far better,' he said. 'Come with me.' He turned his back on her and walked towards a door set in the far end of the gallery wall.

Alex felt the flutter of fear growing with every passing second into something more electric and enticing. She stood frozen by the archway, afraid and yet some how compelled to follow. He opened the door, his face now obscured by the evening shadows. They stood there, unmoving, for what seemed like an eternity. She could feel the pulse rising in her throat.

'Come.' His voice was stronger now; firm and authoritative. He held out his hand and Alex knew then that she was lost. Slowly she walked towards him through the fading evening light, knowing that some part of her longed to experience whatever Peter Tourne had to offer her.

Above her, unseen amongst the verdant green climbers, the housekeeper watched from her apartment window. The old woman let out a thin, bitter sigh.

'You should be a man, Alex Sanderson,' she whispered, and closed the window quietly.

CHAPTER 2

The room beyond the gallery was gloomy, lit only by skylights that caught the last rays of the evening sun. Alex stood in a pool of light, losing Peter Tourne in the shadows.

'Where are you?' she said unsteadily, unable to disguise the tremor in her voice.

'Here,' said he from behind her.

Alex trembled. 'Please... what do you want me to do?'

He stepped closer. 'Everything,' he purred. He stroked her neck. He touched her gently, his tenderness surprising her. She let out a thin hiss, jumping at his caress. His fingers were cold, almost unnaturally so.

'You will learn to obey me,' he murmured. 'You won't need to ask me what I want, you will know instinctively. You will be available for everything I desire.' He paused. 'All the time, night and day.' As he spoke his fingers caught in her hair, jerking her head back. The pain made her gasp. 'Do you understand?'

Alex shrieked as his fingers tightened in her curls, his lips pressed into the soft curve of her neck. 'Tell me you understand,' he said.

She grimaced and twisted as his fingers tightened again, pulling her closer. She whimpered and then whispered, 'Yes - yes I understand! Please, you're hurting me!'

Peter Tourne stepped away from her. His expression was one of triumph.

'Good,' he said. 'Now take off your clothes.'

Alex flushed. 'No,' she said immediately.

He pouted in displeasure. 'You tell me you understand,' he said flatly, prowling around her. 'But you obviously don't understand, or you would obey me at once - like Gena does.'

Alex started to justify herself, but to her horror he sprang forward fluently and grabbed hold of the neck of her dress, his fingers closing tight round the fabric. Alex shrieked, feeling the cloth bite into her flesh. Before she had a chance to resist he pushed her violently against the wall. Hitting the cold bricks knocked the breath out of her. She struggled to regain some shred of control, fighting her fear and surprise.

Peter Tourne's fingers tightened on her dress, wrenching at the thin material. She twisted and turned under his grip.

'Let go of me!' she hissed in terror. Looking up into his face all she could see were his eyes, bright and catlike in the gloom. She knew he was relishing her struggles - the realisation unnerved her and she froze. He gave the material another sharp tug and the summer dress ripped to the waist, revealing her delicate lacy bra beneath.

He grinned as she instinctively tried to cover herself. He pushed her hands away and traced the soft curve of her breasts. She whimpered as his fingers tracked across her nipples, roughly brushing and nipping at their sensitive peaks. She let out a sob and then pushed against his chest, trying to break away.

He let go of her, the smile fading. 'Why are you fighting me, Alex? We both know this is what you want. Take off the rest of your clothes.' His voice was low and hypnotic. 'Do it now before I lose my patience with you.'

Alex watched him like a hunted animal, glancing instinctively towards the door. He followed her eyes.

'You may leave if you wish,' he said evenly. 'But we both know you want to stay, don't we?'

He was right - and she knew now why Gena had said Peter Tourne understood her. She shivered and caught hold of the ragged remains of her dress, pushing it down over her hips. In the gloom he watched her coldly.

She stood on the stone floor in her underwear, the dress around her ankles.

He waved his hand towards her. 'And the rest, take everything off,' he whispered. His eyes travelled down over her body. 'Come along don't disappoint me now, Alex. I have so much to teach you. Tonight is merely your first step of a wondrous journey.'

It suddenly seemed to Alex as if her body had a will of its own. She undid her bra, letting it drop to the floor, then slid down her knickers; both excited and at the same time frightened and acutely conscious of her vulnerability. From the shadows she could see his eyes and knew he approved of what he saw.

'Turn round slowly,' he murmured.

She did, teasingly, deftly. When she had her back to him Alex felt his hands on her shoulders. She yelped as his fingers pressed into her flesh. His voice was a threatening murmur in her ear.

'Don't flirt with me, Alex. There is no need, you are mine already.'

As he spoke he pushed her to the floor. She stumbled forward onto the cold flagstones, landing heavily on her hands and knees. Before she had time to recover he grabbed hold of her arms and jerked her towards him. His face was impassive as he produced leather cuffs from the pocket of his dinner jacket. She watched in stunned surprise as he slipped them round her wrists and then tied them down into rings set in the floor. It wasn't until she had let him put them on that she realised he had rendered her completely helpless.

'Mr Tourne,' she gasped in horror, suddenly afraid. His response was to turn his attentions to her ankles. When she started to strain against the straps he tightened those around her wrists, jerking her face closer to the floor, so that she was crouched on all fours. She let out a thin desperate sob as his hands moved slowly across her body, 'oh Alex, you will be perfect - just perfect,' he said on an outward breath. 'I knew it as soon as I saw you. It will give me the greatest of pleasure to be your first teacher.' He paused as his fingers circled her hardening nipples. 'A good teacher can always bring out the best in his pupil, I will bring out only the very best in you.'

Alex shuddered as his hands moved slowly round to the curve of her buttocks. As he got to his feet, the feelings of vulnerability and exposure overwhelmed her. She trembled, listening to his footfalls in the gloom. She wasn't sure what was more frightening - the sound of his moving away from her, or the sound of him returning.

The shadows subtly changed and she guessed he had altered the lighting in the room so that he could admire his new prize. As he stepped closer she held her breath. He let something cold trail along her spine. She could hear his breathing in the empty silence and closed her eyes, fighting the growing sense of terror.

Peter Tourne let the leather belt rest for a moment on Alex's beautiful bound body. He smiled to himself, relishing the fear and the anticipation he could feel rising from her. She looked divine. Her buttocks were thrust up towards him, accentuating the erotic 'hour glass' shape of her body. Between the cheeks of her bottom he could see the lips of her sex, just parted to reveal the delicate inner pleats, and above them the tight dark bud of her anus. Her sex was

14

framed with a delicate flush of coppery curls. The kiss of the belt made her shiver and wriggle, revealing a little more, opening her a little wider. Already he could make out the glistening moisture of her juices, gathering in the sensitive folds, betraying her excitement.

He let the belt move on, relishing his sense of power, drinking in the heady cocktail of emotions her body created in him. As the seconds passed, he could see her desperately fighting to retain some vestige of dignity, or control. Her breath came in shallow gasps as if she were straining to hear his every move. He saw her relax momentarily, and in that instant he drew the belt back and hit her squarely across the plump orb of her buttocks.

Alex screamed, twisting away from him, her belly dropping to protect the soft exposed areas of her body, while her face pressed down onto the cold floor. Before she could brace herself for the next stroke he brought the belt down again, harder this time.

Peter Tourne grinned, relishing the desperate noises of her humiliation and pain, delighting in the angry red glow that flushed across her skin. She struggled and writhed, trying to avoid the next blow, but he had bound her too well, and the stroke exploded across her buttocks, which clenched as she fought to evade his attentions. Between the heavy curves he could still see the lips of her sex gaping, glistening in the soft light. As if she could read his mind she clenched her muscles tighter still, trying to hide the secret parts of her body from him as the belt swept viciously back again.

Alex gasped as the next blow struck. The soft leather bonds creaked quietly as she jerked and vainly tried to twist away from her assailant. Tears of pain and shock bubbled up in her eyes. Whatever she had anticipated from Peter Tourne's instruction, it had not been this. The overwhelming red hot bite of the leather belt made her gasp and buck with surprise. She could feel the glowing pain in her buttocks spreading up through her whole body. She tried hard to control herself, not wanting to cry out to let him know how much it hurt - or more telling still - how much the hot stinging sensations and the sense of exposure and helplessness were awakening something deep and hungry in the darkest recesses of her mind.

She arched against his next blow, letting out a strangled sob as her face and breasts pressed down onto the cold floor. Behind her, she heard Peter Tourne moving. For a few seconds, she thought the beating was over and let out a thin whine, letting the tension ease in her back.

Before she had time to catch her breath the belt caught her again, hard and hot. The sensations spread out from her bottom in incandescent ripples. She knew she was losing control and let out a dark wailing moan as he hit her again, her rational thoughts were being overcome by the scorching arc of sensations. She bucked and strained against her restraints, letting instinct take over. She felt as if everything she had ever known was slipping way, as Peter Tourne ministered his own particular brand of instruction.

Suddenly there was stillness. The only sounds in the room were those of her desperate and ragged breaths. This time Alex didn't relax, fearing that it would herald another volley of blows from the belt. Instead she held herself taut, waiting for whatever torment might follow.

After a few seconds Alex felt fingers splaying the glowing, stinging contours of her buttocks. She shuddered as long fingers dipped inside her - she knew she was wet - and whimpered as they commenced their exploration.

From behind her, she heard the raw metallic sound of Peter Tourne's zip, and then the brush of his engorged cock against her inner thighs. The contrast to the hot angry glow of her bottom was electrifying. Brutally his fingers opened her sex and he slid into her without prelude. She bayed as his cock filled her and stifled a sob as he grabbed her hips and dragged her exhausted body back against his.

The friction of his clothes against the tender, glowing swell of her bottom made Alex shriek, but Peter Tourne was oblivious to her discomfort. He hauled her into his groin again and again, plunging deeper and deeper into the wet confines of her body, his fingers crushing down on the delicate folds of her inner lips.

Despite the sense of pain and humiliation, or perhaps she realised with a sense of horror - because of it - she could feel the pleasure growing deep inside. Dark crystals of excitement glistened and grew as he locked his fingers into her hair, arching her back against his thrusts. She screamed again as he jerked her hair harder, his fingers now moving to nip and drag at her breasts. As his fingers tightened around her engorged nipples she felt the glowing crystal sensation in her belly explode into glistening shards that ripped through her. Her bruised, aching body closed frantically around the shaft, sucking at him, milking him, and a second later she heard him groan and then join her in a wild and desperate race towards oblivion.

Finally Alex collapsed onto the cold hard floor, huddled to save her screaming shoulder muscles and glowing buttocks. Peter Tourne remained buried deep inside her, his breath ragged and uneven on her bare skin.

Eventually he slowly peeled himself away from her, leaving her feeling open and exposed.

Alex eased herself into a more comfortable position, afraid to speak. He turned his attention to the leather ties around her ankles and relief swept through her. It was short lived though; once he had untied the straps around her ankles, he moved away. She stretched out on the flagstones, waiting for him to come to free her hands. Instead he lifted her head and slipped a thin pillow beneath it. She started to protest but he seemed unreachable. She wanted to see his face, his eyes, but could only focus on his expensive shoes as he walked slowly past her. She felt him fold a blanket over her bruised and sated body, and then she let out a thin unhappy cry as she realised he intended to leave her there, tied to the floor.

'Mr Tourne,' she sobbed, all her senses alight and afraid. 'Please, Mr Tourne. No, don't leave me here! I'll do whatever you want. Please, untie me...' but her cries fell on deaf ears. She heard the sound of his footfalls recede as he left the room, and seconds later she was plunged into total darkness. She screamed out at the indignity, the unfairness, and the memory of the dark insistent call of her own desire.

Finally she realised it was pointless. Peter Tourne had gone. She began to cry aware that in her struggles to call him back she had dragged the blanket down off her shoulders.

Between her legs the sting of the belt still throbbed, while her sex, wet and bruised, still glowed with the aftermath of her excitement. She lay still for a few seconds, hot tears rolling down her cheeks, wondering whether she could untie herself. Her fingers fumbled with the thongs, but in the dark she couldn't see how or where the ties where held.

She listened to the unfamiliar sounds of room and the night outside. It seemed as if she were totally and utterly alone. The tears came back with a vengeance - tears of fear and tears of shame, for she knew that some part of her relished what the virtual stranger had done to her, however much her rational mind denied it.

In the darkness Alex rolled over onto her side, making the joints in her shoulders scream. She tried to slide down under the blanket to keep warm. Her body protested as she felt the cold floor beneath her biting into her hips and knees. She shivered. It was going to be a long, long night.

Easing herself onto her back she concentrated on the stars, which were clearly visible through the skylight above, trying to take her mind off the pain and the strange dark thoughts that emerged again and again in her mind. Slowly, despite everything, she felt exhaustion creep over her aching body, and did not resist as she slipped into a light and fitful doze.

It was still dark when something woke Alex. Instantly she knew exactly where she was. Her body was cold, her muscles and bones aching with strain and cramps. She peered into the gloom, wondering if Peter Tourne had taken pity on her and returned to untie the straps. His name conjured up the images of her excitement and of his body pressed intimately against hers, but more compelling still, the memories of the belt biting into her delicate flesh.

Alex swallowed hard and listened. Close by she could hear someone moving about in the room. She licked her dry lips, struggling to find her voice.

'Mr Tourne?' she asked uncertainly into the darkness. The movement in the shadows stopped. Alex held her breath. 'Who's there?' she eventually called uneasily, unable to keep the tremor out of the words.

She heard the soft footsteps moving closer, and then in the starlight caught the glint of dark eyes. Instinctively she drew herself up into a small tight ball. Her unknown visitor moved closer - so close that she could hear his breathing. He was excited, struggling for control.

There was the sudden flare of a match, and in the flickering light she saw the heavy features of the driver who had picked her up earlier in the day. His lips were slack and wet, his eyes bright with excitement. He lit a candle and stood it on the flagstones beside her. His face contorted into a lustful grimace as he took in the details of her vulnerability.

Alex shuddered, fearing the sickening desire in the swarthy man's eyes. He knelt at her feet, which she protectively curled up against her body, and grabbing hold of the corner of the blanket, whipped it away. Alex let out a thin, strangled squeal.

'No - no please,' she whimpered, as his lecherous eyes roamed eagerly over her naked and bound body.

He grabbed hold of her ankles and jerked her legs apart so that she was totally exposed. He leered at the junction of her legs where her sex, the curls damp and matted from Peter Tourne's use of her tied body, gaped to reveal the damp folds within.

He grinned triumphantly, but didn't look at her face. Instead his stubby fingers moved to her sex, splaying the lips wider so that he could explore her. His thumb brushed her clitoris and she gasped as a lightening bolt of sensation roared through her slim body. The driver grinned again and plunged his fingers inside, playing in the mingled juices of her orgasm and that of his employer's. He spread the moisture out over her thighs, letting it dribble onto her cold skin then bent closer, sniffing at her sex like a dog. Alex flushed scarlet as he lapped tentatively at the pooled moisture.

'Please,' she whispered as he pressed her legs further apart, drinking in the flavours from her helpless body. 'Please leave me alone. Mr Tourne said he would come back. Mr Tourne...'

The man snorted in derision as Alex's voice faded - they both knew she was lying.

Her body felt leaden, touched by cold and cramp and the hideous hypnotic caress of the peasant driver. He sat up, his lips obscenely slick, and grinned as he moved his fingers to open the cheeks of her bottom. For an instant his finger caressed the dark forbidden closure behind her sex. Alex, suddenly terrified, squealed and tried to wriggle away from him, realising the direction in which his desire was developing.

The horrible man sniggered, pressing his finger speculatively against the tight, puckered closure.

'You should be a man,' he murmured dryly.

Alex snorted. Fear fuelling her anger, she tried to disentangle herself from his disgusting fingers.

Grunting, he knelt on his haunches, the same wet fingers working now on his ragged trousers. His cock - dark and meaty - sprung forwards like a wild animal. She let out a terrified sob as his hands moved back to her bruised sex. Dipping into her with his dirty fingers he spread the fragrant juices of his employer and Alex around her quim, lubricating, spreading. The thick liquid cooled as it touched her body, leaving shiny slick trails. He grinned and leant forward, outlining her nipples with the juices. She could smell the warm ocean musk of her sex.

The driver crouched over her, the pungent smell of his sweat overwhelming and repulsive as he lapped at her breasts, dragging them into his mouth, milking her, sucking her breasts as if he were feeding.

Alex tried to unseat him, but it was impossible, he was far too large and heavy to fight off. Roughly he spread her thighs, twisting her body painfully and stroking her juices over his dark and threatening cock. She shivered and then gasped as he drove his phallus home into her open quim. His yellowed teeth closed around her nipples, biting hard. She yelled out in desperation, and her body bucked instinctively, impaling her further onto his vile cock.

The man sat back a little, his eyes fixed on the junction were his body entered hers, and then he began to pump deep into her, his fingers returning again and again to the tight dark closure behind her quim. She bucked as his finger tried to work its way inside her. He leered down at her and then spat onto his other hand.

She flinched - she knew now that he was intent on buggery and there was nothing she could do to stop him. As she felt him working the saliva into her anus she struggled to blank out the terrifying sensations. His fingers eased their way into the forbidden place, making her flinch as he finally breached the tight band of muscle. With each passing second her rogue body gave him greater access, until through the walls of her sex she could feel him stroking his own cock.

She shuddered, bright tears of pain rising behind her eyes, fearful that if she fought too hard he would hurt her.

Unbuttoning his shirt he pulled her up towards him so that he could brush his torso against her pale breasts. His chest and shoulders were thickly carpeted with wiry, grey hair that scraped her sensitive nipples. He sniggered again as their skin touched, then he leant forward to kiss her. His thick wet lips tasted of beer and cheap cigars - and the heady aroma of her own body.

As his lips brushed hers again she bit him. His reaction was to growl angrily and sink his teeth into her bottom lip. She felt the bright metallic taste of blood, then surrendered, knowing it was pointless to resist; tied to the floor, what Alex didn't give him, he could easily take. Fighting her revulsion she opened her mouth to his filthy, invasive kisses.

Above them, unseen by Alex or the driver, Peter Tourne watched the desperate attempts of his gorgeous new guest to unseat her unwanted lover. He lifted a wine glass to his lips and smiled. He'd let his driver know the girl was available, and the man had needed no further encouragement to go and explore his employer's new house guest. He moved closer to the glass at the edge of his hidden gallery. He knew his driver's special predilection and wondered if he would indulge himself.

Below, the man pulled his thick cock out of Alex's slim pale body and lit another candle. It seemed he wanted to see his victim better; wanted to revel in her bondage. Peter Tourne sat back and watched as the man moved closer to Alex and slid his hands under her buttocks. He lifted her pelvis up to his lips, plunging his tongue deep into her sex, lapping and lubricating, whilst, even in the gloom, Peter Tourne could see his driver's fingers moving back between his victim's buttocks, fingering the dark tight closure that he preferred.

Alex's face was contorted, fighting the sensations that threatened to overwhelm her. Her body moved instinctively against the man's broad tongue, unable - despite her fears - to resist the temptation to accept his caresses. Beneath her the driver's slick cock glistened in the candlelight, waiting for Alex to submit, waiting for the moisture to smooth the way into her most secret place.

Peter Tourne held his breath. The driver lifted the girl higher, holding her open so that his mouth could lap greedily at her tight little arsehole. Peter Tourne could sense Alex's horror and the driver's growing desire. The man moved back to Alex's clitoris; she moaned, afraid even now to relinquish her control. Her beautifully pert breasts were flushed, her nipples puckered and dark from the excitement and the cold.

Peter Tourne could sense Alex's climax approaching as her body began to tremble. Just at the instant when it seemed she would tumble headlong into ecstasy, the driver pulled his mouth away from her and spat into his hand again, rubbing his saliva between her buttocks. The girl's expression changed and froze as she anticipated what was to follow. The driver eased forward, his raging phallus all but invisible between the cheeks of her bottom.

Alex mouthed the word *NO!* but the man was relentless, and then Peter Tourne heard her throaty groan as the driver slid his cock into the darkest recesses of her body. She seemed afraid to move, her face pale and desperate, unsure of whether she hated this new sensation... or whether she adored it. The driver looked down at her, his eyes glittering with triumph. He crept closer, sliding deeper and deeper, then his thumb moved to Alex's clitoris, and roughly, persuasively he began to circle it. Peter Tourne could see the pulse twitching in her throat, while her face was still frozen with confusion.

Fear flickered in her eyes as the driver began to move - gently at first, slowly, feeling his way into her. Suddenly she twisted instinctively against his circling thumb and then screamed out as she dropped down, unable to hold herself up any longer, completely impaling herself onto his cock. Her body twitched and turned with the first desperate flurries of the orgasm the driver had lit in her belly, while he began to work more insistently, set now on his own frantic release. His fat lips contorted into a maniacal grin as he reached his climax, fiercely driving his phallus as deep into her as he could.

Finally there was calm; an eerie brittle stillness that hung like smoke between the two figures on the floor. The driver slid out of Alex's body without a second thought. She shuddered, her breath coming in ragged sobs.

The driver grinned at her, his fingers moving back and forth across her body, slipping inside her sex. He leant forward to drag her nipples deep into his mouth, sucking and biting. Alex lay motionless, staring up into the dark night. The man shrugged, pressing his lips against her sex for one last caress, and then slung the blanket over her. She didn't respond, her eyes were focused on the middle distance as the driver leant over her to blow out the candles, his cock dragging, wet and flaccid across her exhausted body.

CHAPTER 3

'Wake up.'

Alex blinked, hearing a female voice close by. She tried to turn over, feeling unbelievably uncomfortable. Her waking mind was flooded with images from the night before. She gasped and struggled to sit up. Her arms were so numb she could barely feel them. The tight leather straps still held her firm. She groaned and then licked her lips, aware of the stale taste of sleep in her mouth. Above her the face of the elderly housekeeper came into view. Alex blushed furiously. The older woman shook her head.

'I tell you Mr Tourne is wicked man,' she said flatly. 'You should not come here.'

'Have you come to let me out?' Alex asked, wincing at the ache in her bladder.

The woman sighed theatrically. 'Yes, I let you out, but first Mr Tourne he want you shaved. Turn onto your back.'

Alex began to protest, thinking about Gena's slick and exposed sex.

The woman above her just shrugged. 'If I don't shave you, you stay tied on floor. Mr Tourne, he say so.'

'I want to use the bathroom,' snapped Alex, turning so that she could catch the woman's eyes. The housekeeper shrugged as if she didn't understand.

'The toilet,' Alex repeated desperately. 'Please!'

Comprehension dawned at last, and the older woman smiled. 'I shave you first, then you go to toilet.' As she spoke she jerked the blanket back off Alex's body. She looked over the girl's slim well - proportioned frame with something akin to professional coolness.

'You have nice body,' she said as she fingered Alex's tender breasts. Alex flinched at her touch, the single pain awaking a thousand others. 'Mario, he come to you also?'

Alex pulled a face. 'Mario?'

'Mr Tourne, his driver, he like to bite, you have bruise here.' She poked the sore area again and Alex winced.

'Mario, he like boys best.' She lifted a questioning eyebrow at Alex, who felt hot threads of humiliation course through her. The old woman's words conjured up the driver's leering, ugly face and his thick meaty phallus pressing home into her. Alex reddened; there had been no way to stop him. She could still feel the pain.

The old woman pouted. 'But he don't mind girls too, and you can't stop him like this,' she indicated Alex's bonds. 'Now, I shave you.'

Alex looked way, feeling her colour deepen under the woman's scrutiny. What could she say? She was as powerless to resist the old woman as she'd been to stop Mario or Peter Tourne from doing exactly as they wished with her.

The woman made a clucking, motherly noise. 'You stay very, very still. I

21

don't want cut you.'

Alex shivered at the possibility, listening now to the slosh of water. The woman returned.

'Open your legs, little one,' she said, prising Alex's aching thighs apart. 'Open them real wide.'

Alex closed her eyes as the housekeeper began to lather the coppery curls around her sex. Her hands were practised and confident. Alex shuddered as she felt the first cold rasping stroke of the razor and then froze, remembering what the housekeeper had said about staying still. She tensed, listening to each compelling stroke, resisting the desire to shudder at her exposure. She held her breath, willing herself not to move, trying not to even think, until the old woman finally struggled back to her feet.

'There, you are done now,' the housekeeper said with a smile. 'You need to rinse soap off.'

Alex wriggled. 'Let me get up now, please.'

The woman mumbled something and then reached above Alex's head. Alex felt the leather thongs give and them lifted her hands slowly until she could see them. Every muscle in her back ached.

'Thank you,' she whispered as she struggled to sit up. Her head span.

The woman crouched over her with a look of concern on her face. 'Slowly,' she said, 'don't rush.'

Alex nodded and finally, if unsteadily, sat upright. The icy touch of the floor was like a balm against her glowing buttocks.

The woman glanced across the room. Alex followed her eyes - the interior was bare except for a series of rings in the floors and walls and ceiling and an expanse of cupboards. At one end of the long room were two doors set into the wall.

The old woman handed Alex a thin cotton robe. 'There is bathroom there,' she said, pointing towards one of the doors, and then glanced down at the remains of Alex's dress on the flagstones. 'I bring something clean to wear.' She bundled up Alex's clothes and then, carrying them and the bowl of water, hurried away.

Once she'd left, Alex grabbed the robe and dragged it around her shoulders. Her body protested, every muscle and sinew felt knotted and sore. She clambered unsteadily to her feet, and hobbled towards the bathroom door. As she walked the slick fragrant remains of her night spent with Peter Tourne and Mario trickled out onto her thighs. She shuddered and pushed the door open.

In the bathroom the walls were lined with more built-in cupboards. She opened the first one - it contained perfume and toiletries, the next one a pile of thick luxurious towels. Alex turned on the taps, ran a deep bath and then gratefully slipped into the warm water. She sighed as the water eased away the pain. Stretching, she took in the startling, naked contours of her sex. The clean lines were shocking, and at the same time deeply erotic. She looked way, feeling the mixture of intense emotions bubbling up through her. Soaping herself, her fingertips sought out the aftermath of the damage from the previous night.

On her breast were the deep navy teeth marks of one of Mario's bites, other lesser bruises pinched and ached as she touched them. Finally she let the soap slide down between her legs. The naked mound of her pubis felt strange under her fingers. She opened her legs wider, wincing as she felt the bruising inside, and behind it the sensation of raw violation that she didn't feel ready to contemplate.

A picture of Mario's eager, lascivious face filled her mind. She shook her head and tried to drive his image away when she succeeded his features were replaced by the cool and aristocratic face of Peter Tourne. She swallowed hard and slid further down into the warm water, willing it to heal her body and soak away the desperate aches and stiffness.

Finally dried and feeling somewhat restored, Alex glanced into the mirror above the basin. Her blue eyes were bright, despite her lack of sleep. Her lips and breasts were bruised from Mario's attentions - but what surprised her most was that other than the obvious bruising she looked no different; she was unchanged by the events of the night before. Thoughtfully she ran a finger over the livid purple mark inside her bottom lip, wincing as she found the tender spot where Mario had bitten her. Her mouth still felt dirty. She shuddered as she remembered the driver's filthy kisses and the odour of tobacco and beer. She opened another cabinet and found a toothbrush and paste. Gratefully she spat into the sink and attempted to scrub away the last physical remains of the peasant's invasion of her body. She pulled the robe tight. Glancing back at the mirror she smiled; at least her body now felt clean - although her mind was a very different matter.

Outside the bathroom, on the floor, lay one of her favourite floral dresses that the housekeeper had obviously collected from the guest cottage. Alex picked it up and pulled a face - the woman had forgotten to bring her any underwear, and had already taken away the things she had been wearing the night before. She sighed and pulled the dress over her head, ignoring the complaints from her body as she moved.

By the rings in the floor where she had spent the previous night were her sandals, discarded at some point, but not forgotten. Alex slipped them on and then made her way out into the bright sunlight.

It took her a few seconds to work out exactly where she was - she had no desire to go back into the house - instead she went back to the steep path around the outside of the villa and climbed up until she found a way into the garden that would lead to the guest cabin.

Inside, on the table in the sitting room, someone had set out a breakfast tray with orange juice, coffee and hot light rolls. Alex ate ravenously, cramming the delicious bread into her mouth as if she hadn't eaten for a week.

She had barely had a chance to collect her thoughts and finish her breakfast before Gena appeared at the open door. Her sudden appearance made Alex jump. Gena's expression was dark and unreadable, but there was a split moment when their eyes locked, each female understanding fully what the other had recently experienced.

Gena was the first to break the silence. 'Peter wants to see you in sitting room.'

Alex hesitated. 'I'm not really dressed,' she began, glancing down at her thin dress. Through the lightweight fabric she could make out the shadowy outline of her nipples, and the curve of her breasts.

Gena's eyes flashed. 'He said you are to come.'

Alex nodded, remembering Peter Tourne's reaction to her disobedience. 'All right,' she said quickly, standing the cup down.

Gena turned so that the sunlight shone through her elegantly tailored dress. Picked out by the sun her silhouetted figure was stunning. Alex swallowed hard, knowing from the events of the night before that Gena too, was naked beneath her dress.

She followed the blonde down into the main house, struck once again by the peaceful qualities and the elegance of the hallway and the rippling sounds of the fountain. Ahead of her Gena mounted the staircase that led up to the sitting room.

The blonde opened the door and let Alex go in first. Peter Tourne was sitting across the room in an armchair, looking out into the garden below. Starn was standing behind him. His eyes roamed slowly over Alex and then to Gena as the two women stepped into the room.

'You wanted to see me?' Alex said softly.

Peter Tourne said nothing - he didn't even move. It was Starn who stepped closer, his eyes resting on the curve of Alex's body where it touched the thin fabric of her summer dress. Under Starn's unsettling gaze Alex was astounded to feel her nipples hardening, pressing forward to reveal themselves through the material.

'Did you have her shaved?' asked Starn over his shoulder to Tourne. His eyes gleamed as he noticed the outline of her nipples.

Peter Tourne was still looking into the garden outside. 'Show him,' he said flatly.

Alex felt herself flush scarlet, and she hesitated.

His voice lowered to a menacing purr. 'Don't make me ask you again, Alex. You know how I reward disobedience.'

Knowing she had no other choice but to obey, Alex gathered up the hem of her skirt, lifting it slowly to reveal the soft vulnerable curves of her naked sex. Starn licked his lips greedily. He stepped forward as if he intended to touch her. Alex flinched and instinctively stepped back towards the door.

Peter Tourne turned to look at her, his eyes resting first on her sex, and then her face. He smiled. 'Very good.' He glanced across at Gena. 'Take off your dress, Gena, then come here and stand by me.'

Without any hesitation Gena began to undo the buttons of her shirt-dress, revealing the heavy swell of her breasts. Alex stood motionless, her fingers knotted in the thin material of her frock, while Gena let her dress fall into a silky puddle around her feet.

Peter Tourne glanced back at Alex. 'I want you to kiss Gena,' he said softly. Alex shivered but didn't move. His penetrating eyes never left her face. 'Am I not making myself clear?' His tone hardened. 'Let me explain. I want you to kneel in front of her, part her thighs, and then kiss her, caress her. Use that tongue and those pretty lips of yours to bring her to the very brink of ecstasy.'

Alex gasped; she had thought he meant a real kiss on the lips - and that prospect had abhorred her - but what he actually meant completely astounded her. She dropped the hem of her skirt.

'No,' she stammered, 'I won't, I can't!'

Peter Tourne lifted his hands in resignation. 'Why do you insist on fighting me, Alex? What I ask is so easy. All you have to do is give yourself to me. Let me guide you show you, teach you. Ah well.' he looked at Gena and then at Starn. 'Lift your skirt up again, Alex.'

She did so very slowly, with great reluctance.

'Now Gena will show you how it's done.' He fixed her eyes with steely determination. 'And you will let her. Do you understand me?'

Alex couldn't bring herself to answer him.

'Do you understand me?' he snapped again.

This time she nodded and Starn stepped behind her. One of his hands slipped round her wrists, holding her fingers tight in the skirt. He jerked them higher until her whole belly was exposed. His other hand snaked around her shoulders until one of her breasts rested in his palm. He squeezed firmly, his thumb and fingers seeking out her nipple, which to Alex's horror, hardened again under his touch.

Gena walked slowly across the room. It was impossible for Alex to ignore her pale and delicate eroticism. Peter Tourne nodded towards a stool and the gorgeous blonde pulled it up in front of Alex, before arranging herself onto it on all fours.

She glanced up at Alex, her eyes glittering as she ran her tongue around her red painted lips. Alex let out a desperate whine and then closed her eyes as she felt Gena's warm breath on her belly. An instant later she gasped as Gena planted the lightest of kisses on the junction where her heavy outer lips met. Behind her she heard Starn sigh and felt him tighten his grip on her. He slid his knee between her thighs and forced her legs wider apart.

In contrast to Starn's touch, Gena's tongue was soft and enquiring, her mouth planting delicate kisses on the lips of her quim. Her tongue eased Alex's sex open, probing and seeking out the hard ridge of her clitoris. Alex gasped softly as the blonde found her goal and then started to nibble and suck at the little throbbing bud. Behind her Starn changed position, his fingers now dropping from the hem of her skirt to the naked contours of her sex. She tried to push him away but he was strong and persistent. His fingers slid down to hold her body open for Gena's probing tongue.

The blonde girl's attentions were frightening in their intensity. Within seconds Alex could feel the spiral of her excitement growing. Gena's fingers joined her tongue, stroking and caressing and teasing. Alex gasped, feeling as if she was losing the control of every part of her body. She found herself leaning back against Starn, and could make out the pressing of his penis through her dress. She moaned as Gena plunged her fingers up into her willing body, exploring her sensitive and moist interior. Her fingers stroked along the inner lips, dipping in and out of the wet slit between. Alex let out a long wild sob as Gena returned her attentions to her clitoris and dragged a perfectly painted fingernail across the throbbing hood that protected the little bud.

The sheer intensity of the sensations threatened to drown her. Alex writhed helplessly, opening her legs wider, her body's desire suppressing her mind's revulsion. She thrust herself onto Gena's waiting tongue, straining to catch every last electric caress.

Moaning and twisting, with Starn supporting her, Alex surrendered herself totally to the feelings Gena lit in her. All restraint and all embarrassment was pushed back by her body's single-minded struggle for satisfaction.

Suddenly Alex knew she couldn't resist the spirals of excitement any longer. She screamed, letting the heat of the climax engulf her. As though in a dream she heard Starn laughing softly, still holding her tight. Even before the last waves of pleasure had crashed through her she heard Tourne say:

'Very good, Gena. Now come to me.'

Alex opened her eyes in time to see the luscious blonde crawling towards her master. As she reached him she lay her head in his lap.

He looked up at Alex whilst he ruffled Gena's hair playfully - it looked as if he were stroking a kitten.

Alex watched, mesmerised, as Gena began to undo the zip of his trousers. Before she could free his cock, he tipped her head back and kissed her full on the lips. Alex shuddered, imagining the salty taste of her own juices on Gena's mouth.

Behind her Starn relinquished his grip. His voice was thick with excitement.

'Take off your dress, bitch,' he said huskily. Alex looked over at Peter Tourne in desperation.

He merely smiled arrogantly as Gena ran her expert tongue along his engorged shaft. 'Do exactly as Starn tells you,' he said quietly.

Alex thought about the night before. Hadn't he said that she would learn to obey him? She could hear his voice in her spinning head: 'you won't need to ask me what I want, you will know instinctively. You will be available for everything I desire. All the time, night and day'. Was this what he meant?

Alex pulled her dress up over her head and dropped it to the floor. Naked, she turned to face Starn.

'That's better,' he said, and sneered victoriously. 'Now come closer.' She did as he ordered, trembling as he lifted her right breast to his lips and lapped at the bruise Mario's bite had left. Cradling her breast in his fingers he closed his lips around her nipple, sucking it hard into his mouth. Below, he delved into the fragrant moist confines of her body. Her sex, so close to orgasm, tightened around him. Starn grunted appreciatively.

Eyes alight with sexual hunger, he guided her back towards a sideboard.

Resting her weight against the edge, he slipped his hands under her thighs, lifting them to encircle his waist. With one hand he unzipped his trousers, letting them slide towards the floor.

His cock was slim and arched towards Alex with a single glistening drop of moisture clinging to its tip. He let the swollen helmet nuzzle between her throbbing lips. The sensation made her shiver. He sneered again as he saw her reaction, and then pulled her forward roughly so that he could slip into her.

As her body closed around him, his face contorted into an expression of pure victorious pleasure. She glanced down and was shocked by the image of his slim phallus sliding into her, her naked sex gathered and puckered around the junction were their bodies met. Above his cock, the little bud of her clitoris throbbed, revealed and then hidden by each of Starn's eager thrusts.

Alex could sense it wouldn't be long before Starn lost control. Across the room Peter Tourne watched their coupling dispassionately, despite the ministrations of Gena. In his lap her red lips closed again and again on his erect penis. Only a slight tightening around his mouth and jaw gave lie to the sensations the blonde was lighting in him.

Alex held his stare, watching every nuance of his expression, whilst Starn forced himself deeper and deeper into her. His thrusts were wild and ragged now, making her already aching body feel sore and beaten.

From across the room, perched as she was on the ornate piece of furniture with Starn thrusting maniacally at her, Alex watched Peter Tourne swallow hard. He seemed to momentarily lose his concentration, and she knew he too was losing control. In his lap Gena moaned as she swallowed, lapping against the pulsating ejaculation of his phallus.

The sound of Gena's muffled little cry was enough for Starn. He lurched forward. Deep inside Alex felt the energetic throb of his orgasm breathlessly he leant against her, his heat seeping through into her naked skin. She gasped and trembled again as she felt his seed fill her to the brim.

Peter Tourne pushed Gena away, letting her collect her clothes, whilst Starn stepped away from Alex, his spent cock trailing its juices onto her thighs. He grinned lazily at her, his eyes glistening.

Peter Tourne stood up, still holding Alex's gaze.

'I want you to begin the preliminary sketches for the mural today,' he said, as if they were both stepping away from a consultation meeting. 'Perhaps you would start after lunch. I'm sure you could now do with a little rest - after all your exertions.'

Alex nodded, 'I'll begin this afternoon,' she said with equal coolness, and stooped to pick up her dress, slipping it easily over her shoulders. She followed him to the door, her expression as impassive as that of the man she knew she would learn to relish; the man she knew could guide her to the dark heights of ecstasy.

Back in her cabin Alex showered quickly, her mind desperately trying to blot out the exotic images of Gena crouched between her legs. She turned the water to a roaring bore to drive away the smell of Starn's body and the warm glow that still pulsed from deep within. Naked and still damp, she threw herself onto the bed and dragged the quilt up and over her body. Seconds later she fell asleep, her dreams alight with the new sensations Peter Tourne's tuition had awakened in her.

When Alex awoke the afternoon sun was streaming into the comfortable bedroom. Outside in the cabin's sitting room someone had opened the French windows and left a tray of food on the table outside on the terrace. The tray was complete with a bowl of tiny roses. Alex stretched, feeling the aches and pulls of the exertions of the last twenty-four hours.

As she dressed she caught sight of herself in the bedroom mirror - her shaved pussy gave her whole body a strange alien quality. She stopped for a few seconds to examine her reflection. Her eyes glittered, fresh from sleep. Below on one breast were Mario's teeth marks, like a livid blue badge. Lower, below her waist, her body ached, but even so it was still only the exotic naked lips of her sex that really marked the changes that had taken place.

She slipped on a light Indian cotton smock with sandals, deciding - in view of Peter Tourne's apparent tastes - that it might be better to leave her underwear off. After she'd eaten she collected her shoulder bag, picked up a sketchpad, pencils, and her tape measure, and then set off into the garden to begin work on the site of the mural.

The long gallery was deliciously cool. It was thrown into deep shadows, and it didn't take Alex long to find a comfortable spot to contemplate her new commission. She chose not to consider what lay beyond the door at the end of the gallery.

In Vernis restaurant she had painted a banqueting scene, showing wild revellers in beautiful medieval costume. The overall effect had been rich and colourful, not unlike a tapestry. But what would she create for Peter Tourne?

She smiled to herself - a Bacchanalian orgy would be most appropriate, she thought darkly, as she began to make a few preliminary sketches.

On the ceiling of the long gallery the reflections of the swimming pool below shimmered and glinted. She stretched, enjoying the luxurious setting and the quietly calming sounds of the water. She didn't hear Peter Tourne's soft footsteps as he came in through the archway, and she jumped when he appeared in her field of vision.

He smiled at her discomfort. 'I'm sorry, I didn't mean to startle you.'

Alex shook her head, glancing up at the enigmatic man who had discovered the way to set her body alight. 'I was miles away, thinking about what I could do with this.' She lifted her hand to indicate the blank walls.

He moved a little closer his eyes were dark and mischievous. 'How quickly your mind moves onto other things - I'm impressed. May I ask what you have decided to paint for me?'

Alex sighed. 'That isn't exactly how this works. You're the client, you tell me what you want, and then I do it.'

He stared at her. 'An arrangement I approve of.'

Alex blushed and lay down her pencil. She could feel his eyes on her body. She stood up to face him, feeling the little flurry of excitement and fear returning in her belly. He lifted a hand and ran it gently over her breasts. Her nipples hardened at his touch. Lower still he stroked at the contours of her sex. She moaned as his knowing fingers traced her heavy outer lips. He smiled at her, like a dark and dangerous wolf, and then stepped back as if satisfied.

Alex was astounded by the intensity of feelings he lit within her, realising too that he had been exploring her to see if she was wearing anything beneath the smock.

'I like my pupils to be ready for my lessons, whenever I want to instruct them.' His voice dropped to a low purr.

Alex shivered.

Tourne glanced towards the door at the end of the gallery.

Alex laughed nervously and tried to tear her mind back to the mural. She focused unsteadily at the blank gallery wall. 'What do you imagine when you look at this wall?' she said as lightly as she could.

The question seemed to break the spell. He stepped forward to touch the smooth white plaster. 'A forest,' he said. 'A magical, wild, green place, full of angels and devils and exotic mythical beasts.'

Alex nodded it was an idea that smacked of sheer genius. The gallery, with the water below and its backdrop of tangled rich green creepers, would be an ideal setting for his fantasy forest.

'That's a wonderful idea!' she said enthusiastically. 'Do you want people in your magical forest?'

Peter Tourne looked back at her, his eyes alight and glistening. 'Oh yes,' he murmured. 'What would fantasy be without people to enjoy it?' He touched the wall again. 'Lost souls playing games in amongst the trees.'

Alex looked at him levelly. 'Lost souls?' she murmured.

He shrugged. 'Players then, lost souls is not quite what I mean.' He paused and stared at her. 'What I am striving to create here at KaRoche is a game,' he said softly. 'A dark magical compelling game.'

Alex swallowed hard and forced her eyes to hold his, knowing that somehow they had strayed away from the mural and back into the electric desires of Peter Tourne's mind.

'And what do you want me to do with your mural, Mr Tourne?'

'I would like you to reflect my intentions,' he whispered. 'Hint at the magic that can be had if you just submit to it; lay yourself bare to its enchantment.'

Alex felt her colour rise. 'And if your players submit themselves to your magic?'

He moved closer, his fingers returning to the hard puckered buds of her nipples. 'Then they can choose how long their enchantment lasts. Some will choose to stay in my wood forever. Others will leave and plant a fantasy of their own.'

Alex shivered, but did not resist as his lips pressed to hers. His fingers on her breasts became rougher, twisting and nipping at the sensitive buds. Alex moaned, feeling the heat rekindling between her legs. She pressed herself to him. Instantly he froze and pulled way, his eyes darkening into unfathomable pools.

'Let us not forget, Alex Sanderson, who the master is here, and who the pupil is.'

Alex blushed. 'But I thought...'

He ran his hand down over her belly. His touch was totally possessive.

'There is no need for you to think, Alex, I will think for you. You have chosen to stay, now you must realise that you have joined my game and you will play by my rules.' He let his hand drop away and walked back towards the archway. 'I will see you at dinner.'

Alex nodded instinctively and picked up her drawing pad, clutching it like a touchstone against Peter Tourne's dark enchantment. After he left she stood staring at the blank wall of the gallery, her mind reeling with erotic images that he conjured in her mind, and a peculiar sense of frustration.

It took time for Alex to regain her composure. Despite Peter Tourne's unexpected intrusion she knew she had to get on with the sketches and lay her tape out to measure the walls. A residue of excitement glowed in her belly with an intensity that both surprised and unnerved her. Her hands shook as she scribbled down the measurements and then some ideas for the mural. The words 'dark enchantment' appearing again and again on her list. Finally she sat down by the poolside and began to sketch.

Drawing was like an addiction to Alex. Its magic pulled her in so that it was easy to forget everything else - or at least, almost everything else. She worked single-mindedly until the fading light made it impossible to continue. Glancing at her watch she realised with surprise that most of the day had gone. She lay the sketchpad down and collected her pencils together. As she took one final look at the pictures she had drawn she realised that every man's face bore an uncanny resemblance to that of Peter Tourne.

She stared at the drawings as if she was seeing them for the first time: Between two trees a nymph was tied and blindfolded, awaiting the attention of her master, her pert breasts pressing through the gossamer of her robe, her sex open and exposed. On the adjoining page a second girl lay spread-eagled. She struggled and fought, her hips lifting instinctively, while the satyr who crouched above her looked on with a riding crop in his hand. On the next sheet, in a shady woodland glade, two women embraced, one kneeling before the other, her tongue deep in the other woman's quim, while their master looked on with pleasure. Alex reddened furiously and snapped the sketchbook shut. Stuffing it into her shoulder bag she hurried back to the cabin in time to change for dinner. Back at the cabin Alex quickly got ready for dinner. Sitting by the dressing table, adding the final touches to her make-up, Alex wondered if Gena would come to call for her again. She leant closer to the mirror, adding a final touch of lipstick. The soft coral pink complemented her light tan. As she drew the stick across her lips she thought about Gena's mouth pressed close to her sex, its contours working on the delicate folds of her body, bringing her closer and closer to the moment of release. The intense images brought a flush to her cheeks. How was she going to face Gena or Starn after the earlier events in the sitting room?

Meeting Peter Tourne had changed her life forever. Trying to dismiss the erotic thoughts she picked up her bag and turned off the lights. Standing in the darkness she wondered for a moment what other lessons he had in mind for her. Outside, the night closed around her like black silk, adding to the sense of expectation. She nibbled her lower lip; was it possible to live so close to the edge? With every minute that passed something seemed to make her think about passion or pain. As Alex reached the doors to the villa she hesitated, hearing the sounds of voices from within. She wondered what she might discover inside.

The doors opened before she touched the handle. Peter Tourne's housekeeper stood in the hallway, her dark eyes expressionless. Alex nodded her thanks, wondering whether the old woman's tense demeanour was one of excitement or anger.

'They waiting for you upstairs,' she snapped and hurried away into the shadows.

Alex climbed the stairs and found Gena and Starn sitting on one of the long leather sofas in the sitting room. They were each cradling a glass of rich red wine. Alex felt herself blush even before anyone had a chance to speak.

Starn nodded towards the next flight of stairs that led up to the dining room. 'Peter is waiting for you, he would like you to go up to him.'

Alex went without hesitation, relieved not to have to make polite conversation with her two morning lovers.

Peter Tourne was standing by the window speaking into a mobile phone.

'Yes, it's working out fine, we're just about to have dinner,' he said, watching Alex's progress as she crossed the room. 'In fact she's here now, would you like a word with her?' He handed her the phone. 'It's your agent.'

Alex felt a sense of relief; Laurence Russell represented normality and real life. While in London he'd always seemed a little disturbing, on D'arnos even the sound of his name lifted her spirits. She glanced at her host, and immediately realised he had no intention of leaving. 'Hello?' she said.

'Hello, Alex. I thought I'd give you a day or two to settle in. How's it going?'

The tension in Alex's stomach eased with the sound of Laurence's familiar voice.

'I hope Mr Tourne's treating you well. He's a very important client of mine.'

Alex swallowed hard, staring at Peter, who was standing beside her.

'I'm fine,' she murmured. 'I've started the first sketches today.' She imagined Laurence in his London office. He often worked late, and as he made enquiries about the job she visualised him seated behind his impressive oak desk, his grey eyes flashing. Odd, she thought, until she'd met Peter Tourne she'd always found Laurence Russell intimidating. He had an upright, military bearing that made her feel uneasy, and sometimes she sensed, when she looked up at him, that he'd been watching her. She had wondered several times whether his interest in her was purely professional. Now she was just relieved to hear him - a voice of normality and reason amongst confusion. Laurence Russell's artistic empire couldn't be further away from the events at KaRoche.

As Alex spoke Peter Tourne lifted the hem of her dress. She shivered.

'The only thing is that they were expecting me to be a man,' she said.

Laurence laughed dryly. *'Really?'* he said. *'Perhaps I ought to have warned Mr Tourne that you're all woman. It hasn't caused you any problems, has it?'*

Alex felt strong fingers seeking out the folds of her sex. How on earth could she answer Laurence's question? 'No,' she said softly. 'I think he's quite pleased with me.'

'You sound somewhat subdued. Are you okay?'

Before she had a chance to reply Peter Tourne took the phone from her, and in doing so he let a long finger snake around to find a way inside her. She let out a strangled gasp as he found his mark.

'I am very pleased - I just wish you'd told me. Alex is proving to be extremely talented,' he said with a smile, tucking the phone under his chin. 'I am delighted with her efforts so far.' His fingers moved to and fro in an intimate, invasive arc. 'I think she'll do very well here.'

Alex didn't quite hear Laurence's reply at the other end of the line, but Peter Tourne laughed. 'Oh yes, I'm sure she'll prove to be more than satisfactory. I'm afraid we have to go now, we're just about to eat.' While he made his goodbyes his finger remained in place. Alex stood frozen to the spot, afraid to move.

He looked at her as he placed the phone on the side table.

'Well done,' he said softly, while pulling his finger from her body. She flinched, but didn't resist as he lifted his hands to her face and pressed the finger into her mouth. The heady musk of her own body flooded her taste buds.

He smiled. 'We will eat, and then later we'll continue with your education.' Alex's eyes didn't leave his. He took her hand and led her to the table, seating her beside him. A second or two later Gena and Starn appeared, and dinner was served.

As each course was completed Alex couldn't help but wonder what would happen once they had finished their meal. A little spark of tension hung in the air, and by the time coffee was served the atmosphere was so expectant that Alex could hardly bear the wait. Finally Peter Tourne looked at her.

'Go down to the room near gallery and wait for me there,' he said softly. She felt a little tremor of excitement and hesitated for an instant - did she really want her education to continue? He looked at her again, but by this time she was on her feet and moving.

Afraid to look back in case her courage failed her, she hurried down through the house and out into the garden, imagining his footfalls on the stairs behind her. Scurrying through the velvet shadows of the gallery above the pool she opened the door of the room where she had spent the night, and gasped - waiting inside was Mario, his dark feral eyes glistening in the gloom.

Alex glanced back over her shoulder, wondering where Peter Tourne was.

Across the room Mario leered and licked his lips.

'No - you shouldn't be here,' she stammered, as the rough looking man crept towards her. 'Mr Tourne said,' she began, and then remembered that he'd told her to wait for him. She had to obey his instructions - she couldn't leave. She had to stay if she wanted what Peter Tourne had to offer.

Alex moved towards the door until her back was against the wall. She trembled slightly. Mario's eyes wandered over her body, as cruel and obscene, as his fingers had been the night before. Alex was desperately aware that her clothes offered little protection from the him. She was wearing the thinnest of cotton dresses and was naked beneath, in anticipation of Peter Tourne's needs.

Mario continued to leer at her, and slowly extended a hand. Alex shook her head violently, and started to side step towards the door. As her fingers closed around the door handle Mario lunged forward and grabbed hold of her arms. Her first instinct was to bring her knee up, but to her horror Mario anticipated the move and dodged the blow before it hit home.

His dark eyes flashed with a mixture of anger and amusement.

'You want hurt me?' he said gruffly. Alex wriggled to try and free her hands, pulling desperately to escape him. As she did the door opened behind her and she spun around to see Peter Tourne and Starn framed in the opening. She sighed with relief.

'Oh, thank God,' she whispered. 'He was already waiting when I got here. He—' To her abject surprise Mario didn't release her, in fact if anything his grip tightened.

Peter Tourne smiled thinly. 'I know he was, my dear. He was dutifully obeying my orders, as he always does.' He turned to the driver. 'Tie her up, Mario.'

Alex stared at him in astonishment. 'No,' she pleaded. 'Please, Mr Tourne, tell him to stop - please! You know I'll do exactly what you want!'

As she begged Mario pulled a pair of handcuffs from his jacket pocket and deftly snapped them onto her wrists. Her heart began to race. It seemed the encounter with Mario was part of the education Peter Tourne had in mind for her.

Part of her wanted to laugh; this was silly, just a game - but she wanted them to stop now. She looked from face to face, desperately hoping to find a hint of compassion in the eyes of one of them. Instead she found an unnerving mixture of desire and contempt that knocked every ounce of resistance out of her.

With a slight nod of his head Tourne signalled to Mario, who dragged Alex to the centre of the room. Glancing up she noticed for the first time a hook suspended on a length of chain from the ceiling. Surely it had not been there before? She squirmed as Mario held her with one strong arm while he pulled her hands up and attached the hook to the centre of the chain, which linked her cuffs. He leered constantly, obviously enjoying his work, and then adjusted the chain so that her hands were lifted above her head, her feet just resting on the floor. Alex was trussed like an animal carcass.

Tourne nodded his approval. Mario moved away, and Alex couldn't help but notice his disgusting erection jutting forward through his chinos. Another almost discernible nod from his boss, and Mario rubbed his hands together, and then opened one of the cupboards set in the far wall. From inside he produced a set of leg irons; a long steel bar, with an ankle cuff at each end.

'Please,' Alex begged softly. 'There's no need for all this. I've already promised to do everything you want. Surely you know that? I—' Her ramblings were cut short as Mario grabbed each of her ankles. She shuddered and instinctively tried to draw away from him. He snorted and grabbed her foot, dragging off one of her shoes. He unbalanced her, and the sockets in her shoulders screamed out in complaint. If she fought too much, he would tip her over and then her whole weight would be suspended on her arms. The thought horrified her. Mario lifted one foot higher to snap the ankle cuff into place and as he did he lifted her foot to his mouth and ran his tongue between her toes.

Alex gasped in horror. The sensation turned her stomach to liquid. Spreading her legs wider Mario pushed the bar into position and snapped the second cuff into place. He knelt back on his heels to admire his handiwork. Alex's sense of panic was growing with every passing second. She was totally at the mercy of the three men - nothing she could do would prevent them from doing whatever they pleased with her. She twisted and tried to meet Peter's eyes. Surely now that his henchman had secured her he himself would take over?

'You have to understand the true nature of obedience, Alex.' Peter Tourne said quietly. 'This is a game we are playing, but you have to understand it is I, not you, who makes the rules.'

His voice shook her to the core. She stared at him. 'Mr Tourne...' she began, uncertain as to what she actually wanted to say.

He held up his hands. 'Speak only when I tell you to. You make the mistake of believing that who you are and what you think is important to us here. In this game the only things you have to offer are *a* - your body, and *b* - your total obedience to my every wish.' As he allowed his words to sink in, he nodded again to Mario.

The burly driver stepped closer and pulled a handkerchief from his pocket. Before Alex could protest he blindfolded her.

Suddenly plunged into darkness, Alex felt her terror mingling with the same dark, unnerving wave of expectation that had haunted her since her arrival at KaRoche. Rough hands clawed at her dress, ripping it away like tissue. She mewled in fear as the cool evening air hit her body. Now she was truly defenceless. She strained to try and hear what was going on in the room. Her head span. She was on the edge of hysteria when she felt the touch of a hand. Was it Mario or Tourne or Starn who was exploring her intimately now - pawing and licking her vulnerable breasts and nipples? Her sense of smell gave her the answer she needed; the stench of Mario's beer-soaked and sweating body threatened to overwhelm her. And she knew, as Mario thrust a rough finger into her, that the master and his guest were quietly watching while the servant played.

The sense of humiliation made her flush scarlet. Did Tourne and Starn plan to watch while Mario indulged himself? Did they intend to watch while he forced his thick cock into whichever orifice took his fancy? Tears welled up inside her, soaking the blindfold, while Mario's fingers opened her sex wider and teased at the tight bud of her clitoris.

What stunned Alex more than her fear and her sense of shame was that some rogue part of her mind was breathlessly excited by what was happening. Despite everything, Mario's crude fumbling sent a ricochet of pleasure up through her belly. As he pushed and prodded, making her shriek with fear and secret pleasures, she imagined Peter Tourne's eyes on her, savouring every detail of the erotic scene.

Picturing his expression in her mind, she didn't feel Mario's teeth closing on her nipple until too late. She gasped in anguish as he bit her, and then tried to pull away from him, fighting her own mounting desire as much as her tormentor's touch. She heard him snort and step away.

For a moment Alex wondered if Mario would stop now - perhaps her punishment was over. They would leave her tied and alone with her feverish thoughts and fears. Her sense of relief was short-lived. From behind the blindfold she heard the unnerving sound of something cutting through the air, and an instant later a corona of pain exploded in her mind as a lash bit her squarely across the shoulders. She screamed and tried to fight. She twisted and turned against her restraints, oblivious suddenly to the pain in her shoulders. She span so far that the second blow caught her breasts, burning across her already sore nipples like a firebrand. The sensation was so astonishing that she leapt into the air. In her solitude it seemed as if she was defying gravity; almost flying away from the pain.

Before she had time to recover another blow wrapped around her waist, and she knew with blinding certainty that Mario was using an old-fashioned horsewhip. Another blow seared across her shoulders before the pain of the previous one had had a chance to ebb. The sensations threatened to consume her, like a flame speeding along a fuse and leaving a white-hot residue on her flesh and in her mind that refused to be extinguished. Every nerve ending in her body felt as if it was alight. More unnerving, along with the pain, plaited and twisted in with everything else, Alex could still feel terrifying threads of pleasure weaving themselves together. She heard a voice begging and mewling, and was stunned to realise it was her own.

For an instant she wondered if she would go mad. Would the sensations she was feeling catch light and consume her? How was it, that in all the years she'd lived, she'd never been aware of this dark seed growing within her? Out beyond the pain and the pleasure she suddenly understood what was compelling her to accept Peter Tourne's education - it was the act of total surrender. She gasped as the realisation flooded over her, struggling to catch her breath as Mario applied the whip again and again. She had given herself totally to Peter Tourne - an act of trust beyond anything she had ever thought herself capable.

'Let go,' whispered a voice close by. For an instant Alex wondered if it was her own inner voice speaking, and then she realised it was the voice of her master, Peter Tourne. Had he been able to read her mind?

'Let go,' he urged again as the whip bit into her back. She whimpered, finally letting all rational thoughts trickle away as her body was caught up in the maelstrom of pleasure and pain. As Mario struck again all that remained was sensation - as electrifying and all engulfing as a summer storm.

Peter Tourne sensed the moment of surrender, that split second when Alex Sanderson abandoned everything she'd ever known and committed herself to him completely. He had witnessed it many times before, and had an instinctive understanding of when a pupil became his slave. Whatever else happened to Alex Sanderson, she would never be the same again. The seed that had lain dormant for so long would blossom and grow under his expert tutelage.

He signalled to Mario to bring the whipping to an end. A trickle of sweat ran down between Alex's straining breasts. Her body, though trembling, was relaxed now, accepting the whip like a lover's kiss. He smiled and walked over to the blindfolded girl. He gently traced a finger down over her taut nipples. He knew she sensed it was his touch and not Mario's. She whimpered and rubbed herself against him like a cat seeking attention. He motioned to Mario to release the chain so that her arms would drop. She was understandably unsteady. He caught her before she could fall, and guided her down to the floor while Mario worked to free her ankles from the irons. She pressed herself against him, wordlessly seeking his approval. Kneeling over her he guided her face towards his groin.

Although hampered by the intense sting in her back and by the limiting and awkward restrictions of the handcuffs, Alex struggled feverishly to free his aching shaft and pull it into her mouth. She needed the comfort of his closeness. She curled onto her side, drawing him deep between her lips, lapping and licking at his phallus in an act of complete submission. Her fingers cradled his balls, her tongue and mouth eager to suck him dry. He shivered and pressed deeper, relishing the heat and the tightness around him. She moaned in appreciation.

He parted her thighs and stroked the soft naked rise of her sex. Without hesitation she opened her legs wider for him, offering herself up for whatever he wanted to take. She was so wet her juices coated his fingers like a fragrant tide. He smiled and sought out the pleasure bud that nestled like a ripe cherry between the lips of her sex. Her moans of delight vibrated through his shaft, taking him to the very edge of oblivion.

He pressed a single finger deep inside her quim, and at once felt her begin to tighten rhythmically around it, her moist heat perfectly echoing the rhythm of her mouth. He had barely touched her, but it had been enough to trigger her orgasm.

'Yesss...' he murmured as he surrendered to the call of his own pleasure, and flooded into her eager and gasping mouth.

Under his expert fingers Alex writhed like a wild animal, giving him every part of herself. It seemed that for an instant their minds met, each sensation replayed and echoed in the other. For that moment master and slave were equal and the same - riders on a storm of ecstasy.

When he'd done with her, Peter Tourne gently pushed her away. She licked her lips as if afraid she'd missed a drop of his precious essence, and then curled back into a ball. Across the room Starn Fettico grinned and began to unfasten his trousers. Tourne shook his head.

'Leave her,' he murmured. 'There'll be plenty of time for that later.' He turned to Mario. 'Take her to one of the cells and leave her chained. This is just the beginning.'

Climbing to his feet, he looked down at the naked English girl, her narrow back crisscrossed with welts, and smiled. It wouldn't take long though, he thought; Alex Sanderson was a natural submissive, even if she hadn't previously realised it herself. She would go far, and he would help her on her way.

Mario unfastened the chain from the handcuffs and hefted the girl up into his arms. His face was a mask.

Tourne stared hard at him. 'Let her rest,' he said, hoping the man would have sense enough to leave the girl alone when he got her to the cell; she'd already given him exactly what he wanted, and had earned herself a rest. He leaned over her and untied the blindfold. Alex's eyes were closed, her face totally expressionless.

Alex's consciousness had retreated into a dark safe corner of her mind, and it took a few minutes to feel she was once again in control. She'd almost felt as if she was watching herself suck Peter Tourne dry. Her body had been working on instinct alone, taking what it craved from the man who would be her master. Now, held tight in Mario's burly arms, she wondered what would follow.

Ridiculously, she felt somehow safe and secure, as if a great weight had been lifted from her. Slowly reason began to reassert itself as Mario carried her across the room to the door beside the bathroom. It was ajar, and inside Alex could just make out a long corridor from behind her half closed lids. It was gloomy and cold. As the chill hit her naked flesh, Alex struggled to suppress a shiver.

Mario walked slowly, though there wasn't the slightest suggestion he might drop her. At the end of the corridor was another open door. Alex stiffened as she glanced inside; it was a cell, barely taller than she was, with a platform along one wall. On the platform was a thin mattress and a rough grey blanket. Beside it was a toilet and a shower. Other than that the room seemed totally bare.

Mario rolled her unceremoniously onto the mattress, caught hold of the handcuffs she was still wearing, and clipped them onto a chain that hung from above. It was arranged so that she would be able to move around the cell, would be able to use the toilet and shower, but would not be able to leave this prison. But what disturbed her more than this alarming form of imprisonment was the expression on Mario's face. He sniffed as he peered down at her, and ran his tongue over his fat lips. He didn't look at her face. Instead his gaze rested on her nakedness, and he casually ran a hand up over her flank.

'You like man to beat you,' he said thickly. 'It make you wet.'

Alex stared at him, struggling to find her voice. 'Mr Tourne said you were to leave me alone,' she said timidly, curling into a tight ball.

Mario snorted. 'He don't care, he not come down here. He just say, 'Mario, fetch the girl. Mario, beat the girl', but he don't come down here. Down here there only me to look after you. If you don't do what I like, then...' he lifted his hands in an all encompassing gesture. 'No food, no water, no blanket... *no nothing!* I make your life very - how you say,' he struggled over the last word, fighting to find sufficient English. '*Difficult!*'

Alex felt her stomach contract. Left under Mario's care her life would be hell. She took a deep breath. 'Mr Tourne will be angry with you,' she said with a confidence she didn't feel.

Mario laughed. 'If you tell him, I make much worse for you. Now, shut up and open legs.'

Alex stayed still. Her jailor's face contorted into a maniacal grin. 'I can make very bad for you, now open legs, you English whore!'

Alex knew resistance was useless, and probably very foolish; it would only succeed in angering him further. She slowly parted her knees.

'Is right,' hissed her tormentor. 'You give Mario pleasure now.' He smiled and spread her legs wider still, driving his fingers deep inside her. She shrieked at his brutality, but his only reaction was to grab hold of her knees and drag her onto her back, scraping the welts across the rough surface of the mattress. He jerked her towards him so that her feet were on the dusty floor, her hips on the edge of the platform, and her tender back on the cold rough concrete. Forcing her legs wider still he stood between them and began to paw at her breasts and quim with one hand, whilst unbuttoning his fly with the other.

Before Alex had time to recover, he plunged his cock home, making her shriek with surprise and fear. He was deaf to her cries and drove on and on, dragging her onto him time and time again. Her back screamed out in agony as it rubbed against the concrete, but nothing she said or cried made any difference. Mario ploughed into her relentlessly, gasping and snorting, and clawing at her nipples until she knew he was close to the point of no return.

Totally disgusted, Alex squeezed her eyes tight to blot out the abhorrent image of his red and contorted features slobbering over her like a madman. She knew he was about to come. At the last second she felt him drag his cock out of her and spurt an arc of semen over her belly. As it splattered onto her skin she felt sick and empty.

Mario wiped his loose mouth with the back of his hand and turned away without a second glance at her.

Alex started to shake, tears coursing down her face. She had to get away from the villa. Whatever Peter Tourne had to offer her it was not worth this. If she stayed she would be at the mercy of any man who wanted her, master or servant, whether it was forbidden or not. The cell door clanged shut and she took a deep breath. Mario's seed clung to her belly in an unnerving puddle. Slowly, steadying herself at every step, she crossed to the shower, the water was icy cold as it hit her, but Alex didn't care. All she wanted was to be clean but she doubted whether water alone would be enough.

CHAPTER 4

Upstairs in the sitting room, Peter Tourne poured himself and Starn a glass of brandy each. Starn's expression was set, his manner cool and offhand. Tourne knew that by denying his friend the opportunity to make use of Alex Sanderson's vulnerability he had infuriated him, and quite enjoyed the sense of power it gave him. He handed Starn the glass.

'Gena is still waiting for you downstairs,' he said, indicating the door. 'Would you like me to call her up?'

Starn snorted. 'If I'd wanted Gena I wouldn't have bothered to come up here with you. What are you planning to do with Alex Sanderson once you've broken her?'

He shrugged. 'You're tired of Gena, already? I'm surprised I thought she was perfect for you. You want to sell her on? If you do I'm sure I can find a buyer. She's a very beautiful young lady. She would command an excellent price.' He knew it wasn't what Starn meant at all, but enjoyed playing with him.

Starn stared into his brandy balloon.

Tourne continued, 'Armande the Frenchman, Bene, Michael - they would all jump at the chance of owning one of my girls. Would you like me to make a few calls?'

'No,' snapped Starn. 'It's not that I'm tired of Gena you know it isn't. It's just that I thought, as we are friends, you would let me sample your new girl's delights as well. Hell, that greasy slob of a driver of yours gets to have more fun than I do!'

Peter smiled. 'What about this morning? You are so impatient, my friend. You haven't lost the chance to have some fun with her again, it's just that at the moment I feel she will respond more quickly if I alone teach her.'

Starn snorted derisively again. 'You didn't think that earlier when she was here with Gena.'

Peter wondered how he could possibly explain what he had seen in Alex's demeanour that had changed his opinion about her fate. Alex hadn't just been broken she had given herself over entirely to sensation and submission. It was an instinctive thing, part of her nature that Peter recognised as something of great value. Alex Sanderson wouldn't just resign herself to being man's slave;

in time, when she came to terms with what she felt, she would learn to relish her new role.

'Of course, Starn, you're quite right. Eventually I will auction her,' he said after a second or two. 'Unless a bidder comes forward in the meantime with a sizeable offer. Just give her a little time more to settle in. In another day or two, when she understands what we expect of her, then of course you can have your fill. Don't let's fall out over one woman, for God's sake - the world is full of them. Here, let me top your glass up.'

Starn seemed appeased. 'An auction? Will you hold it here?'

Tourne shook his head. 'To be honest Alex's arrival at KaRoche has come as a total surprise to me. I haven't had the time to give it a great deal of thought. It might be interesting to let her be sold off with Simon Bay's surplus girls when the time comes. He's staying on the island for the summer. He gave me a ring a week or so ago to say he had a rather good stable at the moment, and suggested I might be interested in taking a look. When Alex is ready we ought, perhaps, to take her over there.'

Starn grinned. 'Simon has a good eye. Perhaps he might even buy your protégé for himself.'

Both men looked at each other knowingly. Simon Bay's girls were famous. A slave master, unrivalled amongst his contemporaries, he was an entrepreneur and businessman who used his frequent business trips around the world to acquire girls from everywhere on earth. If Simon Bay bought Alex for his own use it would be the ultimate accolade.

Tourne smiled, aping nonchalance. 'It would depend on what he offered. Now, are you going to call for Gena, or would you prefer another glass of brandy?'

Starn stood his glass on the bureau. 'I'll go and find her, and God help her if she doesn't satisfy me. After the exhibition with your little artist friend, I need more than just a little light relief!'

Tourne grinned. 'I've had Mario take Alex down to the cells, perhaps you'd like to take Gena to the Gallery room and make use of the facilities there? It never hurts to remind your slave who is in control.'

Starn nodded.

He watched his friend depart, wondering for a few seconds whether he should go and settle himself in the hidden room overlooking the gallery to observe what would undoubtedly be a fine performance by Gena and her master.

He was disappointed that Starn was so easily distracted from the exquisite blonde. Originally Gena had come here to work as a secretary, but he'd known the second he'd laid eyes on her beauty that her obvious talents would be wasted behind a desk - over a desk would be a different matter! He sipped his brandy, closed his eyes, and let his thoughts drift back to that most enjoyable morning when he first had the pleasure...

At Gena's interview, after their preliminary discussions, and as she handed Peter Tourne a letter of recommendation from her previous employer, he 'accidentally' nudged a sheaf of papers off the corner of his desk and onto the floor. Gena instantly and elegantly dropped to all fours to retrieve them. As she gathered them back into a neat pile, Tourne stood up and moved around his desk. At once Gena's instinctive reaction was to look up at him. When their eyes met, she blushed, aware that something other than a simple interview was taking place. As her colour deepened and she began get to her feet she lifted a hand.

'I think,' he said in a low voice, 'that you should stay exactly where you are.'

The blonde girl swallowed hard. 'Stay?' she murmured innocently. 'Here?'

He nodded. 'You understand precisely what I mean...' Peter took another sip and allowed his brandy and his memories to warm him...

He picked up a pair of scissors from his desk and, as if it was the most natural thing in the world, cut along the back of Gena's blouse, through her bra strap, down through her pencil slim skirt and flimsy white panties, tearing away the fabric as he worked, ruining her expensive little interview costume. While he worked, Gena stayed perfectly still, her pale body trembling as the cold blades brushed her skin.

Finally, naked except for her sandals, she crouched amongst the ruins of her clothes. She looked exquisite, a pale creamy-skinned Madonna, cowering, subdued awaiting whatever her superior had in store for her. For a few seconds they were both still - master and slave awaiting each other's pleasure.

When Gena finally looked up to him her dark eyes were bright with fear and anticipation. She remained crouched on all fours, her heavy breasts swaying like liquid silk, breathes coming in short frantic bursts as she waited for his next move.

Surveying her, Tourne knew that beneath the thin veneer of sophistication Gena was still a peasant at heart - her hips were curvaceous and broad, her breasts, now pert and full, would one day be pendulous and heavy. Between her pale thighs was a thatch of glistening black hair, at odds with her bleached blonde curls. She might well have a clutch of diplomas from secretarial college, but her body betrayed the fact that she was born to serve. He indicated she should stand.

Gena clambered to her feet without a word, pushing off the last remnants of her clothes. Tourne ran his hand over her haunches, assessing her body as he would a good horse. She turned instinctively under his fingertips, moving obediently to his unspoken commands. He brushed his fingers over her back and shoulders, letting his hand linger on the curve of her waist.

Already, despite her ripeness, her figure showed signs that it would thicken. For a few years she would serve her master faithfully and later, when she had lost the peach moist richness that suffused her body now, she had the hips to become a breeder, producing a whole new generation of submissive slave girls. He lifted a hand to cup her breasts, fingers working over the pert nipples. She shivered but said nothing. He knew then that Gena was an excellent find.

She was naturally quiet and still - an attribute that many men favoured. Her natural demeanour was meek but sensual. She was the ideal submissive companion.

'Would you like to work for me?' Tourne asked, letting a single finger trail down towards her soft, rounded belly.

Perhaps afraid to speak, Gena nodded. He could detect the pulse in her throat fluttering like the wings of a tiny bird. Amongst the trappings of his expensively furnished office her nakedness seemed extreme. Her pale creamy skin was a stunning contrast to the backdrop of dark corporate grey and silver.

'To be honest, I'm not sure you're suitable. My business clients are sophisticates, where you are barely one step away from the vineyard.' He caught hold of one shapely breast, twisting the nipple savagely. He felt her flinch. 'Wouldn't you be happier back down on the farm, barefoot, with some country boy sniffing around you, and a baby sucking on your tits?' He watched her face for a reaction. Her eyes flashed but still she didn't speak. He smiled triumphantly. Walking confidently around her his fingers continued to trace a careful pattern of intimate exploration.

Finally he plucked a long flexible cane from amongst a Japanese arrangement that graced a side table by his desk. He flexed it thoughtfully, eyes never leaving hers. Still Gena did not bolt or cry out.

'Are you still a virgin?' he asked. It would not be unusual for a Greek girl of her age to be unbroken. Country people had always valued virginity as a prize to be held on to until marriage. Blushing, Gena shook her head. It was obvious that even though she was no longer a virgin, she wasn't experienced either.

'Who?' asked Tourne relishing her discomfort.

Gena's colour intensified, but significantly she didn't refuse this complete stranger an answer to such an intimate question. 'My cousin, Giuseppe. Last summer we...' the words dried up as he moved closer to her. 'We only did it the once,' she stammered.

His expression remained impassive. 'Your cousin? You country girls are all the same. How do I know you aren't lying? How do I know you haven't fucked every man you've laid eyes on with those big tits, that arse - how many hands have played around in that wet little cunt of yours? How many cocks have you sucked dry? Or do you prefer it when they fuck you? Or do you prefer other girls?'

Gena's eyes widened in horror. 'Mr Tourne,' she began to protest in astonishment.

'You're no better than a whore!' he snapped. 'And then you come to my office, pretending to be respectable so that you can get a job with my company! What were you thinking of?'

Gena stared at him open-mouthed, too shocked to speak.

Peter Tourne indicated his desk. It was a huge single slab of black marble supported on trestles.

'Bend over,' he said. 'Let me show you how we used to treat the peasant whores on my father's estate.'

A tiny bead of perspiration broke out on Gena's upper lip. The smell of her reluctance and fear were as tangible as her perfume. She didn't move, but he could see her anxiously pondering the distance to the desk, as if she had already taken each step. He lifted his hands in a gesture of dismissal, and as he did so Gena walked slowly towards the austere piece of furniture as though she was taking her last few steps to the guillotine. Her eyes were firmly fixed on the middle distance as she submissively draped herself across the icy marble.

He heard her gasp as the cold stone sucked the heat from her body.

'Open your legs,' he directed. 'Let me see the sweet little honey pot that attracts all those other men.'

Gena complied without a word, revealing the merest glimpse of her quim beneath the shapely contours of her bottom. The muscles in her buttocks were rigid in expectation of what he had in store for her. He stepped behind her and, catching hold of her hips, pulled her off the table a little so that more of the glorious moist pit was exposed and accessible.

First, he thought, he would administer a good sound beating and then, before the pain and humiliation had faded, before the red glow left her flesh, he would slide inside her. She was so mouth-wateringly ripe - there was part of him that adored her peasant fullness and natural subordination.

Stepping away he lifted the cane and brought it down with a resounding crack across her backside. She screamed out in a mixture of surprise and pain, bending into a contorted arc before slumping back onto the black marble. Her breasts spread beneath her, as pale and full as the harvest moon. Back swung the cane and exploded again. She squealed and arched up towards him, but not so violently this time. He hit her again, striking over and over until the rounded orbs of her backside were raw with a tapestry of welts.

Between Gena's thighs he could see her quim was flushed crimson, the moisture clinging like gossamer to the lips of her sex. Stepping closer he undid his flies and guided his raging shaft deep inside her. She squealed again and struggled unconvincingly to unseat him.

As she twisted round he locked his fingers in her hair and jerked her back up towards him, his other hand scooping up one of her ample breasts, fingers nipping and twisting her cold, erect nipples.

Gena shrieked madly, writhing under him like a frightened animal, but still he held on, riding her, pulling her back onto his cock again and again, grinding his pelvis against the soft expanse of her glowing arse.

'Please,' she sobbed. 'Please no, I am good girl, Mr Tourne. I am not a whore. Please, please don't do this to me. I am good girl.' But while her mouth said one thing her body told Peter Tourne something totally different. Her quim tightened around him like a clenched fist, pulling him deeper, her hips instinctively pressing against him, driving him towards the point where even his inscrutable exterior threatened to crack and display some emotion.

Gena gasped and sobbed, tears streaming down her face. He took her hand and urged it down to her sex, guiding her fingers to seek out the bud of her own clitoris.

'Touch yourself,' he hissed in her ear. 'Let me show you what it is that all those men want from you.' As he spoke he pressed her fingertips hard against the engorged ridge. She mewled in astonishment, almost convulsing as crystal circles of pleasure formed in her belly, bucking and roaring as he began to circle the little nub, pushing her fingers to and fro until finally her head fell back onto his shoulder and he could feel her fingers moving of their own accord.

With Gena's pleasure building, Tourne began to move in earnest, dragging her back hard, tightening his grip on her hair, his free hand returning to weigh and knead her full breasts. She was moaning and breathing hard, struggling to pleasure them both. He felt the first intoxicating ripples of her quim tightening around his erection as orgasm overtook her, and knew then he was lost too.

An incandescent wave flooded through him, driving away all reason as he plunged into her again and again, on and on until he felt he was drowning in a sea of pure pleasure.

When, finally, Peter Tourne slumped onto her back, his body utterly drained, he opened his eyes and smiled.

Beside Gena's tousled, sweat-soaked hair, was the letter of recommendation that she'd handed to him only a short time before. One sentence in the main paragraph caught his eye - it read: *I have always found Gena to be an extremely willing and able young woman.*

Peter slid out of her and adjusted his trousers. What a shrewd judge of character Gena's previous employer had been.

Now, standing alone in the villa, he wondered whether to go and watch Starn re-enact that first conquest. It might be interesting, but it would never be as magical as that first time when Gena had not known what to expect. He decided, on balance, to refill his glass - after all, he had Alex Sanderson to think about now.

Downstairs in the prison cell behind the gallery, Alex huddled into a foetal ball, trying to block out the sounds of Gena and Starn in the room beyond. Even through the thick walls she could hear Gena's impassioned cries and Starn encouraging her on and on as he laid on the whip. The blonde's voice seemed to echo from every surface.

Alex closed her eyes, pressed her fingers to her ears, and struggled to fill her mind with the images of the mural she intended to paint on the wall overlooking the pool in Peter Tourne's garden. How likely was it now that she would ever have the chance to fill the cool shadowy space with pictures? However tempting the lessons Peter Tourne had to teach, she was afraid to think of what might happen if she abandoned herself to this madness. If the chance presented itself she would try to escape, even if it meant abandoning her possessions at the villa. Surely someone would help her? Perhaps the old housekeeper, who'd tried to warn her off in the first place, could be persuaded to help her break free.

As Alex tried to settle more comfortably on the thin mattress every muscle in her body ached. It seemed there wasn't a part of her that Peter Tourne or Starn, Gena or Mario had not touched, kissed, beaten or bitten.

Finally, as the light darkened in the cell, Alex slipped into an uneasy sleep, her mind suffused with images of passion and pain. Again and again in her dreams she was torn between the desire to stay and the desire to escape. As she raced through the feverish dreamscape Peter Tourne thwarted her at every turn, and waited for her with a vicious whip in hand.

The sound of footsteps brought Alex back to consciousness with a start. The cell was now grey with early morning light. She felt cold and stiff. When she heard the key turn in her cell door her immediate reaction was to curl back into a ball in case it was Mario coming back for more. The door swung open slowly to reveal the wrinkled features of the housekeeper bearing a breakfast tray. The contents were meagre; a tin jug of water and two bread rolls and an apple, but to Alex they looked like a feast. The woman set the tray on the floor and then eyed Alex thoughtfully, her eyes moving over the girl's nakedness. Her expression was not unsympathetic, and Alex knew she had to take a chance.

'Will you help me?' she pleaded quietly.

The old woman shrugged. 'Is too late for help now. He already work the magic on you.'

Alex felt a ripple of fear run through her as the old woman continued. 'You should go when first I tell you about Mr Tourne. You not listen then, why I listen now?'

Alex struggled to her feet, regretting it instantly as her body groaned in complaint.

The old woman nervously backed away through the open cell door. 'If you give me trouble,' she said, 'I leave you to Mario - and he not always here. He forget to feed you. He *very* bad man.'

Alex stared at her. 'I won't give you any trouble,' she whispered. 'But please, you have to help me. If you go to my room and find my telephone book, look for Laurence Russell's number. Please ring him. He's my friend. He'll come and get me. There's money there, take it all...' as she spoke she heard the sound of approaching footsteps, and the woman's attention was drawn back into the corridor outside the cell.

There was a tirade of words in Greek and then the cell door slammed shut. Alex stiffened as she recognised Mario's voice drowning out the old lady's mumbled protests. In amongst the foreign words she recognised a few English ones - perhaps Mario was adding them for her benefit.

'Not open door!' the driver bellowed at the old woman 'She is mine. Understand? I look after her you not interfere. No one to see her except me. She is mine!'

His words made Alex shudder - if she couldn't speak to the housekeeper and persuade her to help she might never get away. Perhaps, though, she had already said enough. If the old woman rang Laurence she stood a chance of escaping.

While Mario continued to berate the housekeeper outside the cell, Alex, despite the handcuffs, hastily grabbed the apple from the tray and thrust it under the thin mattress. She then took a mouthful of the cool clear water straight from the jug, in case Mario decided to punish her by taking her breakfast away.

Seconds later the cell door slammed open and Mario stood framed in the opening, his face contorted with fury. He strode across the cell and, without warning, hit her hard across the face with his open hand. The power and surprise of the blow made her stagger backwards. Unable to steady herself because of the cumbersome handcuffs, she toppled over onto the floor, banging her head on the corner of the bed as she did.

'You not talk to her!' Mario roared.

Alex's head span, though through the swirling confusion she could see the brute bearing down upon her. For one awful moment she thought he was going to kick her and tensed up, curling into a tight ball, waiting for the blow. Instead he stooped over, grabbed her hair, and yanked her back onto her feet.

'You make me angry!' he spat, throwing her down onto the mattress. Despite his fury his eyes moved hungrily across her naked body. She sensed that for him anger and desire were emotions that were always dangerously close to the surface of a very thin line.

He glanced back at the ruined contents of the tray - the bread was crushed on the stone floor, and the water jug lay in its own puddle.

'You hungry?' he said thickly.

Alex nodded. Perhaps he wasn't such a monster after all.

Grinning, Mario clambered up onto the platform and knelt astride her. She stared up at him in horror as he unzipped his fly, trying to make some kind of contact with the cruel mind behind the bright flashing eyes. She could smell the rank odour of his masculinity even before he pulled out his cock.

'Eat this then,' he snorted grimly, flexing his hips as he thrust his engorged shaft into her mouth it was pointless to try and fight him. Struggling to control the feelings of nausea Alex began to suck, her mind revolted and ashamed as Mario grunted with satisfaction, his fingers seeking out her breasts, his body moving rhythmically against her face. Alex prayed that while Mario was busy abusing her, the old woman had gone to the guest cabin. Mario snorted as the pleasure overwhelmed him, and he pulled her closer. She could feel the tension building in his body and braced herself for his orgasm. Seconds later her mouth was flooded by a wave of thick semen. Alex gagged. She tried to spit his seed out but he clamped her jaw shut tight around him so that she had no option but to swallow.

· He closed his eyes and slouched with his chin on his chest, and his whole body in a state of total relaxation. He remained kneeling over Alex with his hands on his thighs, and his shrinking cock being soothed by the natural fluttering of her tongue. She looked up at his bulk and wondered when he would leave her in peace. His cock felt like a slug in her mouth.

At last he slipped from between her lips. He lifted his considerable weight from her aching breasts and clambered off the platform. He grinned down at her. 'I bring you coffee now,' he said, waving towards the discarded tray. 'Hot coffee and more breakfast. You just remember not to speak to old woman - you are mine. I look after you now.'

Alex sniffed miserably, her mouth still thick with the taste of his semen. Glancing up at her gaoler's face she hoped she'd already said enough to the housekeeper. Mario left the cell, slammed the door shut behind him, and turned the key in the lock. Alex stared into the gloom and waited for him to return.

CHAPTER 5

Peter Tourne sat alone under a parasol on the terrace and ate his breakfast. From his vantage point he could see the fishing boats sailing out of the tiny harbour, and the first of the ferries arriving. Although it was early the sun was already hot. He glanced at his watch. Hearing soft footsteps he looked up into the wrinkled brown face of his housekeeper. She was carrying a jug of coffee. He smiled.

'I thought for a moment you were Miss Sanderson,' he said in English.

The old woman frowned. 'Mario is too rough,' she said flatly in her native Greek. 'He'll hurt her unless you speak to him. Miss Sanderson isn't like Gena, not a local girl. If you're not careful you could get into trouble. She's too delicate to be left to a ruffian like Mario.'

He smiled. 'I understand what you're saying. Would you please ask him to bring Miss Sanderson up here? After all, I commissioned her to paint a mural. There's no need for her to be locked up all day long.'

The old lady nodded and turned away. He watched her leave; Mario wouldn't dare touch Alex out in the open, but locked in the small cell was another matter. What he didn't want his housekeeper to know was that he knew exactly the kind of man Mario was, and that his driver's brutality was a useful addition to every girl's training.

He waited in his study for Alex's arrival. When she stepped into the room he regarded her carefully. He noticed that she didn't lift her head to meet his eyes, which was a good sign. Naked, and with her hands still cuffed, she looked so touchingly vulnerable.

He nodded to Mario.

'I think we can dispense with the cuffs, Mario. After all, Miss Sanderson is an artist, and we can't expect her to work with her hands so crudely bound, now can we? I think I have something here that will do just as well.'

He opened his desk drawer and brought out a narrow leather collar, set with silver studs. Alex looked up towards him for the first time since entering his study. Her face was pale and gaunt. There was a livid red mark on one temple

- perhaps the housekeeper was right; Mario was taking his role as gaoler a little too seriously. Tourne had no wish for any of the girls in his care to sustain permanent damage - that would be counterproductive.

He held the collar out to her and turned it in his fingers so she could see what he had in store for her. It had a ring set in it, from which could be hung a chain and handle - like a dog lead. At one end of the collar was a tiny lock fastening that snapped shut and which couldn't be opened without a key. He handed it to Mario. Alex didn't move as the heavy man slid the collar round her throat and snapped the lock shut. When it was snugly in place Mario removed the handcuffs.

Tourne nodded his approval. 'And how is my servant treating you, Alex?' he asked, encouraging her to look at him. Alex glanced up with dark unhappy eyes. He could guess.

Alex shot a quick sideways glance at the swarthy driver, her eyes suddenly flashing with fury and hatred. 'Fine - Mr Tourne,' she said quietly - and wisely.

Peter Tourne smiled. She learned fast. 'Good, then in that case I think it's time you started work.' He looked her up and down. 'I'll have Mario find you something appropriate to wear. The sun is very fierce today and you're so fair skinned.' He paused. 'Fair skins always command a good price at auction.'

He watched Alex stiffen and stare at him.

'At auction?' she repeated, unable to keep the note of astonishment out of her voice.

He nodded. 'What did you think happened to girls like you?' he said softly, seeing the fear moving across her face like water rising. 'When I'm ready I'll sell you on, like Gena, and like a dozen girls I've trained before you. Don't make the mistake of thinking you're special; you're just one of many.' He paused and let the realisation sink in before he continued. 'Fair skin always brings a good price.' He waved to Mario and handed him a leash that matched the collar. 'Get her showered and dressed, and then take her down to the garden so she can begin her work.'

Alex sat in the long cool gallery by the poolside. Around her were the tools of her trade, brought down by the housekeeper and arranged on a small folding table. She had had no chance to speak to the old woman again. Mario had watched them both like a wolf awaiting his chance to pounce.

Alex stroked the boxes of familiar brushes and paint tubes, trying hard to regain some sense of control. It was difficult. A length of chain extended from her collar to a ring set in the floor, which meant she could easily move around but could not escape.

She'd assumed when Peter Tourne had told her she would be found some clothes that he meant something of her own - she had been wrong. Mario had brought her a sheer white cotton shirt, so thin that she might as well have been naked, and a skirt that looked as if it had belonged to the elderly housekeeper. It reached the floor, and was made of rough wool. Barefoot and with no underwear she felt like a peasant servant girl, chained and ready for her master or any other man that passed her way. Every movement made the rough wool brush against her sensitive skin, electrifying her bruises and scratches.

Alex stared down at her drawing pad, wondering how on earth Peter Tourne expected her to work when so much had happened. The ideas forming in her head had nothing to do with art or painting, but of pain and passion and an overwhelming realisation that she had to escape from the clutches of Peter Tourne before it was too late. She could still feel the whip cracking across her back, and still feel Mario's brutal touch...

She picked up her pencil thoughtfully glancing down at the wildly erotic images she'd drawn the day before. Perhaps she could create a moral fairytale - a parable that would warn other girls what Peter Tourne was like. The idea began to take shape. Turning to a new page she began to draw frantically, filling sheet after sheet of paper with rough sketches. Perhaps, if she could do nothing else, she could help warn other girls what fate awaited them in the luxurious villa called KaRoche.

Once the form of the mural began to take shape, Alex became totally immersed in what she was doing. Time passed without her being aware of it. Oblivious now to her surroundings, the only thing that registered were the pictures forming on the page. Almost triumphantly she tore a leaf from her sketchbook and began to transfer it onto the squared paper that would help her scale it up for the long wall. Peter Tourne had promised her that she could create whatever she wanted - she intended to take him at his word.

Alex didn't hear the footsteps approaching from the garden behind her. The first time she registered a presence was when a shadow fell across her sketchpad.

'I've been looking for you,' said a low voice. Alex froze, all thoughts of the mural instantly flooding away as if a dam had burst. She turned slowly and looked up into the grim face of Starn Fettico.

She swallowed hard, knowing she was completely vulnerable. 'Mr Tourne is upstairs, I think,' she offered. She placed the pencil and pad on the table and sat with defensive expectancy, like a Wild West gambler preparing for an assault by a sore loser; she knew he wasn't looking for his friend.

Starn nodded. 'I know that. It isn't Peter I wanted to see,' he confirmed her fears. 'He's busy this morning.'

Alex felt a growing sense of panic. She watched Starn's eyes move to the contours of her cleavage and breasts, and then fix themselves on the dark peaks of her nipples where they pressed through the thin cotton voile. She shuddered as he looked away, his gaze moving on to trace the silver chain from the ring in the floor to the collar she wore around her neck. Before she could protest he grabbed the chain and jerked it hard, dragging her to her feet. The table at which she had been working tipped dramatically, spilling pencils and paper all over the flagstone floor. The collar slid sharply up under her chin, making her gasp with discomfort.

Starn pulled her closer, ignoring the chaos he'd created. One hand cupped her breast through the thin blouse while he thrust a foot between hers and forced her legs apart. She could feel his hot and stale breath on her cheek - and an ominous lump against her belly.

'Do you like what you're learning?' he hissed. 'Peter tells me you're a natural - but I'm not so sure.'

'Please,' Alex whispered, 'leave me alone. I have work to do for Mr Tourne.' She knew she had to divert his attentions. 'Tonight. Come to my room tonight. I'll be good - I'll do anything you want. Please... you're hurting me.'

'Shut up!' Starn hissed. He jerked the chain again, his hand dropping now so that he could fumble with her skirt, dragging it up to allow him unobstructed access to her tensed body.

'Peter doesn't want me to *have* you yet,' he said thickly, pawing at her thighs. 'He seems to have forgotten that women like you are meant to be used.' He paused. 'He'll sell you on, you be sure of that. He's already making plans to have you auctioned off. I might make a bid myself. You and Gena would be *so* good together.' He grinned, nodding towards her sketches where they lay on the floor. 'I saw you drawing. Are you the princess in the pictures? Gena the peasant bitch and Alex the little English princess. You'd make a superb pair; you with your sexy tongue up inside her cunt, crouched over, lovely cute arse in the air, while I take you from behind. Oh yes, I'd like that.'

Alex shuddered. Without Peter Tourne there to control him, Starn seemed almost as brutal as Mario.

His searching fingers finally found her sex beneath the skirt. 'You'd like that too, wouldn't you?' he grinned as he ran his palm over the close stubble that had re-grown on her quim. He forced his hand experimentally between her legs, cupping the outer lips and teasing a finger inside her.

Alex squirmed and held her breath. She felt him stiffen even more against her belly.

'You're wet already!' he snorted. 'Perhaps Peter was right about you after all - you are made to serve.'

Alex could feel the tension building in the pit of her stomach. The muscles tightened in her shoulders. She had to get away.

Starn probed deeper, his concentration slipping for an instant as he found the goal he'd been seeking. She felt him relax, and suddenly twisted round violently, breaking free from his clutches. She clenched her fists and thumped them down onto his chest, pushing him so hard that he lost his balance and stumbled backwards. With her pulse hammering in her ears she turned to run. In the split second before she took flight, Alex remembered the collar and chain - but it was too late. Starn, breathing heavily, was already ahead of her. Although she didn't see him she felt the chain jerk so violently that it almost choked the breath right out of her. Another violent tug sent her crashing to the floor.

Before she had time to recover Starn pushed her down hard on the cool stone. His fingers closed painfully on her shoulders. His expression was grim, but his eyes flashed with excitement.

'Oh yes!' he panted, dropping down across her chest so that she was pinned down. 'I like it when they fight!'

Alex's survival instinct was taking control. As the adrenaline began to pump she twisted back and forth, struggling to shake Starn off her. Her rational mind knew it was madness; there was nothing she could do with the chain still attached to the collar. It would be far more sensible to submit, but her body had other ideas. Fighting, biting, and writhing she struggled to get away from Starn, and as she did his hands jerked her skirt up. She screamed as she felt his fingers tearing at her thighs, before they plunged into her again. This time it wasn't a curious exploration but a cruel violation. His expression was predatory.

'You have to learn to do as you're told,' he said thickly. 'I want you - so I can have you. It's that simple.'

Alex glared up at him, and then spat in his face. It wasn't something she'd ever done before, and she was almost as surprised as Starn. His reaction was to slap her face hard, making her shriek. Wiping his cheek he clambered off her and jerked her back up to her feet.

Alex was trembling wildly. Her breath came in ragged sobs.

'Leave me alone, you bastard,' she gasped.

'Now, that's pretty unbecoming language for a little English princess. You deserve a good spanking for that.' Starn mocked. 'I'm surprised Peter hasn't taught you the fundamental rule of this wonderful place; you belong to whoever wants you, whenever they want you, however they want you. You have no say in the matter, do you understand?' As he spoke he spun her round to face the wall, and jerked her skirt up.

'Bend over,' he said, in a low and threatening tone. 'And open your legs. I'll show you what we do to slaves who forget their place.'

Alex longed to resist him, and was about to begin fighting again when she heard Peter Tourne's voice above the sound of her thumping heart. Her momentary relief quickly vanished when she realised what he was saying.

'Good morning Starn, I thought I heard your voice.'

There was no hint of rebuke for Starn in his tone; not a word to protect her or defend her.

Starn snorted. 'Your little bitch spat at me.'

'Tut, tut,' said Tourne, turning Alex round to face him. 'I had hoped she would know better.'

She glanced up into his eyes. His expression was impassive, and she felt a sudden chill that cut to the bone.

'I thought she was beginning to understand,' he said, addressing his remark to Starn. 'It seems we have to take more stringent measures to ensure she understands exactly what is excepted of her.'

'Mr Tourne,' she began, with a note of appeal in her voice.

He caught hold of her chin suddenly, his fingers closing like a vice. 'Speak only when spoken to!' he snapped.

Alex looked away, unable to make sense of the complex emotions that coursed through her. Something about Peter Tourne and his cool voice made her stomach contract with fear, and lurch with a dark, eager desire.

He stroked her cheek. 'I really had hoped that you would learn the rules more quickly, Alex. It seems I was mistaken.'

Alex was filled with a sense of foreboding, only his order not to speak made her hold back from begging. She wanted to tell him she did understand - let Starn have her now, she didn't care. She would do whatever he asked. She did understand!

But Peter Tourne had already turned away and unfastened the end of the chain that secured her to the stone floor.

He didn't jerk the leash, but instead he indicated the door at the far end of the gallery, and Alex obediently and silently moved towards it. Whatever punishment was to follow she had brought upon herself, but the thought did nothing to comfort her as she stepped into the cool and shadowy room. Beside the bathroom in the far wall she could see the door that led down to the cells. Perhaps he would simply lock her up... or perhaps Mario would return.

She stood in the centre of the room without moving an inch, aware of how ridiculous it was to wait so meekly. The chain had been released. She had a hint of an opportunity to escape, and yet she couldn't bring herself to take it. Standing in the doorway Peter Tourne's expression was one of disappointment rather than anger. Did he want her to have more spirit? Did he want to see her attempting to escape? Alex was confused.

Starn's expression by contrast was almost gleeful, as if he'd got some absurd childish delight in getting Alex into trouble.

Tourne took hold of her wrists, and from his pockets produced the handcuffs that Mario had removed earlier. His eyes moved over her body, lingering on her face. She blushed furiously. Snapping the cuffs into place he moved away to where a thick rope was looped around a large cleat on one wall. The rope passed up through a pulley system hanging from the ceiling, and had a large metal hook attached to its dangling end. He unravelled the rope from the cleat and lowered the hook.

Alex almost felt as if she was an observer to her own punishment. She watched, rather than felt, as he slipped the hook through the cuffs and then pulled the rope back up towards the ceiling. With her arms above her head she waited meekly for whatever was to follow. He stepped back and looked her up and down, as still and assured as a big cat hunting game.

The cool room was unnaturally silent. Time seemed to slow until every second was a minute, and still Peter Tourne watched her.

Alex's stomach tightened and the hairs on the back of her neck prickled; this was not the passionate retribution she had expected, but a cool display of superiority that verged on indifference. Would he whip her now? Or would he let Starn loose to do with her as he pleased?

Finally he sighed and turned to Starn. 'Go to my office,' he said in a voice barely above a whisper. 'You know where to find what I want.'

Starn grinned. His obvious delight filled Alex with dread. As soon as he'd left the room Peter Tourne stepped close to Alex.

'You should have obeyed Starn,' he whispered menacingly. 'I thought you understood that I demand total obedience. I'm disappointed with you, Alex. You've let me down.'

Alex's eyes filled with tears, and her view of him became blurred. 'I am sorry, Mr Tourne. I'll try harder next time - I promise...'

Peter Tourne casually stroked her unprotected breasts through the thin voile blouse. Her nipples hardened instantly at his undeniably arousing touch. 'You belong to me,' he whispered. 'Perhaps Starn was wrong in trying to take advantage of you, but even if he was that is none of your concern; you are meant to do whatever he - or anybody else - requires of you. If there had been a fault - a wrong - it would have been his and not yours, had you obeyed him as you should have. Do you understand what I'm saying, Alex?'

Reluctantly Alex nodded. She was nothing more than a possession. Her will was subject to Peter Tourne's. She shivered. He moved away, apparently still unhappy with her. Her breasts felt cold without his touch. Moving across the room he pushed a bell on the wall. Alex closed her eyes, certain that he was summoning Mario. She was right - it only seemed an instant before the swarthy driver appeared.

Peter Tourne barely looked at him. 'Get me the frame,' he said quietly.

Mario's eyes flashed for an instant and then he vanished into the gloomy corridor that led to the cells. After a few minutes he reappeared carrying and dragging something that looked like a single wooden bed frame. A threatening pair of manacles was set at each end, and the body was crisscrossed with slats. Halfway along its length was a broad leather belt, and at one end was a depression, set with two fastenings. Alex realised with a growing sense of trepidation that this depression was there to support her neck and head. She swung round to beg for Peter Tourne's mercy, but his expression - as cold as an ancient glacier - froze the words in her mouth.

He waved Mario closer. The driver manoeuvred the frame into position in the centre of the room, and then set about lowering Alex's aching arms.

Peter Tourne watched Alex with a mixture of pleasure and pride as she allowed herself to be strapped to the wooden frame. He could see the trembling pulse in her chest, and the rise of nervous perspiration between her breasts. He was angry with Starn for disregarding his orders about leaving Alex alone, but even so, Alex had to learn that obedience was everything. The lower manacles secured and held her ankles wide apart. Mario worked slowly and diligently up over her prostrate body, tightening the belt around her waist, snapping the little locks into place on either side of her collar, and then finally taking the handcuffs off and pulling her arms apart and above her head so that he could secure each wrist into the manacles set in the heavy wooden frame.

Alex's eyes flashed with fear, but Peter Tourne knew exactly what had to be done; better now while she was still in doubt about her feelings - it would serve as a proof that she really was his to command.

He nodded to Mario, who slid the final restraint from the back of the frame -

a leather hood that covered her head and eyes totally. Framing her nose it strapped securely under her chin, cutting out every shred of light and most sounds. All that would be left when they had done, would be her sensations and her thoughts.

As Mario jerked the tight mask over her face she began to cry out. It was a shriek of fear and uncertainty. Mario looked at his boss, waiting for instructions. On one side of the hood was a flap with a ball gag attached. Another buckle and the girl would be silenced. Peter Tourne considered this, and then shook his head; he wanted to hear her cries. Also, he didn't want to alarm her too much, and if she panicked in such a heightened state of awareness she might choke. Better to leave the gag off on this first occasion.

Starn reappeared carrying a stainless steel box and a similar leather one. Peter Tourne smiled thinly. Beckoning to Mario he stood back while the large man hooked the frame up on the rope and then hauled it up so that Alex and the frame were hanging at an acute angle to the floor. He waited while the man secured the frame so that it was stable.

Alex Sanderson looked divine; an innocent beauty in her thin blouse, her coarse skirt, barefoot and totally at his mercy. He could sense that she was struggling to make out what was happening, and wondered if she had any idea of what he had in mind as her punishment for defying Starn.

He ran a hand over her breasts, and was rewarded by a faint ripple which spread out from under his fingertips. He could almost feel every nerve ending straining to make sense of his touch.

Roughly he pulled her skirt up, exposing her ripe quim. Her lips were open a little, like a ripening bud. Already a light gloss of hair was returning. Mario had already anticipated his boss's needs and hurried across the room with a bowl of water.

Tourne smiled and opened the stainless steel box Starn offered him. From inside he took a tube of liquid soap. Gently, almost reverently, he soaped Alex's sex. He felt her stiffen as his fingers worked the lather over her mound. He took the razor from the bowl of hot water, and with skilled hands he removed every last trace of hair. Alex held her breath as the razor sliced through the stubble. When he'd finished he rinsed away the soap.

Before he began the next stage he bent forward and pressed a single kiss to the peach-soft lips, his tongue lingering for a second on the peak of her aroused clitoris. Alex responded instantly with a guttural moan and grind of her hips.

Tourne smiled - she would be *so* good, if only she would trust him; give herself over entirely to his desires. He moved his attention back to her breasts. Fingers catching in the gossamer thin fabric that covered them he ripped it open and, taking a swab offered to him by Mario, began to circle the tight little peaks of her nipples with surgical spirit. He felt her flinch and then snort in disbelief. It seemed she may have guessed what he intended to do - after all, she had seen Gena naked.

With the air of a top surgeon he pulled on a pair of thin latex gloves from the stainless steel box, and then removed the piercing gun. It took him only seconds to slip the pre-sterilised surgical steel nipple ring into place. Taking hold of one of Alex's breasts, nipping it tight so that the nipple protruded like a cherry pip, he positioned the gun with great professionalism before she had time to protest. When the head was flat against her skin he pulled the trigger. There was a faint hiss as the spring released, and then a frantic shriek from Alex as the metal bit home.

'No!' she screamed as the ring slid into place. Her whole body flexed and strained against the leather strap and manacles. Her sobbing echoed off the walls of the little room. When Tourne lay the gun against her other breast the sounds ceased and Alex froze. He could smell her fear, her anger, the sense of humiliation rising from her body. When he'd finished she would be wearing the mark of a slave. Her body would proclaim his possession of her. His fingers closed again around her delicate flesh. The only sounds that broke the tense silence were those of her laboured breathing - followed by the malevolent hiss of the gun.

This time Alex did not shriek or fight, but let out a long low wail of despair that made even the inscrutable Peter Tourne shiver with delight. When the second ring was in place Alex began to tremble. Her shivering was enough to make the sunlight catch and glitter off the two new pieces of body jewellery; they looked magnificent!

Glancing down at the vulnerable folds of her quim, Peter Tourne slipped a long stud into the gun. Today he would pierce each side of her labia and put a stud through each of the holes. Later - when she was ready for sale, he would slide a ring in to join the two; it was a symbolic gesture of closure that marked the completion of any girl's training. When the ring was in place he would be ready to pass her on.

Before he began again he gently ran a finger over one of the nipple rings. He considered it added a strange vulnerability and beauty to the female body; tangible proof of a woman's submission to her master.

Pouring more antiseptic wash onto a ball of cotton he swabbed the thick outer lips of Alex's sex. He felt the tension building again in her body as he parted them, and looked at the pale flower petals within. Occasionally he'd seen girls with the inner lips pierced too, but had always considered that a private matter, something a master did to his own woman, whereas the outer ring could be seen and understood by everyone.

He nuzzled the cold steel head of the piercing gun up under the moist folds of Alex's quim. She whimpered. What little he could see of her face was contorted with fear and apprehension. He calmly squeezed the trigger. A flash of silver traced the path of the steel pin.

Looking up he saw that Starn and Mario had moved closer to observe him at work, their eyes betraying hunger and lust. Though Peter Tourne counted Starn amongst his oldest friends, and considered Mario a good and trustworthy servant, he had little respect for either man.

Starn would never understand the subtle blend of cruelty and kindness, of passion and pain that always brought out the best in a woman. He only ever pursued his own pleasures, and in doing so he never commanded the full obedience, or experienced the full beauty, of a woman's unquestioning adoration that was possible. Mario, he knew, was a brutal and self-seeking bully. Though it served him well to have a man with such drives, he'd always suspected that left to his own devices Mario could brutalise a woman so much that she would be of little use for anything thereafter.

He swabbed the other labia. Already the first had begun to swell, plump flesh rising like new bread around the head of the stud. He rested his hand on Alex's firm smooth belly, stroking her gently to calm her. She was sobbing, but made no further attempts to resist him as he pressed the stainless steel gun into place.

He took one final glance at Starn, who licked his lips, salivating at the exhibition. He made a mental note not to sell Alex to his friend, whatever price he offered. Starn had no appreciation of what a fine creature the young English artist was; she needed someone special to help her fulfil the full promise of which she was capable.

He squeezed the trigger that drove the final stud into place. As the pain ricocheted through the girl's body, despite the straps and restraints, she lifted up towards him. For an instant it seemed as if she was offering herself in her entirety into his hands. He smiled - Alex Sanderson was a feast, an exquisite banquet.

Starn was at his friend's shoulder, eyes alight with desire. Tourne could read his mind; he wanted Alex Sanderson and he wanted her now. He sighed and signalled again to Mario. His driver grinned and cranked the rope up so that Alex was now almost vertical.

His friend grinned and stepped closer to Alex, his hand working at the fastenings on her skirt. He dragged it down over her hips, leaving her naked except for the ragged remains of the thin cotton blouse.

'I'll teach her to do as she's told,' he whispered thickly and ran his hands over her newly pierced breasts.

Peter Tourne turned away and picked up the piercing gun. 'Get Mario to put her back in her cell when you've done here,' he said flatly. 'I'll be in my office if you want me.'

CHAPTER 6

Alex came to feeling as if she'd surfaced from some feverish nightmare. She knew she hadn't been unconscious, but very close to it. Peering around she tried to make sense of her surroundings. She was back in the cell. The little room was cool, dark, and totally silent. The chain glittering above her and joined to the collar around her neck brought back a flood of intense images. The abstract, dreamlike quality of her memories hardened into reality.

As Alex turned towards the door she felt the tension in the sensitive peaks of her breasts. Glancing down she saw the malevolent glitter of the rings and lower still, her sex echoed their subtle gleam, but strangely the pain of the piercing was somehow less disturbing than the memory of the events that had followed.

She knew it had been Starn who'd taken over from Peter Tourne, though how she could be so certain was beyond her. She couldn't remember the mask being taken off, but her mind was full of images of Starn circling her, his hands and fingers working into her most secret places with cool brutality. She could visualise his face, cruel and triumphant, as he drew his fingers over the rings that pierced her nipples - and then there was the kiss of the whip as it had exploded across her buttocks.

Tears threatened as she remembered Starn's voice, as cold and unfeeling as the grave: 'Peter Tourne's gone now. You're all mine. He's so concerned with his ideas about educating that he forgets what you're really here for... pleasure - my pleasure. You won't ever deny me again, you miserable little bitch.'

The whip had curled back like a snake and hit her again. It seemed as if the beating went on without end, one blow running into another and another in a tapestry of breathtaking pain, heat, and noise. And finally, when there was calm, she'd hung on the wooden frame, exhausted, struggling to control her mind, every inch of her body raw and aching - and it was then that she felt hot breath on her thigh, followed by a tongue plunging deep inside her quim. The merest contact against the new metal studs electrified her, sending wave after wave of pleasure and pain through her exhausted body. The next touch of the unseen tongue was across her clitoris, sending a bright glittering paradox through her body as the sensations twisted and tumbled together, cutting though her thoughts like a river in full spate.

Just as she was beginning to be drawn in by the growing heat in her belly, a second pair of hands brushed the cheeks of her backside. Against the raw heat of the beating the touch felt almost icy. Her unseen tormentor pressed a finger into her quim, exploring roughly, dipping into her again and again. She felt the brush of an erect penis on the backs of her thighs, and then gasped as it struggled to ease its way into her.

Afraid that he might hurt her she had moved to try and let him have easier access, only to have the man crouching between her legs grunt furiously and grab at her thighs, holding her still. Behind her the man finally found his mark and slid his cock home. She groaned as he buried himself to the hilt with one swift lunge, his hands slithering round to cup and tease her throbbing breasts.

Alex felt the sense of panic growing and struggled to keep a tight hold of her sanity. Behind her the man - she thought it was most likely Starn - grunted like a pig and forced himself as deep as possible, while the man kneeling in front of her continued his relentless tonguing. She felt to be drowning between the two of them. There was no part of her body that seemed to be her own - every inch was alive with pain or pleasure inflicted by another.

The pulsing erection inside her was close to release she could sense it by the way it jerked and by the rasping breath against her ear. But to her horror - and what frightened her more - was that between her legs the dark fire, kindled by the man's tongue, had taken hold, and a great shadowy flame of pleasure was growing in her belly, as raw and terrifying as a forest fire. The thick animal cries of pleasure that she could hear were her own. She screamed as her unseen lover exploded deep inside her and in the same second the flames engulfed her, driving away all reason, all consciousness, until all that was left was sensation.

Now, alone in her cell, Alex flushed crimson. Humiliation replaced her fear. Unlike Peter Tourne they had taken her coldly, used her without feeling... and yet some part of her had revelled in their abuse. Memories of the intensity of her orgasm made her tremble with pleasure. She huddled under the thin grey blanket, careful to keep the fabric away from the tender wounds, and struggled to find sleep.

The beast Peter Tourne had unleashed in her followed into her dreams, where she relived every stroke of the whip, every touch, every dark compelling sensation.

When Alex woke again it was dark. She stared into the gloom wondering what had disturbed her. A light flickered on in the corridor outside her cell, casting a jaundiced pattern through the bars in the door. Mario's distinctive face peered in through the grating. Alex curled into the corner. The driver grinned as he struggled with the lock.

'Get up. Mr Tourne says you join him for dinner.'

Alex stared at the driver. Dressed only in the remains of the ruined blouse she was hardly ready to eat a civilised meal, or perhaps this was yet another part of Peter Tourne's education. Mario swung the door wide. Beside him, standing in the shadows, was the housekeeper. She looked at Alex with a hint of pity in her eyes.

'Come with me,' the old lady said in a tiny voice. 'I get you ready.'

Mario unfastened Alex, and then snapped a long leather lead onto her collar. With Alex secured they walked in procession to the bathroom in the room beyond the cells. She tried hard to concentrate her attention on the gentle ministrations of the old lady rather than the dark lustful stare of Mario, who watched the preparations for her dinner invitation with interest. All the time the housekeeper worked the driver gripped the lead tightly, just in case Alex had any foolish ideas about escaping.

The old woman bathed her, washed her hair and helped her to get dry before turning her attention first to her bruises and welts and then to the new rings and studs. With knowing hands she worked cool balm into the tender pierced places. Her touch was so delicate and gentle that Alex thought she might cry.

When she was finished the old lady twisted Alex's stunning auburn curls into a chic knot. Alex wondered fleetingly why it was she didn't feel self-conscious of her nakedness - and then realised with a start that there wasn't a single piece of her body that either Mario or the housekeeper hadn't seen or touched. The old lady held out a hand and beckoned for Alex to follow her back into the main room. It was bare now. Not a sign of the day's activities remained.

After the warmth of the bathroom Alex felt the chill of the night air on her skin. The woman looked her up and down thoughtfully, and then opened a cupboard. From inside she produced a black leather corset set with studs and chains, and held it up to Mario for his approval. The driver grunted and nodded, his gaze still lingering on Alex's naked body.

Alex shivered as the old woman returned to the cupboard and reappeared with a pair of matching ankle boots; a thin silver chain ran between them, effectively hobbling the wearer. Alex remained still, reluctant to dress in the bizarre outfit her train of thought was broken by Mario jerking at the lead.

'Hurry,' he snapped. 'You not keep Mr Tourne waiting. He get angry.'

The old woman wrapped the corset around Alex's shapely body and then began to fasten it. It was secured by a combination of buckles and laces that nipped Alex's skin firmly as the old woman began to adjust them. Alex gasped as the woman cinched it in over her waist. Glancing down she saw that the skilful boning and cut forced her breasts up and forward, laying them out for her master like a restoration banquet. Below her breasts the corset tightened dramatically around her waist before flaring out into shaped points over her hips. The dark leather framed her naked sex, emphasising the pallor and vulnerability of her body. The woman crouched down to help her slip on the stiletto-heeled ankle boots, before kneeling back to admire the overall effect. Once the boots were on she smiled and then nodded to Alex, as if to imply it looked right.

Alex blushed, imagining how she must look. The old woman struggled and creaked back to her feet and went over to the cupboard again; apparently the outfit was not quite complete. She returned with a pair of long black satin gloves and a mask that covered the top half of Alex's face, the eyeholes framed with tiny silver studs. Alex shuddered; in the mask she became anonymous. Stripped of her identity she was transformed into a creature of pure pleasure. As a final touch the old woman reached into the pocket of her apron and produced lipstick. It was blood red. With steady hands she outlined Alex's full lips, and then stood back to admire her handiwork.

Mario sniffed and then nodded; it seemed he was satisfied with the results. He gave a sharp tug on the lead and Alex had no choice but to follow him. She found it hard to walk in the ridiculous boots; her stride was reduced to tiny steps by the chain and the heels were so high that it was difficult to keep her balance. As if this wasn't enough, the mask restricted her field of vision and the leather corset, tight and unyielding around her cinched body, nipped her flesh making her aware of every weal and ache.

The progress up through the gardens was slow, with Mario tugging impatiently at her lead, making the walk all the more difficult. She caught glimpses of her reflection in the windows as they climbed the steps to the main villa. Her appearance was startling - she looked like a wild erotic ornament; a creature of elicit pleasure. The fragmented reflections, despite everything, increased her sense of expectation, and a tiny flare of excitement formed again in her belly.

Her rational mind struggled with the notion that her ongoing predicament could excite her so intensely. How could this costume and this sense of being nothing more than a possession be so electrifying? Even Mario, her burly minder, somehow added to the growing feelings of arousal. The sea air caressed the naked plains of her body, tightening her pierced nipples into scarlet peaks. Between her legs the same breeze brushed the contours of her sex, teasing back and forth over the creamy folds. Alex shivered; she was wet, she was excited, and yet every shred of her rational mind demanded to know why.

Alex was relieved when they finally stepped into the entrance hall with its bright sparkling fountain. It seemed a lifetime since she had arrived at the villa and first met Peter Tourne. Was it possible that the naively talented artist who had arrived to paint the mural was the same woman that stood there now, dressed as a gift for her master?

The lights were low in the hallway. Candles in glass vases had been set around the poolside. The tumble of greenery around the water reflected the moisture and light, giving the room a magical quality. For some reason Alex was certain that Starn and Gena had left - whatever was to be played out tonight was for her and Peter Tourne alone. As her mind formed his name he appeared from the shadows. She wondered how long he had been standing there watching her. He held out a hand and Mario silently passed him the lead. He looked at it thoughtfully, and then at Alex.

As their eyes met she began to understand her foreign emotions; this enigmatic man had - from the first moment they'd met - instinctively recognised the kind of woman she was. He fully understood the needs and desires even she didn't dare acknowledge existed within her. Did he know her better than she did? For a few seconds they stood facing each other, and in that breathless moment each recognised the true nature of the other: Master and slave, two halves of a complex puzzle that defied all logic and rationale.

'I think we can dispense with the lead tonight,' he said quietly and stepped closer. Instinctively Alex leant into his touch, like a sleek cat seeking the comfort and approval of her owner. Peter Tourne smiled and stroked her neck. She could sense his approval, and felt a disproportionate sense of pleasure. His fingers worked at the fastening on her collar, and then he dropped the lead to the floor. Without a word he turned and made his way up to the dining room. Alex stopped struggling to make sense of what was happening to her, and followed him.

Upstairs the elegant room was lit by candles and the grand table set with just a single place setting. Beside the carver chair at the head of the table was a footstool. Alex had no doubt where her place was meant to be. She would sit at his feet, doing as he willed, obeying his every command. A servant appeared from the shadows and pulled the chair out.

Like Mario, Peter Tourne's houseboy was a local peasant, and Alex immediately sensed his interest in her arrival. His eyes - which rested on her body for no more than a few seconds - gave her a peculiar sense of self-assurance. Stripped of her identity, all she had left to offer was a pure sexuality that was as raw and alluring as a hunger. While the boy busied himself with serving the meal Tourne settled himself at the table and shook out his napkin. Alex curled gracefully onto the stool beside him without a word.

Peter Tourne smiled inwardly as he began his meal, sitting back to allow his houseboy to pour the rich red wine. He wished it was possible for Starn to be there unobserved to watch Alex's unquestioning obedience, but knew it was impossible. Starn had always preferred overt displays of submission, whilst he relished Alex's sweet capitulation. No amount of beating or pain could engender her reaction, unless it was already part of her nature.

He tore the bread on his side plate and offered a piece to his slave girl. She leant forward carmine lips open a fraction to feed from his hand like a tame dog. As her tongue grazed his fingers he could sense the emotion coursing through her veins.

The meal was exquisite, and from each course he saved a little for the girl who awaited his pleasure so willingly. There was a strange erotic charge to the way her lips worked around each morsel, her tongue seeking to retrieve each scrap. If his fingers brushed her cheek she would press against him lightly, her skin warm and inviting beneath his fingertips.

Finally he took his coffee and a liqueur over to the window to look down at the sea below the villa. Glancing over his shoulder he saw Alex waiting for his next command. The leather corset accentuated her subtle curves and the creamy richness of her English complexion. She did not meet his eyes but instead looked down, meek and humble, his command to obey. How much Starn missed with his insensitive fumbling, he thought.

He saw Alex shiver - well aware, no doubt, that he was observing her. As she moved a fraction the candlelight reflected in the silver rings nestled under each nipple and below, between the soft shadowed folds of her thighs he could just see the studs that pierced her labia. She glanced up momentarily, and he beckoned to her. She appeared to slither across the floor, crawling on all fours as if afraid to get up from the stool. As she reached his feet she pressed her face against his thigh. He could feel her breath and smiled. This was all he could have hoped for, and more. He extended a hand and slowly she uncurled and got to her feet.

He nodded towards the table. 'Lay down, my dear,' he said. 'I want to look at you.'

Without a second's hesitation Alex crossed the room and lay down amongst the remains of his meal. He left her there, waiting until he had finished his coffee. When he finally turned to observe her he could see a light sheen of perspiration had risen in the deep valley between her breasts. Her breathing was light and excited. He understood only too well the power of anticipation. He examined her lazily, stroking her sex and running a finger over the swollen places where the studs nestled. As he touched her again she opened her legs to give him greater access and freedom.

He was amused that she should think she could control him so easily. Hadn't he taught her the game was his, and not hers? Between her open thighs he could see the glistening juices clinging to the folds of her quim. She was offering herself up for his pleasure - a touching but unnecessary gesture.

He glanced at the glass of cognac in his free hand, and then with slow deliberation he poured the contents over the sensitive lips of her sex, and as he did so he plunged his fingers deep inside. She groaned as the alcohol seeped over her, startled by the sting and the coldness of it.

'Oh, Alex,' Tourne said as he nipped and pinched at the sensitised peaks of her breasts. 'How clever you think you are. How many times must I tell you, it is I who makes the rules - not you?' He twisted her soft flesh, making her groan again with pleasure, pain, and confusion.

Slowly he backed away, leaving her panting with uncertainty. He was delighted to see she instinctively remained on the table eyes closed, legs still apart, breasts rising and falling deeply. He plucked a candle from its holder, snuffed out the flame, and pressed it into her gloved hands.

'Here we are,' he said softly. 'This is for you. I have no use for your body tonight.'

Alex stiffened, her fingers closing reluctantly around the thick wax shaft. She lay quietly, nibbling her soft lower lip nervously.

'Oh, please don't make me wait,' Tourne whispered. 'Show me what pleasure really can be. Amuse me.'

'Please Mr Tourne...'

'Do as you're told - now!'

Slowly Alex lifted her legs until her booted feet rested on the polished table edge - opening herself as she did. He could sense her fear and humiliation as she guided the candle deep between the sensitive lips of her quim. For an instant the candle withdrew - it glistened with her juices - and then disappeared very, very, slowly as she pushed it all the way home. Her movements were self-conscious and stilted. Her cheeks flushed delightfully, and she nibbled her lip all the more urgently.

Tourne snorted derisively. 'What kind of half-hearted nonsense is this, Alex? Don't be so foolish it wouldn't do to make me angry. Now, I want to see you touch yourself properly. Show me what pleasures your body can offer a man. Show me some passion.' He paused. She was trembling, her fingers still closed tightly around the thick stem. 'Or would you prefer it if I called Mario in to help you?'

He saw her flinch at the mention of his driver, and then suddenly, leaving the obscene wax stem embedded in her succulent sex, she moved one hand to her clitoris where her fingers rubbed vigorously and the other lifted to cup and squeeze her breasts. He hardly needed to see any more of her performance - beautifully arousing as it was; her unquestioning obedience was the goal he sought.

As he turned away from the gorgeous scene he noticed a flicker of movement from the corner of his eye, and realised that he hadn't dismissed his houseboy; he'd been so intent on Alex that he'd forgotten the boy was there.

A thoughtful and mischievous smile slowly lifted the corners of his mouth. He moved smoothly back to where Alex lay quietly panting, shook loose a crisply starched napkin, and blindfolded her with it, whispering assurances as he worked.

When satisfied that she could see nothing, he nodded towards the shadows, his gesture an explicit invitation. The boy's bright eyes stared back at him, unconvinced.

Tourne waved him closer and whispered in Greek, 'Do what you want with her. Whatever you like. While she is on this table she is yours.'

Alex lifted her head from the table and strained to hear. 'Mr Tourne, what are you doing?' she asked timidly. 'Is somebody with you?'

'Sssshhh my dear. Of course not - it's only me here. You look so wonderful, well, I don't think I can resist you after all. It would be such a waste...'

The boy still looked a little uncertain, but bowed his respectful gratitude. His face was an amusing mixture of anxiety and enthusiasm as he dragged his thin cotton shirt off. Watching him, Peter Tourne realised the boy was barely out of puberty - seventeen or eighteen at the most. Underneath his shirt he was as willowy as a reed, with a straggling triangle of dark hair that extended from between his nipples on his undeveloped chest to the waistband of his drawstring trousers.

Peter Tourne watched the boy gazing longingly down, clearly unable to believe his luck at the beautiful English girl spread before him. He smiled with amusement at the youthful erection that strained and threatened to split the front of his trousers. Of course, the lad had seen everything that had gone before, and it would be impossible for him not to be excited. His anticipation and excitement were as tangible as Alex's.

As Peter Tourne watched like a teacher monitoring the capabilities of his favourite student, the boy's hands worked clumsily down over Alex's slim hips. He slipped the candle out, replacing it first with his finger, and then his tongue. At first his caresses were experimental and tentative, as if he expected his employer to call his explorations to a halt at any time. As he slowly realised this wasn't going to happen, he grew more confident, and began to relax and enjoy himself. Tourne warmed to the boy's clumsy eagerness and tried to remember his name, but nothing formed in his mind.

Much to his delight, the boy grew more rough with poor Alex as he grew more confident, although his abrasive fumbling came about more through ignorance than design. He turned Alex this way and that, exploring every inch of her vulnerability as if she was a new toy.

The surprised confusion was etched on Alex's face; these were not the ministrations of one so experienced and refined as her host and patron. 'Mr Tourne...' her whisper was barely audible above the eager sucking of the boy. 'Mr Tourne... please.'

'Sssshhh...' Peter Tourne soothed again, and Alex moaned and stiffened as the boy accidentally found the spot.

Peter Tourne doubted the boy had ever had a woman before, and if he had it had never been like this. Perhaps the boy had shared some guilty fumbling with a village girl in a dark alley, but certainly never had he had one totally at his mercy - his to command. Tourne grinned, imagining the houseboy having his face slapped by a peasant girl as their wills clashed over what part of her he might be allowed to touch or kiss. With Alex he would have no such trouble - she had relinquished herself completely to their control. The boy groaned hungrily, biting and nipping with his sharp white teeth at the soft places between her thighs. She squirmed and twisted exquisitely from side to side, moaning and rolling her head as his explorations grew more and more urgent.

Suddenly he pulled away, eyes alight as his hands continued to nip and squeeze at her submissive flesh. His lips were glossy with her pleasure. He scrambled up onto the table. He straddled her waist, jerked down his trousers, and lay his bursting cock into Alex's perspiring cleavage. He cupped and moulded her breasts around his erection, and thrust his narrow hips ever more urgently, until with an excited shudder he ejaculated over her throat and breasts. His seed exploded over her like an arc of milky stars.

Peter Tourne smiled, thinking that the impromptu exhibition was over, and then realised he was wrong.

The boy, sweating heavily, crouched lower, his cock still jutting forward and glistening with his own juices. He began to lap hungrily at Alex's face and throat, and then sucked and chewed her budding, sperm-coated nipples. Easing himself further down the table his fingers returned to her sex and, pushing her fingers aside, he began to drag and paw at her clitoris.

Alex groaned softly, relinquishing her body to the unseen stimulations. The boy grinned as she continued to writhe under his touch. His attentions turned to the candle which still lay between her legs on the table. He picked it up and buried it into her with one smooth movement. Alex whimpered, and her whole body convulsed. Her back arched and lifted from the table as the boy's fingers returned to her pleasure bud. His tongue lapped and circled the pierced peaks of her breasts. Peter could sense her impending orgasm and was stunned that the boy could put on such a spectacular show.

Alex expelled a long low mewl of utter pleasure and slumped motionless on the expensive tabletop. The boy finally collapsed onto her exhausted body, and lay with his contented face between her magnificent breasts. After a few minutes, suddenly remembering where he was, he quickly scrambled to his feet, and dragged his trousers up to hide his withering embarrassment from his employer's perceptive gaze.

Glancing furtively at the man by his side, the boy blushed furiously. Peter Tourne shook his head and mimed a show of applause.

'You've done very well,' he whispered. 'What's your name?'

The boy's colour intensified. 'Raymond, Sir,' he stammered, unable to meet his elder's eye.

Peter Tourne nodded. 'Good. Fetch some fresh coffee, Raymond. I'll be out on the terrace. You may tidy up in here later.'

The boy nodded and hurried away.

When they were alone Peter Tourne looked down victoriously at Alex.

'Get up. Come here,' he said in a low, even voice. Alex slithered from the table, her body slick with sweat and the remains of the boys' excesses. The candle was still buried inside her. Her face was flushed.

Peter Tourne ran his hands over her breasts and then down to her belly, his fingers fixing tight on the slippery wax. She gasped as he pulled it free. Slowly he trailed the wet shaft over her breasts where her soft flesh was still smeared with the boy's glistening seed and saliva.

'Tell me Alex, whose game are we playing?' he asked, catching hold of her chin and tilting her face up towards him. 'Whose rules do we abide by?'

Her eyes were glassy. 'Yours, Mr Tourne,' she murmured.

'Good. You have to understand that above all else.' He rolled the candle thoughtfully between his fingers and then ran it across her lips. She shuddered. Her carmine lipstick left a smear on the white shaft.

'Open your mouth,' he whispered.

Alex swallowed hard, quite obviously fighting her revulsion, but slowly her lips parted and he drew the candle back again. This time her tongue, moist and pink, trailed along the glistening cylinder. He angled it and pushed the tip against her pouting lips. They peeled open, and he slowly but firmly fed the inanimate object into her hot wet mouth before turning to pull the bell that would summon Mario.

Alex open her eyes and stared at him with a mixture of arousal and surprise as the candle was slipped from her mouth. It was obvious he was dismissing her.

'But, I thought—'

Her host's face hardened. 'I have already told you - you are not expected to think, or to talk. Is it so hard for you to understand?'

Alex looked down at the floor. Because he'd invited her to join him for dinner she'd assumed her reward would be to make love to him. Certainly she had not expected to be abused by him as she had been on the table, or to be manhandled again by his servant. She wondered if he would punish her now for her disobedience - but to her regret he turned away. Such exquisite torture, she thought miserably.

Mario opened the door. His boss didn't even speak. Mario had the lead in his hand and Alex knew then that whatever attentions were to be metered out it wouldn't be Peter Tourne who provided them. She shivered; Mario's expression suggested he'd been waiting for this moment. Alex looked desperately at her host as he casually dismissed them both with a wave of his hand and then headed out towards the terrace.

Mario clipped the lead back onto her collar and gave it a sharp tug to let her know that he was now back in control. Alex nibbled her lip anxiously.

The driver rubbed the back of his hand across his wet lips and then greedily stroked one of Alex's breasts. He grinned and jerked the lead again. This time Alex followed him - she had no choice. Glancing back just as Mario led her through the door, she saw Peter Tourne out on the moonlit terrace - he was staring out to sea, oblivious now of her presence.

CHAPTER 7

After that night with the houseboy, days at the villa KaRoche began to take on a regular pattern for Alex. Each morning Mario would unchain her and lead her out from her cell to the long gallery beside the pool, where she would work on the mural. At first Alex thought it would be impossible to paint under such circumstances, but soon discovered creating the mural was the only vestige of normality that remained, like a touchstone, in her new and strange life.

The way she was dressed was dependent upon Mario's lecherous whims. Sometimes he left her naked, other times he dressed her as a peasant in cotton blouse and skirt, or sometimes he strapped her into a tight leather concoction.

In the heat of the afternoons she was allowed to rest, chained back in her cell. The hours of siesta were always fitful and uneasy; if Mario was not required to drive his boss anywhere or had no other work in the villa he would visit her. Sometimes his visits were purely for sexual relief, on others, if the day had gone badly, he came to take his frustration out on her body with a whip or a leather belt. She dreaded the sound of his footsteps outside the cell door.

In the evening Mario and the housekeeper would appear to dress her for Peter Tourne's pleasure. She would be perfumed and painted, and then dressed according to his instructions; sometimes in exotic ball gowns, sometimes in an elegant evening dress - most often though it seemed he preferred her in a boned leather basque or corsets, her features obscured by a masquerade mask.

Upstairs in the dining room Tourne would feed her by hand as she knelt at his feet. On some nights he required nothing more than her silent companionship. On others she was expected to exchange social niceties or embark on long conversations about art or literature. Part of the game he played with her was that she was supposed to guess which it was he required. If she made a mistake and was unable to guess, her punishment was to be handed over to the houseboy, whose taste for oral sex and ejaculating on her exposed flesh seemed endless. As Tourne ate his dinner she was always aware of the boy waiting eagerly in the shadows - waiting for his turn to make use of her body. Whenever Tourne beckoned the boy over his youthful eyes would sparkle intensely. Alex had felt totally humiliated when she'd learned the truth about that first night on the table, and the humiliation lessened little with each subsequent occasion she was given to the boy. Peter Tourne always preferred his servant to make love to her - if that was indeed what it was - on the table, so that he could enjoy their exhibition. Sometimes he would offer words of encouragement to the youth, guiding him and educating him in the ways of taking her. When the youth had had his fill Tourne would wave them both away and Mario would take her back to the cell to begin the ordeal afresh.

Though it seemed impossible, Alex began to settle down to the peculiar rhythm of life at the villa KaRoche. Within a fortnight her life in London was but a distant memory, and all the while the mural, the finest thing she had ever painted, took shape along the gallery walls, recording forever a coded warning of the events that had overtaken her at the villa.

Her plan for escape rapidly became a dream to sustain her in the long dark nights, chained to the bed, waiting for a footfall in the corridor that would announce one of Mario's late night visits.

Starn didn't reappear at the villa for some time. At first she thought it was Tourne's way of punishing him for trying to take advantage of her while she'd been painting in the gallery, but overhearing a telephone conversation while she was at dinner with her host, she realised that it was because Starn and Gena were away on a business trip in London. Knowing that Starn was staying in the city in which she lived made her wistful. Would she ever be allowed to go back to the life she had known?

As the days passed, it was obvious to Alex that the elderly housekeeper couldn't have rung her agent, Laurence. If the old woman had done as she'd asked, Laurence would surely have come to rescue her by now.

Sitting at Peter Tourne's feet in the dining room one night she wondered fleetingly if Laurence had contacted him since that first phone call. Normally she would have expected her agent to have rung her at least once or twice a week while she was working on a commission, to see how the work was progressing. It seemed that nothing at KaRoche was as normal. She wondered what excuse Tourne had cooked up to explain why she never came to the phone.

'You seem distracted this evening, my dear,' he said, running his hand down over the curve of her shoulder.

Alex blushed and looked up. 'I'm sorry,' she whispered.

Tonight she was dressed in an elegant white shift dress and high gold sandals. Under different circumstances she might easily have passed for a society beauty dining with her lover.

Tourne smiled indulgently. 'I went to see how the mural was progressing this afternoon. It's very good. I am extremely pleased with what you've created for me.'

Alex nodded; she'd learnt it wasn't wise to be too forthcoming. He got to his feet and poured them both a glass of wine.

'How much longer do you think it will be before it's finished?'

Alex stiffened; finishing the mural was something she hadn't given too much thought. When the mural was complete would he let her go home, or would he sell her on as Starn Fettico had predicted? She glanced up at him, trying to suppress the strange mix of hope and fear that formed in her belly. His expression revealed nothing.

'A few more days,' she said carefully. 'Perhaps a week, at the most.'

'Good,' he said. 'Starn and Gena are due back from England tomorrow. I intend giving a dinner party to welcome them.'

Alex wondered whether he meant to include her too, but decided to say nothing.

He turned his glass thoughtfully in his fingers. Alex couldn't help but notice the houseboy hovering hopefully in the shadows. He was watching her with interest, his stare burning with intensity. As their eyes met he licked his lips and lewdly rubbed the already considerable swelling in his trousers. Alex shivered. She knew he was hoping she would make some small mistake that would fire his employer's displeasure.

As she turned away she realised to her horror that Peter Tourne had been speaking '...We've been friends for years. Like you he is English. I'll be interested to see what he makes of your progress.'

Alex struggled desperately to reconstruct the words she hadn't paid any attention to, but fortunately her host didn't seem to have noticed her rude lapse of concentration. He beckoned to her.

'Now, stand up, my dear. I'd just like to assess your progress.'

She did as he asked without thinking.

'Good. Take off your dress.'

Alex reached round to find the zip. He shook his head in exasperation and clicked his fingers toward the houseboy. 'Help her with the dress.'

Alex felt the youth's hands on her back his breath was warm and moist on her skin. Was Peter Tourne giving her to this enthusiastic but clumsy boy yet again? What had she done wrong? The boy struggled to unfasten the zip and then pulled the thin fabric down off her shoulders. The delicate dress slithered to the floor like liquid. Beneath it Alex was naked. The boy didn't move away - Alex could almost feel his excitement scorching her bare flesh.

Peter Tourne studied her beauty thoughtfully. 'Turn around,' he instructed her with quiet confidence.

As Alex obeyed she lowered her gaze to the floor; she couldn't bear to witness her own humiliation in the victorious expression of the young lad. She knew he was taking advantage of her closeness to drink in every inch of her nakedness.

Tourne murmured his approval. 'The bruises have gone,' he said, almost to himself. 'And there are no weal marks. Good. I'm sure you'll meet with Simon's approval.'

Alex completed her slow turn. As her compliance had grown Mario had been less vehement in his beatings. She'd quickly learnt, however repellent his desires, it was far better to do as she was told than risk his fury. As a result, he'd been less quick to use the whip or belt on her.

Tourne leaned forward in his chair, and then began a more thorough examination of her. It seemed he was particularly interested in the rings that pierced her nipples and the studs that pierced her labia. Though far from healed, they were no longer sore or inflamed.

'They've taken very well,' he murmured as he ran a finger over them. Alex shivered - the nipple rings in particular made her feel totally vulnerable. 'You are very nearly ready, my dear.'

Alex's mind raced. Ready? Ready for what?

'My dear friend Simon has expressed an interest in you. He will be here tomorrow night, and then, when the mural is complete, and if he thinks you are suitable, you will join his stable for auction.'

Alex's stomach churned sharply while her urbane host turned her to the left and to the right, holding her at arms length, making a cold appraisal of what he saw as though he were an antiques dealer assessing a fine piece of porcelain.

He continued: 'I'll make certain Mario doesn't mark you before tomorrow tonight. Simon isn't very keen on bruised fruit. You're a little small for his tastes - but beautifully proportioned, and *so, so* succulent.' He cupped and squeezed her breasts as if he were weighing apples. She blushed. He stroked her belly with a flat palm, and then slid a hand down between her thighs. A single finger probed and then opened her sex. 'And still nice and tight here,' he continued his commentary, 'that's good.' He moved his attention to the studs that nestle in the plump outer lips of her quim. There was no emotion in his touch; it was simply a cold assessment of her flesh. 'I'll change these for my family mark once Simon has given his approval. Turn around again, and bend over.'

Alex flushed crimson. The houseboy, as if anticipating his master's requirements, gripped her shoulders to support and ease her forward until her face was almost level with his groin. She could make out the clear swelling before her eyes, and despite herself she was gripped by an almost overwhelming desire to open his trousers and swallow the young cock deep into her throat. Her mouth was parched. It wasn't the houseboy that interested her - it was the near virginal erection hidden within that stretched material.

Suddenly she gasped, and her attention was drawn to Peter Tourne's exploratory fingers. He spread the cheeks of her bottom and ran an inquisitive finger over her anus. Alex shivered; it was the focus Mario's particular pleasure, and the memories of the driver plunging into those most secret places of her body made her stomach churn anew.

She felt something cold and oily trickle down the crease of her backside, and then felt a rush of humiliation as he worked a finger into the tight and dark closure. Her whole body tensed. Tourne grunted as he tried to breach the tight band of muscle.

'Still very tight here too. Relax and pant, my dear, I need to get inside you.'

Alex felt the houseboy's hands tighten on her shoulders. Her shame excited him even more. She gasped as the finger pressed insistently at her entrance. She struggled to control her breathing, so that the tense band of muscle would relax and allow him entry without causing her unnecessary discomfort. Suddenly she emitted a long low groan as she opened and the digit slid home.

Without warning the finger left her as quickly as it had violated her, and the satisfied Peter Tourne moved away, leaving Alex feeling embarrassed and exposed. She was about to straighten up when his voice stopped her.

'Don't move. Stay as you are.'

Alex took a deep breath, wondering what would follow. It didn't take long for the answer to arrive. From the corner of her eye she watched Peter Tourne cross the room and open the door. Mario was already waiting outside. He grinned salaciously when he saw Alex bent over, supported by the houseboy.

Peter Tourne told his driver to enter, and then settled himself in a comfortable armchair. Alex couldn't understand what was said between the two men, but she guessed that her host intended to observe and enjoy whatever was to follow. She watched him top up his brandy balloon from the drinks trolley by his side, and then wait for the show to begin.

Between them, Mario and the houseboy manhandled Alex over to a stool and lay her across it. The corpulent driver knelt behind her, and the houseboy unleashed his raging virility.

A charming little *ménage à trios*, thought Peter Tourne with pleasure. He knew that if he indulged Mario's lusts now it would help ensure Alex arrived at tomorrow night's dinner party unmarked.

Mario grinned lustily down at the houseboy's youthful cock, closed his fingers around it with surprising tenderness for such a big man, cupped and raised Alex's chin with his free hand, and fed the straining erection into her mouth. The boy gasped with delight and threw back his head. Mario undid his young accomplice's shirt. His thick fingers worked at his plump purple nipples. He leant forward and planted a delicate kiss on each, his tongue working around the buds.

Peter Tourne wasn't repulsed by the display of affection between the two males; he was enchanted; he had never observed this side of his driver's nature before. If indeed Mario did prefer the muscular charms of the peasant boy it would explain his preference for buggery.

Alex's delicate English rosebud mouth closed around the houseboy's shaft. Her red lips were stretched, and her eyes were shut tight. Mario shuffled behind her, struggled to free his own bursting cock, and then buried himself to the hilt in her unprotected quim. Crouched between them she was rapidly becoming just a vessel for their mutual desire.

Peter Tourne suppressed a smile as Mario began to plunge in and out of her; it seemed that in front of his master, Mario was conforming to a more usual course of pleasure. Perhaps he was afraid he would incur disapproval if he drove home into his preferred orifice.

Alex let out a thick guttural grunt as Mario began to move in earnest. He slid his rough hands up under her ribcage, turning his attentions to her nipples. His fingers twisted and teased at the engorged peaks, making Alex want to cry out - although the houseboys' cock muffled her cries.

Mario's attentions returned to his accomplice, whose expression was one of absolute ecstasy. Seemingly oblivious to the girl squashed and huddled between them, Mario pulled him closer and planted a long kiss on his gasping mouth. The houseboy groaned and held Mario to him. Alex, humbled and reduced to a mere vehicle for the two males' pleasure, was completely forgotten as they grunted and rutted enthusiastically towards release.

As Mario's lips worked against his, the houseboy groaned again and flexed his hips, driving his cock deeper into Alex's waiting mouth. Mario snorted, almost as if he could feel the boy's excitement directly, and renewing his rhythmic thrusts in and out of Alex, began to gasp and moan as orgasm overtook them both. The houseboy's eyes opened to reveal a strange mixture of pleasure and fear, and then he convulsed. His seed exploded into Alex's mouth and seeped from the corners of her lips. Mario shrieked in delight, clawing the boy closer, sweat pouring down his face as the convulsions and contractions of his own climax closed over him.

When their passion was spent, Peter Tourne got to his feet and waved his driver and houseboy aside. Alex, still crouched over the stool, was wet with their perspiration. He helped her to her feet. Mario's seed trickled from her sex, and a smear of the houseboy's semen clung to her chin.

Peter Tourne smiled warmly. 'You are ready,' he said softly, and handed her back to Mario.

Returned to the darkness of her cell and chained for the night, Alex lay staring up into the blackness. She could still taste the houseboy's excitement in her mouth. Her body's raw desire for satisfaction dispelled even her dreams of escape.

The two servants had been oblivious to her own needs; they had used her, and wanted nothing but her body. That knowledge - dark and compelling - made her ache with a strange sense of pleasure. Peter Tourne was right; she was ready. There was no possibility of going back or unlearning the lessons he had taught her.

She slid a finger between the lips of her quim. Mario's seed coated her fingers, lubricating her caresses as she stroked the soft folds of her sex. Need rose up through her belly like an angry roar. She instantly found the tiny bead that was the seat of all pleasure. Circling the hood with a deft knowing finger she drove another deep inside her quim. The need for release was so close to the surface that the first brush was enough to light fantastic fires in her mind.

As the pleasure began to build Alex imagined Peter Tourne's face; imagined him watching as the two servants had taken her; imagined their bodies penetrating her depths - and instantly she was lost. Deep inside her sex began to contract, sucking her fingers down as orgasm drove away everything but the intense image of Peter Tourne's dark flashing eyes.

When Alex rose and showered the next day the villa KaRoche was already humming with activity. Mario brought her breakfast early, but was so preoccupied that he barely looked at her. Later, while Alex worked in the gallery, the sound of voices from the main villa filtered down to her. She could hear vehicles arriving, the sounds of male voices, and muffled banging and thumping.

71

Mario had barely seemed interested in the ritual of deciding what she was to wear for the day; she had ended up dressed quite comfortably in a thin summer dress and sandals. Had it not been for the collar and chain she could easily have passed for a houseguest. Alex guessed that this was Mario's intention; should a deliveryman inadvertently find his way into the gallery it wouldn't do to find a woman, naked except for a leather basque, chained to the wall.

She worked without interruption all morning, and instead of Mario arriving at lunchtime to take her back to the cell, the housekeeper arrived with a tray. The old lady's expression was tight and preoccupied. She avoided Alex's eye as she slid her lunch onto the table alongside her paints. It seemed that the dinner party had taken precedence over everything else. Alex really didn't mind. It made a pleasant change to sit in the shade by the pool and eat her food.

After she'd eaten Mario arrived, dressed in a clean and tailored uniform, and without comment he took her back to the silence of the cells. His face contorted into a grimace as he chained her.

'He say not to touch you,' he said with obvious frustration. His expression hardened. 'Not to touch, pah!'

Alex felt a sense of triumph; it appeared that Peter Tourne's will did extend to events in the cells after all. Her delight was short lived as Mario unbuckled the belt that held up his tailored trousers. 'He means I should not mark you.'

Alex stiffened. 'I'll tell Mr Tourne—' she began, but instantly regretted it. Mario's eyes flashed with fury. Drawing back his hand he slapped her face with the open palm.

'You tell him nothing!' he snapped, and slapped her again. As she stumbled he stooped and grabbed her calves with surprising agility, and flipped her onto her back on the platform that served as a bed. She shrieked in surprise at his swift assault. Mario jerked her legs apart and moved forward sharply so that her feet rested on his shoulders. 'You make big mistake. Mario can do things to you that leave no marks.'

Alex flinched as his fingers tore at her dress - but as he pulled it aside she knew it wasn't her sex that drew him, but the dark closure behind. He spat into his hand and stabbed a finger roughly inside her anus; with hardly any lubrication her body screamed out in protest.

'Tonight,' he hissed between gritted teeth as his fat finger plunged in and out, 'when Peter Tourne and guests have finish with you, I and the boy will be down to give what you deserve! No one will hear you cry - all people be too drunk to care!'

Alex shivered. 'N-no, Mario, p-please,' she stammered. 'There's no need to be rough with me. I'll be nice to you, and your boy!'

Mario snorted and spat into his hand again. Dragging his finger out of her he unceremoniously flipped her onto her belly and spread his saliva over the tender puckering. With her face forced down into the thin blankets she tensed as she felt his cock brush her thighs.

An instant later he breached the tender skin. She held her breath - she wasn't ready. Terrified that he might tear her she willed her body to relax. Mario was oblivious to her concerns. Alex screamed as he forced himself deeper. A hand clawed round and over her face, covering her mouth.

'Quiet, bitch!' Mario snorted. Alex clenched her fists and bit down on his hand, trying to find a way to combat the pain. Behind her she heard Mario laugh. 'You not hurt me,' he sneered, 'and if you do, you pay later!'

Upstairs in the villa preparations for the evening's dinner party were well underway. Peter Tourne kept only a handful of staff at the villa: Mario, his housekeeper, and a procession of local boys to wait on table and tidy the garden. For any formal or important occasion he would hire in the staff he needed and arrange for the meal to be catered by an exclusive catering company - his housekeeper's cooking, though adequate for his own private tastes, was more often than not little more than simple peasant fayre.

For Starn and Gena's reappearance and the visit of Simon Bay, he wanted something more spectacular. Flowers had already arrived from the mainland, a chef and his retinue were busy working in his kitchen, and various lackeys were preparing the dining room.

Tourne glanced at his watch. He had no particular need or desire to impress Starn - but Simon Bay was a different matter. In his office he had a gown that had arrived on the ferry, delivered by courier that morning, for Alex. He wanted Simon to be impressed by his latest pupil. It would be extremely convenient if Simon could be persuaded to allow Alex to join his stable for his annual slave auction.

Tonight he would oversee Alex's preparation's himself. He sighed - in a way he would be sad to see her go, but for him it was the challenge of the initiation that gave him the greatest delight. Once a girl was broken he would rapidly tire of her company. He much preferred it if they left KaRoche before they lost their appeal. It would be sad if that happened with Alex. A month at his villa should be enough - after that he would let Simon Bay do what he could with her.

As the florist carried a huge display of lilies into the hall, Peter Tourne's mobile phone rang.

'Tourne.'

'*Hello, Peter,*' a familiar voice at the other end of the line laughed. '*It's Laurence here. I've just rung to see how Alex is getting on.*'

Tourne glanced over his shoulder at the milling servants. 'One second,' he said in an undertone. 'I'll just take your call upstairs to my office.'

Laurence laughed again. '*No chance I could have a word with her?*'

Tourne sighed. 'My dear friend, it's siesta time here.'

'*Ah yes, how foolish of me to forget.*'

Peter Tourne, cradling the mobile phone, climbed the stairs to his office and closed the door.

CHAPTER 8

After Mario finally left Alex's cell the day seemed to pass slowly. Alex dozed spasmodically, her dreams suffused by images of Mario, superimposed upon Starn, the willowy houseboy, and last of all Peter Tourne - who, in the frantically erotic dreamscape, watched Alex's every move, his eyes alight with vicarious pleasure.

She had assumed that at some time during her imprisonment he would make love to her, but it appeared, since that first night when he'd shown her the delights of the gallery, that his real pleasure lay in voyeurism.

Tonight he would introduce her to his friend, Simon Bay. He had no intention of keeping her at KaRoche once the mural was complete - and she knew without a doubt that the plans that had formed in her mind for escape had to be put into action now. She had no desire to be the plaything of yet another unknown man. She closed her eyes, trying to imagine what it might be like to be auctioned off to the highest bidder. Her fear and anger were balanced by a darkly erotic counterpoint; there was a strangely erotic frisson in the idea of being bought and sold like a common slave, tied and naked for the eyes of her would be masters.

As evening fell Alex heard the sound of approaching footsteps and stretched, readying herself for the arrival of Mario and the housekeeper. She wondered what they had brought for her to wear; Mr Tourne's tastes were eclectic to say the very least. She was surprised when the door swung open and Peter Tourne himself stood framed by the shadows. He was dressed in an elegant dinner suit, his hair slicked back and tied into a knot at the nape of his neck. The darkness gave his lean features a predatory, wolfish cast.

Behind him, Mario and the housekeeper waited expectantly. For a few seconds the atmosphere in the cell seemed tight with anticipation. He held out his hand towards Alex, and she was stunned to realised that the feeling she experienced in the wake of the simple gesture was akin to love. Something caught in her throat, tears bubbled, unbidden, behind her eyes. She wanted to beg him to let her stay at KaRoche, to let her serve him and him alone. The words that formed in her heart wouldn't form in her mouth. The moment of intense emotion passed and Mario silently unclipped her leash and led her to the room beyond the cells.

Someone had set a tin bath in the centre of the gallery, and beside it stood a large solid table. Lamplight threw the objects into sharp relief. Alex felt as if she was about to step onto a stage.

Peter Tourne settled himself against the wall in the shadows and watched while his servants prepared her for her introduction to Simon Bay. Despite everything the sense of theatre remained, as if she was taking part in a strange ritual. The old woman soaped and shaved her quim. Mario washed her hair then lathered her breasts and back. The two of them worked in complete silence as if they had performed the same rite a thousand times before. The only sound in the room was the water lapping over the side of the tub and splashing onto the flagstone floor.

With every passing second Alex felt more and more like a prize possession being prepared and polished for a final exhibition. None of the others in the room seemed to care who she was - it was her body they were preparing, not her mind. Waves of panic closed over her just like the water that washed over her ripe breasts and slim hips. Finally the old woman helped her out of the tub, dried her with fluffy towels, and then guided her to the table.

Mario took her wrists and lifted her onto the cool wooden surface, urging her down onto her back. The tabletop was set with manacles that snapped around her wrists with an unnerving finality.

Her ankles were next.

Spread-eagled and naked Alex held her breath as Tourne approached and ran a proprietorial hand over her breasts. He cupped and stroked them thoughtfully. Mario appeared at his shoulder carrying a small stainless steel box. Alex stiffened, knowing with an uncanny certainty that the box held the tools that had pierced her.

She hoped he would look at her, his expression giving her the reassurance she needed, but instead he seemed intent on the contents of the box. From inside he produced a fine silver chain and a pair of pliers. She flinched as he cupped first one breast and then the other. With a cool professional touch he slipped the chain though the nipple rings, and used the pliers to close the links at each end to link the two rings together.

Next he moved down to the studs that pierced her labia. Alex winced as he forced the studs up. Mario handed him something from the metal box. Alex strained to watch the journey of the object he was now holding. He was replacing the studs with a single heavy silver ring. A small ornate medallion bearing a tiny coat of arms hung from it. It was a sign of her origins, a mark of ownership. Alex closed her eyes. The first and last time she had seen a ring like it was when she had been making love to Gena. She shivered. The ring slipping through the lips of her sex seemed like a gesture of finality. The mental anguish she felt was far greater than the physical pain of the studs being removed.

When satisfied with his work he turned away and Mario unlocked the manacles holding her ankles and wrists. Alex watched the housekeeper approaching with her outfit; a long sheath dress of gold voile. The fabric was so sheer it looked like gossamer. The old woman slipped it over Alex's head, gently lifting it over the chain that now linked her breasts. Mario added a pair of high golden sandals while the housekeeper set about dressing Alex's tumble of titian curls. Tourne watched without a word until the old woman added the customary slash of scarlet lipstick.

'Do her nipples too,' he said. The old woman undid the high neck of Alex's dress, carefully folded it down, and traced her nipples with the scarlet stick. They hardened instantly under the housekeeper's deft touch. The old woman pulled the dress back into place.

Tourne nodded his approval. Alex reddened; the approval was not for her but for the servants who had transformed her. Helping her to her feet, the housekeeper turned Alex round so that he could admire their handiwork further. As Alex turned she gasped; for the first time since she'd been held prisoner here she was confronted by a full-length mirror, which had been brought into the room without her noticing. What she saw made her freeze.

The exquisite gold evening dress fitted her like a second skin. Intricate gold embroidery emphasised her slender yet shapely form, revealing tantalising glimpses of her breasts and sex. Her tinted nipples pressed in dark invitation against the fabric, the silver chain and rings adding a strange glittering counterpoint to her creamy flesh.

The housekeeper had spun Alex's long hair out into a halo of curls, and subtle make-up made the most of her fine bone structure. Under any other circumstances her appearance would have been a thing of simple beauty - but instead Alex was aware that the outfit subtly proclaimed her submission; the fine studded leather collar still encircled her neck, and the silver chain hung down invitingly between her breasts. Any man alive seeing her dressed in the beautiful gold confection would instantly know she was nothing more than the slave of a very wealthy master; a pretty bauble created for pure pleasure.

Peter Tourne appeared in the mirror beside her. His eyes moved over her reflection, appraising what he saw with a detached look. After a few seconds he offered his arm to her, and Alex felt powerless to resist him. It seemed he was ready to present her to his guests.

Outside the night was already dark and starry. The confident man and the beautiful girl walked in silence to the villa. She longed for him to say something - to offer her some words of comfort or support, but instead his eyes remained firmly fixed on the steps ahead.

Inside the main hallway a uniformed lackey handed them a glass of champagne each. Peter Tourne turned towards the front door, awaiting the arrival of his friends. Beside him Alex trembled as she heard the soft purr of a car engine and the crunch of tyres on the drive.

Starn Fettico appeared first, dressed in a white dinner jacket. Tourne grinned as Starn crossed the room.

'Starn,' he said warmly. 'How good to see you again. How was London?'

Starn grunted and embraced his friend. 'Wet, cold - a perfect English summer.' He eyed Alex, who instinctively looked down at the floor. 'I see you've nearly done with her then?'

Tourne shrugged. 'Almost. I've invited Simon Bay to join us tonight. I hope you don't mind, I want him to take a look at her. Where's Gena?'

Starn took a glass of champagne from the proffered tray. 'I met Jack Casman whilst in Bonn. He offered me a good price...' the Greek shrugged dismissively. 'What can I say?'

Alex stiffened as she realised what Starn was saying. Gena had been sold off like an unwanted puppy.

Tourne nodded. 'So, you're in the market for a new companion too now?

How is Jack?'

Alex's mind was reeling. There wasn't a shred of emotion in Peter Tourne's voice - not the slightest hint of concern for the fate of the beautiful blonde he'd trained.

'He's fine,' Starn had continued. 'Actually, I picked up something that might be of interest to you.' He turned and waved to his own driver who was standing in the open doorway. 'Jack took me to a little club near his mansion - Carmino's - perhaps you've been there? They deal mostly in imports. I would suggest the next time you're in Germany you take a look. They had some interesting things on offer there...'

His voice faded into the background as Alex's eyes were drawn to the doorway. The driver had reappeared, his gloved hand holding two leather leads, attached to which were two girls. Alex stared in astonishment. At first they seemed but mere children, but as they stepped into the light Alex realised they were in fact two exquisitely beautiful young women, perhaps seventeen or eighteen years of age.

Identical twins. They appeared to be Eurasian, with waist length oil-black hair and huge brown eyes. They were naked except for sheer white silk shifts that came down to and swayed around the tops of their thighs. The fabric was so finely woven it revealed every intimate curve. The girls' breasts were small but firm and thrusting, and topped with pert mauve nipples, and their genitals were hairless and oiled. The two of them stared around the opulent interior of the villa, and then giggled nervously. They seemed to bloom like perfectly ripened fruit.

Starn smiled indulgently at his latest purchases. 'Bring them inside,' he said to his driver.

Tourne whistled appreciatively. 'Very nice... very nice indeed.'

Starn sipped his champagne. 'They cost me a mint. A matching pair, fresh from their village - certified virgins. They'd been in Bonn for only three days when I saw them. Barely long enough to have a medical check and arrange some paperwork.'

Starn took a cigar from his top pocket and lit it. The twins meanwhile stood very still, holding hands, obviously apprehensive, watching their new master for some kind of signal. He beckoned them further into the room, and they scurried over to him. Starn relieved his driver of the leads and the girls immediately sank down and knelt either side of him on the cold tiled floor.

Peter Tourne smiled. 'A very nice find. Are they broken yet?'

Starn grinned and took a long pull on his cigar. 'What do you think? It felt just like Christmas, they were so ready for it.'

Alex stared down at the twins. They were naturally subservient. Everything about their body language implied their unquestioning obedience. They looked so sweet and vulnerable. Alex hoped Starn had been kind to them, but doubted it. One girl nuzzled Starn's thigh, seeking attention and favour. Starn appeared oblivious to her. As she moved her glossy hair fell forward, and Alex could see a fine red weal across her shoulder. It seemed almost an obscenity to mark her silky gold tinted skin.

Alex's attention was broken by the sound of Tourne greeting someone else. She looked up and the breath caught in her throat.

'Simon! How wonderful to see you again. I'm so glad you could make it,' the suave host said with genuine warmth as he stepped forward to embrace his guest of honour. 'We were just admiring Starn's latest acquisitions. You remember Starn, don't you?'

Simon Bay - the man invited to come and examine Alex - stepped into the room flanked by two dark skinned women of Amazonian proportions. The girls were both over six feet tall. With spiked shoes that added at least four inches to their natural height they appeared quite awesome. Their voluptuous curves where strapped into fabulously cut leather body harnesses, but, for all their astonishing beauty, it was Simon Bay who captured Alex's attention.

She stared at him in open-mouthed disbelief, recognising his aristocratic features instantly. This wasn't the anonymous slave master she'd been expecting, but a face from the gossip columns - a member of one of the richest and most well known families in England, who's photograph she'd seen time and again in the society pages, squiring some titled beauty or other to a gala, or a ball, or a first night.

He was dressed in a long Edwardian style jacket. His mouth was cruel, and his eyes flashed like a bird of prey as he met her gaze and unashamedly took in the contours of her luscious body. Alex dropped her gaze, feeling her cheeks colour furiously. It seemed the guest of honour hid his real name, but not his nature, behind a pseudonym.

As Tourne, Starn and Simon Bay exchanged social pleasantries, Alex could feel the latter's hungry eyes crawling over every inch of her.

'So,' said Bay, accepting the glass offered to him without interrupting his blatant inspection. 'This is your latest pupil, Peter?'

Tourne nodded. He'd sensed his friend's interest as soon as he'd walked into the room. Good manners had required he show him Starn's new girls first, but he knew that Simon's preference was for European or black slaves; they offered a real challenge.

Simon Bay pensively turned the glass in his long slim fingers. 'Physically she's not quite to my taste,' he said flatly as he slowly began to circle Alex as though stalking his prey.

Tourne nodded. He'd expected as much. Simon liked muscular, heavy breasted women.

Simon Bay teased out a lock of Alex's hair and twisted it thoughtfully around his fingers. 'That isn't to say I couldn't sell her for you. She looks presentable. Interesting colouring. There'd be no need for a master to hide this one away.' As he spoke he glanced at Starn's matching pair of fillies as if to make his point. 'I'd need to have my doctor look her over - put her through her paces.'

He stopped his circling and stood close behind Alex, looking over her shoulder and admiring the slow swell of her breasts. He gripped the hem of her dress and began to pull it up. His thin hand slid between her smooth thighs, making her catch her breath and shiver. His face registered disapproval. 'She's dry.'

Tourne sighed. 'My servants just bathed her.'

Simon Bay shrugged. 'I always prefer them unwashed. Their scent is part of the appeal for my clients.' He pulled his hand away and looked round. 'Have you some oil, and a towel?'

Tourne nodded towards one of the lackeys, cursing himself for not being prepared; a girl sold by Simon Bay had great cache.

Beside him Starn grinned and lifted the leads on his two Eurasian girls. 'Perhaps you'd like to look over my new stock too? I can guarantee they're good and wet. And I'd appreciate your opinion, though they're not for sale.'

Simon Bay nodded. 'Of course, my dear chap. I've always liked twins, though they can be harder to manage. Don't be tempted to split them up - together they're worth at least four times their value as individuals.'

The servant reappeared and Simon Bay slowly poured the olive oil over his fingers. Peter Tourne glanced monetarily at Alex, willing her to behave as he knew she could. She looked at him, her eyes glassy with unshed tears. He nodded his approval and silent support. Without a word she opened her legs, bending forward a little so that Simon Bay could begin his examination without hindrance. She bit her lip as his fingers explored her most intimate parts. He mumbled his approval as his finger slipped comfortably into her quim.

'Nice and tight here. Shame she's so dry, it really spoils the overall effect. She's supposed to be ready whenever she's required.' His finger slipped out and he sniffed it speculatively like an expert wine taster. 'Subtle bouquet,' he mumbled again. 'But difficult to judge when she's so clean.' He oiled his fingers again.

Peter Tourne watched Alex stiffen, and knew from the exquisitely confused expression on her face that his distinguished guest's hand had slid between her buttocks; he knew where Simon Bay would inspect next. As a persistent finger pressed home Alex let out a soft mewl of discomfort.

'Perhaps a little too tight here,' Simon Bay said casually as though commenting on a piece of clothing, 'though she is very tense. If I take her on I'd have to insert a stretcher. A lot of my clients would be reluctant to purchase her if she couldn't take them anally as well.'

Tourne nodded his understanding as Simon Bay wiped his hands on a towel the servant held out for him. He circled Alex again and stroked her breasts through the sheer dress. Her nipples hardened at once under his knowing touch.

He nodded thoughtfully. 'All in all, not too bad, Peter. I'd certainly be happy to put her on the auction list - providing you can let me have her for a few days before hand. Not that you've done a bad job, old chap - she's a fine specimen, but she still requires a little more work. A little... fine tuning, so to speak.'

'I see.'

'Don't look so worried old man, I'm certain she'll make a decent price for you.' He grinned. 'When can you deliver her?'

Tourne's delight at his friend's words was tinged with a sense of regret. He suddenly experienced strange feelings towards Alex. 'A week, she has to finish the mural I told you about.'

Simon Bay nodded. 'Ah yes... By the way,' he said as he took his glass of champagne and instantly changed the subject with a bizarre air of normality. 'Did you hear that Monique is coming to my party tomorrow night. She's calling in on her way back to the States. I've already invited her to fly back to my place for the auction...'

The conversation moved away from Alex and on to wider things. Peter Tourne glanced back as his friend warmly threw an arm around his shoulder and invited him to look over his new body slaves - a single tear was trickling down Alex's exquisitely made-up features.

The dinner party was a great success. Wine - served by Alex and Starn's new Eurasian girls - flowed like water. Simon Bay's intimidating slave women stood sentinel by the double doors of the dining room, their faces impassive, and their eyes flashing as the men indulged in a magnificent meal.

Alex couldn't reconcile the feeling of pain she felt as Peter Tourne played host to his two guests. He seemed oblivious to her now that Simon Bay had given his seal of approval. Her mind was wandering as she refilled their wine glasses for what must have been the sixth or seventh time, and - while not concentrating - the neck of the decanter caught the top of one of the glasses and tipped the contents over the table. Instantly the conversation ceased.

Nervously Alex began to dab at the spreading scarlet pool with a napkin, feeling a tiny flurry of fear in her stomach; it almost seemed the men had been waiting for her to make some kind of mistake. Simon Bay looked at Peter Tourne, and then beckoned Alex nearer. Drunkenly he slid his hands up under her skirt, and teased the lips of her quim.

'Not so dry now, eh?' he purred with amusement.

Alex swallowed hard and looked at Tourne.

'I'm very sorry about the wine,' she began.

Simon Bay grimaced theatrically. 'She speaks too readily. Haven't you taught her that slaves are expected to be quiet?' he said to Tourne. His fingers pawed further. 'In some places they'd cut out her tongue if she refused to obey.' He grinned crookedly. 'Always seems such a shame; a tongue can be used for so many lovely things besides talking.' The wine had made him rough. Alex flinched as he clumsily prodded a finger up inside her. He sniggered and burped quietly. 'Maybe your protégé is not as obliging as you would have me believe, Peter. It's her European upbringing. One of my handsome coloured girls, or either of those pretty little twins of Starn's, would have their legs open the instant you touched them, eager to satisfy their master.'

Peter Tourne, his cheeks similarly flushed with wine, snorted 'that's what makes her special, Simon we both know that. She is yours to command - do what you like with her, you'll see she's better than all of them put together.'

Simon Bay sniggered again and jabbed another finger into Alex. 'She's still too dry.' His fingers slipped out and he turned her to face him. 'My good friend Peter tells me you're willing to please.'

She nodded warily; she knew there was little else she could do.

'Very good,' Simon Bay blinked slowly as if it took a great deal of effort, and then slurped his wine. 'Then lift up your dress.'

As Alex obeyed, Simon Bay - his eyes firmly set on the pierced lips of her quim - lifted a hand and beckoned to the Negro girls who flanked the door. He looked up into Alex's eyes as the coloured girls approached. 'They will make you wet for me,' he said softly. 'Open your legs.'

The heavily built women moved with deceptive grace and silence. Before Alex could compose herself one girl dropped onto all fours between her and Simon Bay and ran her snakelike tongue across the lips of Alex's naked sex. Alex gasped with a mixture of shock and surprise. A moment later the second woman closed behind her and reached round the stunned girl to cup her breasts. Her alien sex brushed Alex's back.

For an instant it felt to Alex as though they would overwhelm and consume her. Between her legs the tongue flicked back and forth across her pleasure bud, while the pinching fingers sent wonderful sensations through her nipples and breasts. She struggled to catch her breath.

Starn snorted and refilled his wine glass.

Simon Bay looked across at him through slightly blurred eyes. 'You have something to say, Mr Fettico?'

Starn leered drunkenly. 'If it were me,' he waved a finger unsteadily in the air, 'I'd punish her for being so bloody clumsy, not let your trained tigers lose on her. She's bloody enjoying herself. She should be whipped!'

Simon Bay nodded. 'Patience, Mr Fettico, patience.'

As the men spoke Alex felt a flash of pleasure lighting in her belly. The black women knew exactly where to touch her. A long tongue slithered over the engorged ridge of her clitoris, caressing the silver ring on its journey through her labia, while strong hands glided up over her thighs. Simon Bay would have had no worries now; Alex could already feel the wetness forming deep inside her. The two women encouraged her to let them take her weight. She leant further and further back against the giantess behind, opening her legs so that the woman crouched between her legs could have greater freedom to kiss and caress her. Long fingers pressed deep inside, exploring the moistening contours with surprising tenderness.

Alex felt the tension in her spine begin to fade. The instant she began to relax her unlikely seducers seemed to sense the change. The woman behind grabbed her ribs. The woman at her feet grabbed her thighs, and they unceremoniously picked her up and threw her face down onto the table amongst the remnants of the dinner.

Alex shrieked. A strong pair of hands grabbed at her legs and jerked the beautiful evening dress up around her waist. Alex began to struggle, but she hadn't bargained on the tenacity and strength of Simon Bay's two black slaves.

One of them mounted the table with feline agility, held Alex's arms before she had time to respond, and pinned her down against the wine soaked cloth. To Alex's utter horror she could feel the seeds of arousal that had formed in her sex now glowing white hot - screaming for release. She swooned under the treatment of the two women.

She heard Simon Bay laugh arrogantly. 'Perhaps this is more to your taste, Mr Fettico?'

A few moments later something hissed through the air and a lightening strike exploded across her naked buttocks. Alex screamed in astonishment. The woman tightened the grip on her shoulders, and Alex realised that in a strange way that touch was meant to reassure. An instant later the whip struck again. This time the blow was harder. The sensation was so intense that every cell in her body seemed to register it; the sensation swept through her like a volcanic blast, driving away every thought, every shred of consciousness that could not be registered as feeling.

Blow after blow detonated across her naked back and buttocks until she couldn't tell where one stroke ended and another began. She thought she might lose consciousness, her mind driven into a corner by the pain, and worse still, the terrifying knowledge that the same pain and feeling of humiliation fed the dark creature Peter Tourne had created in her.

Suddenly the hands on her shoulders rolled her over onto her back. They manoeuvred her effortlessly until her sore bottom was perched on the edge of the table and her legs dangled towards the floor. She closed her eyes, unable to face the gaze of the assembled diners and their slaves.

All she could hear was the ragged sounds of her own breath, and then she smelt something that made her gasp. She knew immediately what it was, and then she felt the brush of warm flesh against her cheek and lips. Someone was straddling her shoulders. She opened her eyes and saw the gaping quim of one of the slaves. The musky smell of the woman's sex was almost overwhelming. Before Alex had time to protest or resist a hand lifted her head up towards the folds of dark wet flesh.

Alex trembled as she breathed in the unmistakable scent. Her body seemed to be covered in a blanket of the female perfume; the odour flooded her every sense. To her horror her mouth began to water. In the instant before Alex pressed a tentative kiss to the woman's body, another tongue opened her own quim and slid effortlessly over the swollen bud of her clitoris.

Alex mewled, the noise buffeted and echoed against the closeness of the woman crouched above her.

Peter Tourne was absorbed by the tableau being enacted in front of him. The two amazons looked as if they were eating Alex alive. They crouched hungrily over her prone body, both facing her feet. The one whom Alex was tonguing had her finger's buried deep in her companion's sopping sex, who was in turn lapping enthusiastically at Alex's unprotected quim. Beneath them their victim was gasping and twisting wildly from side to side, her whole body and mind caught up in the intensity of the moment.

Simon Bay, standing now between Alex's open legs, looked on in triumph. The English girl's cries were getting more and more instinctive as pleasure and passion unseated pain and reason. He dropped the riding crop he'd used on her, opened his trousers, and unceremoniously drove his cock into her dripping sex. Alex arched herself to take him, while his slave's long pink tongue lapped at his shaft as it slid home.

On the far side of the table Starn Fettico grinned slyly. Moving closer, ignoring both his slave girls, he too unfastened his trousers. His cock jutted forward like a scimitar. As the coloured girl squatting over Alex's face moved, her quim opened and closed like a gaping scarlet mouth. Starn gripped her broad hips and pulled her a little closer. Climbing onto the table he guided his shaft into the hot wet depths of her body, his hands sliding along her sweating torso to cup her pendulous breasts.

Peter Tourne saw Alex hesitate for a moment as the coloured girl above her wriggled back a fraction to allow Starn Fettico to drive deeper. He imagined the thoughts and sensations going through her mind as she felt the contours of Starn's knarled cock sliding over her tongue, the brush of his balls against her forehead and closed eyes, and the smell of his body; he could imagine it all.

Alex suddenly let out a long guttural screech of pleasure, and her whole body stiffened and convulsed as the first waves of orgasm ripped through her. As she began to writhe those around her were caught up in its wake. Like a house of cards the lovers began to quake and fall way - all sated, all pleasured.

Peter Tourne smiled, topped up his brandy balloon, and settled himself back in his chair; Alex Sanderson had surpassed anything he could have expected of her. He was certain that Simon Bay would feel the same way.

When she emerged from between the coloured woman's thighs, Alex's face was flushed, her lips slick with the juices of the dark beauty, her sex pink and moist from the attentions of the other slave and Simon Bay's orgasm. She blushed furiously as she realised Peter Tourne had been watching her. He extended his hand and she took it without a word. He pulled her close and kissed her, relishing the taste on her lips. She looked around nervously as the others began to tidy themselves.

'Can I go to the bathroom?' she whispered, her colour intensifying as she spoke.

He nodded. 'Don't be long,' he said softly. 'I'll be waiting for you.'

When she'd gone he went over to the ice bucket and poured three glasses of champagne - after all, he had something to celebrate.

CHAPTER 9

Alex hurried from the dining room, still trembling from the events that had taken place under the cool eyes of Peter Tourne. She was certain she'd passed the test that he'd set her. Her whole body hummed from the intensity of her orgasm. She glanced left and right, struggling to regain her composure and get her bearings. There was a cloakroom in the main hallway. She scurried downstairs - a trickle of semen already running onto her thighs.

As she passed Peter Tourne's office she realised that the door was open - and in the lamplight she saw the phone on his desk. An idea took shape in an instant, and before she really had time to consider any possible consequences she hurried inside, picked up the receiver and tapped in a London number.

To her immense relief Laurence Russell picked up the phone on the second ring. She sighed and thanked God that her agent was a famous workaholic who seldom left his office before midnight. Glancing anxiously over her shoulder she whispered, 'Hello?'

Laurence coughed. '*Hello? Who's that? Is that you Alex? Where the hell have you been? I've been worried about you.*'

Alex felt a lump form in her throat at the sound of his familiar voice. 'Laurence,' she said unsteadily. 'Please listen to me. I haven't got the time to explain. You have to come and get me. I'm still at the villa KaRoche.'

'*What's the matter? Can you speak up? I can barely hear you, Alex. Is there a problem at the villa? You sound different.*'

Alex looked up, catching sight of her reflection in the enormous picture window that overlooked the sea. Her skin was glowing her eyes alight with the after-effects of pleasure. The lamp on the desk reflected in the chain that linked her nipples - She most certainly was different.

'I can't talk to you now,' she whispered hurriedly. Where would she begin even if she had the time to explain? 'Please, Laurence, just come and get me. Something has happened.'

'*All right,*' comforted Laurence. '*But I—*'

Alex jumped and squealed as a pair of hands grabbed the receiver from her fingers and slammed it back into the cradle. She spun round, her expression taut with fear. Mario leered at her.

'Who do you ring?' he snapped, gesticulating towards the phone.

Alex felt her colour drain. 'No one,' she said, backing away from the desk. 'I couldn't get through, that was... that was... the operator.' Alex cringed at her own feeble answer.

Mario's face contorted into a sickening grin. 'I tell Mr Tourne,' he said flatly.

'No!' snapped Alex, holding her hands up to keep a distance between them. 'Please don't, Mario. I'll do anything you want - anything. Please - just don't tell Mr Tourne.'

Mario looked her up and down. His fingers snaked forward to cup her sex. He snorted, rubbing the fabric of her dress up into her quim. 'You're very wet - how you say, *very horny*.' He sniggered. 'They all fuck you, already? You save a little for later. I and the boy - we want our share.'

Alex reddened as the driver pulled his hand away and sniffed his fingers.

'What's going on in here?' Peter Tourne's voice from out in the hall made Alex jump again. Mario grinned at her, and then turned to face his employer.

'I catch her here,' he said nodding towards the phone. 'She going to ring someone.'

Tourne stared past him at Alex. 'Is this true?' His expression was stony.

Alex knew that Mario had already lied for her and that she was now beholden to the brutal driver.

'Well?' snapped Tourne. 'It is true, Alex?'

Looking down, Alex struggled to conceal her guilt, and nodded miserably.

'Yes,' she mumbled. She could sense his displeasure. When she finally looked at him she realised he was more disappointed than angry.

'How could you defy me, Alex? I instruct you. I show you your true nature. I invite one of the world's most respected masters to come and examine you,' he stopped and shook his head. 'And yet you still try to escape?'

'Oh, Mr Tourne,' Alex said softly. The tears that had threatened earlier when she'd spoken to Laurence Russell trickled down her face. 'I don't know. I don't know what I want. I don't understand what's happening to me.' She paused. 'I'm afraid of what you make me feel.' It was true. She was afraid of losing herself in the maelstrom of emotions that Peter Tourne had shown her; afraid that in submitting to her darkest instincts she would lose everything.

Peter Tourne sighed and touched her face. 'Afraid? Oh Alex, what is there to be afraid of? Haven't I told you this is a game - a complex charade that feeds the pleasures of those who lead and those who follow.' He paused. 'Trust me, Alex. Let go and relish the pleasure.'

Alex pouted. 'But you're going to sell me. That's why Mr Bay is here tonight, isn't it?'

He nodded. 'That is true. Another games master, another game.'

'But I don't want to be a slave.'

He smiled wryly. 'Are you so certain of that?'

She felt a flicker of panic. 'But what if—?'

'When you tire of the game all you have to do is walk away. But I don't think you will; you like what I've shown you too much. Something you have to understand is that I'm your master because we have an unspoken agreement that allows me to dominate you. To teach you. To show you all that can be shared. You just have to trust me, Alex.'

She stared at him, trying to grasp what he was saying, but sensing that he was right. Didn't her whole body glow whenever she obeyed him? Hadn't the greatest moments of sexual satisfaction she'd ever experienced come when she gave up her whole mind and body into the hands of this man? Didn't she relish the fact that he took what he wanted from her without question?

Tourne stroked her hair with surprising affection. 'Simon is prepared to sell you at his auction. He's invited us to his villa for a party tomorrow.' He looked at her thoughtfully. 'At the end of the week I'll hand you over to him. You have a day, perhaps two, to finish the mural.'

Alex felt sick. 'Another games master?' she whispered.

He nodded, indicating the phone on his desk. 'Or if you prefer you can walk away now. The choice is yours.'

Alex struggled to make sense of the tumult of feelings that bubbled inside her.

Mario, still standing at his employer's shoulder, leered at her. Voices from outside the office broke the tension, and Tourne turned away to greet Simon Bay and his entourage.

The guest of honour again looked Alex up and down before he spoke, though his remarks were directed towards his host.

'I wondered where you'd got to, my friend. Your houseboy is ready to serve more coffee and liqueurs, and your friend Starn is anxious to show off his latest toys.'

Tourne nodded. 'I'll be there in a second or two Simon.'

Simon Bay's eyes hadn't left Alex. 'Trouble?' he asked.

Tourne shook his head. 'Not really, is there, Alex?'

She had to make a decision. Swallowing hard, she shook her head. 'No,' she stammered. 'There's no trouble.'

Simon Bay slapped his friend on the back. 'Oh come on, Peter. Why don't you let me take her with me tonight? It'd solve everything. Let me have her for a day or two extra.'

Tourne held out a hand to guide his illustrious guest back upstairs. 'No, thank you, Simon. It's a very generous offer, but she has to finish the mural first.'

As they left he turned back to look at Alex. 'When you've been to the bathroom come back upstairs and join us. Don't be long.'

Alex nodded. Mario grinned. She knew that the sophisticated game of passion Peter Tourne had taught her was lost on Mario - and she now owed him.

She hurried to the downstairs bathroom and turned the taps on full. Splashing her face with cold water helped restore a sense of balance. When she returned to the dining room Starn's latest acquisitions were staging a lesbian exhibition. Despite their writhing and moans Simon Bay looked thoroughly bored. The beautiful little Asian girls were self-conscious and ill at ease as they went through the stilted routine Starn had obviously taught them. Despite their beautiful bodies and sinuous curves, it was far from stimulating.

Alex took her place at Tourne's feet and rested her head in his lap while the girls stroked and whispered their way through a mockery of true eroticism. Starn however was delighted, and had no hesitation in joining them, making love to one while tonguing another. Finally, breathlessly, at the point of orgasm he sunk his teeth into one of them. For the first time Alex felt the shriek of pain that followed was close to the reality of sensations that Peter Tourne had so cunningly taught her.

Her eyes felt heavy, and she was surprised when the next thing she saw with any clarity was his face not more than an inch or two away from hers.

'They've all gone home,' he whispered. 'It's time you were in bed.'

With a yawn she uncurled and stretched her knotted limbs. She rubbed her eyes and looked around for Mario. He was nowhere to be seen. No doubt he was lurking somewhere outside, waiting to extract the price for his silence once they had reached her cell. To her surprise Peter Tourne extended his hand and helped her to rise.

'Come with me,' he said softly.

Tenderness was the last thing Alex expected.

Silently he led her into a part of the villa she'd never seen before. At the top of what seemed like an endless flight of stone stairs, double doors opened onto an enormous vaulted chamber. The room was lit by candlelight and appeared to have been carved out of the hillside the centre of the room was dominated by a huge bed. He turned to her as they stepped inside.

'Until you leave here you are my slave, and mine alone.'

Alex nodded and followed him into a marble lined bathroom. Set in the floor was a bath already filled with steamy aromatic water. With trembling hands Alex set about undressing the man who had initiated her into the dark game. As her fingers struggled with his clothes she realised that in all the time she had spent at KaRoche she had never seen him naked. The thought made her stomach flutter with anticipation. She wondered if there was some way she could convince him that she ought to stay with him at the villa. She could be everything he wanted.

Every touch was an act of worship - she unbuttoned his shirt, slipped off his jacket, undid his dress tie, all the time aware that he was watching her. As she pushed his shirt back off his broad shoulders she pressed a kiss to his dark hair trimmed nipples, her tongue paying homage to him, like a supplicant at an ancient altar. She knelt down to unfasten his trousers, eyes chastely lowered to the floor.

Tonight she was Peter Tourne's handmaiden, his body slave, and every cell of her mind and body relished her submission. His cock was magnificent; broad and curved it sprung into her fingers like a sword. She ran her tongue along it, pausing to kiss the engorged scarlet crown. He moaned softly, stroking her hair as she lapped and caressed his shaft. Lifting her hands to cradle his balls she drew him deep into her mouth. She felt the tension growing in his body, and smiled.

'No, not yet,' he said in a husky whisper. 'I want you to bathe me.'

Denied her prize, Alex nodded and moved aside, reluctantly letting go of him.

His body was quite beautiful; slim and muscular, his skin had a soft golden glow to it that made her mouth water. There was nothing she wanted more than to service him, to feel him deep inside her, to give him whatever pleasure he demanded. She trembled, ripples of desire forming and reforming in her belly.

He smiled at her and stepped down into the water. Alex slipped off her evening dress and hurried to join him. With gentle hands she soaped every inch of his glorious body; every touch, every single gesture confirming his status as her lord. He closed his eyes and lay back in the warm water. Alex felt almost overwhelmed by her tenderness towards him. The feelings were so intense she thought she might cry.

When they were done, he allowed her to wrap him in a thick towelling gown and pour him a glass of wine from the tray arranged on the sideboard in the bedroom. Alex noticed that beside the tray was a finely tooled leather strap with a split end. She bit her lip, momentarily touching the cool leather before carrying the wine to him, eyes humbly downcast.

Naked and still wet from the bath she curled at his feet, awaiting his instructions. Tourne set the glass down on the arm of his chair.

'You've forgotten something,' he said.

Alex shivered; she knew what he meant. Struggling to control her racing thoughts she rose and brought him the leather strap. He took it from her and ran it thoughtfully between his fingers, his eyes working up and down her naked body. She felt the anticipation in her belly growing under his undisguised examination. Her body was already crisscrossed with the weals from the beating given by Simon Bay - but what filled her mind was not the painful marks, but the ever growing sense of expectation. She tensed as he got to his feet and swung the strap back.

'Come here,' he ordered, indicating the rug in front of him. She stepped closer. 'Put your hands on top of your head.'

She did as he said - and closed her eyes.

The first blow hit squarely across the tensed peaks of her breasts. She shrieked, astonished that he could still be so cruel. The second blow hit her across the belly, lifting a broad red plain of tender flesh. The pain from the strap was different from the whip; the sensation was more diffused, dissipating through her like molten magma. The third stroke caught her sex, exploding across the ring that pierced her labia.

Her mind flared - hadn't she already proved she was his slave? Hadn't she already given herself to him completely? Why did he still have to punish her? The answer was as obvious as the question; it was all part of the game. She was his to do with as he pleased, and if she wanted to partake in the pleasure of submission she must never forget that truth.

The fourth and fifth strokes hit her low on the buttocks, making her gasp.

'Open your eyes,' Tourne said.

Alex stared up at him. His eyes flashed with desire and pent-up emotion. He threw the strap to the floor, crossed the room, and lay on the bed. She hesitated, wondering what he wanted next. He glared up at her.

'Come over here and give yourself to me, Alex. Show me what a good slave you have become. Show me that you understand the rules of the game.'

She swallowed hard. In some ways, after the beating, she knew this would be the ultimate test; to come willingly to her tormentor, and to surrender unquestioningly to his desire. She walked towards him as gracefully as her trepidation would allow; aware that with every step she was getting closer and closer to losing herself forever in his passion. His eyes remained dark and devoid of emotion.

Slowly she climbed onto the bed and straddled his calves, touching herself as she did. She could feeling the moisture forming in the innermost recesses of her sex.

Tourne glanced down at her fingers. 'Are you wet?'

Alex nodded.

He smiled. 'Good. Now show me what you've learnt. Give me the undivided devotion and pleasure I deserve.'

Trembling, Alex crouched over him, crawling up over his warm muscular body, fluttering kisses over every inch of his frame. Her tongue lapped at his balls, caressing and stroking the intimidating curve of his shaft. Her lips closed around its head. She ran her tongue around its edge, then across to kiss the single moist eye. Whatever else happened to her, Peter Tourne was her first master and every thought that formed in her head was concentrated on giving him pleasure.

Eagerly she drew him deeper, sucking and lapping, willing his approval. When she sensed he was ready she moved over him, replacing lips and tongue with her hands as she lifted herself up to guide him into her. As his cock parted her delicate inner lips, as she felt the sheer strength of his need, their eyes met. He looked into her mind. His gaze was suffused with tenderness.

Without hesitation she impaled herself on him, drawing him deep into her throbbing quim. For the first time she saw a look of pure uncomplicated joy on Peter Tourne's face. She began to move up and down, giving herself to him entirely, her feverish grinding taking them both to the edges of madness. He groaned. Unable to hold back any longer he thrust into her. His face contorted and his movements became wild and instinctive. Alex cried out, feeling the rush of an ancient passion that exploded inside her mind and her body, as they fell into the abyss of orgasm. Down and down they both tumbled, twisting and turning, gasping for breath, until finally it was over and they were still.

Peter Tourne pulled her close to him, his lips brushing her forehead. She sighed - exhausted and completely spent. She was pleased with herself. She curled up under his arm and slipped effortlessly into comfortable sleep.

The next day was the strangest Alex had spent at the villa KaRoche - strange because of its normality. She woke up still beside Peter in his bed, got dressed in her own clothes which were brought to her by the housekeeper, and then after a breakfast they shared on the terrace she went to work on the mural. Peter spent the morning with her, sitting in a garden chair and reading. He even joined her makeshift picnic lunch.

He was a wonderful companion. For once he was more lover than master, but even so Alex could still feel the subtle strength of his power as they chatted and laughed. He was still her master despite appearances, of that she had little doubt. Finally, as the long hot afternoon began, he dismissed her.

'Go back to the guest cabin and rest,' he said softly. 'Tonight, at Simon's party, another phase of your education begins.'

Back in the guest cabin Alex stared at her possessions. Everything was exactly as she'd left it. It seemed so long since she'd unpacked her clothes and arranged her toiletries in the bathroom. She glanced up at the open door, imagining that Gena would appear at any second. She stared sadly at the void - was Peter letting her have one day of freedom before handed her over to Simon Bay? He'd told her it would be at the end of the week, but the way he now looked at her and the gentleness with which he was treating her made her suspect that he might have changed his mind.

Outside in the raw heat of the day the cicadas were buzzing. The fragrances of the exotic flowers wafted on the warm breeze from the garden into her room. She slipped off her clothes, lay down on the bed, and closed her eyes she was intoxicated by the heat and the strange sense of expectation.

She wished there was some way that she could persuade Peter to let her stay. She couldn't imagine anything she wanted more than to be with him Pulling a sheet up over her shoulders she felt the ache of the bruises on her back - that only served to feed her hunger.

CHAPTER 10

As soon as Alex awoke she was aware that someone else was in the cabin. She opened her eyes and was astonished to see Peter gazing down at her. Aware of her nakedness she instinctively tried to cover herself. He smiled.

'How enchanting. I shall miss you very much, Alex.'

She stared up at him. A wave of grief fluttered through her. 'Can't I stay here with you?' she pleaded. 'Please, I'll do anything you want, just let me stay.'

He shook his head. 'No. I'm afraid that's impossible. I have always seen my role as a teacher; a mentor. Here, I want you to wear this for the coming evening.' He handed her a large flat dress box he was carrying.

Alex crept across the bed and undid the ribbon. Inside the box was a long copper coloured dress. She held it up. It looked like something from a medieval painting, with a richly embroidered buttoned yoke and long thin sleeves. The bodice had a low square neckline, below which the body of the dress hung in soft folds. She ran a finger over the silk. It must have cost a fortune, and was very much like a gown she'd painted on one of the figures in the mural. It was a fairytale costume, and certainly unlike anything she had expected.

Peter Tourne nodded towards the box. 'At Simon's party there will be every extreme pleasure you can imagine on offer. His girls and the girls of his guests will be dressed as slaves - in leather, in furs, naked. Only you will be presented as you truly are - a mythical princess amongst slaves. Isn't that what you painted for me in the gallery?'

Alex swallowed hard. 'It's beautiful. Are you leaving me with Mr Bay tonight?'

He shook his head. 'Not tonight - but very soon. Now get ready. Would you like me to send my housekeeper to help you dress?'

She shook her head; she needed to be alone.

Later that evening Peter Tourne's limousine purred along the hilltop roads. Alex stared out into the fading light at the rocky landscape and the sea far below. How easy it was to forget that there was another life outside the villa KaRoche. Sitting beside her in the back seat her current master seemed preoccupied. Before they'd left he'd snapped a fine chain leash onto her collar; a sharp reminder, even a mythical princess could be tamed by the right man.

Alex couldn't take her eyes off the scenery. Olive groves and tiny white houses clung to the steep hillsides. Here and there groups of men meandered along the roads on the way to their local taverna. All these things had eluded Alex until now; she hadn't stepped outside the walls of the villa KaRoche since her arrival. It seemed impossible that life continued normally outside her prison.

Down and down the car went, swinging left and right along the steep roads, until finally below them Alex could see a string of bright silvery lights twinkling through the encroaching darkness. She knew without being told that this was their destination: Simon Bay's luxury seaside villa.

'Ah, at last, Peter. I thought perhaps you'd changed your mind about coming tonight,' Simon Bay welcomed his friend as they made their way up onto the enormous terrace that skirted the villa. Between the palms and neatly clipped hedges music was carried towards them on a soft breeze that blew up from the gently rolling sea.

Alex glanced around. She had never seen such a beautiful house or such a breathtaking setting.

'I should have known you'd arrive fashionably late, even when pleasure is available in abundance. I see you've brought your little protégé. Good, several of my regular customers are here this evening. Come in, come in, everyone else is here already.'

As Simon Bay guided them towards the main party Alex's attention was drawn to the other guests nearby. On the terrace an Arab Prince in long flowing robes sat on a chaise longue. A double ended chain rested in his long fluid fingers, securing two blonde girls at his feet. They were naked except for tiny loin cloths. Behind them, Starn Fettico stood with his two new Asian girls - they too were naked. By the double doors into the main villa a plump well-heeled woman in a sparkling evening dress was being served by a subservient teenage boy clad only in sandals and a mask. As the boy moved Alex could see that his foreskin had been pierced, and a single diamond drop hung from the sensitive skin; it matched those hanging from the woman's ears.

Simon Bay led them through the doors, chattering to Tourne the whole time. Alex was stunned by the number of people in the main reception room there seemed to be a mass of bodies. Some were dressed in opulent splendour, while their slaves were dressed in every erotic and exciting variation of clothing the imagination could create; some in leather, some in harness, some naked except for a bauble or chain. Most of the slaves were masked; rendered anonymous so that only their bodies and their obedience remained on show.

91

Simon Bay directed his friend towards a small group of people standing by the stairs. Alex found it difficult to concentrate on what was being said as the group exchanged the social pleasantries. The room around them was full of guests and slaves of every hue, shape and nationality. She had no idea that Peter's game had so many players.

A discreet tug on the leash from him brought her attention back to the small group who surrounded them. The Arab she'd seen earlier on the terrace had joined this inner circle. His two girls crouched at his feet.

'And so this is your latest find, Peter?' purred a statuesque blonde holding a champagne cocktail in one elegant hand and a cigarette with a vivid smudge of bright red lipstick on the filter in the other. Her accent betrayed a soft, cultured American burr. Her clothing, a sleek black evening dress, discreetly whispered wealth. 'We've been hearing so much about her.' She pouted her red lips suggestively towards Alex.

Tourne nodded. 'That's right, Monique. She's an artist.'

The woman laughed and proudly swelled her generous bosom towards the beautiful topic of conversation. 'An artist is of no use to me whatsoever, my dear. And why is she dressed like that? What is it you're hiding?' 'I'm hiding nothing I can assure you. It's just that I'm growing a little tired of naked flesh.' Tourne replied as he sipped at the drink Simon Bay had given him.

Monique dismissed this comment with a derisory wave of the hand that sent silvery cigarette smoke curling up towards the high ceiling, and then she nodded towards Alex. 'May I?' The request was directed towards Tourne.

He nodded politely. 'Of course, be my guest.'

The woman gave her drink and the cigarette to a nearby waiter, and casually unbuttoned the bodice of Alex's dress. She slipped a hand inside in a manner that told Alex she was a woman who was used to getting exactly what she wanted. Alex felt her colour rise. The woman squeezed her breasts as though they were ripe fruit. A long fingernail traced the rings that pierced her nipples and the little chain that linked them.

'Very nice,' she breathed and ran her tongue over her full lips. '*Very* nice.' She glanced back at Tourne. 'Not growing tired of marking your conquests then?'

He shrugged. 'Just a trade mark, my dear.'

Alex's humiliation and colour intensified as the woman rolled her nipples speculatively between her fingertips. In seconds they hardened into tight peaks. In spite of the shame Alex felt a lovely ripple of desire that unnerved her.

The American woman continued. 'She's quite lovely, and very responsive, but really far too fragile for my tastes. I like them coarser. Bigger tits, bigger bones. Something with a bit more meat on it. It's a pity, I'm in the market for another girl. This one might break if you played too rough.' Her last comment brought a flurry of polite laughter from the other guests.

As her hands dropped away Alex felt exposed and vulnerable. The open bodice of her dress framed her breasts, her tight pink nipples, and the little rings and chain that glittered as she trembled under the group's undisguised examination. Monique waved a hand towards her. Alex knew what the American wanted, and slowly began to inch her skirt up over her legs. Her hands shook as the silky material brushed her thighs, exposing the naked contours of her sex.

The Arab lifted an eyebrow thoughtfully, and then indicated that he wanted her to lift the dress even higher. Alex silently did as she was told.

The Arab nodded his appreciation. 'Very good. She is almost boyish. I have a cousin, Ahmed, who might like her.' He smiled evilly and ran a hand over her creamy flank. 'Soft skin too. Ahmed has a liking for boys. Perhaps I might put a bid in for her - I could buy her as a present for him.'

Alex shuddered, her strongest urge was to turn and run. As the thought passed through her mind she felt the leash tighten and glanced at Peter. His expression revealed nothing.

The prince turned one of the heavy rings on his long fingers. 'I presume we may sample the goods before we make a serious offer?'

Simon Bay nodded. 'Of course, my dear Mustafa. I may not have trained her myself, but our normal house rules apply. Would you like me to have one of the servants take her to your room now?'

Monique stepped forward holding a fresh champagne cocktail and cigarette. 'Whoa, hang on just one minute! If anyone should be trying her out it should be me! I was here first, remember? I really can't believe you men sometimes!' She looked at Tourne. 'I didn't say I wasn't interested, Peter, just that she wasn't to my usual taste.' She smiled as though contemplating disgustingly naughty thoughts, and her eyes returned to Alex's exposed body. 'Mind you, they do say a change is as good as a rest... now don't they?' She pouted sexily and ran a cool hand down Alex's flat stomach to the soft folds of her quim. Alex shivered.

The brash American grinned. 'Sensitive... I like that.' Her fingers slid provocatively into the crevice between Alex's outer lips. Her fingertip brushed the long ridge of Alex's clitoris, and before she could stop herself, Alex let out a soft moan. The American smiled knowingly, and then pressed her finger deeper still.

Alex hadn't realised she was so wet. Her body offered no resistance as Monique explored her. After a few moments the woman, obviously satisfied, withdrew her finger and rubbed it speculatively against her thumb. 'Tight and wet. What more could a woman ask?' She nodded toward the Arab. 'Why don't you feel for yourself, Mustafa? Tight, hot, and wet. Seems a real shame to waste a body like that on a man who prefers boys.'

The Arab smiled slyly and slid his hands between Alex's legs. She closed her eyes against the humiliation. Mustafa smelt of lemons and something spicy that lingered on her senses. Whereas the American's touch had been deft and businesslike, the Arab's slow and callous inspection made Alex's flesh crawl.

His fingers were like claws, and the rings he wore bit into her tender flesh as he pressed and prodded. As he breached her sex a single finger strayed further back, stroking the dark puckering of her anus. Alex stiffened - it seemed that Mustafa's brother wasn't the only one interested in the delights a boy could offer. He moved closer, sniffing at her neck and hair.

When he finally stepped away Alex struggled to suppress a shudder of contempt.

Mustafa nodded to Monique. 'You are right. She smells good, almost wholesome. I have a suggestion. What if you try her out tonight, and I have her tomorrow?' He glanced at Simon Bay for confirmation. 'It won't be a problem will it, Simon?'

Alex stared at Peter, waiting for him to protest, but knowing he wouldn't; it seemed he'd handed the responsibility for her further education over to Simon Bay. She didn't like Simon Bay.

'No Mustafa. No problem at all.'

The enormity of Alex's predicament suddenly hit her. More than ever before she realised just how powerless she was to prevent these people from doing anything they wanted with her. Things started happening around her and she was unable to do or say anything.

Monique glanced over her shoulder and beckoned to someone Alex couldn't see. A few seconds later a broad woman pressed between the guests. Alex stared at the new arrival in horror; this was quite obviously the kind of woman Monique preferred. Her slave was no more than five feet tall and almost as wide. Her voluptuous curves were tightly encased in a finely tooled leather basque that squeezed her heavy breasts forward. Her body was contorted into a stunningly exaggerated hourglass. On either side of her cavernous cleavage a small white scar marred the creamy rise of her ample flesh. As Alex looked at the marks she realised with a chilling certainty that the little scars, each about an inch across and in the shape of a rose, where in fact burn marks the woman had been branded by her mistress!

Monique smiled warmly at her slave. 'Gerta, I would like you to take...' she paused and looked at Tourne. 'What's the girl's name?'

'Alex,' he replied. 'Alexander Sanderson.'

Monique nodded and then held out her hand. Without a word he dropped Alex's leash into Monique's palm.

'Take her to my room, Gerta, and get her ready. I'll be up to try her out after we've eaten.' She spoke without taking her lustful gaze from the promising morsel who would be her entertainment for the evening, and passed the leash on to Gerta.

Alex gasped as the plump woman tugged sharply at the strap. She prayed that Peter would grab the leash from Gerta and take her away from Simon Bay and his corrupt hedonistic guests. She looked beseechingly at him, but as she followed Gerta across the crowded room he turned away and took another glass from the tray the waiter offered him.

Peter Tourne dabbed the napkin to his lips and picked up the wine glass at his fingertips.

Sitting opposite him, Starn Fettico grinned. 'A superb meal.'

He nodded.

'You're very quiet tonight,' Starn whispered. 'Simon tells me your latest little kitten has created quite a stir. If Monique and Mustafa are interested you're sure to get a damned good price for her. Not bad, bearing in mind she turned up out of the blue. I wish I had your luck.' He paused, looked at his friend for a second or two, and then snorted. 'Oh come on, Peter, that isn't why you're so damned quiet, it is? For God's sake man, you told me yourself the world is full of women - all ready to serve us.'

Tourne nodded. Starn was right - but even so he'd thought about nothing but Alex since Monique's intimidating slave had led her away. He'd insisted that Alex be returned to him before he left for the villa KaRoche. Mustafa had complained - after all, wasn't Alex supposed to be his for the next day? Reluctantly Tourne had agreed to Simon's arrangement, and then confirmed that he would have Alex delivered to Mustafa first thing in the morning.

He glanced around the room. Monique was lighting a cigarette from the candelabra in the centre of the table. In her everyday life she was an executive in a top New York merchant bank. In her secret life she had a stable of handmaidens - mostly women like Gerta. Tourne acknowledged the nod she gave him.

He'd always thought her choice of plain and homely bed partners reflected her insecurities about her handsome rather than traditionally beautiful face. Whatever her motives, she certainly had the money and influence to indulge her tastes. He'd also met Sven, the Swedish harem master who travelled with her. Ostensibly he was her personal trainer, while the posse of young women masquerading as her PA, her secretary, her housekeeper - each had a fictional role to play in the life she led outside in the real world.

He wondered fleetingly what Alex's role might be in the household if Monique followed through on her promise and bought his protégé - but as he watched her, logic told him that the only reason Monique had insisted on sampling Alex's charms was to assert herself - to prove once again that she was more than equal to any of the men present.

Across the table the rich American woman aped a yawn.

'I'm sure you gentlemen will excuse me,' she said with a sly wink. 'I've had a very busy day. Jet lag, you know how it is.' She fooled no one, least of all Tourne. Monique was eager to get her hands on the exquisite English girl upstairs. Around the table the diners shuffled to their feet, their innate good manners acknowledging Monique's abrupt departure.

Simon Bay smiled and lifted his glass towards Tourne. 'Here's to pleasure,' he said, his eyes firmly fixed on his guest. 'Perhaps you gentleman would care to join me in the drawing room?' he addressed the whole table. 'I believe Tony has organised a little display for our amusement.'

There was a murmur of approval as all eyes turned towards Tony, another of Simon Bay's party guests.

As Peter Tourne got to his feet Mustafa pushed his way through the crowd.

When he reached his side he caught hold of his arm and whispered furtively: 'I have no wish to see any more trained apes perform. Simon tells me he has given Monique the Chinese suite.'

Tourne stared at him uncomprehendingly. 'I'm sorry?'

'The rooms overlooking the sea,' the Arab continued whilst trying to contain his obvious enthusiasm. 'Surely you must know about them... the mirrored rooms?' He grinned, and Tourne instantly understood. Several of the suites in Simon Bay's villa were fitted with large mirrored walls. Those in the know were aware that the mirrors concealed secret rooms where the events played out could be observed by a select band of his inner circle.

Tourne discreetly followed the Arab across the room. He wasn't surprised to see that Simon, having waved his guests into the drawing room, was making his way towards them. In one hand he was clutching a bottle of Krug, and in the other three glasses.

He smiled and shrugged philosophically. 'Is there anyone who hasn't already seen Tony's show? They won't notice we're gone.'

Tourne glanced back over his shoulder, hoping that Starn Fettico hadn't seen them leave the main group.

'This way,' said Simon, waving the bottle towards his left. 'Outside, down the steps, through the garden. Just follow the path, but quietly my friends, we have no great desire to give the game away, have we?'

Alex was growing increasingly uneasy. Since her arrival in Monique's room she'd been stripped naked by Gerta, with the help of an intimidating Swede called Sven, and now she hung, powerless, bound to a frame in the centre of the room while her plump little captor oiled her body with some kind of perfumed unguent.

Peter Tourne's indifference had knocked the fight out of her - though she knew she wouldn't be able to overcome Gerta and Sven anyway.

When the doors to the suite opened she struggled to turn to see who had arrived. The collar around her throat made any movement virtually impossible, but from the corner of her eye she saw Monique reflected in one of the huge mirrors that lined the room. Her suspicions were confirmed by the sound of the American's distinctive purr.

'Bring me a scotch, Gerta. Christ, my feet are killing me.'

Alex wondered if the American would give herself a few seconds respite before she turned her attentions to her - she was wrong. The American stroked her back.

'It seems that someone has already taught her about the whip.'

Alex winced as the woman pressed her fingers against one of the weals that marked her spine. A hand circled her torso and cupped a breast, fingers teasing at her nipples.

'I'm not certain about the rings,' Monique continued. 'I much prefer branding - so much more permanent.'

Gerta mumbled her agreement and Alex shuddered as Monique's hands snaked lower to stroke her sex. 'Though here, when the mount is shaved, it is quite effective. Perhaps it's an option I might consider.'

Alex wondered how long this cool and analytical assessment of her body would continue - perhaps the American's only reason for bringing her here was to ensure Mustafa didn't touch her first.

'How did she behave when you stripped her?'

'She did as she was told,' Sven grunted from somewhere close by.

Monique stepped round in front of her. Alex looked away, intimidated by the merciless look in the other woman's eyes. Monique pensively swirled the ice around in her glass, and then suddenly reached forward, grabbed hold of Alex's hair, and jerked her head up. Fiercely she pressed her lips to Alex's, forcing her mouth open to accept her tongue. As she did, Alex felt something brush her nipples, sending a chill right through her - it was the cruel ice cubes. She stiffened, trying to resist the woman's searching lips.

'Kiss me you little bitch,' hissed the American.

Alex, fighting her revulsion, struggled to respond. The scotch splashed over her breasts, while Monique's hands, still cupping the ice cubes, roamed wherever they pleased. Alex shuddered again in horror as she felt the ice traverse the lips of her sex, and then gasped as Monique slipped the cube inside her. The first was followed by another - and then another. They were so cold they seemed to burn; a hideous combination of ice and fire that made her feel dizzy. Monique's lips and mouth were wet and tasted of wine and acrid cigarette smoke. Instinctively Alex tried to turn away from her, but Monique pulled her closer. Alex squealed as the tormenting fingers returned to her nipples, twisting and pinching at their delicate peaks.

'Please,' Alex whispered in desperation. 'Please...'

Monique stepped away and looked contemptuously at the poor girl. Alex could see the dark outline of the woman's nipples pressing through her expensive evening gown and trembled - Monique was clearly very excited. Deep inside Alex felt the ice beginning to melt, trickling out like chilly fingers over her thighs as the scotch dripped from her belly.

'I think our little friend here needs to be taught that I always get what I want, and I don't expect to have to fight for it. Bring me my toy box, Sven.'

Behind the huge mirror that overlooked Monique's suite, Peter Tourne, Simon Bay and Mustafa were already enjoying the events being played out before them. Tourne was monitoring and savouring Alex's shocked expression as Monique approached her carrying a small ornately cut box, from which she produced two evil looking nipple clamps. Designed like crocodile clips, they were encrusted with precious stones. Alex gasped in horror as Monique lifted then up for her to see, and then groaned as the first one bit home.

The second made her squirm in agony, her fingers clenching and unclenching in anguish. Monique looked triumphant.

'Oh, that's *much* better,' she purred and ran her tongue over Alex's flat tummy.

Tourne felt a warm excitement in his groin as he imagined the delicate cocktail of sweat and scotch.

Gerta circled the English girl slowly, and then tied a blindfold tightly around her head. Once satisfied with her handiwork she handed her mistress an old fashioned teacher's cane. It seemed Alex was to be taught a cruel lesson.

Monique grinned maliciously as the girl struggled in vain against her restraints. She bent the cane into a semi circle before releasing it with a malevolent hiss. Alex whimpered. The American teased the tip along the crack of the girl's sex. As the cane slid over her skin she stopped struggling and began to tremble.

Monique licked her lips hungrily as she circled the girl, letting the tip of the cane trail over her sweating body. Finally she stood behind Alex, flexed the cane once more, and then let go with a stroke of the most astonishing venom. The whole of Alex's body convulsed in the restraints. Even behind the glass the men could hear Alex howl as the pain ripped through her.

'Tourne's playthings are always so soft,' Monique sneered and beckoned Sven to her. The tall blonde slave undid his mistress's evening dress and guided it down over her shoulders. Beneath it she was wearing a leather basque that matched that worn by Gerta. In those few seconds while Monique was undressing, Alex began to sob, struggling frantically to get free of her bonds. Monique smiled without humour and drew the cane back again. Already there was a vivid crimson weal on Alex's slim buttocks.

The second stroke was, if anything, more vicious than the first, and caught Alex on the base of her spine. She sobbed miserably, mouth gaping and gasping for breath. Tourne noticed the trickle of liquid running down between her thighs. Alex slumped forward, gasping as Monique lay on the third and fourth blows. The cry of agony seemed to catch in the girl's pulsating throat.

The cruel American again drew back the cane and brought it down with another terrifying crack. Alex could only whimper now, and Tourne sensed the subtle change in his pupil as she gave herself up to the pain, allowing its dark enchantment to drive away her fear. He wondered if Monique had noticed the change - but knew from her stance and the expression on her face that she had. The girl seemed to almost offer herself up for the next blow, writhing provocatively in the frame. The next blow made her gasp but her hips thrust back, revealing the plump contours of her quim.

Monique smirked. 'Perhaps she isn't so soft after all.' Another blow. Alex moaned and stretched. Monique hastily threw the cane to the floor. 'Cut her down.'

Behind the glass Peter Tourne smiled; Monique was good.

Gerta looked at her mistress for some kind of explanation as to why the punishment should stop, but was waved away.

'Take off her blindfold, too. I want to see her adorable face.'

Alex stumbled from the frame and was steadied by the powerful arms of Sven. She was still trembling, her eyes glazed, but she turned instinctively towards the sound of Monique's drawl.

'Come here, my little one,' the American woman purred, standing with her legs apart, hands on hips. Alex dropped to her knees and crawled to the woman's feet. Without a word she nuzzled at the proffered and naked sex, her tongue begging entry.

Monique grinned. 'Oh, you *are* good,' she whispered thickly. '*Very* good. No wonder Tourne is so proud of you.' She opened her legs a fraction more to allow the girl greater freedom.

Understanding precisely the requirements of his mistress, Sven handed Monique a huge black dildo. She looked at it with longing while the beautifully inexperienced face continued to work between her legs, and then slipped it into the kneeling girl's hands. Without any instruction Alex lapped at it, her tongue lubricating its thick rubber shaft, and then slowly she pushed it into the mistress's open quim, smoothing its path deep inside with her tongue.

In the hidden room Tourne could feel the growing excitement of his two companions.

'Oh yes!' Mustafa hissed between gritted teeth whilst leaning forward to get as good a view as he could. 'Your young lady is quite, quite superb. Whatever Monique offers you, my friend, I'll double it.'

Tourne smiled. He could sense Alex was almost sharing her mistress's pleasure - it seemed to flow through the two women, rolling back and forth like a tide.

Alex pressed the dildo home, her tongue lapping urgently at Monique's pleasure bud. Her whole body was alive with sensuality as she set a compelling rhythm with the huge phallus. Above her, Monique locked her fingers in Alex's silky hair, ground her hips down onto the thick stem, and then threw back her head, drinking in the attentions of her new and willing slave.

As the first waves of the American's orgasm rolled through her, Simon Bay grunted his approval. 'Are you sure you won't let the girl stay here tonight? I'd most certainly like to slip into that wet little quim of hers myself. Seems such a waste to leave it all to that bull dyke.'

Tourne shook his head. 'Not tonight,' he murmured, his eyes still fixed on the continuing activities inside the room. Still trembling with after shocks of pleasure Monique knelt on the floor beside Alex. Without a word passing between them, Alex gently withdrew the dildo from Monique's body, and impulsively licked the juices which coated it. Monique's whole demeanour had softened significantly, and she looked into Alex's eyes with apparently genuine affection. She gently took Alex's hands, guided the dildo away from her lips, and with no resistance she eased it down and into her grateful sex.

The English girl gasped as the impassive column impaled her, and then lifted her hips to welcome the dark intruder.

Peter Tourne turned away - his job was done. His own intense excitement now needed release. The hard arc of his cock strained angrily inside his expensively tailored trousers. Later, on the way home, he would take his pleasure with Alex. It might be his last chance before he had to hand her over to her new master.

CHAPTER 11

In the early hours of the following morning, in the intimate darkness of the limousine, Peter Tourne ran a warm hand over Alex's smooth thigh. She flinched, but didn't resist.

'Lift up your dress,' he said. 'Let me see where Monique marked you.'

She turned to look at him. 'You should know where Monique marked me,' she said softly, 'you watched her doing it, didn't you?'

He nodded.

'I knew you did. I could sense you there.' As she spoke she slid the dress up to her waist and turned so that he could see her back and legs. Her delicate creamy flesh was covered with livid weals and bruises. Between her legs - even in the gloom, he could see the marks on her thighs where Monique had bitten and pinched her skin as she drove the dildo home. He bent forward and tenderly pressed a kiss to each purple spot. Alex shivered as his tongue traced the perimeter of her injuries.

'Open your legs wider,' he said softly. 'Let me kiss you.'

This was a reward for them both. He gave her tenderness and pleasure where before there had been pain. His tongue caressed and flicked around her clitoris. Alex moaned and sank into the soft leather seat. She allowed his attentions and the quiet movement of the car to relax her. She lifted herself to him, thighs opening, giving everything she was to him. He didn't have to demand her obedience; it was his already.

She moaned deliciously, writhing under him, opening herself wider and wider for his intimate caresses. He could sense that in her heightened state her pleasure was so close to the surface that it wouldn't take a great deal to unleash a maelstrom of delight. Gently he turned her over so that she was crouched on all fours, her knees pressed into the thick carpet, and her face and elbows sank into the seat.

She looked exquisite; ready for him, legs apart, her sex framed by the rich curves of her sore buttocks.

'Hold yourself open for me,' he whispered as he undid his trousers. She did as she was told, and more as her fingers sought out his raging shaft. Eagerly she pulled him closer, her fingers parting the lips of her quim in readiness for his entry.

He took her from behind, letting her guide his throbbing cock into the depths of her weary but excited body. She bucked as he slipped home, pressing her buttocks into his groin and then whining like a puppy as he slipped a hand down and began to toy with her engorged pleasure bud. His other hand sought her nipples. They were as hard as cherry pips brushing against his fingers. Alex began to climax almost before he started to touch her.

Her sex closed around him tightly like a closed fist, milking him dry with every stunning contraction. Mutual waves of pleasure roared through them, echoed and intensified by each wild excited thrust - on and on and on until

Tourne thought he could happily die inside her. It seemed an eternity before they were still.

As Alex turned over and tidied her dress she caught sight of Mario watching her in the rear-view mirror. She had little doubt that he'd enjoyed her exhibition with his master. Seeing his glittering eyes was an unpleasant reminder that she was still beholden to him. She wondered fleetingly what dark favour Mario might demand as payment for his silence about her phone call to Laurence.

Staring out into the dark balmy night she wondered whether Laurence had taken her plea for help seriously - surely it wouldn't take him long to arrange a flight to Greece? Where was her rescuer? She tried to block out the events that had taken place at Simon Bay's villa, but it was impossible; there wasn't one part of her body that didn't bear reminders of her time spent with Monique. Her nipples throbbed, the tender folds between her legs felt raw and swollen - and yet, out beyond the humiliation and the pain was a sense of elation and pleasure that drowned almost every other emotion. Peter Tourne's tender caresses had brought the pleasure to the surface. She swallowed hard, confused again by the fact that her rational mind rejected the ecstasy her body demanded. Her rational mind was the part of her that demanded rescue. She slipped down in the seat, trying to avoid Mario's penetrating eyes.

They travelled the rest of the journey back to the villa in silence. Peter pulled her close. She rested her head in his lap, relishing the sensation of closeness. By the time the car drew to a halt Alex was almost asleep. She yawned stretched and uncurled, easing the cramp from her back and shoulders then followed her master inside. As they entered the main hallway Peter turned and said:

'For the remainder of the night you will stay in the guest cabin. I'll have the housekeeper wake you up early. Mustafa has asked that you be delivered first thing tomorrow morning.'

Alex stared at him aghast. 'But... but what about finishing the mural?' was all she could think to say. Every time she felt she was making headway with Peter Tourne he knocked her back by reconstructing the wall between them.

He shrugged. 'It's almost complete, isn't it?'

Alex nodded. 'Yes,' she said sadly. 'Almost complete... but—'

He turned and began to climb the stairs. 'In that case I'll ask Mustafa to return you as soon as he's finished with you, so you may finish it. Simon's auction is to be held next week, so I want it finished by then...' his voice faded.

Alex nodded sadly. She already knew that Simon Bay wanted her to go to his villa as soon as possible. 'Another day should be enough.'

Peter Tourne didn't reply. With a great sense of loss Alex opened the French windows that overlooked the garden. Someone had lit the lamp in the guest cabin. It glowed at the window like a beacon in the velvety darkness. She hesitated for a few seconds on the steps of the villa, drinking in the perfumed night air, and feeling tears prickling up behind her eyes. It would soon all be over. She rubbed her eyes. Peter had already made up his mind; it didn't matter what she did to try and persuade him otherwise, he intended that she should leave KaRoche.

As she picked her way carefully along the pathway towards the cabin a slight rustling close by caught her attention. Before she could determine what the sound was a hand clamped firmly over her mouth.

She knew at once and with little surprise who her assailant was - Mario, come to collect his debt! One arm locked firmly around her waist, pinning her hands. Alex knew it was pointless to fight or resist. He pushed her down into one of the flowerbeds, turned her over roughly, and knelt heavily across her heaving breasts.

He quickly undid his flies and leant closer. His erection was ivory white in the darkness, a fearful scimitar that he pressed to her face. She tried to turn away as he brushed the swollen helmet against her cheek, although she knew it was pointless trying to resist.

'Suck me, English girl,' he sneered as he trailed the moist tip over her closed lips. 'You leave here soon, and I not tell Mr Tourne about your phone call. You owe me.' He grinned and shuffled closer. 'We not got much time. No time to sleep. The boy wants you before you go. I say he could.'

He smelt of raw male musk, his whole body sweating and ripe. Alex felt numb - yet strangely excited - as he guided his throbbing flesh into her stretched mouth. Closing her mind to the discomfort and the taste and smell of his body, she began to work on him. From the undergrowth she heard the houseboy's heavy breathing; it seemed they both intended to make her pay for Mario's silence.

A few hours later Alex rolled off the bed in the cabin. The copper coloured evening dress was stained with earth and splashes of semen. Mario and his accomplice had taken their payment in full. She pulled it off unsteadily and made her way to the bathroom. Looking at her reflection in the steam kissed mirror she wondered how on earth she'd allowed herself to sink so low.

The morning sunlight caught the links of the chain that linked her nipples. Either side of the rings were two tiny bruises like fingerprints; the reminder of the nipple clips that Monique had applied to her.

As Alex turned slowly she could see the purple stripes that curled across her narrow shoulders. Her whole body was a map of the journey taken through the realms of pleasure and pain.

She stepped into the shower and let the refreshing water course over her. It warmed her skin and muscles, soothed away the aches and pains, and massaged her bruises as attentively as any lover could.

She closed her eyes and turned her face up into the torrent. The sound stilled her mind and the drumming heat soothed her body - the perfect combination.

When she went back into the sitting room, wrapped in a fluffy white robe, she was surprised to see that in her absence someone had delivered a breakfast tray. Alex had hoped that Peter would invite her to eat with him. She had barely a chance to pour the coffee before the housekeeper appeared in the doorway.

'Mr Tourne say the car be ready for you in half hour.'

Alex nodded, but the old woman didn't move. 'Was there something else?' she asked.

The old woman stepped into the cabin, glancing nervously over her shoulder. 'He ring again for you.'

Alex stared at her. 'I'm sorry?'

The old woman held a bony finger to her lips. 'That man, the one you tell me ring. He ring here last night when Mr Tourne out, and then he ring later when Mr Tourne in.'

Alex stiffened. 'Laurence? He rang here?'

The woman nodded. 'I answer phone. He talk long time with Mr Tourne.'

Alex's stomach knotted. She wondered what Peter had told her agent. What excuse had he spun for her absence? She only hoped that Laurence would still arrive in time to save her - perhaps he'd phoned to confirm his arrival.

'Do you know where he was ringing from?'

The housekeeper shrugged.

Alex pressed on. 'Did you hear what they said?'

This time the old woman shook her head emphatically. 'No,' she said angrily. 'I not listen.'

Alex realised that by asking she was implying that the woman spied on her employer. 'I'm sorry, I didn't mean,' she said quickly, but the old woman fixed her with a cold stare.

'I not listen,' she repeated. 'But I think your man, he is in Greece - the line sound very bad. The local exchange is very old.'

Alex nodded. 'Thank you,' she said softly. She hoped the old woman was right.

She finished breakfast and reluctantly got herself ready for her trip to Mustafa's villa. As she dressed her mind wandered again and again to Laurence Russell. He was hardly a friend, but even so he had to help her. She visualised his face and smiled; she knew his interest in her was not purely business. She'd clearly seen that in his eyes the last time they'd spoken in his office. She picked up her jacket and bag - she only hoped his arrival would be soon. Once the mural was complete there was no telling how long Peter would let her stay at the villa KaRoche - but she knew it wouldn't be for very long.

The car journey back across the island seemed to take hardly any time. Alex peered out of the tinted windows of the limousine, looking again at the sights she had seen on the previous evening. In daylight the island was even more beautiful than she had supposed. It struck her that under different circumstances she could have relished her stay on D'arnos.

As the car headed out along the coast road the beaches below looked magical; each rocky inlet giving way to another with spectacular views out over the rich blue ocean. Mario, divided from the seating compartment by a glass panel, seemed distant and cool. They passed what looked like Simon Bay's villa, curled like a sleek white sphinx at the mouth of a rocky cove. Turning back inland they followed the line of the sea until, amongst a grey green rise of olive trees, Alex saw what looked remarkably like the minaret of a mosque.

She stared in awe as they approached and more and more of the palatial buildings were revealed. Set high on the hillside Mustafa had built or bought what looked remarkably like a Moor palace.

Mario guided the car between a stand of trees towards ornate wrought iron gates. Alex felt her stomach tighten. Until now she had been enjoying the scenery, but as the gates swung smoothly open she realised with a start that she was seconds away from meeting a man who could be her new master - or worse still - was trying her out to see if she might suit his cousin. Alex swallowed hard, grateful that the trees along the steep driveway cast a shadow inside the car, hiding her expression of trepidation. She was being delivered like a parcel - on a sale or return basis. Alex struggled to control the growing sense of panic. She remembered the feeling of unease she'd felt the previous evening when Mustafa had run his hands over her body, and she remembered the strange smell of his cologne. She wished she could go back to Peter Tourne.

She trembled; panic mingling with expectation. It was as though there was another part of her - a dark twin soul - who, far from being afraid, was relishing the moment.

Ahead, in a semicircle of sunlight, Alex could see two dark-skinned men, dressed in long flowing white robes. As the men turned to watched the car approaching Alex saw they were carrying guns, and tucked in their cummerbunds were curved ceremonial swords. They had to be Mustafa's private bodyguards.

The car slowed and stopped in front of imposing double doors.

Mario turned to her. 'I will see you tonight,' he said malevolently as he slid out to open the door for her.

Alex ignored him, her attention was firmly fixed on the entrance to Mustafa's luxurious home. Across the sweeping driveway the doors opened, and in the shadows Alex could see a tall woman, dressed in traditional Muslim robes. Jet black, the robes covered her from the top of her head and down to where they brushed the tiled floor. Only the way the figure moved revealed the fact that she was female.

Alex took a deep breath; this was the moment of truth. In the doorway the woman beckoned to her. Alex climbed nervously from the car, and without looking back she hurried inside.

The smell struck her as soon as she stepped from the sunlight; the perfume of citrus fruits and rich oil. Her hostess - if that was what the woman was - had turned and was already gliding away from her through the opulent hall. Alex followed.

The cool interior of the huge building was quite astonishing. It was decorated in a subtle mixture of traditional Arabic and European styles. When they were beyond earshot of the guards the woman caught Alex's arm and said, in a low and melodic voice, 'I will take you to the harem, to prepare you for my master.'

Alex nodded. She could just see flashing blue green eyes through the black lace eye mask. Silently Alex followed her deeper into the building through a warren of passages. Finally they stood in front of a pair of heavily carved doors; smaller versions of those at the entrance to the house. The woman touched them with a slim pale hand, and at once they folded back on silent hinges to reveal a huge marble lined room. Alex gasped - it was like looking into an ornate bird cage.

On couches around a central fountain girls of every colour and caste relaxed in luxurious splendour. Every one of them was dressed in the traditional costumes of the harem. Every one of them was swathed in jewel bright colours with gems to match. Some were playing cards, others reading, some small groups were talking. Mustafa's harem must have had at least twenty-five exquisite girls in it - and they all turned as one to look at the latest arrival.

'Would you like some tea?' asked the mysterious woman in the black robe.

Somewhat bemused, Alex nodded as a statuesque negress came over to introduce herself.

'Hiya,' she said cheerfully, extending a hand. 'I'm Antia.' Alex was surprised to hear the tall coloured woman had an American accent. She thought for a second of Monique.

'A redhead,' the coloured girl continued whilst eyeing her up and down appreciatively. 'You're not Irish by any chance, are you?'

Alex shook her head. Antia grinned. 'Shame, we think Mustafa is secretly trying to recreate the United Nations. You'd better come with me and have your tea later. I'm supposed to be getting you ready.'

Alex hadn't expected such a warm welcome, and was pleasantly surprised by the confidence and kindness the woman showed her. She began to relax - just a little. As if sensing her confusion Antia took her hand.

'Come on, I'm not going to bite you. We're all sister's here. There's really no need to be so nervous.'

'But... but aren't you all Mustafa's slaves?'

Antia smiled. 'Yeah, and it'll be easier on you if you don't forget that. But we're all here because we want to be with him.' She paused. 'We know what he can offer us, and we all enjoy it.' She lifted her hands to encompass the splendid room. 'It's wonderful the things modern slavery can provide,' she added with a grin. 'Now, come on, I've got to get you ready.'

She indicated another carved door set into one wall. Alex followed her. Beyond the door was another large and splendid room; finished in marble it was much like the previous one. In the centre was a huge sunken bath, and beside it a massage couch and table. It reminded Alex of pictures she'd seen of ancient Roman baths.

Antia nodded to her. 'Take off all of your clothes so we can get started.'

As Alex began to unbutton her summer blouse she glanced up and froze. Set high up in the wall was a balcony. Mustafa was sitting there watching, his face expressionless. He'd come to witness his beautiful sample being made ready. Reddening, Alex slipped off her blouse and skirt. She was naked underneath.

Antia looked at her marked body and winced. 'Wow, who did that to you?' she asked. Alex looked away shamefully, and Antia said: 'Never mind, you don't have to tell me. It's just that it's been a long time since I've seen anyone cut up like that. Mustafa only marks us if we misbehave, and so everyone learns very quickly not to.' She scooped up Alex's clothes and dropped them into a laundry hamper. 'I'm going to wash you down first. Get into the bath.'

Without questioning the woman's instruction, Alex did as she was told, aware as she stepped into the bubbling water that Mustafa's eyes were on her. She couldn't help but admire the graceful negress as she slipped off her harem pants and thin top. Her body was the colour of dark coffee and intimidatingly yet beautifully muscled. Her sex was also shaved, and in one of her outer lips three silver studs sparkled. Seeing Alex's eyes resting on her shaved pubis Antia grinned and stroked them fondly.

'Three sons,' she said in a proud voice.

Alex stared in astonishment. 'You have children?'

Antia nodded. 'That's right. Three sons and a daughter. Mustafa likes his women to breed. He's particularly proud of the boys. He sends them home to be raised as little princes. The more sons you bear him the higher you rise in the pecking order.' She stroked her tight flat belly. It seemed impossible to Alex that she had any children at all.

Slipping effortlessly into the scented water, the coloured woman soaped her hands and began to wash Alex's body. Her touch was both deeply soothing and strangely erotic. Alex's feelings of anticipation were heightened by Mustafa's presence, seated above them bearing silent witness. Alex moaned softly as the coloured girl cupped her breasts, easing away the tension and bruises with her skilful touch. When her long fingers worked lower, down over her belly, Alex felt a tremor of pleasure that shook her to the core. The woman really knew how to excite - was this part of Mustafa's plans for her preparation, or was Antia making the most of the situation? She heard Antia moan softly as a finger found its way into her tight quim. She knew she was already wet, and opened her legs a fraction so that Antia could stroke her with a cupped hand.

Antia's caresses were stunning in their intensity; if this as the treatment she could expect in Mustafa's harem perhaps it wouldn't be so terrible if he did bid for her - this was sheer heaven. Just as the first acute spirals of delight began to form in her belly, Antia's clever hands disappeared. Alex opened her eyes dreamily.

Antia smiled. 'Sorry babe, but we've got to get on - after all, the master's waiting.'

Alex glanced up towards the balcony. Mustafa was staring down into the bathroom, eyes glittering darkly. Alex struggled to suppress a shudder - her previous sense of calm rapidly dissipating. Antia helped her out of the soothing water and up onto the couch. She arranged her so that she was facing the balcony. Totally exposed as she was, Alex wondered what might follow. To her surprise Antia continued the massage, using the same oil that suffused the house with its pungent odour.

This time the coloured girl's touch was deft and professional rather than erotic. Alex winced as she eased her knuckles deep down into her tender flesh. It was deeply satisfying, in an odd way, to be handled with such skill. Glancing up she saw Mustafa had moved closer to the rail to get a better look at the body he would soon be exploring. His expression was intense.

'Now,' purred Antia. 'A little garnish.'

Alex stiffened. 'What do you mean?' she asked softly.

Antia smiled down at her. 'Relax, it won't hurt.' From the table by the couch she took a large bowl containing a brush. 'This is a special stain, it was used by ancient courtesan's at the palace of some king or other to heighten their allure. Mustafa likes us all to use it.' As she spoke she began to outline Alex's nipples. Where the oily paste touched her skin it darkened to a rich crimson. The contrast to her milky white skin was vivid.

'Oh yes, that look's good. You're going to make our master very happy. Now, open your legs.'

Alex glanced up at her hesitantly.

Antia smiled. 'I promise, it won't sting. I just don't want to spill any - it stains whatever it touches.'

Alex did as she asked, closing her eyes tight as the brush worked its way across the most secret recesses of her body. She flinched as Antia opened her legs a little wider, trailing the soft brush back so that it circled her anus. She could imagine the view that Mustafa was enjoying.

Thinking her preparations were over Alex relaxed a little and opened her eyes, just in time to see Antia cracking open a long necked plastic vial.

'Please, what's that?' she queried anxiously.

Antia's eyes sparkled eagerly. 'Lubricant. Breathe deeply, and try to relax - this won't take more than a few seconds. It won't hurt if you don't fight it - I promise. I just want to make sure you're ready for our master.' She paused and eyed Alex, recognising the slight confusion on the English girl's face. 'This'll help to smooth the way.'

Alex blushed deeply as the coloured girl's skilful fingers splayed the tight corona of muscles around her bottom and slid the neck of the vial home. She breathed deeply as advised and waited, and then an oily warmth permeated through her most secret place. She gasped as Antia withdrew the slender container and began to stroke her tightly puckered entrance, working the ointment in deep. After washing her hands in a basin she cracked a second vial and urged it deep inside Alex's sex. The ointment also filled her there to the brim.

Alex lay for a few seconds watching the coloured girl tidying away the remains of her work. Antia smiled down at her.

'Do exactly as he tells you, and don't - whatever you do - fight him. It won't be long now.' From somewhere beneath the couch she produced a pair of ornate wrist bands which were linked by a silver chain. Alex stiffened anxiously as Antia gently but firmly took hold of her wrists and snapped the cuffs into position.

Antia's expression was gentle and comforting. 'Remember,' she whispered, 'just do everything he says - everything. He'll only hurt you if you give him cause to; if you try to resist him.'

Alex stared up into her dark feline eyes; all her fears suddenly returning. Antia helped her to sit up, added ankle chains which matched the wrist chains, and then wrapped a wisp of sheer blue silk around Alex's throat. She folded a matching sliver of silk between her legs, tying it on each hip. Standing back she glanced up towards the balcony and her master. Mustafa nodded.

Antia took a cloak of blue silk and wrapped it around Alex's shoulders. Finally, she produced a matching scarf and used it to blindfold her trembling charge. She took the opportunity of closeness to whisper furtive words of encouragement; she understood the turmoil of emotions the English girl was experiencing.

Alex felt Antia's strong hand close around her elbow.

'He's waiting.'

Alex nodded, her throat suddenly too dry to speak. She allowed Antia to guide her through the cool building, the soft padding of their bare feet on the cold marble the only sound to accompany them.

Peter Tourne hadn't intended to accept Mustafa's invitation to watch his protégé's initiation into the harem - but the temptation had ultimately proved too strong to resist. He'd followed the limousine driven by Mario, to Mustafa's villa, in his Porsche. He'd watched Alex's preparation on close circuit TV, and now sat on one of the plush couches in Mustafa's private first floor suite, sipping strong sweet coffee, and awaiting his host's arrival. Mustafa grinned as he threw open the doors to the room.

'A few minutes more, my friend. I'm very pleased with the way she behaves. You've taught her well, Peter, but then again, I should expect nothing less from you. Would you care to stay here and participate? Or perhaps you would prefer to watch from the privacy of one of the guest suites? There are camera's set up and ready to capture the moment.' The Arab paused. 'I could send one of my girls in to keep you company?'

Tourne hesitated, and then nodded. He knew very well the direction his host's tastes were likely to take, and wasn't sure he wanted to be in the same room when Alex was exposed to them.

'That would be perfect,' he said as evenly as he could. Mustafa clapped his hands. From nowhere a houseboy appeared, dressed in flowing robes that mimicked those of his master.

'Take Mr Tourne to the Peacock Room, and see to it that he has everything he requires.'

Tourne followed the boy from the room. Looking down into the hall below he saw the blindfolded Alex being led by the black masseuse to join Mustafa. She was completely oblivious to his being there.

Alex strained to work out where she was being taken. She could feel a little of the warm oil Antia had applied smearing between her thighs. Her companion was silent now, guiding her only with the lightest of touches on her elbow. They climbed a flight of stairs, and then she heard a knock. Doors opened in front of them.

She guessed from the rich smell of oils in the air that she was finally in the presence of Mustafa. Something brushed the chain that linked her wrists - and then she was jerked forward. It took a second or two for her to realise that a leash had been snapped midway along the chain. The thin robe she was wearing was peeled away with a grunt of satisfaction.

As the seconds passed, Alex shifted nervously from foot to foot, aware that unseen eyes were savouring the details of her nakedness. She tried to imagine what Mustafa could see - and what he was thinking. Firm hands turned her around. Fingers brushed intimately between her thighs, and she wondered what on earth would come next... The dark side of her mind had already guessed.

Peter Tourne, ignoring the girl crouched at his feet, watched on the TV screen as one of Mustafa's servants pulled the leash down between Alex's legs; connected to her wrist chain it had the effect of bending her double like a hairpin. It was designed to snap onto the chain that linked her ankles.

He knew that the Arab wasn't interested in the girl's breasts, her face, her talents, or her company; his only real pleasure was in the tight dark closure that nestled between the cheeks of her darling bottom.

The servant untied the loincloth from around Alex's narrow hips and pulled it away. Across the room Mustafa stood unmoving, while the black girl who had prepared Alex ceremonially parted his robes with the air of a squire preparing her brave knight for battle. The Arab was hugely endowed. The coloured girl knelt before him and respectfully cupped his shaft in her fingertips, pressing a kiss to its head before beginning to oil it.

Across the room another servant - a handsome boy - was standing in front of Alex, supporting her shoulders.

Mustafa pushed his attendant away and took up his position behind the bending Alex.

The coloured girl crawled after him, and without any further preliminaries she guided his cock straight into Alex's sex. Tourne could see Alex flinch as the huge bulk of the Arab breached her. After a stroke or two he saw her stiffen as she felt the Arab withdraw. He saw her hold her breath as Mustafa's cock brushed her tensed buttocks. Tourne willed her to relax - to submit, to give herself over to the insatiable Arab. He watched her mouth open, and then heard her gasping shriek as the coloured girl fed Mustafa into her lubricated anus.

Tourne knew that Mustafa was a far bigger man than his own driver Mario, and he could see Alex's body instinctively trying to repel his advances. He watched Mustafa lock his fingers in her hair and jerk her head back.

'Come along, little English flower,' he heard the Arab hiss. 'This is not what I expect. Let me in or I'll have one of my servants flay the skin off your back. Ahhh, that's *much* better - pant, relax, and let me take you.'

Alex shrieked again as every muscle in her body complained at the cruel contortion. The Arab slid a little deeper into her, making full use of the lubricant Antia had meticulously applied. She understood that compliance would ease the path, but found it hard to overcome her initial revulsion. As the Arab began to move deeper still she thought she would tear. Aside from the throbbing pain in her backside, her whole body complained at the way she was bound. The chain that linked her ankles and wrists was so short that every thrust threatened to rip her arms from their sockets.

Alex struggled for every breath. As she gasped for air she suddenly felt sick, overcome by the pungent odour of the body oil Mustafa was wearing. She felt a delicate touch between her thighs and realised someone else was trying to ease her discomfort.

She guessed it was probably Antia. A fingertip brushed her clitoris, and despite the demanding column of flesh in her bottom, she shuddered with a pleasure that could not be denied.

As Mustafa finally reached his goal and his hairy belly came to rest against the up-curve of Alex's perspiring buttocks, she felt dizzy with a mixture of humiliation, suffering, and undiluted rapture.

CHAPTER 12

It was barely lunchtime when Antia took Alex to Peter Tourne's waiting limousine. Used and discarded, Alex felt filthy. Her body was so sore that she could hardly sit down on the plush leather seats. She flushed with shame at the memory of how her body had responded so positively to the strange demands and desires of Mustafa. Once he'd had his fill of her he'd simply walked away, leaving her to be freed by unseen hands. The blindfold had been removed, and she'd been taken back to the bathroom to collect her clothes.

Alex stared unseeing at the countryside as Mario drove her back to the villa. She wondered if Mustafa would now bid for her at Simon Bay's sale; the idea of which horrified her. Worse still, there would be others there, unknown men and women who might demand even more from her.

She shivered and wrapped her arms across her chest - she couldn't let Simon Bay sell her, there had to be a way to escape from these people. Where on earth was Laurence? And how could she possibly explain to him what had happened to her since her arrival on the island?

Alex was so deep in thought that it only seemed a few minutes before the car drew up in front of the portico to the villa KaRoche. She barely looked at

Mario. Not waiting for him to open the car door for her she slipped across the seats and hurried inside the villa. The housekeeper was dusting in the hallway, and looked up at the sound of Alex entering.

'Is Mr Tourne in?' she asked, some of her old confidence returning.

The old woman shook her head. 'No. He go out after you leave. I not expect him back until after lunch.'

Alex nodded, her mind formulating a plan. 'I'm going to shower and then work on the mural this afternoon,' she said in a firm voice that brooked no contradiction.

To her surprise the old woman was almost deferential. 'Of course. Would you like me bring some lunch?'

Alex paused; the very thought of food made her feel nauseous, but perhaps it was because she still smelt of the Arab's pungent perfume. After a second or two she nodded - she might feel different after a shower, and besides, if she was planning to escape it would be foolish to leave on an empty stomach.

Once back in the guest cabin she sorted through her luggage and found a pair of faded jeans, a thick black cotton shirt, walking boots and a light jacket. Stuffing her passport, wallet, driver's license and a few other essentials into a canvas holdall, she stowed the things at the back of the wardrobe and went into the bathroom. She didn't look in the mirror, afraid of what she might see. After a long shower she ate lunch, then picked up her art box and went downstairs to the gallery. It was cool and silent by the pool. She opened the box and began to work.

Outside, in the heat of the day, Peter Tourne arrived home from his luncheon with Mustafa. He was as preoccupied and distant as his slave girl.

Part of him regretted accepting the Arab's invitation; Mustafa had used Alex like a mindless vessel, as unfeeling and dispassionate as anything he'd ever seen. For Peter Tourne this was not how the game should be played.

He climbed the stone steps to his bedroom, wondering how his protégé was feeling. At the door he hesitated and considered what he might do if he found her waiting for him.

His room was empty the windows open a little to catch the breeze from the sea. Picking up the phone he tapped in a number - he had to ensure that Mustafa didn't get the chance to buy the English girl. His first call was short.

'What do you want me to do with her?'

The reply was a barking laugh. *'You're not getting sentimental are you, Peter? I thought we'd already agreed that I should buy her once she was trained.'*

He felt a sense of relief. 'At the auction? Will you go to the auction? Simon Bay's very keen to take delivery as soon as possible. What worries me is that there's at least one other purchaser who's very keen to get their hands on her. The bidding will go through the roof.'

There was a thoughtful pause at the end of the line. *'Perhaps we can come to a private arrangement then? I'd like to see her on the block, but if you're prepared to deal now...'*

Tourne nodded. 'Yes - yes I am,' he said quickly. 'I'll ring Simon and let him know there's been a change of plan.'

'Good, if we can come to an arrangement over the price I can pick her up tomorrow, if you like.'

He relaxed a little. 'That would be perfect. What'll you offer me for Alex...?'

When the deal was concluded he dialled Simon Bay's number. After that brief call was finished he pulled off his soft leather shoes and threw himself back onto the large bed.

It was early evening when he went in search of Alex. To his surprise she was sitting downstairs at the poolside staring at her completed creation on the wall. She was so deep in thought that she didn't hear his approach, and for a few seconds he had the chance to watch her unobserved. Alex Sanderson was exquisite - as tiny and delicate as a perfect English flower.

The last of the evening sunlight blazed in her auburn hair, whipping the tumble of curls into a flaming halo. For an instant his eyes moved to the mural she'd created - it was exactly the fantasy woodland peopled by strange mythical animals that he'd envisaged. Erotic images suffused the greenery. It was a masterpiece. Tourne realised that somewhere during Alex's education and initiation he'd lost sight of the work she'd created. It was almost as if he were seeing it - and her - for the first time ever.

Finally sensing his presence she turned, her face tilted towards him, eyes alight and bright with tears.

'It's finished,' she said in a voice cracking with emotion. In her hand she had a small brush, and as he watched she leant forward and signed her name with a flourish. He stepped up behind her and stroked her hair. She let out a long thin sob and turned to embrace his waist, pressing her face into his body. He could feel the tears, hot and angry, soaking into his shirt.

'Please Peter,' she whispered, 'don't make me leave here. Don't send me away with those other people. I don't like them.'

'Let's go and have dinner,' he said quietly. He was afraid if he embraced her or answered her plea he would lose his sense of resolve.

Alex rubbed away the tears with the back of her hand, sniffed miserably, and then nodded.

They ate in virtual silence. Strangely, as they went out onto the terrace for coffee, Alex felt completely at peace for the first time in days. The mural was finished - her work was done and now she would find a way to go home. She had to; if Peter wouldn't protect her, then she had to. She glanced across at him.

'I'm leaving tomorrow,' she said softly.

Tourne nodded.

It was an ambiguous thing to say. She knew he intended to deliver her to Simon Bay's villa - but she had other plans. If he let her spend the night in the guest cabin it would be a simple matter of waiting until the household was asleep and then creeping away into the darkness. Instead of being driven the following morning across the island by Mario, to the fate that awaited her, she would catch the first ferry back to the mainland. Almost exactly as the thought formed in her mind Tourne turned to her.

'You will spend tonight in the cell.'

Alex stiffened. Was it possible he could read her mind? She stared at him, considering her reply, afraid that if she protested too much he might guess her plan. After a few seconds she said softly. 'Why can't I sleep in the guest house?'

'You really are quite astonishing,' Tourne snapped. 'How dare you question my decision? Surely by now, Alex, you've realised that it's extremely unwise to do so? I am the master here - I set the rules. I'm certain your new master will correct your disrespectful failings as a matter of priority.'

Alex felt a flutter of anxiety.

Tourne continued. 'Mario will take care of you tonight, and then I'll have my housekeeper bathe and shave you in preparation for your delivery tomorrow.' He beckoned her closer. She obeyed without another word. 'And don't *ever* question me or any other master or mistress again. Do you understand?' As Alex was about to reply he caught hold of her hair, his face contorted angrily. 'Even now you try to play this game by your own rules. Will you never learn?' He pushed her away roughly. 'Take off your dress.'

Alex lowered her eyes and began to unbutton the bodice. In arriving back from Mustafa's in such a defiant mood, she had accidentally stepped too far back into her old recusant frame of mind. She fumbled nervously with the tiny pearl fastenings. She could sense his growing displeasure, and was relieved when the buttons gave way and she could slide the light cotton dress down over her body. She was afraid to look up at him, and simply stood in the pool of fabric, naked except for her sandals and the rings that he'd inserted.

'Turn around.'

She did so, moving slowly, careful not to let her body posture suggest defiance or flirtatiousness. Even now she was his slave and relished the sensation of his eyes moving over her nakedness. If only there was a way she could stay at KaRoche with him. The thought glowed in her mind like a flare. There was nothing she would not do for him or give him; he owned her in every sense of the word, and she couldn't imagine ever feeling the same way about any other man.

Her train of thought was broken by the arrival of the houseboy carrying a mobile phone. Tourne took it from him, and as he began to speak Alex realised with a jolt that the caller was Mustafa.

'Actually, she's with me now,' Tourne said, once the niceties had been exchanged. There was a pause and he laughed without humour. 'No, my mind is already made up, though I'm not saying your offer isn't a good one. On the contrary - it's highly flattering.'

Alex felt a cold chill of fear trickle down her spine - it seemed that Mustafa was pleased with her, and wanted her for his own. She prayed for Peter's resolve to hold, and that he wouldn't be swayed by the obviously tempting offers coming from the insatiable Arab.

Tourne was still speaking. 'My dear friend, you know I would never set out to offend you, but the decision has already been made.'

Alex's mind was racing. She assumed Mustafa was attempting to put in a bid before the auction to secure her services. She shivered. Only moments before she had brooded for the umpteenth time whether escaping was what she really wanted, and that what she longed for deep down was to stay with Peter Tourne, but she now realised that was impossible. For her own sake she had to finally accept that he had no intention whatsoever of keeping her - and that being the case, she had no choice but to escape from KaRoche.

As he continued to speak he beckoned her closer. She moved to his side, and trembled as he began to stroke her breasts with idle familiarity. Oddly his touch was of great comfort, and she crept even closer to him, relishing the smell and heat of his body as his fingers moved down to the folds of her sex. For a while he toyed with the ring that pierced her, and then casually slipped a finger into her moist quim. It wasn't until he'd finished his conversation and handed the phone back to the waiting houseboy that she remembered they were being observed.

Tourne put a finger under her chin and tipped her face up to his. 'It would appear that you've created a great deal of interest in my friend Mustafa.'

Alex fought to control her anxiety.

He grinned salaciously. 'He just offered me at least twice what I might expect to get for you at auction. Believe me, that is quite a sizeable offer, and tempting to say the least.'

Alex swallowed hard, wondering whether he would be swayed by greed. He pulled her closer, pressing her down onto her knees. 'But I told him your fate has already been decided.'

Alex tried not to show her fear; what did he mean? Had Simon Bay already put in an offer for her? Or perhaps Monique? Or Starn? Or was it someone else who'd been at Simon Bay's party? What was going to become of her?

'Undo my belt,' Tourne said.

With trembling hands and heavy heart she did as he ordered.

'Now, pull it free.' He looked across the terrace to the still hovering servant as her fingers guided the leather through his trouser loops. 'Come here boy, put the phone down. I have a job for you.' He looked down at Alex. 'Give my young friend here the belt, and then get down on all fours. Perhaps I can teach him a few new tricks.'

Alex tried hard not to meet the houseboy's excited eyes as she handed him the belt. She could see his hands trembling as they closed around the buckle. Crouched at his feet she braced herself for the first kiss of leather. She wondered if his lack of experience would make him timid - it didn't.

His first stroke was a terrifyingly ragged explosion that wrapped tight around her waist, cutting into her delicate flesh like razor wire. She heard Tourne say

114

something in Greek, and closed her eyes and hid her face in the crook of her trembling arm in preparation for the second blow. This time it hit her squarely across the buttocks with a terrifying crack. The blow was so hard that it seemed to ricochet through her skull. Her every sinew tensed in readiness for the next strike. She heard her tormentor take a deep breath, and then she yelped in shock as the belt caught her low, flaring against the soft folds of her pouting sex.

The dark twin inside her mind was beginning to stir. She could feel a web of pleasure weaving itself in her belly as the next stroke, as hot as molten steel, blasted across her buttocks. Then there was another, and another, and another. As the boy laboured on the myriad of sensations he unleashed became a blur. She gave herself up to the pain; a willing supplicant, riding it like surf as it crashed over her. Every thought and every fibre of her was fastened to the belt's kiss. When the boy finally stopped she almost felt as if she'd been robbed of her pleasure. Hands grabbed her hips and she felt the urgent press of a cock seeking entry. She had no idea whether her rider was the houseboy or Peter Tourne - her only desire now was to give herself freely.

As the cock opened her, driving deep into her throbbing quim, she shrieked with pleasure. It felt as if she might drown and pull her unseen lover down into the water with her. The merest brush of the groin against her buttocks was enough to spark the first heady contractions of orgasm. On and on the waves swept, rolling out from the centre of her soul, until finally, exhausted and breathless, she collapsed onto the flagstones of the terrace. She was totally drained - all passion was spent.

When the penis eventually slipped away and she opened her eyes, she was pleased to see she was alone with Peter. It seemed his words to the houseboy had been a dismissal. She curled up against his broad chest, making soft noises of pleasure and affection. He gently disentangled himself from her.

'Don't Alex. Put your dress back on, and I'll send for Mario. You must be ready to leave tomorrow.'

Alex stared at him, the sense of cruel reality returning. Despite everything she was still nothing more than a commodity; he'd done with her and now she was dismissed. She got to her feet, eyes downcast to disguise her pain and sense of loss. With clumsy fingers she pulled on her clothes. Once again the truth hit her that escape was imperative, and before the next sunrise.

Mario silent appeared and snapped the lead onto her collar without being instructed. He then led her away from Peter Tourne and away from the villa. His eyes were alight with lust.

'What did big Arab do to you?' he teased with a wicked leer as they made their way into the shadowy garden. Alex suspected he already knew, and wondered how much of the day he'd spent thinking and lusting about what had happened to her. As he jerked her close she could smell stale wine. She could see he was a little drunk.

'You like it maybe? You know Mario like it.' He stumbled a little on the steep steps and held out a hand to steady himself. As he did Alex, without thinking twice, seized her chance.

Grabbing hold of the leash with both hands she gave it a hefty tug, completely unbalancing her gaoler. As he staggered towards her she lifted her knee and felt a satisfying crunch as his testicles squashed against it. Speechless, gasping for air, and completely unable to move, Mario let go of the leash and collapsed into the bushes. He curled into a ball and rolled onto his back, his large hands clutched to his groin. Without considering the consequences Alex grabbed a garden hoe that lay carelessly nearby, and brought the handle crashing down onto the slob's head. He slumped instantly, and ceased moving or making any noise.

Turning sharply, Alex sped away, running down through the archway that led to the guest cabin. Without daring to look back she threw open the door and grabbed the holdall she'd hidden in the wardrobe earlier. It may have lost her a few seconds, but it would be far easier to get away dressed in sensible outdoor clothes with money and a passport. She checked quickly and was relieved to find both her money and passport still inside. She tried not to think of Mario and the enormity of what she'd done, lest her frail courage suddenly desert her. Despite her haste she had the presence of mind to grab a couple of succulent oranges from the bowl by the window for sustenance. Then, bag in hand, she hurried back down through the gardens, desperately seeking a way out that didn't involve going back into the villa.

Removing her sandals she ran down flight after flight of stone steps. As the darkness closed around her she thought she heard voices from the terrace. Perhaps Mario had recovered already. Just as she was about to hide in the relative safety of the bushes, she saw a gate set in the perimeter wall, and headed for it. Carefully easing it open, she was delighted to find it led onto a steep coastal track - it was hardly a road. Panting heavily, Alex quietly closed the gate behind her and slipped into the oily shadows.

In the moonlight she could see the track was cut into a deep gorge, its high sides creating dark pockets of inky blackness. She scurried for cover and changed into the clothes she'd brought with her. Rolling the discarded things into a tight bundle she stuffed them deep into a patch of scrub and headed downhill on what, she hoped, would be the pathway leading to the main harbour. She could now distinctly hear voices on the hillside above. She had no head start to speak of - if she wanted to be safe she knew she'd have to find someone to help her, or somewhere to hide.

The track, which skirted the walls of KaRoche, was steep and uneven. Alex was glad she'd had the sense to bring boots. The heavy rubber soles not only gave her good grip but also muted her footsteps. In the darkness she was certain no one could see her from the grounds of the villa, but her heart still beat a calypso rhythm in her chest, and the downy hairs on the back of her neck prickled. Gingerly she clambered up the steep walls of the track, trying to get her bearings.

Far below, away to her right and along the edge of the shoreline, she could make out the lights of the harbour. Above her she heard the sound of a car starting up - either Mario had alerted Peter, or Mario intended to take the car to search for her himself. He would now be in a foul mood - to say the least, and she certainly didn't relish the thought of being caught and subsequently punished by him.

Overhead the moon broke through the clouds, and for a few seconds Alex could see that amongst the rocks and bushes on the seaward side of her was a path that led down towards the rocky shoreline; it looked impassable to anything but foot traffic. She scrambled up between the bushes and began to pick her way down towards the sea. The path was steep and precarious, twisting backwards and forwards between the tumbles of boulders and wind contorted trees.

It seemed to take an eternity to get down to the shoreline. With every step she was afraid she might fall or lose her footing in the darkness. Finally, though, the path flattened out, and Alex was at last aware of the peaceful lapping of the warm Mediterranean. Another few steps and she was finally walking on sand, and a gentle sea breeze played through her hair. Relief popped in her stomach as she spotted a cluster of lights through the silvery darkness. It wasn't the main harbour, but at least here she might get some much needed help.

A hundred or so metres along the beach she realised that what she could see was a low cottage or a boatshed, with a small fishing vessel hauled up onto the shore beside it. A lantern swung and squeaked in the breeze. Figures huddled around the boat, the sound of their voices and an occasional laugh drifting towards her. As she got closer one of the figures looked up; a pale face in the dark night. Before she considered the possible dangers she called out to them.

'P-please...' her timid voice strained nervously. 'Can - can anyone help me?'

A man called back in Greek. Something about his voice startled her. The lantern swung higher and two of the figures headed towards her at a brisk trot. She sensed instantly that she'd come across a clandestine meeting that was supposed to be secret, though she had no idea what it could be. Calling out had been a terrible mistake. Turning frantically she scrambled around in the darkness for the cliff path. Behind her she could hear raised voices getting rapidly closer, and she knew she'd escaped from one nightmare, only to foolishly stumble into another.

As she stumbled around in the stamina sapping sand a pair of steely hands clamped onto her shoulders. She shrieked in terror. She was utterly unable to resist as her captor flipped her over onto her back. Pinned down in the darkness she struggled and twisted back and forth to try and unseat the shadowy stranger who held her down in the sand. After a few seconds another figure appeared with the lantern, and lifted it up so they could see what it was they'd caught.

Alex, breasts heaving and breath rasping in her lungs, glanced up into the lamp's glare. Four male faces peered down at her. One of them mumbled something in Greek, and a second leaned closer. His rough fingers slipped under the leather collar Peter Tourne had fastened around her throat. The man

117

sitting heavily on Alex said a few words to his colleagues. She didn't need to speak Greek to understand that they knew exactly what the collar meant. The man who'd touched the collar now tugged at the front of her shirt. It was strained tightly across her breasts, and the buttons easily popped open. The delicate silver chain and the rings that pierced her nipples glittered in the lamplight. There was a split second of silence. Alex felt the lust rising in the men as clearly as she could hear the sea rolling in, and had little doubt as to what would follow.

One of the men mumbled Peter Tourne's name, and there was a contemptuous laugh from the man sitting on her as he squeezed and mauled her vulnerable breasts. His breath reeked of cheap wine.

Jerking their prize to her feet, he picked her up as if she weighed no more than a child, and threw her over his shoulder. She gasped and thumped his back with her fists, her feet kicking wildly. Her strong captor merely laughed, slapped her bottom, and tightened his grip on her thighs.

When the party reached the boat the man threw her unceremoniously onto the sand. One of the other's knelt across her and pinned her hands back above her head. She was surprised when another pressed the mouth of a bottle to her lips and grunted something at her. Unable to resist, she took a long drink. Wine poured down her throat, making her gasp for breath. The lamp was put down in the sand and the soft light draped across Alex's bewildered face. Another pair of hands closed around her waist, while someone else pulled and tugged her boots and jeans off.

In the orange arc from the lamp she could see the four men were swarthy local fishermen, on a late night drinking spree. The alcohol had stripped away any vestiges of control. The wine bottle was forced back into her mouth, while she felt a hand pawing at her shaved sex. Eager fingers splayed her open, diving deep into the warm moist confines of her sex. She froze, terrified they might tear the delicate flesh around the ring.

Someone picked up the lantern and held it high, and the man who'd been pinning her down slid off so they could admire their prize. There was an earthy grunt of approval from each of them, and then the one who'd first caught her unbuckled his belt; it seemed he was to be the first to have her; his prize for bringing in such a fine catch. Her legs were forced apart and he straddled her, hauling her back onto his raging cock. Dragging her face closer he pressed a wine-tainted kiss on her lips. His cruel and hungry eyes stared down into hers, savouring her humiliation and distress. He grinned, and stroked her leather collar.

'Slave,' he whispered in heavily accented English.

Alex shivered, and then gasped for breath as he suddenly plunged his cock into her.

The next few hours were a jumbled tapestry of insanely wild sex. The fishermen poured more and more wine down Alex's throat, forcing her to drink, making her head spin and her stomach churn. And they fucked her again, and again, and again. There was not an orifice they did not fill; her

118

mouth, her anus, her quim. If they noticed the weal marks and bruises on her exhausted body it didn't stop them from using her for their seemingly endless round of pleasure.

Alex crouched on all fours in the sand, feeling like a stud bitch as one man slipped his cock into her dripping sex while another lifted her head up and fed himself into her mouth. Every sense was drowned with the sounds, sight, and smell of sex. In her muddled, drink-numbed mind, she begged them to stop, to take her home, to set her free - but her plea's fell on deaf ears.

At long last, as the grey light of a new day began to break, the man who'd initially caught her hoisted her up into his arms and carried her to the hut. It seemed to be the signal for the others to depart.

Alex curled up on his rough bed, assuming that she would be allowed now - finally - to go to sleep. But quickly his hands running between her legs told her otherwise. He rolled her onto her back and began to lap at her sex, awash with the spent semen of his companions. She moaned for him to stop, but he was relentless. He grinned up at her, his lips slick and wet.

'Pleasure. You to give me pleasure, you're slave,' he stumbled with the English. Alex moaned and sobbed as his tongue worked its way over her clitoris. Her exhausted body responded at once. She was so tired, but she adored what this peasant could do to her. She was stunned and ashamed; how could her body find so much pleasure in the aftermath of their squalid orgy? Her tormentor eased his fingers into the warm confines of her sex, stroking her towards the darkest of ecstasies. She writhed miserably, trying to suppress the passion that was growing inexorably in her belly.

'Please don't,' she sobbed as the first white hot shard of orgasm exploded inside her. 'Please let me go. You have to help me, please...' Her whole body convulsed with the wonderful sensations he was inducing, and she knew then that she was beyond help.

Whatever vestige of self-respect she had remaining shattered like glass, and she relinquished every part of herself to the slave mentality that drove her on and on, taking pleasure from her own humiliation and shame. Her captor finally pulled away, still grinning. Almost idly he crawled up alongside her and dragged his cock out of his trousers. He rubbed the rejuvenated shaft across her open lips.

'Pleasure,' he purred again. 'You give me much pleasure, or I beat you too... like Peter Tourne.' As he spoke he ran his fingers through her sweat-soaked hair. She had no choice but to take him into her mouth. As her lips closed around him she could taste her juices mingled with the sweat and semen of his companions. He threw back his head and pulled her up onto him, while her fingers and tongue struggled to give him the pleasure he demanded. He bucked against her face, and she sucked hard as she slowly admitted to herself that she enjoyed the way he used her purely for his own gratification; there was no consideration for her needs, and that realisation re-lit the fire deep in her belly. He quickly groaned and filled her mouth, and Alex swallowed and shuddered pleasurably in unison with the heavy man.

119

When he was still and breathing evenly she curled up like a child against his hairy belly. He smiled and stroked her tenderly. 'You a good slave,' he murmured and dragged a blanket up over them both. Alex closed her eyes, willing sleep to steal her thoughts away.

CHAPTER 13

As Alex's eyes fluttered open the morning light filtering through a small window reminded her of the guest cabin, but the reality of her predicament filled her mind an instant later. She blinked and stared around the rough interior of the beachside building. It was little more than a shed and smelled of rotten fish. On the far side of the room, piled on a table, were a heap of fishing nets. The wooden floor was bare and sandy, the walls covered with faded yellowing whitewash. The odd sticks of furniture were sun-bleached and looked like salvage. Alex rubbed her eyes. The makeshift bed smelt of sweat and sex. She shivered. The only crumb of comfort was that she was alone.

Memories of the previous night came flooding back in an intense rush of disjointed images; her escape from Tourne had delivered her straight into the hands of drunken ruffians. Far from making an escape, it appeared she had merely exchanged one horrible prison for another. Her head ached violently from the after effects of the wine they'd forced upon her, and every other part of her body felt tired and tender.

She gingerly tried to slide off the bed. As she rolled over something caught on the tangle of dirty blankets. She stretched across to free herself, and was instantly horrified at what she saw. The fisherman had tied her to the bed with a length of greasy rope. One end was knotted through her collar, and the other was fastened around the metal frame by her head. It certainly wouldn't prevent her from escaping, but the gesture made her cringe. She was tied in the same way a man would tie a stray dog. Tears trickled down her face. Did the fisherman truly believe she would wait there for him to return? How could she have sunk so low?

Beside the pile of fishing nets her gaoler had left a bucket of water, a tin cup and a half loaf of bread. Alex stared at it and tried to shake off the sense of resignation and despair that threatened to engulf her. Her clothes had to be on the beach - if she found them, got washed and dressed, she could still make her ultimate escape.

It took seconds to free herself from the rope. She hobbled across the rough floor and used the cold water from the bucket to wash away the evidence of the night before as best she could. She was thankful there wasn't a mirror around to bear witness to her degradation. Wrapping herself in one of the blankets she crept cautiously out onto the beach - it was deserted. Under the hull of the boat she found her jeans and boots. She picked them up, trying to ignore the cache of empty wine bottles littered around in a rough circle. It was here the men had held her down, their arena marked by discarded rubbish.

Across the sand in the shadow of the rocks she found her shirt, jacket and bag. Even though her clothes were stained and torn she pulled them on. Dropping the blanket to the sand she dressed where she stood in the cool rising sun, the fresh sea air helping to revive her - just a little. She checked her meagre possessions, and was relieved to find the men had not taken her money or passport. She then started to explore, trying to get some idea of where she was in relation to the harbour.

The cove she was in appeared to be completely encircled by rocks, but as she had come down a steep path from the villa, she reasoned that there had to be another way out which led in the direction of the village - after all, the boat was still on the beach, so her captors hadn't left by sea, and she doubted they'd climbed up to Peter Tourne's villa, because it was situated so far away from the village.

Alex circled the warming beach. Her senses concentrated on any unexpected sounds in the distance; the last thing she wanted was for the fishermen to reappear and find her still there.

After nearly half an hour she came across a well worn trail that seemed to lead up into the hillside but ran in the general direction of where she guessed the harbour to be. There were probably other paths, but she was desperate to get away from the beach and its vivid memories, and the possibility of recapture. Shouldering her holdall, she set off determinedly without looking back; she wanted to put the events in the cove, and at KaRoche, well and truly behind her.

After the first hundred yards or so the path veered steeply up into the hills. What had appeared to be an easy escape route quickly turned into a tortuous climb. The path that had seemed so well trodden close to the cove twisted back and forth between rocks and boulders, at some points fading away totally. The loose stones made it difficult for her to get any decent footing, and the muscles in her thighs and calves soon ached and burned. She considered whether to climb down and try to find another way out, but was afraid she might come across the fishermen again. She was rapidly losing her bearings - which way was the harbour now?

Eventually, after a tortuous climb that tested Alex's resolve to the limit, she clambered up between a rise of steep rocks and found herself in a deserted olive grove. She paused a moment to gain her breath, and then followed the meandering path until she was beyond the trees, where she found a narrow track which she presumed to be the one she'd crossed the previous night. To her right it climbed back up into the hillside towards the villa, and to the left it ran down in the direction of the sea, which glistened far below.

Alex stopped for a quick rest. She quelled her nagging hunger by devouring the two juicy oranges, and despite her desperate predicament, was unable to resist the spectacular views her elevated position afforded her. She shaded her eyes from the sun and watched the tiny dots offshore that were the local fishing boats. Some were stationary, and accompanied by a mass of white flecks which circled and swooped to feed on any discarded scraps, but others were moving slowly in a line, and Alex knew then that they were coming out from the harbour, and in which direction she needed to be walking. Surely she couldn't now be more than half an hour from the village and the harbour?

Slinging the holdall over her back she set off with a new feeling of optimism. Sadly that optimism was punctured fatally as she rounded a large boulder a little way down the track. Below her, parked in the curve of the bend, was Peter Tourne's distinctive Mercedes. She stopped abruptly, almost losing her footing, and inadvertently sent a number of large stones clattering noisily down towards the car. Spinning round to flee back the way she'd come, she came face to face with Peter Tourne and Starn Fettico.

'No!' she screamed in horror and frustration. 'No! Where did you...? How did you...?'

She quickly turned again trying desperately to locate an escape route, and saw Mario was now leaning cockily against the car. They had cut her off. She stared at Mario, then at the track, then back to Mario, wondering if she dare try to run past him. Even from a distance she could see he had a sore looking lump across the side of his head, and she knew that if he caught her he would be eager to repay her for the blows she'd struck the night before. He grinned malevolently as their eyes met. She sensed he would be only too pleased for her to try and make a break for it. She knew she was lost. Her shoulders sagged in defeat, and she turned and looked up at Peter Tourne.

'How... how did you find me so easily?' she asked quietly.

He smiled with his usual, infuriating confidence. 'Your little friends were eager to let me know they'd found one of my girls. I hope you enjoyed their company. We'd already guessed where you were; there are only three paths up from the cove, and someone would've let me know if you appeared down in the harbour.' He paused, his eyes resting on her ruined clothes. 'You wouldn't have got very far on the island anyway - my marks are well known all over.'

Alex's wrists were suddenly seized and twisted painfully up behind her back. She shrieked with agony and arched onto tiptoes in an attempt to decrease the discomfort of Mario's rough and unnecessary treatment. Both Tourne and Starn enjoyed the way her shirt stretched tightly over her vulnerable breasts, her nipples clearly visible, and then the former waved Mario away.

'Let her go, that won't be necessary. Will it, Alex?'

She shook her head miserably as she rubbed her freed wrists.

Starn grunted and mopped his brow with a handkerchief. 'You're too damned soft, Peter. I'd flay the skin off the little bitch if she was mine.'

Tourne smiled. 'Then I'm sure she'll be relieved to know that you haven't bought her, Starn. But as it is, her punishment is no longer my concern.'

Alex stared at him. 'What do you mean?' she whispered.

Tourne reached forward and gently brushed the hair back off her forehead. As he did he snapped the lead onto her collar. 'You are no longer my property, Alex. At lunchtime today I hand you over to your new owner. I think under the circumstances it would be better if we went back to the villa and prepared you for their arrival.'

Alex stood rooted to the spot. Mustafa's face formed in her mind, followed rapidly by Monique's. 'Who is it?'

Tourne smiled and then tugged at her leash. 'You never learn, do you? Let's just say he's an old friend of mine. I'm certain you'll make him very happy.'

Alex's thoughts raced. Was it Simon Bay? Was he to be her new owner? She silently fell into step between Peter Tourne and Starn Fettico, and contemplated the fate that awaited her back at KaRoche as they led her to the waiting car.

When they reached the villa Tourne turned to her. 'I'm going to chain you in the gallery room. My housekeeper will come and get you ready for your presentation to your new owner.' He stared intently into her eyes. 'Don't ever lose sight of the game, Alex. I told you before that I make the rules, and despite how it may seem to you at this moment, I promise I will do all I can to ensure you are well treated when you leave here.'

Alex barely heard his words of scant comfort. She was looking up the garden steps at Mario, who was already standing beneath the shady archway that led into the gallery. He was obviously waiting for her. She wondered with a shudder what revenge he might exact upon her for having the audacity to escape.

Peter Tourne tugged at the lead. 'Come on, we don't have much time.'

The gallery was cool and dark after the glare of the bright morning sun. Alex would have been grateful to have shed her filthy clothes if it hadn't been for Mario watching her undress with his lust filled eyes. He hadn't spoken since his boss had handed him Alex's leash. To ensure she made no further escape attempts the collar was now connected to an overhead chain, like the one in the cells.

The room had already been prepared for her return - she wondered how it was that Tourne had been so confident he would find her so quickly. Once she was undressed the housekeeper re-shaved her sex with deftly confident fingers. Alex could hardly believe she now found such intimacy acceptable. Her sex and nipples still bore the crimson stain that Antia had applied to them. Climbing into the steaming bath Alex tried hard to concentrate her mind. If she thought for more than an instant about who her new owner might be she could feel a sense of panic growing low in her belly. Mario remained unmoving against the wall - his expression was dark, thunderous.

As the housekeeper helped Alex from the bath and wrapped her in a fluffy towel, Mario mumbled threateningly: 'You soon get what it is coming to you, English girl.'

Alex flinched. The housekeeper glared at him, but he continued unperturbed. 'I am everywhere. Every house has a Mario.'

Alex felt an icy chill run down her spine. He was right - every master would have a friend or a servant, who would demand or steal her favours. She straightened her back and squared her shoulders, and challenged him with a confidence she didn't feel. 'I'll be ready for him next time, you've taught me a great deal.'

Mario's eyes flashed furiously and he lunged towards her. It must have hurt his pride to let a girl like Alex escape his clutches. Alex leapt back in alarm as he raised his fist. The little housekeeper intervened.

'No!' she snapped at the corpulent driver. 'I get her ready now! You don't mark her face, you fool!'

Mario spat in disgust. 'Bitch!' he growled. He was genuinely very angry.

Alex prayed that whoever had bought her intended to take her away from KaRoche straight away - if she was left alone with Mario she dreaded to think what might happen. The housekeeper waved her towards the leather surgical couch. Glad to break eye contact with the driver, Alex climbed onto the padded top and stared at the ceiling. The old woman secured her wrists to the framework. It wasn't until she was totally immobilised that Alex wondered why she had been secured.

Mario's distinctive features came into her field her vision. He was grinning like an imbecile.

'He going to brand you now. Your new boss want you marked so everyone know you belong to him,' the housekeeper said as if she could read her mind. Alex gasped and began to struggle frantically, rolling sideways off the couch. With her wrists secured any real chance of escape was impossible. Mario grabbed her and dragged a heavy leather strap around her waist.

'Please! Please don't do this!' Alex pleaded as he turned his attentions to her ankles. 'Let me go! I'll do whatever you want... please Mario!'

The sweating driver merely laughed. She should have known that there was no point in appealing to him; he would be only too pleased to see her hurt and humiliated, as he had been. Despite her frantic despair Alex heard a door open, and then saw Peter Tourne approaching her.

'We've come a very long way, you and I,' he said with a casualness that belied the insanity of her situation. She stared at him, longing for him to untie her. At his shoulder Mario reached across her and took a cloth bag from the housekeeper. Before Alex could really focus on what he was doing, he lifted her head and pulled the bag down over her face, plunging her into stuffy darkness. She heard the door to the gallery open again and strained to pick up any sounds that might give a clue as to who was with Tourne.

'It's good to see you again,' she heard his muffled voice greet the unseen guest. As you can see, we have her ready for you. What do you think?'

The reply was too indistinct to catch. Alex closed her eyes and struggled to concentrate on the voice of the new arrival. It had to be the man Peter had sold her to; her new owner. A cool hand stroked her thighs and then lifted to outline her breasts. A fingertip lingered on the rings that pierced her nipples.

'Ummm,' murmured her unseen examiner. It was impossibly frustrating, not to mention alarming. The hand returned to her thighs, easing them wider and then stroking her exposed sex. Alex instinctively strained her hips against the leather strap that held her waist to the couch, and a low chuckle told her that her rude movement had been noted. A thought formed in Alex's mind, but quickly fluttered away as a probing finger slipped inside her.

'Very nice... very tight. You've done a good job,' said a man. 'I'd like my mark in the usual place.' The finger slid from her and was gone.

Unseen hands loosened the strap at her waist and rolled her over. They pinned her firmly to the couch. Something pliable but hard was pressed between her lips. She bit down hard and held her breath. An instant later a searing lightening strike exploded on her buttock. The pain roared through her body. The scream caught in her lungs. She bucked and twisted against the excruciating heat of the branding iron. Sobbing incoherently, she clenched her fists, refusing to be overtaken by the shadowy waves of unconsciousness that beckoned. Despite her determination the darkness draped over her. The voices around her fragmented and broke into abstract sounds, floating on a swirling wind, and she slipped effortlessly into oblivion.

When Alex recovered she was laying on her side on the uncomfortable mattress in the cell. Surely she couldn't have been unconscious for more than a second or two? She stared around, struggling to get her bearings. The cell door was slightly ajar. As she watched it opened and a figure appeared from the shadows.

Alex stiffened - it was impossible. A name formed in her mind and then on her parched lips.

'Laurence?' she whispered in total astonishment. Her agent, her would-be rescuer, the man who'd sent her to the villa in the first place, stepped into the tiny room. She struggled to lift her head, and repeated his name. 'Laurence? Oh my, it is you.' A great wave of relief swept over her. 'I'm so glad you're here.' Her eyes filled with tears. 'Why did you take so long - ?'

Laurence smiled gently. 'Hello Alex. I've come to take you home. That's what you rang me for, wasn't it? You wanted me to rescue you from Peter Tourne's clutches?'

She began to nod, but something in his tone and expression made her stop. Why was it he showed no surprise or shock at finding her bound and naked in a tiny cell? And why didn't he seem concerned for his own safety?

'Why didn't you come straight away, when I first rang you?'

He smiled again. 'What, and spoil Peter's fun? I don't think so Alex. I came here today because he told me you're ready - and I can see that you are.'

He stared down at her, relishing the details of her body. Alex shivered, realisation trickling down her spine like icy water. Looking up into his eyes she knew exactly why he'd come to KaRoche.

'Was this your idea all along, Laurence?'

'I'm afraid so,' he grinned and shrugged as though he'd merely been uncovered as the perpetrator of a harmless prank. 'Peter Tourne and I have been friends for years. When I took the commission for the mural I didn't tell him you were a beautiful woman, but I knew he wouldn't be able to resist breaking you in once he saw you.' He moved closer, as though about to tell her a secret. 'And that's precisely why I sent you here in the first place. I wanted to possess you from the first moment you came into my office for an interview. You look quite lovely, Alex. But then again, I always knew you would.' He ran his fingers lightly over her forehead. 'Peter gave you a light sedative to help with the pain, are you feeling okay?'

Alex nodded weakly. 'And so you're my new master?'

'That's right, my dear. We couldn't have Mustafa taking you off to God knows where, now could we? The man's an animal, let's face it, Monique is not much better. Such a waste to let either of them have you. I'd planned to bid for you at Simon Bay's auction - it seemed like a suitably melodramatic conclusion to your training - but as you generated so much interest amongst his associates, Peter and I came to a private arrangement; we couldn't risk losing you. I must say, he seems commendably interested in your future welfare. He knows you'll be well looked after in my stable; my companions are part of a very exclusive coterie. You've been marked with my initials, as are all the girl's I own. You can meet the rest of them when we get back to London.'

He gently unfastened the leash from her collar. She made no attempt to escape - what was the point?

Lawrence nodded towards the cell door. 'When we're done here I'd like you to collect your things together so that we can catch the evening ferry. I'd like to get back to London as soon as possible.' He paused and smiled with genuine warmth. 'You'll like the rest of my clique, I'm quite certain. The girls are all like you; artists, sculptors - a very select band of England's most talented young stars...' he gently touched the dressing which soothed the smarting area of the branding. 'It'll look quite exquisite once it's healed, believe me. Oh, I ought to tell you that I've already arranged for all of your things to be delivered to my house. I expect my slave to be on hand for my every whim.' He patted his thigh. 'Now, come here, Alex. Show me that you understand totally what I expect from you.'

Alex swallowed hard, almost unable to believe what she was hearing. Hadn't she always suspected that Laurence Russell's interest in her was more than just professional? Wasn't his carefully hidden desire what she'd hoped would spur him on to come to D'arnos to rescue her?

She slowly slipped from the mattress and crept towards the man who'd delivered her into the hands of Peter Tourne. He was her rescuer turned master. She didn't need to ask what he wanted from her. His penis was jutting forward like a rapier against the soft fabric of his trousers. Catching hold of her collar he pulled her up onto her knees and bent from the waist to kiss her passionately.

'Oh Alex,' he murmured. 'You have no idea how much I've dreamt about this moment.'

Without a word she undid his belt and, kneeling at his feet, ran her tongue along his exposed shaft in an ancient act of worship.

Even as she tasted his first salty offering she could feel the excitement

126

stirring deep inside her own body. Her sex moistened, her nipples hardened, and the dark half of her mind had finally won the battle.

Maggie and the Master
Chapter One

Max Jordan smiled at Katya and ran a hand over her cheek and then down to her shoulders, his fingers moving slowly, tracing the curve of her breasts and the faultless contours of her pink nipples. Under his touch first one and then the other hardened into tight buds.

Eyes downcast, feet apart, hands behind her back; over the past few months Katya had become the very epitome of the dutiful slave, and thought Max, was all the better for it. Since he had completed her training she was altogether calmer, more self-assured, even more beautiful than when they first met. She was the picture of elegance when they were out together and completely wanton, his to command and enjoy, when they were in private.

Katya had been a pleasure to train - a natural submissive, despite her initial resistance. The girl had been remarkably quick to understand what was required of her, and helping her to find the way past her natural resistance, finding the way to make her - and others like her - compliant and eager to serve him was what Max Jordan did best.

She trembled slightly as he stroked his fingertips over her belly and parted the lips of her sex to enter and explore. There was no hint of resistance; rather he sensed her eagerness for his caress, his attentions, his dominance.

Since they'd met Max had helped Katya unlock the natural submissiveness she had hidden away for so long. Now her body and her mind and her very soul were his to use and abuse and pleasure exactly as and when he chose, to give to whom he wanted, to deny her, to indulge her, to beat her until her screams filled the room and lingered in his dreams.

Tonight he thought how exquisite she looked, totally naked, her mons shaved and oiled for his approval, her face betraying just a hint of make-up to emphasise her full lips and deep brown eyes, her short blonde hair brushed off her face making her look almost elfin. Her black and silver collar was cut deep to accentuate the line of her slender neck, and the matching lead - well, he intended to hold on to the lead for just a little longer.

'You understand what is happening, my little one?' he asked tenderly. Max had no need to shout or bark instructions at her; Katya had long since learned the penalties of disobedience and the rewards of complete submission.

'Yes... Master.' Katya's voice was low and soft and faltered over the words.

He smiled again, and tipping her face up to his pressed his lips to hers. He could see the glitter of tears in her eyes and felt the trembling flutter of her lips like a trapped butterfly against his.

'You will be well taken care of, my precious,' he said. 'I wouldn't have it otherwise.'

She didn't have a chance to reply.

'Master, Mr Gilbert is here.'

Max swung round at the sound of his housekeeper's voice. 'Wonderful, Mrs Griffin, would you show him in, please?'

He stepped away from Katya and hung the lead up on the hook alongside her. 'Spread you legs a little wider, my dear; Jack will want to inspect his new toy.' Without lifting her head Katya did exactly as instructed. Six months earlier she would have fought him, answered him back or made some smart remark, and it was interesting how the crop and a firm hand could teach a girl the virtues of silence and complete obedience. For a moment, master or not, Max's heart ached. He would miss her.

'Ah, Max, there you are. How's life treating you?'

Max crossed the room to greet his guest. 'Fine, Jack, how nice to see you again. Come in and make yourself at home. Would you like a drink?'

'Scotch would be good.'

'How was the drive?'

'Very good, hardly any traffic...' Their exchange of pleasantries was brief; Max could see that Jack's attentions were already elsewhere. 'So this is the little creature you told me about, is it?' he said, walking over to the corner where Katya was secured.

Soft lights picked out the delicate glow of her skin; she was so perfect, so very delicately made that she almost looked like a statue standing there.

'Indeed,' said Max. Her delicate appearance belied the way her body writhed beneath his like a hungry animal, the way she opened up under his touch, the silky wetness that pooled in her sex, so much that often as he buried his cock deep inside her it seeped down her thighs.

Jack pursed his lips and looked the girl up and down thoughtfully, as if appraising livestock. 'Not bad... not bad at all,' he said, stepping a little closer. 'May I?'

'Help yourself,' said Max, pouring a generous measure of scotch into the two tumblers on a side table. 'After all, after tonight she'll be all yours. Assuming of course that you want another of my girls in your harem?'

Jack laughed as he surveyed Katya. She stood perfectly still, just as she had been taught, dark eyes resolutely downcast. 'Hardly a harem, Max, and besides, your girls are always so well schooled. I've never had the stamina for breaking and training myself, whereas you - well, it's a gift. A gift we are all pleased to enjoy.'

'Flattery will not reduce the price,' said Max wryly.

'As if I would think such a thing,' said Jack with a grin. He took the drink offered him, and fishing the ice from the glass drew it down over Katya's throat and then traced a slow glittering line to her belly, before easing it slowly across the contours of her sex.

The girl shivered, and with her eyes closed threw back her head as it passed over her clit, letting out a gasp as his fingers found the heat of her.

'Wet already,' he said admiringly. 'My, my, but you train them so very well, dear fellow.'

'Anticipation plays a great part in this game, Jack; you should know that by now,' said Max. 'As a slave Katya already has some idea of what to expect. The secret is to tell them just enough to feed the imagination, but not enough to spoil the surprise.'

'So you keep telling me, in which case let's not disappoint her, eh?' Jack said, pushing the ice home, forcing it deep inside her, his fingers parting her outer lips to find his mark. Katya gasped.

Max closed his eyes for an instant, imagining the way the well-toned muscles of Katya's cunt would close tight around those invading fingers, imagined the sensation as the ice instantly began to melt, glistening rivulets trickling down the insides of Katya's taut thighs, water mixing with the musky perfume of her body.

He could see the girl's cheeks reddening furiously and smiled to himself. It was a fine balance to unleash the wanton in a girl whilst still retaining a certain coy self-consciousness, an ability to feel shame mixed amongst the most extreme pleasures.

Jack's finger explored deeper still, moving rhythmically while his thumb lifted to brush her clitoris, and in the stillness of the room Katya let out a long moan, a heady mixture of pleasure and humiliation.

Pulling out, Jack took the lead down from the hook and snapped it tight. 'Get on your hands and knees, bitch. I want to see exactly what it is I'm getting for my money.'

Wordlessly Katya complied, her head down, hips raised, knees well apart so that every inch of her body was available to the man Max had so recently sold her to. Jack left her there a moment or two so that the extent of her submission was emphasised.

He then crouched beside her and ran his hands over her breasts, cradling their weight in his palms, teasing and pinching the nipples, before working farther back over her flanks and thighs.

'What's this, not a bruise, nor a single welt?' he mused conversationally, passing a hand over the ample curve of her buttocks before turning back to Max.

'No, I thought you might prefer to mark her yourself.'

Jack laughed. 'How well you know me,' he said. 'What shall we say, then? Twenty with the cane? Or perhaps the crop? Or maybe just an old fashioned spanking to begin with?'

'Whichever you prefer, Jack, you know we can accommodate them all here.' On the floor between them Katya remained totally motionless.

Jack glanced at the wall of Max's study, hung with the instruments of his craft. The man smiled appreciatively. 'That's a rather handsome cat you have there. It's new, isn't it?'

'Handcrafted by a dear friend of mine,' Max confirmed. 'Would you care to try it out?' He passed it across, and Jack hefted the weight and tried a couple of practice sweeps to judge how the weight lay before taking off his jacket and moving behind Katya.

'Twenty?' he said again, and Max nodded. Katya was certainly not afraid of pain, although like most of the slaves he'd trained over the years her relationship with it was ambivalent - love and hate combined in a single instant. Max could see a sheen of sweat on the girl's back and detected the slight tremble in her legs as Jack prepared.

His first strike was clumsy, missing her buttocks and instead winding the snapping tendrils around her thighs, biting the silky skin.

'One,' she sobbed, grimacing.

The cat hissed again.

'Two,' she gasped, Jack hitting her squarely across her bottom, making her rock forward. He waited until she was still, waited for that instant when she just started to relax and then struck again, lower this time so the tails cut across the tops of her thighs.

'Three,' she squealed.

Max felt his pulse quicken as she writhed under the cat's attentions, letting the pain echo through her. He could almost feel the crack of it like some electrical charge that lit a fire in his belly. Damn she looked beautiful; her skin reacted quickly, the bite of the cat's tails already lifting narrow stripes and red kisses on her creamy white flesh. Tonight he and Jack would share her and tomorrow she would be gone forever.

As Jack lay on each stroke Katya counted diligently, between cries and strangled sobs, calling out her punishment. When at last he was done she crawled over to him, her eyes bright with tears, and kissed the cat that lay in his hands, thanking him for its hot caress before returning to the position on all fours.

Jack, breathless, eyes bright with excitement, ran his fingers through her hair and then began to stroke her burning flesh. She mewled like a kitten and pressed against him as he worked over the welts, caught up in the heat and power of the pain. Using the juices from her sex he wetted the tight puckering of her bottom and without prelude began to explore her most secret places - places that until now had been Max's alone.

Katya whimpered as he pushed a finger into her bottom, and Max knew her pleasure was mixed with a potent sense of violation, although she knew better than to protest.

Then Jack unfastened his fly and with one seamless motion drove his throbbing cock deep into the girl's tight sex, his finger still buried deep in her rear. Instinctively her back dipped to meet him as he drove deeper still.

Max smiled; it fell to her new master to have the first choice of pleasures and explore his new prize, after all, he had paid well for the privilege. But Max had known her first, brought her to this place, this state of sweet surrender, and nothing and nobody would ever take that away from him.

Contentedly he settled on a chair in front of Katya, and with no fuss guided his aching cock deep into her waiting mouth. Her impatient tongue ran around the tip, teasing his shaft, working feverishly back and forth between it and the single eye before drawing him deep. He eased back, letting her pleasure him. He was going to miss Katya.

As if reading his mind, between gritted teeth, Jack said, 'What are you going to do once she's gone, Max?'

The man smiled. 'Don't you worry about me, Jack; they say when the student is ready the master will appear, and trust me, in my experience it works the other way around as well. A new girl will turn up soon enough. Katya is just the latest. There is always another...' Looking at the face of his companion Max knew he might as well be talking to himself. Buried to the balls in the girl's compliant body, Jack snorted and threw back his head, pleasure suffusing his heavy features and driving away any further need for conversation.

'So, what do you think of this?' said Kay, executing a faultless pirouette across the sitting room.

Maggie Howard looked up from her book at her new lodger and grinned. 'You're not seriously going to go out in that, are you?'

Kay's shapely body looked as if it had been poured into the tiny rubber dress she was wearing, with its thin straps and low-cut neckline. The dress ended six inches above her knees, showing off a good tan and shapely, slim legs, enhanced by high black patent stilettos. With her long blonde hair twisted up into a French pleat, tendrils hanging down to frame her features, Kay looked as if she had just stepped out of some erotic fantasy.

'Certainly am,' she said, handing Maggie a cloth and a spray bottle. 'Mike bought it for me as a present; we're going to some new club over in Moorville. Don't wait up.'

'I wasn't planning to. What's this?' said Maggie, peering down at the bottle. Mike had to be at least ten years older than Kay and sexy in a dark, predatory way that Maggie found both incredibly intimidating and hugely exciting, not that she intended to share that fact with Kay, who was totally besotted with him.

'Latex polish. I want you to buff me up.'

Maggie lifted an eyebrow. 'Meaning what, exactly?'

Kay laughed. 'Polish me; you need loads of talcum powder to get these things on and it kills the shine. Go on, I can't reach.'

Maggie obliged. Although it felt odd to polish something that gave and wriggled and giggled under her touch, but even so a couple of sprays and a whisk over from the cloth and the little rubber dress glowed with a deeply satisfying patina, emphasising the ripe curves and plains of Kay's gym-honed body.

'This would make a great subject for your column,' said Kay, checking her appearance in the mirror.

'What would?'

'Sex under wraps, fetish stuff; you know, whips and chains and leather. Bondage and rubber.' Kay's eyes widened mischievously. 'This new club would be just the place for a bit of research.'

Maggie shook her head. 'I write a lifestyle section, Kay; mid-30's angst, looking for Mr Right, getting a cheap loan to buy the car of your dreams, building a garden, buying a sofa. And anyway, all that kind of stuff, whips and things, it's a joke, isn't it?'

Kay smiled. 'If you say so,' she said. 'Tell you what, I'll give you a couple of website addresses, go and take a look and then tell me what you think. It's another world out there. People who treat sex as a hobby - an addictive game, worth playing well.'

Maggie pulled her best sceptical face, at which point the doorbell rang. 'Prince Charming?' she suggested.

'I should think so, unless you're expecting someone.'

'Hah - don't rub it in unless you want me to double your rent.'

Giggling, Kay picked up the black leather coat Mike had bought her the week before and went to answer the door, while Maggie turned her attention back to the book. She could hear muffled voices in the hall and waited for the sound of the door to close and for silence to descend again.

She'd been divorced for almost two years, and although generally life was better - there being nowhere lonelier or more soul destroying than a bad relationship - any lingering optimism about how good life would be out on the far side had long since faded.

Own house, own job, own lodger taken in to make ends meet. Maggie sighed; it wasn't such an exciting story as she'd imagined. It wasn't that she was short of men, it was just that she was short of the *right* men.

Maggie glanced unseeing at her novel, wondering what was taking Kay and Prince Charming so long, hoping they hadn't decided on a quickie in the hall before going clubbing.

Kay put her head back around the door.

'What, don't tell me the pumpkin and six has broken down already,' said Maggie.

'No, Mike said that if you're at a loose end tonight maybe you'd like to come along with us.'

Maggie laughed. 'Are you serious? What, in my pyjamas?'

'Don't be so daft. I'll lend you something. I've got loads of things upstairs.'

'Thanks,' Maggie said, 'but I really don't feel like it tonight. You go and have a good time.'

'He meant it,' Kay said. 'It would do you good to get out. Treat it as research.'

'I'm touched, but I'd feel totally out of place,' said Maggie flatly. 'And besides, I hate playing gooseberry.'

Kay wrinkled her nose. 'Okay, but here...' she pulled a card out of her handbag and scribbled something on it. 'Go and have a look. Whatever you want, whatever your wildest dreams, you can find it on this site - really. It's where I found Mike.'

Maggie smiled indulgently and took the card. 'And that's meant to be a recommendation?'

Kay smiled, waved, and was gone.

Maggie glanced down at the card, intending to drop it in the bin. 'Darksecrets-dot-com,' she read aloud, and then smiled. What the hell had she got to lose? After all, Simon in the office had asked her out for coffee just last week; Simon Faraday with his thinning hair and bad teeth; Simon who seemed to think he was doing her a colossal favour by paying her any attention at all.

She glanced up at the clock; there was still time enough to do a couple of hours work before turning in, although it seemed like a pretty poor way to spend a Friday evening.

She looked at the phone, wondering who to call. Simon had told her she could ring him any time. She got to her feet and headed up to her office; she could always pick up her email too and maybe just take a quick look at Darksecrets. After all, there was no harm in looking, was there?

Max Jordan rolled back amongst the tangle of sheets, sated. As she had been taught, Katya rested her head on his hairy belly, and took his spent cock in her mouth to lick away the traces of both his excitement and her own.

During the long hot evening Max and Jack had shared her in every possible way, using her arse, her mouth, her hands, her face, her breasts, and her cunt, taking themselves and Katya to the very edge of oblivion. Finally Jack had cried enough, his body slick with sweat, his eyes rimmed with fatigue.

Tonight Katya would sleep between them, ready and eager to please if either man woke and had need of her.

Max groaned softly as her tongue worked its own particular magic over his shaft and balls. Some masters preferred their slaves to sleep on the floor, or be bound or chained to a low bed or mattress beside them, or even kept in separate quarters, but Max always enjoyed sleeping with his possessions. He relished feeling the soft flesh of an enslaved girl curled up against him. It strengthened the bond between master and slave, certainly in the early stages, and taught them what pleasures he expected from a submissive.

There was nothing better than to be roused from sleep in the early hours by the caress of eager lips around his semi-hard cock, or to be able to sink barely conscious into the compliant body of a slave taught that his pleasure was paramount.

In his heyday Max liked the girls to come to his room in rotation or in twos or threes, and he would use them as he saw fit. Now he had to take them one at a time, although it still seemed that he had more stamina than the younger Jack.

He stroked Katya's hair back off her face and pulled her up to him. 'Sleep, little one,' he whispered, and without another word she settled down with her head on his chest. He reached over and before extinguishing the light took a long look at his slave. The last thing he saw before the darkness embraced them was the contented smile on Katya's lips.

Kay was right; it was like another world. Maggie stared at the computer screen completely absorbed in the images on the screen, cradling a mug of coffee. It was nearly three in the morning and she had been surfing Darksecrets and links to various other sites for the best part of four hours. What she found there had taken her breath away. All her life, in her darkest fantasies, Maggie had imagined what it might be like to be used and desired and taken by a dominant man, not that she would ever tell Kay that - she had barely dared acknowledge it to herself. And they were here, all her fantasies and more besides, laid bare.

She took a sip of coffee, wishing it were something stronger. Wasn't that why she married Barry, thinking, hoping he was a dominant male? Hadn't she been looking for a man who would instinctively understand what she needed, a man to look after her, a man to control her, a man who would see her as his possession and relish her submission?

Maggie reddened furiously as the thoughts formed. There was a part of her, a part she had long denied, that wanted a man to use her body, to make her do all those things she had always wanted to do but was too afraid to. Perhaps it wasn't too late to find what she had always known had to be out there, somewhere.

Maggie stared at the page that would let her post a profile in the contact section of the site. What had she got to lose? She didn't have to answer the replies if she got any; she would be anonymous. They wouldn't give out her email address or any personal details. Maggie bit her lip and then began to type, slowly considering every word carefully.

Not long out of a long-term relationship, I'm looking to explore some of the fantasies that have haunted me all my life. I want a real man. A man who understands me. A man who... She paused, wondering how best to put it. *A man who can help me find what I truly am.* She typed with a surety she didn't feel.

Before her courage failed her she added details of her size and age, then watched as the words appeared on the screen, and then very quickly closed the computer down before she had a chance to change her mind. If anyone ever found out about the ad she'd bluff it out, tell them it was research for an article or a story - anything but the truth.

The following morning when Maggie got downstairs, Mike was sitting at the kitchen table drinking coffee.

'Hi, late night?' he said, looking her up and down.

She smiled uncomfortably under his scrutiny. She knew she looked unkempt. 'I didn't realise you were staying,' she said, as lightly as she could manage.

'You don't mind, do you?'

Maggie shook her head. 'No, as long as you don't make a habit of it.'

Kay came in, carrying the post. 'Morning,' she beamed. 'Did you take a look at Darksecrets, then?'

Maggie had already worked out what to say. 'Yes, actually I did, and you're right, it really is amazing. It would make a great article.'

Kay grinned and settled on Mike's lap. It was impossible to ignore the way her nipples pressed through the thin fabric of her T-shirt. 'See, I told you so.'

'Okay, so I was wrong,' Maggie acknowledged.

Across the table Mike looked at her, his expression very different from the puppyish look on Kay's face. Maggie tried very hard not to notice the possessive way his hand rested on Kay's thigh, although as he met Maggie's eye she couldn't help wondering what it was he saw in her face. Did he see her envy, or perhaps her fear?

'Actually, I know someone you should meet,' he said.

Maggie returned his gaze as steadily as she could. 'Really and who would that be?'

'A friend of mine, he taught me everything I know, he's a very interesting man. I'm sure you'll find he's exactly what you're looking for, and maybe visa versa.'

The way Mike spoke hit a raw nerve and Maggie felt her stomach churn. 'To be honest, I'm not sure exactly what I'm looking for, Mike, but if you leave me his number I might give him a ring some time,' she said.

Mike smiled and added milk to his coffee. 'Oh, that isn't how it works,' he said. 'No, I'll tell him about you, and if he's interested then he'll make contact. Did you put an ad up on the Darksecrets site?'

This time Maggie did blush. 'Yes, I thought it might help with my research.'

'In that case give me the nickname you used.'

'Curious,' said Maggie.

Mike grinned. 'As good a name as any, although you know what curiosity did, don't you?'

Maggie picked up her drink; she couldn't bring herself to reply.

'Hello Maggie.'

It was a week later, Friday evening, and Maggie was curled up on the sofa in front of the television. Kay hadn't come home and left a message on the answer machine to say she wasn't likely to be back until Sunday evening, so Maggie had plans to indulge herself. During the week she made up her mind that Mike's offer had been at worst a bad joke and at best an attempt to humour her.

'Hello, who is this?' she asked, muting the television.

'Mike gave me your number.' The man spoke with a soft Irish lilt, his tone low and even, which was both compelling and oddly disturbing.

Maggie felt her pulse quicken. 'Mike? Kay's Mike?'

'An interesting way to describe him; Mike is one of my more able students. He told me you're curious, Maggie.'

She was unsure of what he expected her to say, if anything.

'The thing is, Maggie, do you know what you're curious about?'

She took a deep breath, wondering if she dare tell him; the silence yawned as deep as the ocean and Maggie sensed he had no intention of filling the void.

'There are things... things I've always imagined doing... being part of,' she eventually confessed, wondering what on earth possessed her to tell a total stranger the secrets she had kept hidden for so long. 'Things I've always wondered about, fantasised about. And I write... I was hoping to maybe do an article, about those things, maybe.'

'Things,' he repeated in the same low tone. 'What sort of things, Maggie?'

'I can't tell you,' she blustered. 'I can't...' the words dried in her throat as she realised she longed to tell him but couldn't. 'I don't know how to.'

'Don't worry,' he said. 'I'm sure we can find a way to help you discuss your thoughts and dreams.' He paused. 'We should meet. Sunday, we'll meet for lunch.'

'The thing is...' Maggie began, trying to come up with a plausible excuse.

'Good, I'll email you your instructions. Oh, and Maggie...'

'Yes?' she said.

'My name is Max, but my slaves call me master.'

And then he was gone, and Maggie was left sitting on the sofa with the phone in her hand, the sound of her pulse thundering in her ears.

'Oh, my God,' she whispered, wondering what on earth she'd gotten into, and at the same time feeling a compelling flicker of anticipation.

She hurried upstairs and booted up the computer. As Max had promised there was an email waiting for her.

Maggie,

In future you will refer to me as master.

On Sunday I will send a car for you at midday. You will wear a white blouse, loose dark skirt and high-heeled shoes. You will also wear white underwear and black stockings. You may choose whether to wear a suspender belt or not, although if you make the wrong choice you may expect to be punished. You may wear a suitable coat.

Prior to our meeting you will neatly trim your pubic hair. You will be examined to see that you comply exactly with my instructions. You will stand or sit with your feet parted by eighteen inches.

I look forward to meeting you.

Maggie stared at the screen with a mixture of outrage and excitement; just who the hell did this man think he was? Master indeed! Had she asked for any of this stuff? How dare he assume that she would just do what he said? Trimming her pubic hair? Did he really believe she would just obey and... and... and what?

Angrily she snatched the phone off her desk and dialled Kay's mobile number. This was ludicrous. She didn't care where they were; she needed to speak to Mike.

Just as she was about to press *Call* she read Max's email again and shivered, letting the images trail through her mind; wasn't this exactly what she had always dreamed of?

Chapter Two

The following Sunday morning Maggie stood in front of the mirror in the bathroom and coolly appraised her naked body. She was slim with firm breasts, had a trim waist and shapely hips, and slender legs. At the junction of her thighs nestled a dark triangle of hair, a tight little pelt of curls.

But her mind wasn't just on her appearance. She was mulling over Max's call and the tone of his email.

When the car turned up she would tell the driver or Max or whoever it was driving that there had been a mistake, that she had changed her mind, tell them thanks but no thanks, that she wasn't looking for... for... Maybe she could tell Max that she wanted to talk to him as part of her research, and see how he reacted. He knew she was a writer, so she could ask him for an interview. Maybe she would just go anyway; where was the harm in that? She'd take her mobile, and enough cash to get a cab from wherever it was she found herself.

Still deep in thought she stepped under the shower and let the water wash over her skin. She took the razor off the side of the bath and began to shape the soft curls as Max had instructed. Feeling her excitement slowly begin to build, she let her mind toy with the idea of what it would feel like if she was *really* preparing herself for her master.

It was a compelling thought, and under the torrent Maggie washed and shaved and preened more thoroughly than she had on her wedding day, taking time over every stage.

Of course Max Jordan wouldn't really want to inspect her, she thought, massaging shampoo into her dark hair. It was ludicrous, some kind of mind game to try and rattle her. She soaped her breasts, feeling their warmth and the languid weight of them cupped in her palms, feeling her nipples harden, imagining what it might be like to be made to strip in front of a total stranger. The excitement began to build in her belly, a compelling ache. How would it feel to be in the shower, knowing a stranger was appraising her, watching her every move.

Maggie shivered. It was nearly eleven; another hour and Max would send for her. She threw back her head, relishing the Max of her imagination. If nothing else he had given her a whole new fantasy to enjoy.

Slowly her finger tracked down over her belly, following the path of the razor, Maggie imagining all the while that Max was watching her. Her outer lips were shaved bare now and felt soft and vulnerable. A single finger eased them apart, discovering the moisture already gathering there, her growing excitement clinging to the soft folds of her sex like dew.

With the fingers of her other hand she found her clitoris and circled it, pressing gently down on its sensitive hood. Unable to stop herself she moaned and arched back against the cold tiles; imagining Max Jordan moving closer, his unfathomable eyes fixed on hers; imagining the pleasure in his expression as she touched herself, talking to her, cajoling her, encouraging her to explore her body in the most graphic of terms.

With two fingers deep in her sex, the tight muscles closed around her caress like an eager mouth, sucking them deeper still. Breathing hard Maggie found herself trying to imagine what it would be like to be fucked by the mysterious Max. What would it feel like to have him buried to the hilt inside her? For an instant she imagined an unknown cock driving home, filling her to the brink, making her cry out in a mixture of pleasure and pain as he forced himself deeper than she thought possible.

The first great wave of orgasm took her by surprise, overtaking her like a great flood. Her knees buckled and she slithered to the bottom of the shower, fingers still buried as she thrust onto them, rubbing hard on her clit to milk the last embers of intense heat that had overcome her. And then it was gone and for an instant Maggie reddened furiously, feeling ashamed. How on earth had she got so worked up over a single phone call?

'Maggie?'

She nodded.

'My name is Guido. Max Jordan sent me to pick you up. Are you all ready?'

'Yes, I'm fine,' she said, not quite able to keep the tremor out of her voice, and locking the front door, followed Max's driver towards the black car that sat like a raven at the end of her drive. It was exactly midday and she was dressed as Max had instructed. After all, if she wanted to meet him, for whatever reason, it might be in her best interests to play along.

'Is Max in the car?' she asked the driver. He was dressed in a beautifully tailored black suit that emphasised his broad shoulders and narrow hips. Walking slightly ahead as if guiding her, he swung round and smiled wolfishly.

'Why?' he asked.

It wasn't exactly the response Maggie had expected. 'I, um, just wondered,' she began, and then changed her mind. She would find out in a matter of seconds if her host was there. 'So where are we going?' she did ask.

'Lunch.' As he spoke his eyes moved slowly up her body. 'Mr Jordan is waiting for you.'

Maggie wasn't sure whether she was relieved or disappointed. 'Have you worked for him long?' she asked conversationally. The man opened the rear car door, and taking her hand, helped her inside, waiting while she settled on the cream leather upholstery. His fingers lingered on hers just a little longer than was comfortable, as did his gaze on the elegant curve of her legs.

'Where exactly are we going?' she ventured.

'You ask too many questions.' The driver's gaze did not falter. 'It will get you into a lot of trouble. I'm taking you to a hotel for lunch, not too far. Don't worry, Max has impeccable taste, in food as well as women, and he is very generous.'

Maggie could hear all kinds of meanings in the words. Generous with his woman as well as his money? That was certainly the implication.

The man smiled as if reading her mind. 'And it pays if you don't forget the rules,' he said as he was about to close the door.

'The rules?' she echoed anxiously.

'Your legs should be open,' he said. Maggie had automatically crossed them upon getting into the car. He leant in and slid a hand between her thighs, and Maggie was so shocked she didn't have time to resist.

'Slaves are meant to be available at all times, legs open, you had better get used to it.'

Maggie felt herself colouring furiously. 'But I'm not a slave,' she countered indignantly.

He smiled, his fingers rubbing her thigh. 'Oh, I think you are,' he said. 'And even if you aren't at the moment, you soon will be. Take my advice; make sure you do exactly as you're told. It pays to learn fast with Max.' And then the door closed and he was climbing into the front seat.

Maggie struggled to regain her composure. In her handbag she had slipped a notebook and pen, the tools of her trade, taken almost like a shield to protect her from Max Jordan. As the car drew away from the kerb she tried to convince herself that she was just playing along to get a decent interview. It would make a great story. Slave master in a modern world. She'd be fine. It wouldn't be the first time she'd felt a little intimidated by her subject, but she knew how to wing it, appear at ease and relaxed even if she wasn't.

The car headed towards the coast, and as Maggie settled she was aware of the driver's eyes in the rear-view mirror, and again she wondered what she'd let herself in for.

Max Jordan watched the car make its way slowly along the quay, then up the hillside towards the hotel. He had booked his usual suite with the sitting room overlooking the harbour. Suitably double-glazed, the French windows that opened onto a sunny terrace not only kept the sea winds out, but all sounds in. The rendezvous was far enough out of town to be private, but not so far as to unnerve his guest.

Max's usual waiter took the champagne from the ice bucket and refilled his glass, while the austere man watched the car's progress. Mike had told him that he considered Maggie a natural, someone who had perhaps suspected she was a submissive for years but fought her natural inclinations.

These were the kind of girls Max liked best - spirited and bright with a fire and passion that if harnessed and trained properly would be a delight for him to enjoy both as slave and companion. It was that combination and his ability to recognise it that ensured his girls always brought the highest prices, whether at auction or in a private sale.

One of the reasons Max loved this suite was the view it afforded him; out beyond the harbour a broad sandbank sheltered the little cove, and beyond that was the open sea. And below, as Maggie climbed the stone steps guided by Guido, he could see her clearly, and it appeared Mike was a better judge than he gave him credit for. He could see the mixed emotions on Maggie's face, in the way she moved.

She was nervous, full of expectation and apprehension. He was delighted to see that she was dressed as he had instructed, but wasn't fooled for an instant, for Maggie Howard wasn't obeying him she was humouring him - although it wouldn't be long before she learned the difference.

'Here we are,' said the chauffeur. He stood before the impressive double doors, knocked once and then stepped aside so it was Maggie who waited for permission to enter. As she heard Max Jordan's voice from inside her heart missed a beat. She bit her lip, fingers locked unmoving around the door handle.

'Trust me, it doesn't pay to keep him waiting,' the driver said, and before she knew quite what she was doing, Maggie turned the handle and stepped into the cool room.

Caught in silhouette against a sunlit expanse of glass was a powerfully built man of medium height, probably in his early-fifties, with grey hair, dressed to her surprise in casual trousers and a white shirt, his sleeves neatly rolled up to reveal strong forearms. He had a trimmed beard, heavy but handsome features and a broad mouth. All this Maggie saw and absorbed in an instant. But what she noticed most of all were his eyes - blue-green, glinting, intimidating... yet there was something else, something lurking behind them that was quite impossible to fathom.

'Maggie,' he said in a warm but formal tone. 'How nice to meet you.'

'Max,' she said, with considerably less assurance in her voice. Was she supposed to call him that, or master, and how preposterous an idea was that? She reddened, feeling uncomfortable and unsure in a way she hadn't felt since her teens. Tension crackled in the air between them like the edge of a storm. Maggie shifted her weight, feeling like a lamb waiting for the wolf to decide her fate.

'So,' said Max, taking the champagne bottle from the bucket and pouring a second glass. 'What is it you want? What excuse are you going to use? Are you going to tell me that you're here to interview me, or shall we dispense with the nonsense and the half-truths and the lies, and you tell me what you truly want?' As he spoke he brought the glass to her, all the time his eyes calmly taking in the details of her face and body. It felt as if he was looking into her very soul.

He offered her the champagne and she took it, murmuring her thanks while her heart beat frantically in her chest.

'I don't know, I'm afraid,' she said weakly, almost to herself.

He smiled and gently stroked the line of her jaw. 'I know,' he said.

Maggie trembled, shocked by her reaction to his touch.

'And I do understand, my dear. Drink your champagne then tell me, did you

140

do as I instructed? Did you remove your hair.' His open palm brushed her lower belly so lightly and so fleetingly it was almost like a breath.

'Yes,' she said, eyes downcast, trying to avoid his gaze.

'And what are you wearing under your skirt?'

Maggie felt so self-conscious she thought she might faint. 'White underwear,' she began. 'Although I?'

'Yes, white underwear and what else?' he interrupted. 'Are you wearing suspenders?'

She nodded.

'And you understood my email, that if you made the wrong choice then you would be punished?'

'Yes, but... but surely that was a joke? I mean, you didn't mean punished, not really.'

He pressed a finger to her lips in a gesture so intimate it took her breath away. 'I'll ask you again, Maggie. Did you understand my email?'

'Yes,' she said, still longing to justify or explain her choice, but he held up his hand to silence her.

'Open the left hand drawer of the bureau and tell me what you find there.'

She looked up at him, eyes bright with fear. 'I don't understand.'

'You will, now do as you're told.'

Uncertainly she walked across the room, opened the drawer and let out a little gasp of panic. Inside was a white envelope with her name written on it, but it wasn't that that made her gasp; it was the leather riding-crop that lay across the envelope.

'Well?' he said, sipping his champagne.

'There's some sort of whip in here, and an envelope.'

'Open the envelope, Maggie,' said Max, from somewhere behind her.

She picked it up, her hands trembling. Inside on a single sheet of paper were the words, *For wearing suspenders your punishment is twenty strokes.*

Maggie swung round as if he'd spoken the words out loud. 'But this isn't fair,' she complained. 'It's ridiculous. How was I to know?'

Max held out his hand to her. 'Bring me the crop, Maggie,' he said, as if she hadn't spoken.

She stiffened, determined to hold her ground. 'How was I to know?' she repeated.

Seconds ticked by, seeming like hours. Max Jordan didn't move, didn't reply, while Maggie's mind raced... and then froze. Wasn't this the very thing she had always imagined? Wasn't it the fantasy that had driven her to a potent climax in the shower? Wasn't this the act of submission that had fuelled countless such fantasies? If she walked away now, if she turned and left, then she might be turning her back on the very thing she longed for.

Maggie took a deep breath to try and still her thoughts, and then very slowly she took the crop from the drawer. For a moment she held it in her hands, trying to imagine what it might feel like to have it crack across her flesh. The idea was both enticing and appalling.

'I'm afraid,' she said, her voice tight with emotion.

'I know, come to me,' he said, and she took one step and then another until they were face to face. 'Now give me the crop,' he said. 'Let me teach you, let me show you what your heart already knows,' and as he spoke Maggie did as she was told, struggling all the while to maintain some shred of composure.

'And now, my little Maggie, you must ask me to punish you,' he said, bending the crop into an arch between his fingers.

Her cheeks flared crimson. 'I must what?' she gasped incredulously.

His voice was low and even and yet incredibly powerful. 'You must ask me, you must say, "master, please punish me".'

'But I can't do that,' she insisted. 'I can't.' All the while she could feel a surge of heat rushing through her and a raw flurry of excitement growing between her legs.

Max shrugged. 'Very well,' he said, and set the crop down on a side table.

Standing there in the silence Maggie wrestled with her fears and her inhibitions, until finally she said, in a voice barely above a whisper, 'Master... please punish me.'

'Very good,' he said as he took her hand, and resistance gone she allowed him to lead her to a large leather armchair. 'Bend over,' he ordered, and she did as she was told. 'Lift your skirt.'

Maggie let out a long slow breath, closing her eyes in shame as she fumbled with the garment, imagining the picture she presented to Max Jordan. Then she leant forward, her hips and bottom in the air, her feet apart to maintain her balance over the chair, her white knickers taut across the rounded contours of her buttocks. She shivered, wondering if she was already wet enough for him to see the moisture seeping through the thin fabric. Her stockings and suspenders framed her bottom as neatly as any picture frame.

She felt Max moving closer and held her breath. She felt his hand brush across the contours of her rear, felt them move between her thighs to the intimacy of her sex, cupping and kneading her through the silky material.

Her colour deepened. He must be able to feel her heat, feel the wetness and the excitement. She moaned and without thinking thrust back against him, some instinctive part of her hoping he would brush her pleasure bud.

'You are a shameless little slut, Maggie,' said Max Jordan. 'You are going to be such a pleasure to train.'

Maggie whimpered with fear and embarrassment as he unhurriedly removed his hand, and the next sensation she felt was the flexible length of the crop being drawn very slowly across her buttocks as if it too were exploring her, letting her know what to expect. Max teased the looped tip across her thighs, between her legs, setting every nerve alight as he caressed her.

'Well, Maggie,' he whispered, 'are you ready?'

She held her breath, then nodded.

'Oh no, my dear, you have to tell me.'

'I... I'm ready,' she whispered uncertainly.

'Then count for me,' he said, and an instant later she felt the crop crack across her waiting flesh. The first stroke was hard enough to make her cry out, her body arching under the blow, a dark pain flooding through her.

'Oh, my God!' she gasped. So this was what it felt like.

'Count,' he snapped.

'One.'

He ran the crop's length under the curve of her buttocks, making her painfully aware of its threatening flexibility - and then just as she began to relax he hit her again, no harder but lower. Maggie shrieked, feeling the breath catch in her throat. It was all she could do to gasp, 'Two,' in a voice she barely recognised as her own.

'Good girl,' he murmured, letting the whip hang in the air for a second. Max watched the way the girl reacted, observing her with the eyes of a true master, watching for signs of her panic and fear, reading and relishing them like a good book. She looked exquisite, bent over the chair, her creamy flesh reddening under his ministrations.

The next stroke was a fraction harder and she cried out again, wondering how hard they would get, whether she would be able to stand the pain, whether having come this far she had made a terrible mistake, and whether she should get away now.

He hit her again and Maggie gasped, 'Four,' between gritted teeth.

Max smiled, feeling the stirring in his groin and more than that, the stirring deep in his soul. He adored hearing his women scream - both with pleasure and with pain He drew back the crop for the fifth stroke; it wouldn't take Maggie long to realise that pleasure and pain were just different sides of the same coin and no more than a heartbeat way.

After the sixth stroke he ran his hand over her glowing backside, stroking and kneading the tender flesh. She was wonderfully wet and he could feel her juices soaking into the thin fabric of her knickers and smell the soft musk of her growing arousal.

This time his finger strayed to rub the throbbing bead of her clitoris. As his fingertip found its mark he could feel her whole body tense and then slowly begin to move against him, seeking a release that, although she was unaware of it, was a very long way off.

Just as she found a rhythm Max stopped and pulled her knickers down to her knees. This time there was no tenderness. He felt her flinch and before she could recover he brought the crop down again across her bare buttocks.

'Ohhh...' she wailed. 'No, please... that hurt, that hurt.'

'How many?' he demanded.

'S-seven,' she sobbed, and he hit her again, her body twisting away. 'Stand still and count, bitch,' he growled.

'Eight,' she gasped. He could hear the tears in her voice but didn't hold back.

'Nine,' she cried out and twisted away again, the weals rising white and then reddening on her creamy skin.

'If you move again I will tie you down,' he warned. 'Perhaps I should tie you anyway...'

Maggie, bent over the chair, trembling furiously, said nothing.

'Well?' he said, drawing the loop of the crop across her legs, the merest touch enough to make her stiffen. 'What do you say? Would you like me to tie you down?'

There was a heady silence, and then she said, 'I don't know.'

He smiled. 'Come, come, my dear, isn't that what you've always dreamed of, to be tied and beaten and used for some faceless man's demands? To be fucked, to suck cock until your mouth fills with spunk, to feel him fucking your cunt, and your arse...?'

Her reply was a muffled sob.

'Well, I am that man, Maggie.' And as he spoke he hit her again.

'Ten!' she cried, her whole frame quivering.

He slipped his free hand between the cheeks of her bottom. Her sex opened like a flower to him and he pressed two fingers deep inside her. She offered no resistance, and as he pulled back he smeared the juice from her sex over the tight little rosebud of her bottom. He felt her tense as he stroked it, and then let his finger move to rub down over the hood of her clit. She let out a little sob of pleasure and he pressed a little harder, dipping back into her sex to lubricate his caress.

'Halfway, Maggie,' he said. 'Well, would you like me to stop?' Silence fell and he felt Maggie wrestling with all the fears and doubts she'd ever had.

After a few moments she said, 'No, master,' in a weak voice, and Max smiled knowingly. He let his hand drop away from the wet confines of her quim and brought back the crop, cracking it across her vulnerable buttocks again. She cried out once more, but this time they both knew something had subtly changed.

'Eleven,' she hissed.

At fifteen he stopped again to caress her beaten bottom. Sixteen and seventeen were relatively gentle, allowing her to settle, the rhythm of the strokes he knew was oddly comforting, and then for the last three he struck hard and fast, the count of twenty lost in a tearful scream.

As soon as he was done he stepped closer to comfort her, touching her face and hair, wet with tears. And then he placed the whip by her cheek. 'It's customary for a slave to thank her master for her punishment and kiss the instrument of her pain.' At once he saw the flash of indignation in her eyes, and smiled; oh yes, Maggie Howard was going to be a real challenge and a real delight.

Slowly, very slowly she looked up at him, her face alight with countless contradictory emotions. 'Thank you,' she whispered, and pressed a fleeting kiss to the punishing leather.

He very delicately drew the loop of the crop across her chin. 'Master,' he prompted.

She bit her lip and then let her gaze fall, cheeks flushed. 'Thank you... master,' she said humbly.

'Now, stand up,' he went on, and she obeyed, then as he turned to refill her champagne glass she moved to pull up her knickers.

'What do you think you're doing?' he barked.

'Getting dressed,' she said, bent over, frozen in the movement.

'Did I tell you to cover yourself up?'

'No, but I thought?'

'No nothing, stay as you are. While you are here with me you are mine. You do as I say; you do not act upon some whim of your own. Do you understand me?'

She nodded.

'Now strip completely.'

'Strip?' she echoed.

He nodded. 'And from now on you will not speak unless I ask you a direct question.'

Very slowly, reluctantly, almost as if her hands belonged to someone else, he watched as Maggie began to unfasten the buttons of her blouse, pulling it back off her shoulders. Beneath was a white lace bra, exquisite against her smooth skin. Next she unfastened her skirt and let it slither to the floor. With her knickers around her knees, Max could see she had done exactly as ordered and neatly trimmed her pubic hair.

She hesitated and looked up at him, eyes full of appeal.

'And the rest,' he insisted, waving a hand towards her.

She unfastened her bra to expose her breasts, the nipples erect, before bending to slip off her panties, suspender and stockings.

Totally naked her eyes filled with tears. She looked so vulnerable standing before him. Max indicated she should turn around, and she did. Her backside was beautifully striped with red weals that were already turning to a delicate shade of purple.

As she turned full circle he handed her the champagne. 'You are very beautiful,' he said.

She blushed and he slipped a hand down between her legs to feel the wet contours of her sex. 'Do you expect me to fuck you today?' he asked.

Her eyes widened. 'I don't know, master,' she said, her brain and tongue struggling to express what she expected.

'There are so many things you don't know, aren't there, little one?' He lifted a hand to cup her breasts, fingers pinching the puckered nipples. She winced, and he pondered with relish just how much more she would wince when he clamped them. From a pocket he took a silk scarf and carefully lifting her hair, he blindfolded her.

Plunged into darkness Maggie stiffened with apprehension. She waited for what seemed like an eternity, aware of Max moving, picking out a sound on the edge of her hearing, and realised with horror it sounded like metal on metal. Max Jordan took her wrists one at a time and she gasped as she felt cold metal snap shut around them. This was crazy. What was she doing there?

He led her across the room and guided her back onto a chaise longue. He pulled her hands up above her head and secured them to the frame, and then

145

spread her legs, tying each one at the ankle so that her feet were on the floor on either side of the narrow chaise. The rope was slack so she had a little movement. As he worked she thought how strong and insistent he was, but at the same time how oddly gentle his touch, which put her at ease until she realised that bound and blindfolded Max Jordan didn't need to be rough with her - she was his to do with exactly as he wanted.

Once she was secure he ran his hands over her body, lingering on the curves of her breasts and the mound of her sex.

'Do you know how wet you are, my dear?' he drawled. He teased a finger between the lips of her sex, and she knew then, hearing and feeling the wetness.

She whimpered, wondering what on earth was coming next. And then she knew. She felt his breath on her throat and then his teeth nipped her nipples, teasing them into aching hardness before moving down over her belly, slowly down to the heat of her quim.

Surely he wasn't going to... he pulled the outer lips of her sex apart, holding her open while his tongue eased into her, over and over, his mouth and lips joining in sucking and lapping at her pleasure bud. And then there was pain like a bite on the outer labia as he clamped something to it - and then again on the other - the pressure and the nip making her gasp in shock, she cried out and then winced as he pulled her wide open.

She mewled in pain, although her excitement began to build further. She heard him ripping off some sort tape and fixing the clamps back against her belly so that she was totally exposed. His tongue teased and nibbled a counter point to the pain. She pressed her body up against his face, letting him drink her, surrendering totally to his exquisite caress. Despite the clamps she knew she was teetering on the brink of release and so it seemed did Max. As she groaned, eager to reach the point of no return, he pulled away making her instinctively thrust her hips up to him, seeking his tongue.

'Do you want to come, Maggie?' he whispered, and there was no way she could deny it.

'Yes, master,' she sobbed, pressing herself towards the sound of his voice.

'You must ask my permission.'

'Please, master, may I come, please?' she begged, her voice tight with desire and emotion.

His fingers found her clit again, his touch no more than the tiniest brush, the lightest caress, and for an instant Maggie thought she would go mad if he didn't make her climax. Another finger gently pressed at the tight puckering of her anus, teasing and stroking the sensitive nerve-endings, making her writhe and buck against her restraints, and worse still, making her whole body sing. To her horror she felt his lips working towards his fingers, his tongue licking her dark little rosebud with as much skill as seconds earlier he had lapped her clit.

It was so intense, so all consuming that without thinking she begged over and over, not sure whether she was pleading with him to stop or pleading with

146

him to go on.

'That's it, beg me, Maggie,' Max said.

'Please, please make me come,' she pleaded, wriggling against him, now oblivious of the bite of the clamps.

'When?' he goaded.

'Now, please make me come now.'

'I don't think so,' he said cruelly, and pulled away. Maggie tensed in frustration, her body lifting towards him as far as the restraints would allow, but before she could protest any further he pulled off the clamps ands tape. She wailed and gasped as the blood rushed back into the sensitive flesh. Then he took off the blindfold and freed her wrists. She was stunned by his coolness and found it impossible to meet her tormentor's eyes - while between her legs a fire burned so fiercely she was afraid she might be engulfed by it, the temptation to slide a hand down between her thighs almost too much to bear.

Once he had unfastened her ankles, he tipped her chin up to him. 'Look at me, Maggie,' he said, and reluctantly she did as she was told. To her surprise he was smiling. 'I know what you're thinking. Don't touch yourself, for today your body is mine to do with as I please. Here, drink your champagne,' he said, and handed her the glass.

At that moment there was a knock on the door, and Maggie gasped and instinctively bent forward trying to cover her nakedness and her arousal.

'Stay exactly as you are,' Max snapped. 'If you cover yourself I will give you to whoever it is waiting outside.' And then he called, 'Come in!'

The door slowly opened to reveal Guido, his driver, and the uniformed waiter pushing a covered lunch trolley.

The two men set the table by the window as if there was nothing out of the ordinary happening, and once everything was ready Guido remained behind to serve.

Max indicated the table and Maggie stared at him in astonishment, and then accepted the chair Guido held for her.

'Keep you legs open; I want Guido to be able to see you,' Max said as the driver guided the chair back under the table. 'You must learn that as a slave you are available at all times - to whomever I choose.'

As he spoke the driver, lurking behind Maggie, slid a hand over her shoulder and cupped her breast. As she was about to protest he slipped his other hand down to her tummy, two fingers brushing the little triangle of pubic hair.

All the while Max held Maggie's gaze. 'Enough, Guido, thank you,' he said, without letting his eyes leave hers.

Guido's hands moved away, but enmeshed in the look of relief on Maggie's face Max saw a sense of loss too, and smiled to himself. A willing whore was almost more than he could have hoped for so soon after selling Katya.

Chapter Three

Lunch consisted of chicken in a creamy herb sauce that almost melted on the tongue, served with a selection of vegetables and the sweetest new potatoes. Maggie made an effort to concentrate on every mouthful, trying to regain some sense of control.

Guido acted as their waiter, pouring the wine, serving with enviable ease, his expression totally impassive although Maggie sensed his eyes drinking in her nakedness. As they ate Max asked her about her job, her life, and despite Maggie's initial reluctance and more than a little nervousness, she found herself opening up to him in a way she had never expected.

Max Jordan was urbane and charming, his soft Irish accent inviting and almost hypnotic, but not for an instant did Maggie lose sight of her position, or her vulnerability, or the fact that Max's confidence and easy manner masked a dark need to dominate - although what perhaps disturbed her most was that her body responded to it. For all the pain and humiliation she had already experienced at Max Jordan's hands, there was a sense of relief, almost as if she had finally come home.

Dessert, fresh strawberries and cream, was followed by coffee, and then from across the table Max said in that wonderfully melodious tone, 'A good slave understands her place and is happy there. Her role is to anticipate her master's every wish and obey his every command.'

Maggie reddened. It was the first time whilst eating that the conversation had returned to the subject of slavery, although it wasn't far from her mind. She longed to ask him how he had become a master and why, but despite her curiosity and the supposed article she was supposed to be writing, she couldn't quite bring herself to voice the question.

Max signalled to Guido, who set the two coffee cups down side by side on the tabletop. 'You will serve me, Maggie, my coffee and a brandy,' he ordered.

Maggie nodded and he raised an eyebrow, quite clearly expecting something more.

'Yes, master,' she said hastily, the words sounding somewhat silly and clumsy.

He smiled as her colour intensified. 'And then you will get a taste of what it feels like to be a man's possession. For the rest of the time you are here you'll kneel at my feet, like a good slave, knees parted, back straight. Some masters will want you to keep your hands behind your head or neck, but I prefer them held neatly behind your back. You will sit like that until and unless I instruct you to do otherwise.'

Maggie swallowed heavily.

'Do you understand me?' he pressed.

Her gaze lowered. 'Yes, master,' she said meekly.

'Stand up,' he snapped, the warmth leaving his voice. 'I will have my coffee on the terrace.' Then without another word he stood and headed outside.

Maggie looked at the coffee cups, and then anxiously at Guido, whose face remained as resolutely impassive as ever.

'White, milk not cream, no sugar,' he said as her discomfort grew, taking the second cup for himself and adding cream.

He passed a tray to her with a brandy glass on it.

'Thank you,' she said nervously, arranging the cup next to the glass.

'No need to thank me, slave,' Guido said. 'I'm sure we'll be able to find a way to work your debt off later.'

Maggie stiffened, and would have asked him exactly what he meant if she hadn't caught sight of Max waiting outside for her. 'I've already told you,' Guido said, 'it doesn't pay to keep him waiting.'

Maggie went out through the French windows. The terrace was sheltered, a perfect suntrap, and to her relief extremely private.

Max smiled. 'Thank you, slave,' he said, taking the coffee and brandy.

The light breeze whipped at her hair, making her shiver both with cold and anticipation. She set the tray down on the table beside his chair, and then more reluctantly knelt down beside him on the warm deck. Max waited until she was settled and then ran a hand over her shoulders and hair, leaning forward to cup a breast and squeeze her nipples.

'Slaves aren't just marked by their obedience, little one,' he told her. 'Most wear a mark to show their position, to show who they belong to.'

From the hotel room Guido appeared carrying a flat velvet pouch. Maggie looked up with a mixture of curiosity and surprise.

'Did I tell you to look at him?' Max barked. 'Or move?'

'No, master,' she said quickly.

Max pinched her nipple, making her wince and simper.

'Get up,' he ordered. 'If you become a slave you don't need to think or decide what to do; others will make decisions for you. You have no need to be curious at what things are, because trust me, what is yours will come to you.'

They stood close, face to face, Maggie with her eyes still demurely downcast, trying hard to stop the little tremble that flickered though her body like an anarchic pulse. She wanted to protest, tell him that she wasn't anyone's slave, and that she had no intention of becoming one of his slaves, but something made her hesitate.

Was it a fear that if she said the words aloud then he would send her away? Would he reject her? Although she found it hard to admit to herself, if that happened she would be consumed with regret and would never have or taste the heady secrets this strange liaison promised.

'When you stand you will have your hands behind your back, legs apart.'

Maggie nodded and took a deep breath to try and still her racing pulse, so caught up in calming herself that what Max did next took her totally by surprise. Drawing back his hand he slapped her breast, catching it squarely on the side, making her gasp in shock, and then he struck the other one, catching the nipple. She bit her lip and looked up at him in astonishment.

'Count,' he said flatly.

'One...' she responded hastily.

He struck again, harder.

'T-two.' What was she doing, letting him do this? It seemed even more bizarre than letting him take a crop to her bottom. The sensation of heat and pain spread through her torso. 'Th-three!'

The forth blow made her shriek and twist away from him. 'Guido!' he barked, and the servant handed him a black ribbon with a white ball secured halfway along it. He smiled, eyes narrowing. 'Do you know what this is, my dear?' he asked.

Maggie shook her head. 'No, master, I don't,' she said honestly.

'It's a ball-gag,' he told her. 'Let me show you how it works. Open you mouth.'

The ball sat uncomfortably between and behind her teeth, holding her mouth wide open and making swallowing difficult. Despite her best efforts a trickle of saliva ran down her chin. She looked at Max in horror, who smiled again, drew back his hand and struck her breast harder still. The gag successfully muffled her shriek.

'We can't go disturbing our fellow guests, now can we?' he said, slapping her again. 'And if you move again, Maggie, I'll string you up on the railings.

After twenty he stopped and she hoped he would remove the gag - but no. Instead he took the velvet bag from his driver and from inside produced a black leather collar set with a band of stainless steel. There were three rings set into the steel, and the collar was hinged at the back and fastened with a little padlock, which was stamped with what looked like an heraldic device. As Maggie stared she realised the emblem consisted of the letters M and J.

'Would you like to try it on?' he said.

Maggie shivered, unable to work out the right answer; not that it sounded like a genuine question, and with the ball-gag in place her answer would be restricted to nodding or shaking her head.

'And I did say try,' he said, tipping her face up to his. 'You will only be expected to wear a collar on a more permanent basis if you accept the terms of my contract, Maggie. Well?'

He held the collar out towards her and she stepped closer, afraid to think for fear of where those thoughts might lead her. Max fed the collar around her throat, snapped it closed and fastened the lock. It fitted snugly.

'You look magnificent,' he said, stepping back to admire her, his eyes studying her face, the ball-gag wet with saliva, the collar and then the glowing orbs of her breasts.

'Good,' he nodded, as if speaking to himself, his gaze moving lower still. She felt like a prize animal and tried not to let a growing sense of panic or unnerving desire overwhelm her. It wasn't that the collar was uncomfortable, it was what it and the gag symbolised. Surrender, silence, obedience - and a terrifying glimpse of a trust of the most fundamental kind, that she realised would have to grow if she stepped into this ring of fire with Max Jordan. She would quite literally have to trust him with her mind, her body and her soul.

He sat down and opened his legs. 'Come here and lay across my knees,' he told her, and without a word, still reeling from the snap of the collar, Maggie did as she was told. For a moment she lay totally still, listening to her own heartbeat, feeling the press of his trousers against the sensitive glow of her skin, trying to find a place where she felt balanced, and then Max said, 'You are disobedient and wilful, and yet I know that in your chest beats the heart of a true slave, Maggie. I can feel it, I can see it.'

How could he be so certain when she was so unsure?

He stroked her buttocks, working his fingers against the welts left by the crop.

'I can teach you, Maggie. I can show you.' She closed her eyes, the glow simmering before lunch still there between her legs, hidden a little by fear but nevertheless within an instant of rekindling. 'But you have to learn to obey me. Do you understand?'

'Hmmm,' she mumbled through the gag, wondering why he hadn't removed it, and then she found out why. His hand exploded across her bottom making her convulse, and as she shrieked in horror Max drew her arm behind her back and spanked her again.

She sobbed and shook her head desperately, but his hand found the mark again. Tears coursed down her face and at the same time, and to her shame, the glow in the pit of her stomach began to build again.

Four more spanks were delivered and then he pressed two fingers into her sex, roughly, and her hips lifted to give him access, desperate for his caress. She heard him laugh with pleasure, and no longer cared.

Pushing her off his lap she rolled wearily onto the wooden decking. 'Get up on all fours, you little bitch,' he snapped, and without a second thought Maggie did as she was told, and was utterly shocked to feel his rampant cock drive into the wet confines of her cunt, filling her, making her gasp with shame and delight. She sobbed as he penetrated her, both at the ferocity of his entry and at the relief and joy of finally feeling his erection buried deep inside her.

As he fucked her she met him stroke for stroke, gasping behind the gag as his hands sought her nipples, twisting and tormenting them before moving down to her clit, nipping and stroking the engorged bud until she felt the roaring wave of orgasm about to wash her away.

'You may come,' he panted in her ear, his weight on her back, and she was lost, borne up, carried away by the most intense sensations she had ever experienced. She cried out again and again as he drilled deeper still, riding the tightening of her sex cocooning him, and she knew he was with her every step of the way, driving deep, arching and crying out as the wave overtook him too.

When they were done Maggie turned and slumped into his arms, sated, shivering and raw with emotion.

'You're not done yet, little one,' he said, and she stared at him in weary bewilderment. He undid the ball-gag. 'A good slave always cleans her master. With your mouth,' he added, running a finger around her lips. 'After I have taken my pleasure, you will clean me.'

She looked down at his cock. Even spent it was impressive, long and thick with a smooth helmet, wet and glistening with their combined juices.

'Well?' he said, and without complaint Maggie knelt over him and took his cock into her mouth, tasting their salty flavours. He sighed and stroked her hair, and after a few minutes he gently he pulled her away and kissed her on the lips.

'Come with me,' he said, and together they rose. 'A good slave always walks two paces behind her master,' he informed her.

Maggie did as she was told, trying to ignore the avaricious glint in Guido's eyes as he stood by the door, watching her. He gave her the barest of smiles, and she couldn't contain an uneasy shudder.

Guido let the smile linger on his lips. He had been with Max for over two years as valet and driver, and in return Max was teaching him all he knew. Another couple of months and he would be on his way and begin his own stable. Maybe he'd make a bid for Maggie when she stepped up on the block; it would be nice to start with one of his master's girls as a yardstick. She was certainly extremely appealing, headstrong and bright, but even he could sense that under that apparent self-confidence and independence she had a strong desire to please, to be wanted, to be owned.

The way she had writhed and sobbed under Max's ministrations had truly been a delight. Guido replayed in his mind the way the girl waited on all fours to be fucked. There was no way she faked any of that.

He straightened his tie, already relishing the prospect of the drive home.

'And when dressed, in public,' Max continued as they stepped back into his suite, 'a good slave will always look and behave impeccably, like a lady; elegant with appropriate clothes, good shoes, subtle make-up and perfume. My slaves are always well presented.

'My main interest has always been in the initial training of suitable girls - in recognising those who will make good slaves and interesting companions. I train them in the basics and then sell them on. We have regular auctions. There is always a lot of interest in my girls.'

'Sell them?' Maggie echoed, unable to contain herself.

Max smiled, apparently forgiving her for speaking without permission.

'Yes, sometimes we sell privately but for the most part we auction off our spare stock, or those we're tired of, or whatever. Besides that we often have auctions where slaves are sold for just a night or a weekend.'

Maggie felt her colour draining. He was talking about his slaves as if they were animals, and worse still, as she considered what he said, was the realisation that somewhere - just below the surface of the life she knew - was a culture where this kind of behaviour went on.

The idea not only unnerved her but also, she realised, excited her. Max took her hand and led her into the bedroom.

'Lie on your back on the bed,' he told her. 'Legs parted.'

Maggie stared at him in disbelief, and then at the four-poster bed that dominated the room. Surely he couldn't be ready for more - he'd only just spent.

'Come along, there is no place for coyness now, Maggie,' he snapped, his mood volatile. 'You will follow my instructions instantly and to the letter. Now!'

She looked at him uncertainly, heart beating fast, and then did as she was told, closing her eyes to block out the images that filled her head.

'Very nice,' he said. 'Now hold yourself open so I can examine you.'

Maggie froze... examine her?

'What are you waiting for?' he growled.

'I can't,' Maggie whispered. 'Please, I... I can't.'

The silence and the seconds ticked slowly by, and then Max said. 'For every minute you keep me waiting I will add six strokes of the crop to your punishment. Now open your cunt for me.'

Maggie let her fingers trail down over her belly, eyes tightly closed. This was ludicrous. Why should she obey him? But then taking a deep breath she let her fingers slip between the outer lips of her sex, warm and wet with excitement. She opened herself a little, praying the gesture would be enough.

'Wider,' he snapped.

Maggie did as she was told, feeling herself flush scarlet. It wouldn't have been so bad if Max touched her, but he didn't, he was just watching and waiting.

'Guido, come in here,' he eventually called, and Maggie cringed with shame, wanting to pull her fingers away and close her legs. 'Stay as you are,' Max ordered, anticipating her reaction. 'Did I tell you to move?'

'N-no, master,' she stammered.

'What do you think?' Max said conversationally, and Maggie knew he wasn't talking to her.

Guido mumbled something and she felt him moving closer, felt his eyes and breath on her.

'Get up on all fours so Guido can have a better look at you,' Max ordered, and she stiffened, feeling her stomach tighten with shame and apprehension.

The driver ran his hands over her buttocks and hips, letting his fingers stray down to her sex, thrusting, exploring, probing inside her with none of the finesse employed by Max Jordan.

'Nice and tight,' he observed, as her sex instinctively tightened around him.

'Indeed... indeed,' Max concurred, and embarrassed beyond all measure Maggie let her head fall to the mattress, feeling she would die of shame. Guido parted her further and pushed another finger inside, her flinch doing nothing to halt his invasive touch.

'Help yourself,' said Max. 'I'm going down to the bar for a drink. You can do whatever you like, just don't fuck her.'

Alone with the driver Maggie's heart pounded furiously; ridiculous though it was she already held some trust for Max Jordan, but not this other man. He removed his fingers, and she felt his tongue lapping the backs of her thighs and then wriggle into her sex. She gasped at the intensity and intimacy of the touch, his nose nudging her puckered rear entrance as he devoured her.

She felt shamefully uncomfortable, but there were the first flickers of renewed pleasure too. She cringed; had her body no shame at all? Guido slid a finger up to caress her clit, and she moaned as he brushed the tight little peak. It was all the encouragement he needed. He began to lap at her quim and then worked further up along the sensitive bridge of flesh between her sex and the forbidden entrance above. Maggie whined in horror, trying to wriggle away from him, and then gasped as his tongue brushed over her anus, lapping and teasing.

'Oh!' she gasped. 'No, please don't. Oh!' But her protests seemed to make his tongue work all the more diligently while his fingers teased her pleasure bud.

'Please don't... please don't,' she whispered, his tongue driving her mad with need. It felt wonderful and awful at the same time.

'Enough, Guido,' said a familiar voice. 'We can't have Miss Howard enjoying herself too much, now can we?'

The driver pulled away, leaving Maggie hanging, her sex wet and ready for more, her bottom slick with his saliva.

'Look at you, you filthy little whore,' Max Jordan sniggered, and without prelude he pressed a finger into the tight confines of her rectum. Maggie cried out in shock, her body fighting the invasion.

'Nice and tight,' he concluded. 'Maybe a little too tight at the moment for what I have in mind, but we can cure that. Have you ever been fucked in the arse, Maggie?'

'No,' she gasped in horror, aware that her body was clutching his intrusive digit. Another finger slipped into her sex, the fullness and the intense sensations making her feel heady.

'I like to bugger my slaves,' he mused. 'It's my own special place, somewhere that's mine and mine alone - no other man is allowed to fuck you there. They can fuck your cunt, fuck your mouth, fuck your tits, but your arse is mine.'

Maggie shivered; it seemed appalling and unnerving that such a sophisticated man could speak so crudely about her body, and his desires and plans to use and abuse it. His fingers left her.

'I think that is enough for now,' he said, as casually as if they were taking an afternoon stroll. 'Get up.'

A little unsteadily, Maggie got to her feet.

'Now,' he said, 'before we go any further...' Maggie looked up at him expectantly, and saw the intent in his eyes. 'Every slave I take on must sign a contract.'

'A contract?' she echoed uncertainly.

'Be quiet. I have warned you about speaking so freely. I take no one on without a contract, and once it is signed you are committed to it. I consider it a legally binding contract and so should you. And you also have to understand that at the end of your training, I will sell you.'

Despite everything that had happened Maggie found this revelation unbelievable. It was preposterous, some sort of a joke. No one in their right mind signed themselves away under someone else's rule.

Max continued. 'I am a firm master, but fair,' he told her. 'I understand what you need but I won't rush you to achieve it.'

Maggie squashed the look of derision that threatened. What man ever really knew what a girl wanted?

He raised an eyebrow, as if anticipating a question, and when none came he continued. 'Would you like to see the contract?'

Maggie was intrigued. 'Yes, master,' she said, and Max made a gesture towards Guido, who handed him a briefcase from which he produced a single sheet of paper and handed it to her.

'There we are, my dear,' he said. 'The contract.'

Slowly she began to read. 'I, Maggie Howard, hereafter referred to as the slave, do offer myself to Max Jordan, hereafter known as my master, for his pleasure in a BDSM relationship, as defined in detail as follows...'

Maggie glanced uncertainly at Max, then at Guido, then back at the document in her trembling hands.

'The slave is fully aware that her master is a strict dominant, and that she is a willing slave to be used for his desired pleasures. The slave expects the domination of her master and is willing to endure any and all punishments deemed appropriate by him.

'I hereby grant permission to my master to dispense any punishment he may deem appropriate to the slave totally for his enjoyment and the pleasure of hearing the slave request his mercy.

'The slave will be under her master's complete and total control and will immediately obey and comply with any order or instruction given to her with the full joy of knowing she is his property and his to use however he chooses. If the slave displeases or disobeys her master in any way she expects to endure any punishment he so chooses as necessary for her inappropriate actions.

'The slave also agrees not to make any change in her physical appearance without the prior approval of her master.

'The slave agrees to full participation in any and all activities her master desires as she does not know the extent of her limits with him at this point and desires to learn how complete is her submission to him.

'After thorough training is completed the slave will be sold to the highest bidder.

Maggie reddened furiously and felt her pulse increase as she finished reading. Then she read it again, more slowly this time, not trusting herself to look up and meet Max Jordan's eyes.

It gave her an odd feeling deep in her stomach. In her imagination the scenario of being owned and used and shown off was hugely exciting, but the reality? She had no intention of signing herself away. What on earth did the man take her for? She looked at him levelly. 'I am expected to sign this?' she said.

'No, there is no expectation on my part. The choice is entirely yours, Maggie. But before you dismiss the idea and walk away, let me tell you something about yourself. Even if you don't sign you will never be free. Today you've caught a brief glimpse of those things that have haunted your dreams, maybe even your nightmares, for a long, long time.'

She looked away; he was far too close to the truth for it to feel comfortable. But Max hadn't finished.

'And I know, Maggie, because I see it in your eyes. I know from my own experience that you can never escape those desires that are in your mind.' His tone changed. 'But maybe you've already got enough for your article. Isn't that what you came for?'

Maggie nodded.

'Well, in that case you are free to go.' Her dismissal was so perfunctory it took her by complete surprise. Max pulled a key ring from his pocket, beckoned her closer and removed the collar, which Guido immediately returned to its black velvet bag.

She extended a hand to give him the contract back, but Max waved it away. 'Take it with you,' he said. 'I wouldn't have expected you to sign it here and now anyway. You need to be sure you understand all the implications of something so momentous, but remember you must sign it before your training begins.'

Maggie smiled. 'Thank you,' she said, and went to retrieve her clothes. She had no intention whatsoever of signing his stupid contract. The idea was ridiculous. Utterly ridiculous.

'You have to understand, Maggie,' he went on as she dressed, 'that you will never win and you will never escape.'

She wondered what he meant, and then realised with a growing sense of unease that it was some kind of a threat - except that the threat was from inside her, not from Max Jordan.

'Thank you for lunch,' she said, as casually as she could manage.

He smiled confidently. 'Guido, show the young lady to the bathroom.'

When Maggie re-emerged not more than half an hour later, showered and dressed, the suite was empty, all evidence of lunch and of Max Jordan's presence gone. All that remained was Guido - standing by the door waiting to drive her home, his peaked cap resting lazily between his fingers.

'Well, well, well,' he said with a sly grin. 'Here we are again, Miss Howard. How does it feel now you know what Max Jordan has to offer you?'

Maggie tried to smile with conviction. 'It feels just fine, thank you. I don't want what Mr Jordan has to offer, though. I've seen enough, and I don't want any part of it.'

Guido shook his head, and Maggie wondered if the lie was as obvious to him as it was to her.

'But I am interested in what makes a man like him tick,' she continued; after all, she reasoned, if there really was an article in it, she could do with a bit

156

more background material.

'You should have asked him, then,' said Guido, standing to one side to allow her to pass. 'I'm sure Max would have told you anything you wanted to know.' He paused as Maggie drew level with him. 'And so would I. For a price, of course.'

'What does that mean, exactly?' she demanded.

'Oh, come on, Maggie, don't be so naïve,' he said with mock disappointment, tutting loudly. 'I tell you something and then you pay for it in kind.'

Maggie stared at him indignantly, and without thinking swung her arm to slap his face. But he was too quick for her and caught her wrist in a vicelike grip that made her wince with pain.

'He told me you could be fiery,' Guido mused, chuckling throatily, his smile never faltering. 'A good judge of character, is Max Jordan.'

'Which is more than can be said for you,' snapped Maggie, angrily jerking her hand away from him.

Guido smiled. 'If you would like to wait outside I'll bring the car to the front of the hotel,' he said with infuriating assuredness.

Chapter Four

'Where are we now?' Maggie asked, leaning forward in the back seat of the car and looking out at the passing countryside, trying hard to spot a familiar landmark. To her complete surprise, after the events of the afternoon, she had drifted off to sleep on the drive home. Feeling slightly foolish she repeated her question. 'Where are we, Guido?'

She caught the driver's eye in the rear-view mirror. He smiled lazily. 'Don't worry, it's not far now,' he said. 'Why don't you just sit back and enjoy the ride. I'll let you know when we get there.'

Something about his tone made her uneasy. 'But I don't recognise this road,' she said, trying to keep the anxiety out of her voice. 'How far are we from Richwell?'

He laughed. 'I've already told you, relax. This is the scenic route. There's no rush, is there?'

Making an effort not to look or sound flustered, Maggie turned her attention back to the view outside the car. It was a beautiful evening. The early summer sun was slowly sinking in the west, daubing the undulating landscape with a mellow golden light. Ahead of them the road unfolded like a ribbon, and Maggie looked for some clue as to where they might be, the tension in her stomach building. She had no idea where they were or where they were heading, and just as she was about to ask again the car slowed and they crossed a narrow wooden bridge that led off the road and through a copse of trees.

Maggie didn't like this. On the road they may well have been taking a scenic route home she wasn't familiar with, but this was little more than a dirt track leading to she knew not where.

The car was travelling more slowly now, rising and falling over the uneven surface.

'Guido, what's going on?' she asked anxiously. 'Where are we? You're supposed to be taking me home.'

'Don't worry,' Guido said, his wolfish smile caught in the mirror. 'I thought you wanted to know how it felt to be a slave? Isn't that why you met Max today, to get your hands on a little background information? Well, this is lesson two.'

'I wanted to know about Max Jordan,' she began, humouring him.

'I've already told you that I'm prepared to tell you everything you need to know,' he said, guiding the car into a clearing and switching off the ignition. 'I've told you the deal, it's just that now I've upped the stakes a little.' He indicated the narrow track that led back to the road. 'How about it, Maggie?' he said, the grin holding. 'A ride for a ride. Part of your continuing education, or maybe a little payment on account.'

Maggie forced a smile, trying to mask her trepidation. 'Let's go back, Guido,' she suggested. 'I can pay you something, but not much,' she began. 'Perhaps we could negotiate?'

'You know that isn't what I mean,' he sneered angrily, cutting her short. 'I don't want or need your money.'

Maggie said nothing; she already knew what the deal was. Hadn't he told her as she left the hotel?

'So, I'm going to have the rest of what I sampled this afternoon.' He licked his lips. 'You taste really good.' Maggie reddened and he chuckled. 'Come on, don't tell me you didn't enjoy it. I could feel the way you were moving under my tongue and my fingers. There was no lie there, you were close.'

Maggie shivered. 'Guido, please...' she began.

'No more talk, just get out of the car.' His tone hardened. 'I can take what I want or you can give it to me - simple as that. It's up to you.'

Maggie looked left and right through the trees. They were miles from anywhere. There was no point in running. There was nowhere to hide. What choice did she have? And besides, wasn't there some tiny part of her, some part she would never admit to, that was excited by the idea that the man wanted her so much he would jeopardise his job to have her? Hadn't she relished the humiliation of being given to him at the hotel, to play with just as he wanted? Maggie fought to silence the rogue thoughts.

'This is ridiculous,' she said instead. 'Take me home. I won't say anything about this to Max.'

Guido laughed. 'You really think he'd mind? You have to understand, Maggie, that slaves are mere possessions, toys to be used. I thought Max had made that clear to you.'

She stared at him, trying to gather her thoughts. What could she do other than try and talk him out of whatever obscene plan lurked behind those dark eyes?

'Get out of the car,' he said, his tone icy. But Maggie didn't move, and his expression hardened. 'Now!' he spat. 'And take your skirt off.'

Maggie bit her lip, considering her options. What was she going to do? She guessed Guido would be a lot less controlled than Max, and decided that her best course of action was to humour him.

Slowly, very slowly, heart pounding in her chest, Maggie slipped across the seat and did as she was told, trying to formulate an alternative while unzipping her blue skirt and letting it drop to the grass. Underneath she was wearing the white underwear and stockings and suspenders stipulated by Max Jordan.

Guido's eyes moved hungrily over her body. 'Max was right, you are a natural,' he said, and Maggie reddened under his undisguised lust.

'Guido, please,' she began, wondering if she could appeal to his better nature. But he was having none of it, and instead he lunged and cupped her sex through the thin fabric of her panties, fingers tightening, squeezing hard enough to make her whimper.

'I want this,' he growled, 'and I intend to have it. And as I said, Maggie, either you give it to me or I'll take it.'

He looked her up down as if relishing her growing apprehension. 'Now I want you to strip for me, or would you prefer me to rip your clothes off?'

Without another word Maggie slipped off her knickers and undid her suspender belt, uncomfortably aware of his intrusive stare. Being outside in the woods made her feel doubly exposed, doubly vulnerable.

As she straightened up from removing her stockings Guido, annoyed at the delay, roughly unfastened her blouse, pushed up her bra and grabbed a breast in each hand, dragging her tight against him, his kisses hard and hungry while his hands squeezed the tender flesh until she cried out into his mouth. His cruel touch made her reel with a terrible sense of fear and resignation and also, and to her abject horror, sexual hunger. Was this what slavery and submission truly meant? Slavery to your own terrible desires?

'Take off the rest of your things and bend over the car bonnet,' he said. 'And spread your legs wide so I can see exactly what I'm getting.' He pushed her away towards the waiting vehicle.

Maggie closed her eyes, trembling, going through the motions while her mind was in turmoil. How had it come to this? Naked, shivering and afraid she settled down over the broad polished black bonnet without another word, her forearms supporting her while Guido explored her body, her back, her breasts, her buttocks; no place was spared his crude examination, his invasive fingers investigating the welts Max had striped her with. Then just as she began to find some sense of composure, some safe inner space, he kicked her feet further apart, leaving her even more vulnerable to his explorations.

'Give me your wrists, here,' he snapped. 'Put them behind your back.' She closed her eyes, knowing that some part of her had already surrendered.

Helpless, with her cheek pressed against the warm bodywork, Guido jerked her arms back and tied them together at the wrist with a length of cord.

'Well, well, well,' he said, breathing hard. 'The little madam out to do some research. Did you think it would bring you this far?'

She held her breath, too afraid to reply.

He caught hold of her hair and jerked her head back. 'Well, what have you to say for yourself? There's no Max here now to protect you, no safety net. You're all mine. Did I tell you that Max is training me to be a master too? I've learnt a lot from him, but I've always known in my heart what really turns me on; a delicious girl fighting and struggling against me, crying out, begging for mercy, writhing and sweating... that's what excites me.'

Maggie froze, then heard Guido spitting, felt his fingers work the saliva into her quim and then felt the hard press of his cock probing the lips of her sex, before he plunged into her with one smooth penetration.

The invasion took her breath away, his cock large and stout. She wailed with shock and without thinking begged him to stop. 'Please, you're hurting me,' she sobbed, knowing full well that's what Guido wanted to hear, and secretly experiencing the reawakening of her carnal desires. As she struggled beneath him he pushed deeper still, holding her hips to pull her back onto his rampant erection.

'Please, Guido, no please,' she rambled, even though her treacherous body was responding to him. And Max's driver was already beyond any discussion, turning back or reasoning. He locked his fingers tight in her hair, pulling her up to him, dragging her off the car, bending her back like an archer's bow, her exposed breasts thrusting forward.

As he rutted into her again and again his free hand mauled her breasts and twisted her nipples. Maggie cried out in pain and shock, while deep inside she felt her own dark passion building inexorably, ashamed of what she was feeling. How could such an animal excite her so much? How was it that this violation, this abuse of her body by a man who was practically a stranger, was the very thing that ignited the fires in the pit of her stomach? Maggie was ashamed of herself, even more than she loathed Guido.

He grunted like an animal, driving on and on, excited by her physical and verbal reactions. As he got closer to the point of no return he pulled her fully back against his body and clamped his arms around her waist, biting her neck and lapping her hot flesh.

'You love this, don't you, you dirty little bitch?' he growled between clenched teeth.

Maggie said nothing, trying desperately to retain some last shred of self-control.

'Tell me,' he snapped. 'You like to feel a cock deep in your cunt, don't you? Don't you? Tell me.'

He twisted his fingers tight in her hair and jerked her head back, making her shriek in pain.

'Yes!' she gasped, horrified to hear herself admit it.

'Yes what?' he pressed. 'What is it you like, you dirty little bitch?'

Maggie shivered as he drove deeper still, emphasising his questioning, making her cry out again as his cock filled her. 'T-to feel a cock d-deep inside me,' she stammered, writhing with pleasure and shame. His fingers tightened in her hair and around her nipple and she squealed. 'Deep in my cunt!' And Maggie knew it was true. She wanted him to use her, just as she had wanted Max to use her. She wanted Guido to take her over the edge into oblivion, and instinctively began to move against him, grinding her arse back into his groin, tipping her hips so that his body angled perfectly against hers.

'What do you want me to do then, Maggie?' Guido growled in her ear, as if sensing the change in her.

'I... I want you to fuck me,' she gasped. 'Please, fuck me. Make me come. Please... please, Guido.'

As she begged he snorted derisively, pulled out of her and pushed her down onto the grass. 'On your knees,' he growled, and Maggie, sobbing with frustration, did as she was told, stumbling with her hands tied, knees parted to maintain her balance.

Guido leered down at her, stroking her hair back off her damp brow, running his fingers over her breasts and lips and throat. And then he arrogantly brushed her chin and cheeks with his rigid shaft. It was slippery and smelt of her own excitement, then grabbing her hair again he stroked the bulbous tip across her lips, and then fed it deep into her mouth.

The taste and smell of him suffused her senses; the heady mixture of aroused male musk mixed with the flavours of her own body was almost more than she could bear. Her lips were slick with his pre-cum and more than anything she wished her hands were free so she could touch herself and him. Her whole body was screaming for release.

Guido towered above her, dominant and full of lust, obviously relishing the way her tongue and lips worked over the head of his cock, enjoying the special attention as the kneeling girl submissively lapped and sucked his shaft deep into her mouth. Maggie could feel his pleasure building along with her own. She heard him grunt, felt the tension increasing in his balls and braced herself for the great flood of seed to fill her mouth.

Guido thrust once, twice, and for a moment she was convinced he was going to ejaculate and make her drink his seed, but then at the very last second he pulled out, dragging her head back and splashed her face and breasts and cleavage with this warm spunk. She gasped as it splattered on her flesh.

He grinned triumphantly down at her, catching his breath. 'Now you look like a whore - and you certainly act like one.'

Maggie felt so ashamed she wanted to die, but it seemed her torture wasn't over yet. Guido, his cock still wet and slick with combined juices, dragged her to her feet and back over the bonnet of the car, on her back this time, and to her horror he began to lap up the trail of warm semen that clung to her body, licking and sucking her face and breasts. Seeing the shock on her face he smiled and kissed her, pushing his tongue, slick with spunk, deep into her mouth.

Maggie shuddered and tried to roll her head to one side, tried to push him away. But Guido merely laughed and continued to lick her, her face and her ears, sucking her nipples into his mouth, biting and nipping. Maggie gasped and began to moan, beginning to lose it again, overcome by so many sensations and needs that threatened to engulf her.

But still there was no reprieve. Gradually Guido was working lower, spreading her legs until there was no part of her that was not exposed to his fingers and his lips.

'You taste wonderful,' the driver drooled, plunging his tongue deep inside her and then lapping at her quim like a hungry dog.

Maggie cried out, part of her horrified by the exposure, the other half afraid that he might stop. Finally he sank down amongst the grass and the leaves beneath the trees, and Maggie gasped as he lifted her bodily and set her legs over his shoulders, his tongue moving between her thighs, devouring her sex. He slavered against her and then, just when she thought she would go mad with desire, he located her clitoris.

Maggie cried out with relief and pleasure. Instinctively her hips thrust to meet the driver's tongue, oblivious to everything but the bliss building deep inside. He slid a finger into her quim and another lodged just inside the puckered bud of her bottom. She groaned and writhed against his touch; Guido surely had to be Max Jordan's star pupil.

She closed her eyes tight, all rational thoughts vanishing into the abyss as wave after wave of pleasure rolled over her, but then he pulled away and Maggie whimpered with frustration.

'Come on then, ask me, I want to hear you beg,' he goaded, his tone thick with desire. 'Beg me, bitch. Beg me for what you want.'

'Oh,' Maggie sobbed, 'please don't stop now, Guido, please don't stop. I'm so close, lick me... suck me... please. Please make me come.'

Guido's tongue brushed across her pleasure bud. Maggie groaned again, lifting her hips. He lapped a little harder, and it was almost more than she could bear.

'Please, please,' she sobbed, any last shred of pride lost in the hungry pit of desire as he circled the little peak with the tip of his tongue. For an instant Maggie thought she might go mad and then the wave broke over her.

'I'm going to come!' she shrieked. 'I'm going to... oh... oh!' She shuddered, rolling from side to side, her sex grinding into his face. And as she peaked she felt him rise and sink his rejuvenated cock deep, deep into her sex. Her body closed around him and he followed her into oblivion seconds later, throwing back his head and grunting like a wild animal as he drove his cock into her.

And then finally they were both still and all Maggie could hear was their ragged breathing, the pound of her pulse and the rustling of the trees.

As the car made its slow way back down the uneven track, Max Jordan stepped out from behind the shelter of a tree and watched the red taillights disappear into the distance. Guido was somewhat crude in his technique, but Maggie Howard was far better than he had hoped for.

162

He walked slowly back to his own car considering the way the day had gone and what he had just witnessed. He smiled; he was going to enjoy training this one.

Maggie sat up in bed, her thoughts racing. The room was dark except for a ribbon of moonlight falling through the open curtains and settling across her duvet. It had to have been a dream, didn't it? A dream? More like a nightmare!

She switched on the bedside light, and there on the bedside cabinet was Max Jordan's contract. She closed her eyes, dropped her head into her hands for few seconds and then with a growing sense of determination got out of bed, pulled on her dressing gown and went across the landing to her office. This was ridiculous and dangerous. What did she think she was playing at?

Maggie booted up her computer and began to compose an email.

Dear Max, thank you very much for lunch today, and for your time, and for showing me some of the things your slaves have to endure.

Her mind raced as the memories returned; was it endurance or enjoyment that lingered in her mind? Whichever it was she knew that however appealing the sensation it was also terrifying, perhaps too terrifying.

It was a real struggle to keep her mind on the task in hand, but even so she continued.

But I have, despite your parting words, come to the conclusion that I'm really not ready to be involved in the kind of activities you showed me - if I ever was. Thank you for your time.

Best, Maggie Howard.

She pressed *Send*, and as the message vanished into the ether she sat for a few moments wondering whether it was a great mistake or a narrow escape. Was it relief or a sense of loss that gripped her?

For a few minutes she stared out of the office window into the night sky, trying to still her racing mind by picking out the constellations she recognised. What devil was it that Max Jordan had released? Certainly without his influence she wouldn't have responded to Guido in the way she did. Maggie didn't see herself as a slave or as naturally submissive, but there was no denying the kick of excitement she had felt whilst being at the two men's mercy. Was it too late to put that particular genie back in the bottle?

She padded back to bed, and as she turned off the light and closed her eyes it was Max Jordan's face she saw.

Chapter Five

'So, how about coming out to dinner with me?' said Simon Faraday, leaning across his office desk.

Maggie, looking up from her computer screen, lifted an eyebrow quizzically. 'I'm sorry?'

She had popped in to work to sort out a few things for the piece she was writing on garden design and was - at least to the outside world - totally absorbed in what she was doing.

Simon's crooked smile didn't falter. 'I was just thinking, the last few times I've seen you, you've looked a bit down in the mouth. So I thought you could do with cheering up. There's this really nice little seafood restaurant on the coast and I just thought...'

Maggie put on a strained smile. She had assumed Max Jordan's response would be to try and persuade her to change her mind about his proposition, but what she hadn't been prepared for was the polite email accepting her decision and wishing her well. It was open now on her computer, and she'd read it over and over.

But that, of course, wasn't the end of it. In the week or so since their lunch date Maggie's dreams had been haunted by compelling images of Max Jordan and Guido, and in quiet moments during the day she found her mind recreating a stunning collage of erotic images from her encounter with them. Thinking about it made her wet and excited and left her longing for more. It was the sweetest torture. Maggie closed her eyes, trying to convince herself that if she starved this newfound hunger it would, eventually, wither and die.

'So, what do you think?' asked Simon.

Maggie looked up at him and blushed, hoping he couldn't see what had been in her mind and painfully aware that she hadn't listened to a word he'd said. 'I, um,' she began. 'The thing is, Simon, that I...'

'That I'll pick you up around eight, that's all settled then,' he said cheerfully.

'No, I?'

'We're going to the *Neptune*. It's so popular I was lucky to get a table at all.'

'Eight?' Maggie couldn't quite get her head around what was going on.

'Eight o'clock, that's right, tonight,' he insisted. 'What's the matter, not changed your mind already, have you?' he laughed.

She stared at him, bemused. Surely she hadn't agreed to go out with Simon Faraday whilst daydreaming about Max Jordan?

'I didn't say I'd go,' she said flatly; nothing was so important that she would have forgotten that.

He pulled a face. 'Oh come on, Maggie,' he pressed. 'You didn't say you wouldn't. And anyway, where's the harm? Everyone else is going to be there. This way you can have a drink, relax, and let me do the driving.'

Maggie shivered, recalling in graphic detail the last time someone had taken her for a drive.

'Eight it is, then,' he said, and before she could decline he was heading off across the office at top speed with a huge grin on his face. She looked back at the email and sighed. Maybe it wouldn't be such a bad thing; she could do with a night out. Maybe she was being cruel; maybe Simon Faraday wasn't so bad, really.

Perhaps he was an acquired taste. Perhaps he had hidden depths. Maggie sighed; who was she trying to kid?

'So who's going to the *Neptune* with the delectable Simple Simon from accounts then?' said one of the guys from of the graphics department on his way past her desk.

Maggie growled at him. Evidently bad news travels fast.

'What's all this about you and Simon Faraday, then?' said one of the other freelancers as she queued up in the deli at the end of the street at lunchtime.

By the time Maggie was ready to leave work she was seething. Was there nobody Simon hadn't told?

'Goodnight, Ms Howard, have a good one,' said the guy on the front desk as she crossed the reception area, and as she reached the glass doors he added, 'It's nice that you two have got together at long last. You'll make a lovely couple.'

There was no missing the sarcasm in the security guard's voice and Maggie swung round and glared at him, but he just grinned wryly.

So, it seemed that Simon had told every last soul that worked in the building, and Maggie was beside herself.

Supper was not a success.

'And then I hit it straight down the fairway, nearly three hundred yards, sweet as a nut,' Simon bragged, miming a golf swing.

Maggie looked at him over the rim of her wineglass. Over two hours with him and all she wanted to do was swing at the end of a rope. The 'everyone' Simon had said would be at the restaurant turned out to be a handful of minions and toadies from the accounting office. But at least one thing he was right about was the food, which was excellent, but by the time it was served she knew she had drunk too much to truly appreciate it. It had been a long and very dull evening.

She stifled a yawn, and when some little creep at the end of the bench said, 'Looks like someone's ready for bed,' half the table sniggered.

Simon caught her eye, and Maggie smiled in what she hoped was a neutral sort of way, at which he drained his glass and said, 'Well, it's getting late and we've all got a drive home. Think we should make a move.'

Maggie was about to protest, but then realised that she really did want to get home, and much more time spent with Simon and any pretext of good manners would have gone. So she got her coat and slipped outside.

'Someone's keen,' said the same creep as the rest followed her out into the car park.

As they reached Simon's car he opened her door, but then any sense of gallantry was lost as he grabbed hold of her arms.

Maggie wriggled out of his grasp but even so he pressed his lips to hers in some revolting parody of a passionate kiss. 'I've been wanting to do that all evening,' he rasped. 'God, you look bloody lovely. Good enough to eat.' There was no missing the implication in his tone, and Maggie glared at him.

They drove home in complete silence, Maggie only too aware of the wine in her bloodstream. Bloody man. She might have accepted his dinner date but that gave him no right to maul her, did it? Or was she giving him mixed signals? Did he, like Guido, think she was offering a ride for a ride?'

When they got back to her house it was obvious that Simon expected to be invited inside. Maggie glanced up at the windows; Kay couldn't be home yet, the lights were out in the sitting room and there were none on upstairs. Maybe she was staying over at Mike's.

'Simon,' she began. It was important to nip this in the bud before it went any further, but he smiled at her and slid his arm across the back of her seat.

Maggie sighed. 'Look, Simon, I'm really... really...' she decided upon the truth, 'I'm really pissed off that you told everyone at work that you were taking me out. That's not the way to do it...' He looked hurt and she felt a mixture of relief and contrition, but apparently undeterred he moved closer and this time she hadn't the heart to push him away. He took this as an invitation.

'Maggie, you've got no idea how long I've waited for this,' he whispered, pulling her close and kissing her full on the mouth, his tongue hungrily seeking entry between her lips. As he pressed closer one hand crawled onto her knee and before she could stop him it eased clumsily up her thigh while the other settled on her breast.

He began to move his lips against hers, and for the briefest of moments Maggie tried to let herself sink into it, go with the flow, respond in kind, imagining what it might be like to have Simon as a lover, but every instinct in her body fought against it. She didn't want it. She didn't want him.

Encouraged by her apparent passivity Simon's fingers tightened on her breast while the one between her legs tried desperately to find a way into her panties.

'Open you legs,' he murmured thickly. 'Come on, baby, you know you want me.'

'Simon, for God's sake,' she snapped, pressing against his chest. 'Of course I don't want you.'

'Relax,' he purred, still intent on seduction. 'Let me do the driving.'

Maggie was so stunned she didn't know what to say until his fingertips grazed the lips of her sex and his panting increased in volume. 'Shit I've waited so long for this,' he drawled. 'You feel so good. Come on, open wider for me.'

'For crying out loud,' Maggie yelped, managing to wrestle free and scramble out of the car, 'stop it, Simon.'

Totally bemused he clambered out after her. 'What the hell's the matter?' he demanded. 'I thought it was going really well. Do you want to go inside instead, so we can get a bit more comfortable? I can understand you not wanting to make out in a car.' He looked at her intently, waiting for a reply, and then snapped angrily. 'What? I thought you liked me.'

Maggie shook her head. 'Simon, I need you to understand this,' she said slowly, as though talking to an imbecile - which perhaps he was, she thought. 'I don't fancy you. I've never fancied you, and I never will fancy you. No, I never will, not at all. You're not my type. I think of you as a friend.' She could hardly tell him he made her flesh crawl.

For a few moments Simon looked taken aback by her words, and then he smiled. 'Maggie, I understand what you're going through, and I don't want to rush you into anything you're not ready for. I really like and respect you, and we can take it as slowly as you want.'

Maggie stared at him in astonishment. If only he knew, she thought. She shook her head. 'No thanks, Simon,' she said. 'Goodnight and thank you for a lovely dinner.'

'What do you mean, goodnight?' he snapped angrily, as if the penny had finally dropped. 'Aren't you going to invite me in for a coffee or something?'

She shook her head again. 'No, it really isn't what I want, Simon,' she insisted. '*You* really aren't what I want. I'm trying not to be hurtful; I just want you to understand. I like working with you - but that's as far as it goes.'

'You little tease!' Simon snorted. 'You shouldn't lead men on like you do. You'll regret this, Maggie Howard. I promise you, you'll regret it.'

But she had already turned away feeling both sorry for Simon, and relieved to be away from him. She went up the path without looking back, closed the front door behind her and took a deep breath, waiting for the sound of his car pulling away.

After a minute or two standing in the dark of the hall she heard the roar of the engine and sighed with relief. There was something she had to do and she certainly wasn't going to do it with pining Simon lurking in the street outside.

She went upstairs, switched on her computer and began to type.

Dear Max...

She stared at the screen, trying to work out what it was she really wanted to say. She erased her introduction and began again.

You're right, there is no escape, she eventually continued. *Please may I...* She paused again. How did she ask, how did she let him know that she wanted more than anything else to feel again the kiss of his whip on her flesh? She opened the drawer of her desk and drew out the contract, and then with her heart in her mouth she began typing again.

Humbly beg to be trained by you?
Maggie.

She pressed Send before she had a chance to lose her nerve, and then sat in the darkness staring at the screen. Although she was nervous and worried about what she had just done, she also knew with total certainty that it was the right thing to do.

As the thought settled in her head she heard a noise - a hiss and then a sharp intake of breath. At first she thought it was her imagination, and then she realised with a start that she had made a terrible mistake. The house wasn't empty at all. Kay and Mike were in Kay's room and the noise Maggie had heard was the swat of the crop or a whip. Something in Maggie's belly tightened as she heard Kay's emotional voice call out the number of the stroke.

'One,' she squealed.

Maggie closed her eyes, her body and mind instantly alight with the memory of Max's touch. She crept across the landing and stood for a few seconds outside Kay's door. There was no way she wanted them to know she was there, spying on them, but part of her longed to join in. She heard the whistle of the crop again, and this time a guttural cry as the implement found its mark.

'Oh my, please master, please no,' Kay begged as the crop cracked down again.

Maggie shuddered, feeling her sex tightening, and tiptoed back to her room.

Lying alone in the darkness, all thoughts of Simon receding fast, she listened as Mike thrashed Kay. At twenty-five strokes it finally stopped, and Maggie closed her eyes, imagining the sensation as a hungry cock drove deep into her friend's cunt, filling her as her beaten buttocks ground back against his groin. It was almost more than she could bear. Without thinking she moved her hands down over her breasts, relishing their weight and softness in her palms, teasing the hardening peaks, and then when the need became greater still she moved on down across her flat tummy, finding herself wet and hot. Easing two fingers into the tight confines of her sex she began to circle the glowing bud of her clit, lifting her hips, imagining her fingers working in and out were a cock as she impaled herself again and again.

With her excitement being mirrored in the bedroom across the landing it didn't take long for her to bring herself to the point of no return. As she stroked and explored and let the waves of pleasure wash over her she imagined Max Jordan there in the darkness, watching her every move, his eyes glinting with desire.

Finally Maggie fell asleep with her fingers still between her thighs.

'I didn't hear you come in last night,' said Kay, helping herself to a cup of coffee, dressed in her bathrobe.

Maggie smiled and sipped her tea. 'I was late getting back,' she fibbed, wondering how Kay felt, imagining the pattern of marks on her silky smooth skin.

'And how did your romantic dinner go with the lovely Simon?'

Maggie laughed bitterly. 'It didn't. It was a bit of disaster, really. Did you go out anywhere nice?'

Kay shook her head. 'No, Mike came round and we had a nice quiet night in.'

'Right,' Maggie said casually. For a moment their eyes met, and strangely it was Maggie who blushed, not Kay.

'Are you working at home today?' said the latter, leaning easily against the kitchen unit.

'No,' said Maggie, glancing up at the clock. 'I'm working on some layouts for the garden features, and it's easier to do it at the office.'

Kay nodded. 'Okay, well in that case I'll see you later,' she said, and was gone, taking her coffee with her.

Maggie worked doggedly all morning, keeping her head down and ignoring all questions about the events of the night before from others in the office. Time and again her mind strayed to the sound of Kay crying out in the darkness, intermingled with images of Max and Guido and the way the crop had felt, the way her own body had writhed under its cruel kiss.

Fortunately Simon didn't show his face and by lunchtime she was feeling far less tense, except of course that she found herself checking the incoming email every ten minutes looking for Max's reply. As she stared at the screen countless thoughts ran through her head. What if he didn't respond? What if he didn't want her, after all? What if it had all been a huge mistake?

Before she drove herself mad with worry and self-doubt she decided to go down to the canteen and pick up a sandwich and coffee, and to her surprise when she got back there was a huge bunch of scarlet roses, broken by soft sprays of gypsophila, sitting on her desk. Her first reaction was to look around in case it was a joke. Or worse still, what if they were from Simon?

She put her coffee down on the desk and undid the little note attached to the swathe of cellophane.

Welcome home, slave. Check your email. Your master.

With her heart beating nineteen-to-the-dozen she logged on, and there, tucked amongst at least a dozen other messages was a single line email inviting her to pick up an e-card from a bondage site. As it opened she shivered with anticipation, for on the screen was an image that could have very easily been her. Tastefully shot in black and white a naked female knelt at the feet of a man in full evening dress, her hands bound behind her back with cord. She was wearing a collar, but most of all it was her face that struck Maggie. Her expression was serenely beautiful, totally at ease with her submission. Under the image Max Jordan invited her to begin her training.

I will pick you up at ten o'clock tomorrow morning, from your home. Make sure you bring the contract with you. Signed, unless you change your mind again. I shall expect you to stay overnight. You will wear a full-length coat, short dark skirt and white blouse, hold-up stockings and high heels. You will not wear any underwear, unless of course you wish to be punished.

Max Jordan had an unfailing eye for detail, thought Maggie. She smiled and looked back at the bunch of roses, remembering her punishment last time she got the instructions wrong. Oddly enough, it was a relief to know he wanted her and, stranger still, how much she longed to feel that sense of being owned.

'So what's this then, a little token of affection from a mystery admirer?' said a familiar voice.

Maggie looked up to find Simon standing alongside the desk. She quickly flicked off the screen so he couldn't see the picture on the card.

'Funny you should say that,' she said as casually as she could manage.

Simon managed a weak grin. 'About last night.'

'I think I owe you an apology, Simon,' she cut in, her resolve and confidence boosted by Max's invitation.

'I've been thinking, too,' he countered. 'Maybe I was taking things a bit too quickly. So to make it up to you I was wondering if you would like to come to the cinema with me at the weekend?'

Maggie smiled but shook her head. 'No thanks, Simon. I'm flattered, but I meant it when I said you really aren't my type.'

His expression soured immediately. 'So what is your type?' he sneered. 'Men who send you roses, I suppose.' And with that he marched off across the office in a foul mood again.

Maggie sighed. Men who didn't behave like spoilt children would have been a better description. She looked back at the screen. Men like Max Jordan.

The following morning Maggie stood in her kitchen dressed exactly as she'd been instructed. She had one eye on the clock and shifted anxiously from foot to foot counting off the minutes. Waiting was awful. What if Max didn't show up? What if it was all a cruel joke? She gazed in the mirror - her eyes looked wild and haunted, and when the doorbell rang she almost jumped out of her skin.

It was a sunny, lovely day, oddly normal in contrast to the images and memories in her head. Guido was waiting for her on the doorstep, and if he had any thoughts about her appearance or their earlier encounter in the woods it didn't show on his face.

'Good morning, Maggie,' he said, and touched the peak of his driver's cap.

Maggie reddened, remembering their last encounter. 'Good morning.'

As she walked slowly away from the house she felt as if her life was about to change forever. As she got to the car Guido opened the nearside rear door, and to her surprise Max Jordan was waiting in the back.

He smiled and indicated that she should join him. 'Good morning, Maggie,' he said smoothly, as with her heart in her mouth she slipped in alongside him. 'How nice to see you again,' he said. 'And how are you today?' And then as the car drew smoothly away he added, 'So have you got the contract with you, as I instructed?'

Maggie nodded, not trusting herself to speak. She opened her bag and handed him the envelope.

He nodded. 'Very good. Now, take off your clothes, except for your shoes and stockings.' His manner was firm and concise. Maggie stared at him questioningly, but his expression remained totally neutral. 'Already you disobey me?' he said. 'On one hand you beg to be allowed to serve and be trained by me, and then you fall at the first hurdle?'

Maggie looked around the interior of the car, anything rather than meet his eyes, shivering under his unflinching gaze. 'But... but I can't,' she ventured. 'Not here in your car.'

'Oh but you can, my dear, and you will,' he said confidently, 'because I have instructed you to do so and you will obey me. You want to. You need to surrender, Maggie. Now take off your clothes, I won't tell you again. Or would you rather we turned round and I took you home?'

'No,' Maggie blurted. 'The thing is...' her voice faded as she struggled with the reality of obedience.

Max appeared bored by her resistance and turned his attention to the envelope she'd given him. Ripping it open he pulled out the contract.

'So, Maggie,' he said, 'let us see what it is you've agreed to. "The slave will be under her master's complete and total control and will immediately obey and comply with any order or instruction given to her...' He smiled eruditely, before reading further. 'If the slave displeases or disobeys her master in any way she expects to endure any punishment he so chooses as necessary for her inappropriate actions...'

He studied her closely, his eyes bright. 'Well, my dear?'

Maggie dropped her gaze, and with a sigh of resignation, slowly unbuttoned her coat and slipped it back off her shoulders. As Max continued to read she unbuttoned and removed her blouse, unzipped her skirt and eased it down over her hips, until she was sitting beside him in just hold-up stockings and her high heels. She knew without looking up that Guido was watching her progress in the rear-view mirror.

'Very good, my dear,' Max said, as she folded her clothes on the seat. 'Here.' He handed her the collar she had worn so briefly at the hotel. Without a word she put it on and then turned slightly so he could snap the little lock shut. The sound made her shiver with anticipation.

Max looked her up and down appreciatively and then cupped one breast, rolling the nipple between thumb and forefinger. 'Open your legs.' His tone was crisp and businesslike.

Maggie stiffened. His fingers tightened on her nipple making her gasp, but still she resisted him. 'Maggie,' he growled, squeezing the bud between his fingertips, making her cry out in shock, and this time she let her knees fall apart.

With no prelude his free hand dropped into her lap, fingers roughly prising her sex open, exposing her totally. Maggie gasped; there was no finesse here, just a desire to explore her body in the basest of ways. He drove a finger between her lips, a sense of shame swamping her as he explored her delicate folds.

'Did you find her nice and tight, Guido?' he asked casually, and Maggie looked up in horror, reddening furiously. It hadn't occurred to her that Max would know about her escapades in the woods with his driver. She had assumed it was a secret between her and Guido - and knew in her heart that it would never have happened had it not been for the lingering image of slavery and submission Max Jordan had imprinted on her mind.

'Yes, sir,' said Guido, his eyes twinkling in the mirror. 'Nice and tight, and really hot for it.'

Max brushed her clitoris with his thumb, making the muscles in her belly tighten. Maggie could feel her body responding shamefully.

'So, you let Guido fuck you as soon as my back was turned, did you?' he accused her. 'Is that the kind of girl you are, Maggie? A dirty little slut who opens her legs to any man that comes along?'

What could she say? She felt sick with shame. There was no excuse for the way she'd behaved.

'From now on I will be in control of who has you - who fucks you.' He sank three fingers into her, making her stiffen and suppress a sob. 'And I will decide when you touch yourself and how you do it. You do touch yourself, don't you, Maggie?'

She closed her eyes and wished she could close her ears too, his words goading her.

'Tell me,' he ordered.

'Yes, master,' she admitted.

'Yes master, what?' he pressed. Surely Max didn't really want her to explain. A finger pressed hard over her clit, making her whimper beneath the heady mixture of discomfort and pleasure. 'Tell me, Maggie. Tell me.'

'I - I like to touch myself,' she stammered.

'Where do you like to touch, Maggie?' he interrogated. 'Your nice tits? Your cunt?'

Maggie felt the heat of humiliation growing inside her. How on earth could she say the words aloud? In the front of the car Guido listened and waited, his eyes on the road as he drove.

'Yes, master,' was all she could manage.

Max caught her clitoris tight between thumb and forefinger. 'Don't try and be clever with me, young lady. Tell me, do you like to touch this?' His hand spread to cradle her sex.

'Yes, master, I like to play with myself there,' she admitted meekly, her voice barely above a whisper.

Max nodded. 'Good girl.'

She felt defeated and crushed and humiliated. Max pulled her to him and kissed her forehead. 'Good girl,' he said again. 'Now, as you like the woods so much I thought we might go for a little walk today. Just you and me.' He handed her her coat. 'Put it on.'

Maggie looked at him inquisitively. Did he mean her to get dressed again? He smiled as if sensing her confusion, his voice as warm and personable as some older uncle taking his favourite niece out for the day. 'Just put it on as you are - no need to get dressed again.'

Gratefully she pulled it over her nakedness, but before she could button it he added, 'Leave it open, I want to look at you.' He carefully arranged the garment so that her body remained totally exposed to him, and then added to the bizarre quality of the journey by starting a conversation with her about her work at the magazine, and she found herself telling him about the project on gardens.

As time passed towns gave way to villages and villages gave way to countryside. Guido manoeuvred the car through the trees, along a track that led away from the winding road. The car drew to a halt in a small, leafy area that provided parking for picnickers and ramblers.

'Get out,' he ordered her, and Maggie was about to protest when he added, 'You may button your coat now, for the time being.'

She sighed with relief, for with her coat fastened and stockings on, no one would guess she was naked underneath; a little inappropriately dressed for a woodland stroll, perhaps, but certainly not naked.

Max caught hold of her hand. 'Now, my dear,' he said, 'let me show you one of my favourite places.'

They walked for a while through sun-drenched trees, talking about all manner of things, but just beneath the surface Maggie could feel her expectation and tension growing. There came a moment when silence fell and all she could hear was her pulse in her ears, a counterpoint to the gentle sounds of the woodland and nature.

Despite her coat she was very aware of her nakedness beneath, particularly every time a dog walker or courting couple ambled by, nodded and murmured politely and walked on.

At last Max headed off the main trail towards a thicket, stopped in a slight hollow and from behind a small bush produced several lengths of rope.

Maggie stared at him in astonishment. 'What are you going to...?' she began, her voice tight with apprehension.

'Take off your coat, Maggie,' was all he said.

As Max unwound the rope he watched her closely. It was interesting to watch her hesitation. She was torn between her desire, her fear, and a myriad other contradictory emotions. As if in slow motion she slipped her coat off, letting it fall to the ground. She stood very still in front of him, making no effort to cover herself, her nakedness emphasised beautifully by the trees.

As Max blindfolded her he could feel her trembling. He pressed the ball-gag into her mouth and then took hold of her wrists, feeling the tremor vibrate deliciously through her body. She looked magnificently vulnerable amongst their surroundings, her creamy skin a subtle contrast to the whispering canopy of green and gold. She looked like a delicate nymph.

He bound her wrists tight together in front of her and then threw one end of the rope up and over a branch above her head, pulling it tight so that his newest student was stretched taut, taking her weight on the balls of her feet, hands bound high up above her head. With more rope he tied each ankle apart, spreading her legs wide.

She was totally still and silent, although as he worked he could feel every sense in her body reaching out to him, begging, hoping, searching for clues as to what might happen next. Standing behind her he ran his hands over her, both to enjoy her body and to reassure her. Her flesh was silky and cool.

She moaned behind the gag as his fingers worked down her spine and around her lithe torso to cup her breasts. She gasped, instinctively thrusting her body back towards him. Max smiled to himself; beneath her cultured and rather aloof exterior Maggie Howard had the heart of a whore. When he turned his attentions to her sex he discovered that she was already wet, her silky juices coating the tops of her thighs.

Stepping back he slipped off his jacket and took a flogger from the inside pocket. Very gently he drew the soft leather strands across her thighs and buttocks. Maggie mewled, tugging against the restraints. Max stepped back a little to check his stroke, and then hit her, not hard, but enough to make her muscles tense. She gasped and twisted at the end of the rope, instinctively trying to escape. He hit her again, harder, and she whimpered into the gag. Harder still he struck her and she let out a stifled sob, the noise spilling out from around the gag.

He beat her again and she shrieked as the tail of the cat wrapped around her ribcage and clawed hungrily at her breasts.

Max smiled. Through the trees he saw a flicker of movement and knew his activities were being observed. He hit her again, ignoring their uninvited guest, deliberately lower so that the tails of the flogger wrapped round the tender flesh of her thighs. Her whole body convulsed. Again she cried out, sharp and raw despite the gag, and then he struck again, from the corner of his eye spying an elderly man creeping closer, totally mesmerised by Maggie and her naked, whipped body.

Max hit her again and her head snapped back. He knew from the tone of her muffled protests that even though she was still at some level registering the pain, her mind was floating in a sea of endorphins, the body's natural pain relief.

The next blow wrapped around her waist and she twisted on the rope, gasping, saliva seeping around the gag onto her chin. Her body seemed to glow with an inner light as the pain speared through her. She looked superb, and Max glanced to his left and eyed the old man, his expression frozen with carnal hunger. It was as if Maggie's passion and pain had drawn him out into the open.

'Would you like a closer look?' asked Max.

The old man looked around uncertainly, clearly unable to believe his luck, and then nodded. It was obvious from the bulge in the front of his trousers that he was hugely aroused.

Maggie was trying hard to still her breathing as she reached out for clues as to what was happening. The old man circled her like a hungry scavenger, studying her beauty and her vulnerability, breathing it in. Max stepped close behind her and reached round to open the lips of her sex, so that the old man could see the ripe pinkness within. She was wet, her clit a hard bud longing for release. The old man leered and licked his lips, and fumbling with his trousers pulled out a gnarled and wizened cock.

Max beckoned him closer, so he could touch her, and feeling a second pair of hands on her flesh Maggie let out a shriek of dismay.

'Be nice to our new friend, my dear, or I'll take the whip to you again,' Max threatened, his lips brushing her ear.

The old man wiped his mouth and then ran his shaking hands over her face and throat, before cupping a breast in each hand, then moving even closer, lowered his lips hungrily over one nipple and sucked noisily. His twitching cock brushed against her thigh, leaving a sticky trail across her creamy flesh.

Maggie swallowed as if trying to still her fears, while the old man's fingers and lips pulled and slobbered on her breasts.

'Help me untie her,' said Max, and the old man needed no further encouragement. He stooped stiffly to untie her ankles, his face within inches of her sex, drinking in the enticing scent of her arousal.

Max untied her hands and then turned and eased her forward so that she was bent at the waist, her hands against the tree to support her. The old man leered again as Max undid his trousers and, without prelude, sank his raging cock into Maggie's waiting and vulnerable body.

She moaned and threw back her head, her sex closing around him like a clenched fist, her muscles drawing him deep, deep inside her. Despite the gag she cried out as Max began to fuck her. He could sense her longing for her own release, while beside them the old man groaned too and mauled her nearest breast while with his other hand he avidly pumped his straining shaft.

Max suspected that neither of them would last long. Maggie cried out as he pulled her back onto him again and again. The old man snorted and grunted and an instant later a flood of sperm hit her back and arm and then Max was there too, filling her with his offering.

As he pulled out of Maggie the old man sank slowly to his knees and began to lick hungrily at her quim and bottom. She mewled wearily and then Max watched as her body and her raw animal need began to take over. She began to move, instinctively grinding her wet quim over the man's wrinkled face until his tongue and fingers carried her over into oblivion, the waves of orgasm crashing over her. Between her trembling legs the old man, his face slick with sexual juices, pulled away, leering broadly. Max moved forward and rubbed his flaccid cock across her lips, and watched with satisfaction as her tongue emerged and she performed her duty for him. To his delight she drew his limp wet cock between her lips, and he enjoyed the devoted movements of her tongue.

Chapter Six

Back at the car Maggie sat quietly trying very hard to regain some sense of composure. She was wearing her coat, the leather slave collar, hold up stockings and shoes, the latter now a little grimy from their walk and activities in the woods. In the rear-view mirror Guido watched her discomfort with evident interest.

'Home now, I think,' Max decided, 'for a little lunch and relaxation. You can leave your clothes and bag in the car; Guido will see to them.'

Maggie had almost forgotten that she'd agreed to stay with him, and realised with a growing sense of apprehension that whatever was going to happen to her, the experience in the woods was just the beginning.

Working from home meant that she could come and go as she pleased. Although she had a desk at the magazine's office no one would comment on her absence as long as her stories were filed on time. She sat back and closed her eyes, trying hard not to let her imagination run away with her. For a moment she tried to imagine what it might be like if she never went home. What if Max kept her? What if...? She bit her lip, struggling to get a grip on her rampant imagination.

Max Jordan's home was an elegant four-storey townhouse tucked away in an affluent city side street. They were welcomed at the door by his housekeeper, Mrs Griffin, a tall, sour-faced woman of an indefinable age. She was elegant and icy, dressed in a dove-grey coatdress that seemed deliberately cut to hide her figure, almost as if designed to render her asexual. Her thick straight hair, a shade of grey fractionally lighter than her dress, was pulled back into a severe bun that did nothing at all to soften her angular features or cold blue eyes.

'Would you like me to take your coat?' she said to Maggie as they made their way inside. Maggie stopped mid-stride, and Max turned to look at her. It was obvious that he expected her to hand it over, and Maggie was beginning to understand only too well that it didn't do to keep Max Jordan waiting or to disobey him. The rules of the game weren't so hard to fathom out, but were at odds with everything else she had ever believed in or known. She slipped off the coat and handed it to Mrs Griffin, painfully aware of her exposure, but the older woman's expression didn't change, she said nothing, her eyes taking in both Maggie's nakedness and her discomfort in a single glance.

'Give Mrs Griffin your shoes as well, Maggie, they need cleaning,' Max said, and naked, barefoot, feeling like a well-trained puppy, Maggie padded along behind him into an elegant sitting room furnished with black leather chesterfields and a cream carpet. The drapes at the floor to ceiling windows were black velvet caught back with gold ties, and the room had an air of male elegance, of good taste and understated luxury.

'Today, my dear, you will begin basic training, you will begin to understand how it feels to be a fulltime slave. This evening we have guests coming for supper. But now we will have a little aperitif, lunch, and then I'll have Mrs Griffin show you to your room. You might like to have a little rest before this evening.'

He smiled and settled comfortably on one of the sofas. 'I would suggest you take a nap. It will be a long evening. Now turn around; I want to see if you're marked.'

Maggie did as she was told, reddening slightly as Max turned her first one way and then the other. 'Hardly anything,' he said, sounding disappointed. 'I like to see where I've been, to leave my mark. Go to the side table and bring me my crop.'

Maggie hesitated.

'Did you hear me?' he asked.

'Yes, master,' she said. 'I heard you.'

'Then do as you're told. For a little while you will be allowed some leeway, but trust me, young lady, that luxury will rapidly be coming to an end.'

Maggie went over to the table, where set out in a neat row was a braided leather crop, a whip, the tails arranged in straight lines, a schoolmaster's cane and a leather paddle that looked a little like a short oar.

The tools of Max's trade.

Maggie gulped and picked up the crop as instructed, then with her eyes downcast she returned and handed it to him.

'Get down on your hands and knees,' he ordered.

Maggie got to the floor in front of him, already feeling the rush of adrenaline, stunned at how quickly she obeyed. She remembered how the crop bit into her flesh and made her cry out in shock and pain. Closing her eyes she braced herself for what she knew would follow.

Max, the consummate sadist, trailed the looped tip gently along her spine and over her buttocks, exploring her body with all the self-assurance of a man examining his property.

'Open your legs,' he said, and Maggie obeyed, exposing the delicate folds of her sex. Max cut the air with the crop, a practice swing, but still it made the kneeling girl cringe. 'You're a little nervous, slave,' he commented.

She heard the crop cutting the air again and cried out almost before the blow cracked down across her poor bottom. Even though it wasn't overly hard it sent a white-hot glow through her body.

'One,' she hissed instinctively, knowing it was what he wanted to hear.

'Two,' she wailed as the next strike landed square across the fullest part of her buttocks.

'*Three*...' The pain was intensifying.

'Four,' she gasped. It hurt so much, hot and sharp.

'Five.' The word nearly caught in her throat, vying with a protest for release.

'Six.' Surely Max would stop soon? Surely six was enough?

'Seven... eight... nine... ten...' a volley of rapid strokes.

'Eleven... twelve!' Maggie shrieked, biting her lip to hold back the tears that threatened. And then it was over and she felt Max's cool hands on her skin, comforting the reddening flesh.

'There we are, my little one, all done,' he murmured, and for an instant Maggie sensed and heard the arousal in his voice. He pressed the crop to her lips and without a moment's hesitation she kissed it. How had this happened?

Gently Max helped her to her feet. 'Look,' he said, and stood her in front of a large mirror. Maggie turned and looked at her bottom, the blotchy welts rising across both cheeks. Max slipped a hand between her thighs and she closed he eyes with a mixture of shame and resignation, knowing without being told that her rogue body was wet already and eager for more.

'Now, get me a sherry and then come and kneel at my feet like a good slave,' he said, and Maggie did as she was told, aware of his eyes on her as she moved around the room. Then she handed him his drink and knelt at his feet on the carpet, and he idly stroked her hair as he talked.

'Our guests tonight know you have only just begun your training, but that is no reason for bad behaviour,' he said. 'You will do exactly as you are told, when you are told. Do you understand me?'

'Yes, master,' she acknowledged.

Max smiled. 'I understand this is hard for you, my dear, but you must trust me. I will show you things that until now you have only dreamed of.'

Although he was speaking quietly the tone was strong, the tone of man who had experienced many things, who commanded respect, and without thinking she settled her cheek on his knees, relishing the feel of his fingers stroking her head. It struck her as odd that a man who could be so cruel was also so capable of such tenderness.

Max sat for a while, soothing her as he might a favourite pet, and as he did she felt the tension in her easing. How odd that this man who gave her so much pain was also the one to offer her such a compelling sense of comfort and reassurance.

'So, as I said, we'll have lunch and then you can rest, my little one,' he said, then sipped his sherry.

'Yes, master,' she whispered, and realised how natural the words were beginning to sound.

Maggie's room was on the top floor, tucked up under the eves of the large old house, with a small en suite bathroom attached. The antique pine bed was made up in delicate white bed linen, and fluffy white towels hung from a rail by the open bathroom door. On one wall hung a large ornate mirror, and on a linen chest under the window a vase of white jasmine filled the room with a heady scent.

While she and Max had been downstairs having lunch her clothes were being neatly hung in the wardrobe, her clean shoes neatly tucked onto the bottom rail.

Then once Mrs Griffin had drawn the curtains and turned down the duvet, Maggie slipped into bed and despite everything going on in her life was asleep in a matter of seconds.

For a few moments when she awoke Maggie wondered where on earth she was. The light had subtlety changed as the day slipped slowly from afternoon into evening, and refreshed by her sleep she sat up in bed wondering what she was expected to wear for the dinner party. She'd brought a couple of nice outfits with her that could be dressed up or down as the occasion required. Maybe she ought to try and find her way downstairs and ask Mrs Griffin.

Just as she was considering what to do there was a knock on the bedroom door and the housekeeper appeared, and she quickly pulled the bedclothes up to cover her nakedness.

'The master sent me up to help you get ready,' the woman announced, her expression unchanged.

'I'm fine, thanks, really,' said Maggie pleasantly. 'There's really no need to go to any trouble. I was wondering what I ought to wear though?'

'The master sent me up to help you, Miss Howard.' The woman smiled thinly. 'Surely you know better than to disobey his instructions. I'm to bathe you, wash your hair and then help you dress.' As she spoke she set a box down alongside the vase of jasmine.

'Oh,' Maggie said, a little surprised by the announcement, not sure that she wanted to be treated like a child by the woman. 'And what am I to wear for this evening?'

Mrs Griffin's expression still didn't alter. 'You'll find out in good time.'

Maggie got up, and conscious of her nakedness she headed into the bathroom to use the toilet, when it struck her there was no door.

She looked back at Mrs Griffin, blushing furiously, but if she was expecting sympathy or privacy, none was forthcoming.

'I need to use the loo,' she said, but the woman seemed oblivious to her sensitivities. She followed her into the en suite, bent to put the plug in the bath and turned on the taps, but made no attempt to avert her gaze or leave Maggie alone. Defeated, Maggie sat on the toilet, careful not to catch the other woman's eyes.

When she was done Mrs Griffin added a stream of bath oil that filled the room with the scent of sandalwood and ylang ylang, and helped her step into the deep tub.

Maggie hadn't been bathed by anyone since she was a child, but Mrs Griffin lathered and then rubbed her down, her fingers skilfully working through her hair, down over her breasts and belly, and lower still into the intimate places between her legs. Maggie, although deeply embarrassed, knew it was pointless to resist. It was an odd thing to share so intimate an experience with a complete stranger, and sensual on the most basic of levels. She wondered if the woman could sense the flutter of arousal and pleasure in her belly, but if she did it was not apparent.

When she was done Mrs Griffin held out a fluffy white bath towel and dried Maggie with brisk efficiency.

'Stand still,' Mrs Griffin instructed, standing her in front of the large mirror while she oiled Maggie's body. Maggie shivered, but Mrs Griffin's face remained unerringly impassive while her skilled hands carried on rubbing her breasts, nimble fingers working over her nipples, tweaking them into hardness, sliding down over her tummy, sex, and the ripe curves of her bruised bottom. Maggie blushed furiously, but it seemed to go unnoticed as the woman worked diligently.

Behind the two-way mirror in the small room, little bigger than a cupboard, Max enjoyed a deep mouthful of brandy and settled down to watch Maggie being dressed, enjoying the familiar stirring in his groin.

When she was done the older woman opened the box on the linen chest, and as she lifted out the contents Maggie gasped in shock. Inside was a black leather harness, held together with rings and studs. It went around her torso like a jacket, large rings fitting tight over her breasts, forcing the nipples to jut forward. Straps snapped onto the D-rings on her collar, with another broad strap fastening tightly around her waist, and then between her legs was another

179

one, with a slit in it so that once securely fastened in place it held the lips of her sex open. She swallowed hard and looked across at the housekeeper.

'It doesn't pay to keep the master waiting,' said Mrs Griffin.

Once Maggie was dressed the austere housekeeper handed her a pair of high-heeled knee-length boots, and then looked her up and down before very carefully outlining her eyes in dark brown kohl and her lips in red lipstick. Caught in the reflection of the dressing table mirror Maggie looked like a sexual toy, ready and available, her body a sexual invitation.

Mrs Griffin took a step back to admire her handiwork, and then as a final touch took a lead out of the box and snapped it to one of the D-rings.

Maggie felt a chill; it defined her status. Then she obediently rose and followed Mrs Griffin downstairs, her stomach churning.

'Ah, there you are, Mrs Griffin,' said Max, looking up as they entered the room. 'I was just telling Freya that you've cooked venison for us this evening.'

'Yes, Mr Jordan, although it's farmed,' said the housekeeper, entering into a conversation about cooking with Max's guest, a statuesque blonde dressed in a smart pinstriped business suit. She was sipping a cocktail and didn't even bother to look in Maggie's direction. But what really caught Maggie's attention was the naked man crouched on all fours at the woman's feet. He too was wearing a harness and a collar and lead. He looked at Maggie, drank her in, his eyes bright with lust and a very obvious hunger.

Max noticed Maggie looking at the man, and Freya caught the man looking at Maggie and admonished him sharply. 'Beau!' she said, snapping the lead taut and wrenching his neck.

'Sorry, mistress,' he whined, and Max smiled as Maggie's face registered her surprise and discomfort.

'On your knees, Maggie,' he commanded, and she knelt at his feet, trying to avoid the longing look of Freya's slave. She noticed that around his cock and balls, which were shaved and oiled, was a series of rings and leather straps, linked to the harness that appeared to keep him in a state of semi-arousal.

Mrs Griffin departed to the kitchen and Freya and Max were talking again. Under normal circumstances, at any normal dinner party, Maggie would have been chatting with them, or at least been politely involved in their conversation, a glass of quality wine in her hand. But here, crouched on the floor, it seemed that their chatting bore no relation to her life or where she was in the order of things.

Guido, smartly dressed in the guise of a butler, appeared and announced that dinner was served. Max smiled to his beautiful guest. 'Ah, splendid,' he said. 'Shall we, dear Freya?' and indicated that she should accompany him.

Freya again tugged Beau's leash and to Maggie's total amazement the man scurried behind her on all fours. When Max took her lead she looked up at him in silent appeal.

'Come on, Maggie,' he said, and to her shame she also followed on her hands and knees behind him, cringing with the degradation of it all.

'Nice markings,' Freya said casually, her fingertips brushing Maggie's welted

180

buttocks. Max nodded his appreciation for the compliment; in that instant Maggie felt more like a prize possession than ever.

Across the hallway heavy double doors led into an elegant dining room, decorated in cream and the richest crimson.

A long mahogany table, set with crystal and silver and an ornate silver candelabrum, dominated it. Without being told Beau got to his feet and pulled Freya's chair out. Maggie decided she'd better follow suit for her master, and noticed the magnificent table was laid for only two.

Only two place settings?

She was hungry and had assumed, wrongly and somewhat foolishly it now seemed, that they would all be dining together. Instead Guido handed her a dish and indicated that she should serve Freya and Max, and as she began to she noticed that on a sideboard were two heavy-bottomed dog bowls. As she completed and task and set the serving dish down Guido nodded towards the bowls. She looked at him uncertainly, and then realised that she was supposed put food into them too - food she knew was for Beau and for her. She stiffened and stood her ground, but Guido nodded again and reluctantly she spooned vegetables into the two bowls, and then Beau added meat.

She looked down at the food. No knives, no forks, just fingers and tongues - like animals. This was impossible, but then Guido nodded towards the table where Beau was shaking out a linen napkin and settling it on Freya's lap. The elegant blonde appeared to take no notice of her slave; instead she gave Max her full attention, laughing gaily at some comment he'd made. Maggie looked at Max, who gave her an almost imperceptible nod of encouragement, so she shook out his napkin and dropped it onto his lap. He rewarded her by running a hand over her thigh, but it did very little to settle her.

Beau served the wine, while Max and Freya continued chatting. Beau then stood beside his mistress until she looked up and said, sounding decidedly bored with his presence, 'You may go and eat now.'

Guido placed both bowls on the floor side by side. Beau was immediately on his hands and knees again to eat, while Maggie stood looking down at him and the vacant dish. Guido had cut the food up into small pieces, and she was very hungry, but there was no way she was going to grovel like Beau.

'Is there something wrong with your dinner?' said Max, and it was obvious from his tone that he didn't take kindly to having his meal interrupted.

'No, master,' Maggie said contritely.

'Then eat it,' he ordered, and indicated the bowl with a sharp hand gesture.

Maggie looked at him beseechingly. 'Please, master, I can't,' she began, her voice quavering. There was no way she was going to eat like an animal, no matter how hungry she was. Meanwhile Beau was snaffling up his dinner like some obscene parody of an obedient pet dog.

'Can't, or won't?' said Freya icily.

Maggie looked down at her feet, painfully aware of her nakedness, accentuated rather than covered by the leather harness.

'Answer me!' the blonde snapped angrily, her veneer of refined elegance vanishing in an instant.

There was a long pause while Maggie summoned her resolve, and then at last she said determinedly, 'Won't.' She was instantly aware of the tense silence in the room as Max, his guest, and Guido all stared at her in apparent disbelief, and the grovelling man beside her stopped shovelling his face into the bowlful of food and looked up at her, his chin and nose smeared in rich sauce and his mouth open in shock.

'Won't, *mistress*,' Beau whispered sarcastically, but it was too late for Maggie to retract her insolence.

'Take her away!' Max roared at Guido, waving his hand in dismissal and throwing his linen napkin onto the table beside his meal, as though she had just ruined his appetite and the whole evening. 'Get her out of my sight!'

'Big mistake,' said Guido, as he marched Maggie out of the dining room and down the hall. 'Showing him up in front of his guests. Big mistake.'

'But I didn't,' Maggie protested.

Guido snorted. 'That's not how he'll see it.' He led her upstairs, unlocked a door at the far end of the landing, and pushed her inside, the room beyond making Maggie gasp with shock.

It was a dungeon. There was no other word for it. In one corner was an awful rack, and in another a large, foreboding cross-shaped frame. The walls were hung with whips and crops and gags and manacles, clamps and clips and all manner of other things, many of which Maggie didn't recognise and had no idea what they might be used for.

She turned to Guido. 'Let me go back,' she pleaded, unnerved by the ominous room. 'I'll eat my dinner, I will, it was a mistake. Just take me back. Honestly Guido, it was a silly mistake.'

Guido's smile widened. 'You're right about that,' he said, 'but it's too late to go back now. I suggest you cooperate, because if you don't it will be worse for you... a lot worse.'

Maggie shivered. What choice was there for her?

'Come closer,' he ordered, and caught hold of her wrists.

A while later, after he and Freya had eaten and taken coffee and brandy, Max opened the door of the dungeon room and smiled. Guido had done a good job on his little charge. Maggie was nicely bound, blindfolded, her neck and arms held in a padded wooden yoke, holding her reasonably comfortably with her arms at shoulder level, her legs spread wide apart and manacled to a metal spreader-bar.

He watched his latest acquisition straining to turn, trying to make out who was there and what would follow. Beside him Freya smiled appreciatively and unfastened her tailored jacket, beneath which she wore a shiny black leather bodice. As he watched she dropped the jacket and then her skirt, rather like a seductive snake shedding its skin. Beau appeared and hurriedly picked them up, folding them neatly over a chair, his eyes bright with anticipation as his mistress stripped down to her beautifully styled leather basque. It was cut high to make the most of her long legs and the creamy flesh of her shapely thighs.

'May I?' she asked Max, without taking her eyes off Maggie's restrained form.

He smiled. 'Of course, my dear,' he said. 'Help yourself.'

Maggie trembled, responding anxiously to his voice.

Freya smiled calculatingly and surveyed the tools on offer, before taking down a fine leather whip.

In the restraints Maggie stiffened as she felt the approach of what for her was an unseen figure.

Freya walked around her, surveying her with assurance, pinching her nipples, feeling between her legs, pushing a finger deep inside Maggie's vulnerable sex and then drawing the slick juices out and across Beau's waiting lips. He licked her fingers and whined expectantly for more.

'Nice and tight, Max,' the woman purred appreciatively. 'What's her arse like?'

Max smiled. 'Untried, Freya,' he disclosed. 'It's early days yet and you know my policy; it is for me and me alone. At least the first time.'

Freya laughed, the cultured sound like a tinkling piano. 'You are such a traditionalist, dear Max,' she mused. 'And besides, she'd need stretching whoever fucks her tight little virgin rear passage. Perhaps I can help you with that?' She ran her fingers over Maggie's buttocks, before working them into the warm valley between them.

Max watched Maggie react to the blonde's conversation with interested, seeing the tension in her neck and back, catching the slight nibble of her lower lip.

Beau whined again and leant up against Maggie's legs, like a cat, his expression hungry, and Freya's expression betrayed her affection and indulgent attitude towards her slave. She nodded and he began to touch and stroke, his fingers and tongue working into Maggie's wet quim.

The bound girl shivered as Freya drew the soft strands of the whip across her hips. They dangled against Beau's face and shoulders but he seemed oblivious to them, far keener to explore Maggie's undefended sex.

'Enough,' Freya snapped, and barely pausing for Beau to crawl clear she brought the whip down across Maggie's back. The strands wrapped around her, catching her breasts and making her jerk and shriek, although Max guessed that in her heighten state of anticipation even the lightest blow would extract such a reaction.

'One!' she gasped, her muscles tightening.

Freya laughed. 'Oh, there is no need to count tonight, my dear,' she said. 'There will be too many to keep track of.'

After six strokes Max held up a hand and took something else down from the wall. Freya's eyes sparkled approvingly. 'What a wonderful idea, dear Max,' she purred. 'How very remiss of me.'

Behind her mask Maggie was struggling with a sense of panic, and worse still, the warm glow of pleasure that was already gathering in her belly. What dark magic was this? She closed her eyes tight shut. It was as if Max Jordan had opened a doorway in her soul into a world she had never really believed existed.

A female hand cupped her breast, and she smelt expensive perfume. Freya pinched her nipple between finger and thumb and then drew it between her lips and sucked. She groaned against the supple flesh and began to tease Maggie's sex, teasing the wet lips that were held open by the split leather harness. Maggie wriggled, trying to get away from the fingers, although she knew she was already treacherously wet.

'Oh, don't struggle, honey,' purred Freya, her tone heavy with sensual intent, and an instant later something snapped onto Maggie's right nipple, making her cry out in shock and pain, and immediately the hurt was repeated on her other nipple. Maggie writhed desperately, trying to get away from the intense pain of the clamps as they chewed her erect buds.

'Gently, my pretty,' murmured Freya, and Maggie shivered, letting the sensation settle. It was hot and raw and made her eyes fill with tears, but after a few moments by some miracle her body began to adjust, as if, once the pressure was understood, it could cope. She took a long low breath, letting her body and mind settle. It was going to be all right after all, wasn't it?

And then Freya pinched the lips of her sex. Maggie froze, felt the brush of some kind of clamp on the delicate folds of flesh, and held her breath. 'Please, no... no,' she gasped. 'No...'

The jaws sprang shut and Maggie screamed. The pain was like nothing she had ever felt and tears meandered down her cheeks.

'Steady,' consoled Freya, pressing her lips to Maggie's. 'Don't fight it, breath slowly and relax into it. It will be all right, just breath slowly.'

Maggie tried to accept the throbbing discomfort, and then felt Beau licking her again.

'That's enough now, slave,' Freya intervened, and this time Maggie moaned not with pain but with frustration as the grovelling tongue left her.

Then before she had time to compose herself she heard something cut through the air and then screamed again as the cane found its mark. Her body thrust forward and Freya caned her again across her defenceless bottom. The first scream seemed to have barely died before another surpassed it. As her body arched the clamps on her nipples and labia seemed to bite even harder.

Maggie thought she would go mad from the torment, and then there was another stroke as brutal as the first two. Her nipples ached and her buttocks glowed. Again the blows exploded, and again and again. Maggie could hear someone sobbing and begging for mercy, and realised it was her.

Max's fingers tightened around his brandy glass. His cock ached with desire as Maggie sobbed and writhed deliciously in her restraints. She was truly magnificent. Her toned body was covered with a gloss of perspiration, her whole being alight with the pain, and yet he could also sense the tide of arousal behind it. Beau crouched at her feet like a dog waiting for leftovers. Freya's eyes were like glowing coals, her mouth open, her expression alive with excitement and anticipation.

At last she dropped the cane on the floor and grabbed Maggie's hair, wet with sweat and oil. 'Had enough?' she spat breathlessly.

'Yes, mistress,' Maggie sobbed.

'Good.' Freya caught hold of the clamps on her nipples and pulled her closer still. 'You will do as you're told next time.'

Maggie gasped with pain. 'Yes, mistress,' she promised. 'I will, mistress.'

Freya pulled off the clamps and Maggie wailed again as the woman massaged the blood-flow back, the apparent kindness a double-edged sword for the rush of blood was all the more painful for the stimulation. The clamp on Maggie's sex lips was also removed and then Freya looked at Guido, who was watching with interest.

'Get her out of the stocks,' she ordered, and as Maggie slumped to the floor the woman unfastened the crotch of her leather basque.

Max watched keenly. He suspected that Maggie had never been with another female before, and wondered how she'd react. If she refused to comply with Freya's demands, he knew the severe blonde would have no hesitation in meting out yet more punishment. With Maggie on her knees Freya cupped her face and pulled her to her sex. Freya really was a natural dominatrix, her pleasure truly in inflicting pain and exacting total obedience from those few who passed her stringent selection tests. Max knew she would be ready now for that growing pleasure to be brought to its natural conclusion. He smiled; on many occasions it had been him who'd had the pleasure of taking her to the very edge and beyond.

Crouched on the floor Maggie shivered. There was an instant, a split second when she pulled back with misgivings and revulsion, and then slowly she pressed a kiss to Freya's shaven mound, her tongue inquisitively slipping between the outer labia, easing them apart.

Freya sighed and beckoned to Guido to bring her one of the low dungeon stools. Then sitting upon it she opened her legs wide. 'Use you fingers as well as you tongue,' she instructed, and without hesitation Maggie complied, any resistance quashed. Beau crawled over and unfastened the leather laces of Freya's basque, exposing shapely breasts, and then sucked one nipple deep into his mouth. Guido looked to Max, who nodded, and the driver sank to his knees to suck the other, his erect cock in his hand.

It was all far too much to resist, so Max also got to his knees, but behind his slave girl and pressed a hand between her legs. She moved against him instinctively and he could smell her arousal. He unfastened his trousers and with one long penetration he drove his cock deep into Maggie's sex, and was rewarded by a guttural moan of pleasure as he filled her completely.

Maggie felt the first traitorous ripples of an orgasm reverberate through her body, and knew they weren't hers alone. Above her Freya moaned in delight, and she could hear the guttural snorts of the men as they approached their own orgasms. The climax, when it came, was rapid and destructive, like a hurricane ripping through her, tearing her and the others apart.

She heard Freya cry out and felt her grip her head and pull her face even tighter to her sex, anointing Maggie's mouth with her slick pleasure. She felt a splash on her shoulder, and another on her opposite arm and her back, and felt as if she was drowning in the men's spunk, while deep inside her she felt the final throbbing surge that told her the man thrusting between her legs had filled her with his seed.

Chapter Seven

Maggie woke in the half-light, wondering where on earth she was. A hand was between her thighs, lazily exploring the contours of her sex, stirring her from a dreamless sleep. As she tried to turn over she realised with a start that her hands were secured to a long chain that bound her to a bed. It was Max Jordan's bed. Images and events of the previous evening flooded her slowly awakening brain, and not just images, but also Max's instructions, his rules and constraints, which she must learn to obey as second nature. Max Jordan's rules.

'Slaves are not allowed to urinate in private, nor bathe without their master's permission.'

They had been drinking brandy after Freya and Beau had left in the small hours of the morning, and Max told her exactly what she must expect and adhere to if she continued in his service.

'You will be beaten every time we meet,' he told her. 'Ideally you should be beaten every day, but for the time being we must content ourselves with every meeting. Before your punishment you will tell me the things you have done that you think might displease me.' As he spoke he watched her expression intently, although she wasn't sure whether it was to watch for any sign of dissension or just because he enjoyed observing her reactions.

'From now on,' he continued, 'I will decide who uses your body, and that includes masturbation. These are just a few of the fundamentals, Maggie. When you signed the contract you became mine - body and soul. You fully understand that, don't you?'

Maggie nodded, tired and sated, the brandy relaxing her, unable to believe that a man of his age still had the stamina to go on when all she wanted was to fall into bed and sleep.

Max savoured a mouthful of the amber liquid, and then continued. 'When you are here and sleeping in my bed you are to wake me in the morning by sucking my cock.

'Your body is always to be available to me, or any person I choose.

'Whenever you are awaiting my presence, or any of my guests, unless told otherwise you will always assume the slave position - on all fours, legs apart, head down. Do you understand me, Maggie?'

She nodded sleepily. It was all too much to take in. Her whole body ached, her mind ached and she wanted to sleep, but Max continued. 'And from now on, until otherwise instructed you will keep every weekend free for my pleasure. Guido will pick you up every Friday evening. Other than toiletries you will only need to bring the clothes you stand up in. And whilst on the subject of clothes, as a slave you are forbidden to wear underwear unless it is something I have given you to wear for a specific purpose. This includes when you are at home, out shopping, or at work.'

'But what if someone notices?' said Maggie, instantly thinking of Simon Faraday at work.

Max smiled. 'Such trivialities are unimportant,' he said, easily dismissing her concerns.

'But what if they say something, or use the knowledge to try to take advantage of me?' she asked anxiously.

'Then you are to let them,' he said simply. 'After all, you are a slave now, Maggie. Indulge any such liberties, and then you must report to me every last detail.'

She blushed.

'So,' he said, draining the last of his glass. 'It is time for bed now, my little one. Oh, and one more thing, if I want you at any other time I will ring and have Guido collect you.' He produced a mobile phone and passed it to her. 'This is for you, to be used exclusively for communication between us.'

Maggie took it and nodded.

Totally exhausted, she had assumed that once they were upstairs she would be allowed to sleep, but instead Max had her kneel at the side of the bed and then used her mouth, fucked her as hard there as he had her cunt, then holding her close he filled her mouth with his seed and she had little choice but to swallow every last drop.

Before she had joined him in bed he put leather cuffs on her wrists and fastened her by a silver chain to the head of the bed. As the lock snapped shut he smiled. 'Sweet dreams, slave,' he said, and switched off the light.

Now, in the half-light of the bedroom and wide-awake, Maggie remembered her instructions, eased down under the bedclothes, took his flaccid penis between her lips and very gently began to suck. Her reward was a low chuckle of approval.

'Good girl, good girl,' he mumbled. 'But I want a little something more than your mouth this morning.' He pulled her up to him and stroked her hair back off her brow. 'Come with me,' he said, reaching over to get the key from the bedside cabinet drawer to unlock her wrists.

Max led her across the bedroom to his en suite bathroom, and turned on the shower. He then slipped off his robe and pushed her down to the floor. 'Hands and knees,' he snapped, and Maggie stared up at him in surprise. 'Now,' he insisted impatiently, taking a tube of lubricant from the glass shelf over the basin.

She obeyed, and before she had time to absorb what was happening she felt

187

him work some grease into her anus and immediately felt him crouch behind her and press his erection between her buttocks. She held still, too apprehensive to resist, and felt his cock relentlessly sinking into her tight channel, deeper than she thought possible. Slowly her body gave way to him, filling her until she could feel his balls nestling against the lips of her empty sex. She whimpered, the experience so at odds with everything she had ever considered acceptable.

Max grunted with pleasure. 'Oh yes...' he growled under his breath as he began to move. 'Does it hurt?'

'A little,' she whispered truthfully. 'But it's not the pain. It's just...' How could she explain that it made her feel humiliated? He must surely know what he was doing to her, that in some ways what she felt was worse than any physical discomfort, and yet at the same time strangely, wickedly exciting? Crouched on the floor in the bathroom Max Jordan had reduced her to the lowest common denominator. Kneeling and naked for his pleasure she was only a sexual object, a pleasure to be taken, a good tight fuck. Tears ran down her cheeks as he ploughed deep into her rectum, her cries seeming to drive him on to greater effort.

She was terrified he might hurt her, terrified he might stop and terrified of the strange excitement building low in her belly. What was happening to her?

Above her Max's breath was becoming ragged, his thrusts more instinctive, and Maggie found herself moving with him, longing to slide a hand between her legs to stroke her treacherous, throbbing clit.

'Please, master, may I touch myself?' she whispered, her breath heavy with trepidation and desire.

'Oh yes, my little one, you certainly may,' he snorted as he gripped her hips and pulled her back onto him. So Maggie began to rub her clit, feeling the little bud pulsing under her fingertips, but before she could orgasm Max ejaculated, driving furiously deep, and denied her own release Maggie slumped to the floor tiles, stunned and trembling, his penis pulsing rhythmically inside her tightness. Then when completely drained of his essence Max withdrew and gathered her limp form into his arms.

'Well done, slave,' he said, kissing her ear.

Maggie pressed herself into his embrace, seeking warmth and reassurance, and oddly enough, comfort. Gently he helped her to her feet and together they stepped into the shower. His hands worked over her body, lathering her, his washing her both an act of tenderness and an act of possession. She leant against him, giving him free rein to touch and explore her. His fingers pressed back and forth over her pleasure bud, and then he pulled down the showerhead and played it between her legs. Maggie gasped as the fierce jets found their mark. Skilfully he teased it back and forth over her clitoris and the succulent flesh of her sex and bottom, and she immediately felt the first glowing ripples of an orgasm wash over her.

'Ooohhhh...' she gasped.

'Don't forget to ask,' he warned, nipping her neck and shoulders.

'Please, master, please let me come,' she obediently begged. '*Please.*'

'Very well, you may,' he acquiesced, and gratefully she began to move against the powerful water jets, pressing her hips forward until she thought she could take no more, at which point Max sunk to his knees and gently began sucking her engorged clit. She cried out, this time in pure bliss, and let the sensations absorb her. She held him, crying out in delight, aware only of her body and the relentless ministrations of his tongue. Under his skilful manipulations the wonderful orgasm seemed to go on and on until she thought she would faint from the sheer intensity of feelings and emotions.

At last, after what seemed like an eternity, there was stillness with only the sound of the cascading water. Trembling, Maggie didn't resist as Max helped her out of the shower and wrapped her in a fluffy white towel.

'I have to get on with my day now,' he told her, slipping on his towelling bathrobe. 'I have things to attend to. I want you to go back to bed and rest; it's still early and there's no need for you to be up yet. I'll have Mrs Griffin bring you up some tea and sort out your clothes for the day.' He kissed her forehead and she padded back to the bedroom, and with a sense of relief, slipped between the sheets.

It was almost midday when Mrs Griffin, carrying a tray, woke Maggie. She drew the curtains and plumped the pillows, treating her like royalty.

And Maggie made the most of it. Here she was living on Max Jordan's terms and by Max Jordan's rules. Never in all her adult life had she surrendered so totally to another person, and yet somewhere in that act of submission she found the very thing she craved. Something about it gave her a huge thrill, and yet something about it troubled her to the core. With Max all life changed, the truths she had held so dear for so long altered and contorted in such a surreal world.

After she'd eaten Mrs Griffin returned and helped her dress, apply her make-up and brush her hair. An hour later, dressed in a cream silk basque with wired cups that displayed her breasts like ripe fruit, cream stockings and high heels, Maggie went downstairs. Catching sight of herself in a mirror she saw the face and body of a beautiful courtesan.

In the sitting room Max was busy at his desk, papers spread out in front of him. He looked up fleetingly, barely seeming to register her as she walked into the room. She hoped he would say something, compliment her appearance, but he merely indicated she should kneel at his feet, the perfect slave, the elegant possession of her master.

Max had plans for Maggie. He had already arranged for the next part of her training, but it was essential she learn fully that she was the slave, not the star.

He stroked her hair, her cheek resting on his thigh. She delighted him, she was everything he could wish for, but by the same token it was important that she understood her place in the scheme of things.

'Guido will be taking care of you today,' he told her, and she looked up in surprise. 'You want to say something, slave?'

189

'Um, no, master,' she said, although they both knew that wasn't true.

'Good.' Max rang the bell on his desk before turning his attention back to his papers, and a few minutes later Guido appeared. As his driver crossed the room Max felt Maggie tense, but said nothing.

Maggie looked up at him, and he indicated she should stand. She did as she was told, although her eyes were wide with apprehension. Max smiled; he had the perfect cure for that.

Guido slipped a blindfold over her eyes, gripped her arm and led her away.

Max dropped the papers back into his desk; time for the show to begin.

Maggie tried not to let her fear show, instinct telling her that Guido would take advantage of the slightest sign of weakness. He led her out of the sitting room, that much she could guess, and then across the hall and down some stairs to what she assumed were the kitchens, and then down yet more steps. It was nerve-wracking not being able to see and she shivered, afraid that she might lose her footing, while at the same time her mind was spiralling away at the prospect of what might follow.

As they turned a corner the air became cooler and slightly musty.

'Nearly there,' Guido informed her, and Maggie could hear the mixture of amusement and anticipation in his voice as they moved along a damp and chilly passage.

'W-where are we going?' she asked anxiously.

He sniggered. 'That's for me to know and you to find out.'

The floor under her feet was cold now, and the muffled sound of their voices made her sense the ceiling was low and the walls close around them.

'Here we are,' said Guido, and Maggie swung round to try and track his voice as he let go of her and moved away. 'Relax,' he said. 'I'm not going to leave you. It'll all be so much easier if you don't resist me, although you must know that by now. Do as you're told and you'll be fine.' As he spoke he took one of her hands and snapped a cuff around her wrist, pulling it out to one side and fastening it to something that held her arm parallel to the floor. He did the same with the other and Maggie fought to suppress her panic.

'My, what a pretty sight you are,' he mused, running his hands over her breasts, tweaking her nipples. Maggie squealed at the sudden pain, and with an open palm he slapped first one and then the other, making her gasp with surprise. He slapped each breast again, harder this time.

'So very pretty,' he drawled. 'I really enjoyed watching you with Freya. She's some piece of work, isn't she?' As he spoke he nudged her legs apart and fastened a spreader bar between her ankles.

'You're going to enjoy today,' he told her conversationally. 'Max has arranged something special for you.'

'What do you mean?' she asked.

He said no more, and the next sound she heard was his retreating footsteps and the sound of the door opening and closing.

'Guido?' she called anxiously. Hadn't he said he wouldn't leave her alone?

190

'Guido?' she called again into the ominous silence.

'Guido?' she called more earnestly, increasingly unsettled by her chilling solitude, but still there was no response of any kind. She tried to sense what was going on. The minutes ticked by slowly. She pulled on her restraints, aware even as she tugged at them that it was pointless. She became more anxious and her pulse quickened as panic again threatened to overwhelm her.

And then, just when she thought she could bear it no longer, she heard the door open again. Maggie had no idea who it was - Guido returning, or Max. Her emotions teetered between relief and trepidation. As she strained to pick up any clues as to the identity of the presence, she could just discern the movement of feet and whisper of male voices.

'H-hello?' she stuttered. 'Who is it? Master? Guido? Is that you?'

No one answered, and Maggie tugged desperately on the restraints, twisting her wrists, trying to loosen the cuffs that held her tight.

'Is there anyone there?' she cried again, a little louder this time, at last provoking a response.

'For God's sake gag her,' ordered a male voice she didn't recognise, and then she heard footsteps and someone moving closer. Something round and hard was pushed into her mouth and straps tied tight at the back of her head. It was a ball-gag. Maggie let out a wail of apprehension. Now she couldn't speak or see, but she could still hear and her body froze as a voice whispered in her ear.

'Hello, Maggie,' it said. 'Your master tells us that you need to be used like a proper slave should be.'

Maggie strained hard against the cuffs.

'I'm sure an arrogant little bitch like you has fantasies of more than one man taking you at a time? Don't you, eh? And that's what we're here for. To make you beg for mercy and beg for more. How do you like the idea of that, eh, Maggie?'

As the voice continued to taunt soft tendrils stroked across her breasts and stomach, the touch sensual yet alarming. Maggie groaned behind the gag as her nipples responded, tightening. She shook her head in denial, trying to say no to the cruel goading, then a stinging lash across her breasts made her sex tighten and the moan from behind the gag become a wild sob. More lashes cut across her breasts, buttocks, thighs and belly. Maggie couldn't hold back, she cried and then screamed into the gag, struggling against the cuffs and spreader bar.

Just when she thought she could take no more her tormentor leant close. 'A little word of warning, Maggie,' he whispered sharply. 'You are our plaything today. Max says we can do exactly what we want to you. And trust me, whatever we want to do to you, we will do. Although if you do what you're told we might just let you go when we've finished with you. But if not you might find yourself tied down here for quite some time.'

Maggie shrieked again as six hard strikes of a cane cut across her buttocks. She tried to force herself to stop struggling, her chest heaving as she tried to catch her breath.

Hands began working their way over her body, touching and molesting with callous intensity. Fingers slid inside her wet sex, finding and then circling the hardening ridge of her clitoris, while another eased into her bottom making her wriggle and sob in protest. As she tried to pull away from them a hungry mouth closed over one of her breasts, sucking and biting the nipple, then another mouth started suckling the other, while two pairs of hands mauled between her parted thighs from the front and from the rear.

Maggie struggled to breathe, saliva trickling around the ball-gag and down her chin. She moaned, frightened and anxious, and yet against all the odds she secretly began to enjoy the crude attentions. As if sensing her growing arousal the mouths pulled away.

She sighed, but any sense of relief was misplaced and premature.

'Enjoying it, aren't you, sweetheart?' the voice drooled salaciously. There was a moment's fumbling between her tensed thighs, she held her breath, wondering what was coming next, and then something thrust up inside her without prelude. Maggie cried out with shock as her body opened in its path, and then again as someone gripped her breasts and pinched her nipples tight with a set of cold metal clamps. The pleasure and pain combination was almost unbearable. Her sex began contracting while the thick dildo thrust without compassion in and out of her.

Maggie felt her body spasm, she couldn't hold back. It was all too much. She bit down on the gag as a fierce orgasm swept through her, her body arching as her sex closed tight around the dildo. Still gasping, still in the throws of her climax, the dildo was wrenched out and she moaned gratefully as a rigid penis slid slowly up into her vacant cunt. At the same time something smaller and slimmer was eased into her bottom, a finger slick with lubrication, and then retreated and a cock nudged up to take its place. Maggie sobbed deliriously as it embedded itself in her tight rear passage. Her mind protested but her rogue body seemed only too eager to cooperate. There was no way this was possible... no way...

The stranger screwing her arse eased his meaty erection slowly but determinedly further and further inside her. Maggie thought she would faint with pleasure and shame, writhing between the two naked men.

She sobbed pitifully, but her muffled protests were met with grunts and curses of pleasure as the two men began to find a mutual rhythm, driving in and out of their victim, sandwiched between them, tied, gagged and stretched open for them.

'Want to swap places?' rumbled the man who'd spoken previously, and with that they both withdrew, shuffled around her, exchanged places, then eased back deep inside her and continued fucking.

Maggie slumped between them, wanting it to be over. She was raw with a heady mixture of pain and pleasure. The two men began moving more erratically, fucking her with ever more urgency. She heard one gasp, and despite her fatigue her head rolled back and she shuddered with a violent orgasm as she felt the hot release of semen deep, deep inside her cunt.

'Oh fuck!' snorted the man behind her, feverishly kissing her neck and shoulder, pulling her back onto him as he thrust his cock fully up her arse, his sperm erupting deep. 'Oh, that feels so fucking *good*,' he groaned coarsely, wearily.

Sandwiched between her captors, Maggie struggled to catch her breath while their panting bodies ground hot and sweaty against her. Gradually they both withdrew, leaving her shivering and empty, listening to the muffled whisperings of her two unseen lovers. Was lover the right word? Or was assailant more appropriate?

Firm hands unfastened the gag and Maggie stretched her jaw thankfully. Other hands released the nipple clamps.

But if she had hoped to be set free she was mistaken. After a few moments the voices receded and once again she hung in the restraints straining to hear any clues as to what would happen next.

Max Jordan was the last to leave the cellar. Although he hadn't taken part in any of the activities he could almost feel the tight grip of Maggie's sex closing around his cock, imagine the way her body felt as she writhed against the twin cocks that had impaled her. He smiled and climbed the stairs back up to the sitting room, wholly delighted with his latest acquisition.

'Well, well, well,' said a familiar voice, breaking into Maggie's reverie, and she stiffened as Guido ran a hand over her aching breasts. 'Quite a show you put on there,' he said. 'And look at you now, you dirty little whore.' His finger traced the course of the semen trickling down her legs. 'Look at you - something to be used and then discarded.'

He ran a finger up to her sex and then drew it across her lips. 'I know what whores are for,' he went on, unfastening her arms so that she slumped to the floor on her hands and knees. He caught hold of her hair and Maggie shrieked in protest, but still fastened to the spreader-bar she couldn't get away from him.

She heard the zip on Guido's trousers and knew exactly what was coming next. She heard him crouching, and then from behind he drove his cock into her soaking sex, forcing it deep into her until she cried out. 'Fuck me, you dirty little bitch,' he snorted, driving deeper still and jerking her back by her hair.

'Even after the fucking those two just gave you, you're still nice and tight,' Guido sniggered. 'Max was right about you; you really are a complete slut.'

An instant later Guido gasped, she felt him buck and then he jerked once, twice and came in a pulsing eruption, flooding her sex with his warm seed. He held on to her for support for a few moments, and then hauling her to her feet pulled off the blindfold. She blinked in the dim light of the cellar, but didn't make a sound as he unfastened her ankles, peeled the grimy basque off her and led her to a small shower area off the main cellar. He watched as she washed, eyes still bright with avarice and desire, and she tried not to catch his eye. Wasn't it enough that Max allowed him to use her as and when he wanted, or was there more?

Once she was dry, and completely naked except for her collar, Guido led her back upstairs. As they approached the sitting room Maggie heard voices from within and froze. One of them she knew was the voice from the cellar, but the other one sounded equally familiar.

'What is it?' Guido goaded. 'Don't tell me you're shy.' He opened the sitting room door and Maggie's worst fears were confirmed. Max was playing host, handing out drinks, an unknown man sitting in an armchair sipping one, and by the window, holding and empty crystal glass, she saw to her complete horror stood Mike, Kay's boyfriend!

Max smiled broadly. 'Ah, excellent,' he said enthusiastically. 'Maggie, Mike would like another scotch and soda. See to it, please.'

Feeling utterly shell-shocked Maggie did as he ordered, and as she handed Mike his drink he smiled smugly at her.

'You see, Maggie,' he said, 'I told you I knew someone you'd like to meet.'

From across the room Max interrupted the tense silence that followed Mike's arrogant boast. 'Come here, Maggie,' he said, and indicated the floor beside him, and totally humiliated she did exactly as she was told and knelt at his feet. 'On all fours, I think,' he added. 'We want to see your marks.'

After a perfunctory examination Max nodded and indicated she should stand. The men, it seemed, had some business to conduct. Maggie served them more drinks and snacks as and when required, all the time aware of their eyes on her body. And when she wasn't needed she knelt at Max's feet, the epitome of submission, although all the while her mind was racing.

Max, when engrossed in discussions, toyed idly with her, and it seemed there was no part of her and no time when she was not his property. As the afternoon headed into evening Max suggested they retire to the dining room for dinner.

At the door he kissed her on the lips. 'Well done,' he said, and the two simple words made her heart leap. 'I want you help serve my guests their meal,' he added. 'And then you can go to your room and eat. I'll have Mrs Griffin bring a tray of something up for you.' His expression suddenly hardened. 'And when you've eaten you will go and kneel by my bed until I come up.'

'Yes, master,' she yielded meekly, and realised that for the first time she truly meant the words, that in all senses Max Jordan truly was her master.

Chapter Eight

Sitting at her desk in the office of the magazine where she worked, staring at the computer screen, Maggie struggled to make sense of the articles she had been working on the week before. It felt as if the words and thoughts came from a different life, written by a different person. In fact, it felt almost as if she had woken up inside a dream.

'Maggie?' She looked up without really thinking to find Simon standing beside her desk. Couldn't the bloody man take a hint? But before she could say anything he smiled at her crookedly, giving her an odd sense of déjà vu - hadn't this been the moment that had driven her to seek out Max Jordan?

'I just came over to say that I think I owe you an apology,' he said, surprising her with his unexpected display of contrition. 'I shouldn't have told the world and his wife that you were coming out for dinner with me last week. It was tactless of me, and... well, lunging at you wasn't the most gentlemanly thing I could have done either.' He paused thoughtfully. 'The thing is, I value your friendship, Maggie, and even if you're not interested in me in a romantic way, which I do understand, I'd hate to lose you as a friend.'

Maggie managed to put on a smile. It was a very big thing for him to say, under the circumstances. 'It's all right, Simon,' she said graciously. 'And thank you.'

'There's just one more thing...' he went on, and Maggie sighed, knowing there had to be something else to it. 'I wondered if you could do me a favour.'

'A favour?'

He nodded.

'What sort of a favour, Simon?'

'Would you come out to dinner with me tonight?'

Maggie laughed. She had to admire the cheek of the man. 'That isn't a favour, that's a date.'

'No, no it's not, honestly,' he insisted defensively. 'The thing is, my department is entertaining some very influential clients this evening. I've already roped in three or four of the staff, but to be honest I could do with all the help I can get.' He paused and tried out his pretty feeble little boy lost expression on her. 'I really could do with your help, Maggie. I really could.'

She studied his eyes closely, and then smiled. She still felt a little guilty about the dinner date at the *Neptune*, and came to a decision. 'All right,' she said after a few seconds, 'just as long as you understand that it's not a date, okay?'

Simon grinned, looking mightily relieved - or pleased with himself. 'Okay,' he beamed, and just then a courier approached Maggie's desk carrying a huge bouquet of snow-white Arum lilies.

'Maggie Howard?' he asked, correctly addressing her. 'These are for you.' And she accepted them, somewhat taken aback. They were astonishingly beautiful, if slightly macabre.

Simon looked at her and then at the flowers. 'Someone die?' he blurted with his usual lack of tact.

Maggie opened the card and read the words inside. 'A little something to mark the end of your old life and beginning of the new. Check your email. The master.' She felt her cheeks blush. 'You could say that,' she said to Simon. 'Just someone's idea of a joke, that's all.' Hastily she tucked the card into her bag.

'We'll go straight from work, then,' Simon said.

'I'm sorry?'

'To dinner,' he qualified. 'I've booked an early reservation at *Fernando's*; our clients have got a long way to travel home.'

Maggie groaned. 'I'll have to nip out at lunchtime and get something to wear,' she told him, wishing she'd never agreed to help him out.

'Why?' he asked cheesily. 'You look great as you are.'

Maggie looked down at her faded jeans and black silk blouse. She had complied with Max's edict about wearing no underwear, but he had kind of fudged the rules; after all, he hadn't said anything about trousers or generous fitting blouses so that no one would notice. 'Only a man would say that,' she said scornfully.

Simon shrugged. 'About half-six, then?' he confirmed, and Maggie nodded. No point in trying to backtrack now.

As soon as he was gone she logged on to the Internet, and as she waited for her email to appear she pondered the prospect of dinner with Simon. She didn't really want to go out with him again, but it would probably mean she at least missed seeing Kay, and the inevitable embarrassment that encounter would bring.

Maggie shivered, thinking about Mike and the events of the weekend as her master's address appeared on one of the incoming emails. It had occurred to her that Kay almost certainly didn't know about Mike and his clandestine activities. Maybe she thought he kept his sadist streak just for her. How could she possibly face her lodger and friend ever again, knowing what she now knew?

Maggie opened Max's email. All there was, typed centre page, was an address in a nearby town - no date, no time, just the address and a set of instructions on how to dress. Short skirt, blouse, hold-up stockings, no underwear. Maggie smiled; it was almost the kind of outfit she could wear to dinner with Simon if she chose something subtle.

She stared at the screen, unsure whether to email or ring to ask Max for further instructions. Her instincts told her it was a test. She glanced at the lilies and decided to wait. A man who knew she was at the office rather than at home left nothing to chance. She'd have the information she needed as and when he decided she should.

'Maggie?' She instantly recognised Max's voice on the mobile, and trembled slightly. The last thing she'd expected was for the phone he'd given her to ring while she was out with Simon's clients.

'Be at the address I sent you at eight tonight,' he told her. 'You have your instructions; you know what to wear.'

Across the room a waiter served wine and fruit juice to Simon's corporate guests.

'I - I'm sorry, I'm busy at the moment...' she blustered. 'I'm helping at a business dinner with Simon from accounts.'

'Really?' He didn't sound amused. 'Well get out of it. Unless, of course, you want to displease me? Or is this disobedience? Do you want to be punished?'

'No, master...' she said urgently, her pulse quickening.

'Good, in that case I will see you at eight. I want your help with the training of another slave. I'll be expecting you, the door will be unlocked, come straight in. And try to remember all you've been taught, Maggie. Don't disappoint me...' His voice was low and even, and before Maggie had the chance to reply he hung up.

Just then Simon beckoned her over, and she really didn't know what to do for the best. 'This place is great for a function room, isn't it?' he said, looking tense, clearly keen to make a good impression on his clients. 'And the food is superb.'

She nodded. 'It's very nice, Simon,' she agreed, 'but I'm afraid I'm going to have to leave you to it; something's come up.'

He stared at her, looking agitated. 'Leave?' he whispered furiously. 'But why? We've only just got here. I thought you said you'd help me out.' She could see he was angry, and justifiably so.

'I'm really sorry, Simon,' she said, thinking on her feet. 'But I've just had a call from an interview I've been chasing for weeks. They're only in the country for a few days but the PR guy says they can see me tonight - another magazine has been bumped off the A list. I'm so sorry.'

Simon didn't look very convinced. 'So who is this mystery celebrity, then?' he challenged.

'Look, I really can't talk about it,' she fudged. 'I've just got to go. I'm sorry.'

He sighed. 'Okay, if you must.'

Maggie smiled, the knot in her stomach easing. 'I owe you one,' she said, and with the first hurdle out of the way she slipped into the cloakroom and took off the white lacy knickers and bra she'd bought at lunchtime, and looked at herself in the mirror. It wouldn't take long to get ready. A little more make-up and a button or two more undone on her new white blouse, a little more perfume and she was ready. She smiled at her reflection, aware of the way the outline of her nipples showed through the thin fabric.

'Wow,' said Simon as she reappeared. 'You look great. I hope this mystery celeb is worth it.'

Maggie reddened. 'Were you waiting for me?' she asked.

'I just came to ask if you'd like me to drive you to the interview?' he said. 'After all, your car is back at the office.'

Maggie shook her head. 'No, it's all right,' she declined the offer, 'I've arranged for a taxi. And besides, this is your bash, you're the host, Simon, you can hardly leave.'

Ten minutes later, settled in the back of a cab, she wondered what Max meant about helping him out with another slave. Did he mean Beau, perhaps, or someone else? As she allowed her imagination to run riot she felt a familiar stirring deep in the pit of her tummy, a hot tendril of arousal surging up through her like a lightening bolt. She made a point of keeping her eyes lowered in case the driver could see the desire sparkling in them.

Shortly before eight the taxi drew up outside the address Max had given her. As she climbed out into the anonymous suburban street the evening air touched her nakedness beneath the short skirt.

The taxi driver seemed to sense her apprehension. 'You going to be all right on your own here, love?' he asked as Maggie paid him.

She nodded, not trusting herself to speak, holding her coat tight, certain that somehow he knew that beneath it she was dressed for Max Jordan, as he had decreed she should be.

She shivered, watching the taillights of the taxi disappear around the corner, letting the sense of excitement and isolation thrill her. She drew a calming breathed, amazed at the change that had come over her since Max's phone call.

The house he'd directed her to was a modern suburban villa on an executive estate, hidden away behind neatly trimmed shrubs and an expanse of manicured lawn. Maggie made her way up the drive, aware of her high heels crunching on the gravel.

The house was quiet as she let herself in through the front door. The hall was tastefully furnished but at the same time oddly featureless, as if styled from the pages of a Sunday magazine. Maggie hesitated, wondering what to do next, when she heard a familiar voice.

'Up here,' Max called.

She slipped off her coat and checked her appearance in the hall mirror, tucking the white blouse tighter into her skirt, pulling the thin fabric taut over her breasts so her nipples showed through. She climbed the stairs tentatively. There was only one door open on the landing, light spilling from it. Taking a deep breath she slipped into the bedroom, and gasped. In the luxuriously furnished room was a naked woman, tied facedown on the bed, a pillow under her hips, her raised buttocks crisscrossed with blotchy welts. Maggie stared, there was something terribly familiar about her, and then she realised with horror it was her lodger, Kay!

Her face was turned to one side, her long blonde hair fanned out across the white pillows, a black blindfold covering her eyes. She was breathing hard.

Max Jordan stood to one side of the bed, fully dressed, a black leather riding-crop held loosely at his side.

'Come over here,' he ordered, and as Maggie got close he grabbed her hair and pulled her to him with a brutal ferocity and gave her a crushing kiss. Maggie gasped, she could feel the heat in him and his animal arousal induced by the whipping he'd given Kay. He pressed his fingers between her legs, under her skirt, his fingers demanding entry, prising into Maggie's already wet sex. She sighed with shameful pleasure.

He pulled away from the kiss, grabbed the front of her new blouse and ripped it open. There was no place for subtlety, and clenching his jaw he tore it away from her body completely, heedless of ruining her new garment.

Maggie cried out in shock, yet at the same time felt her body respond to the hungry assault. He leered and swooped to capture a nipple between his teeth, biting hard enough to make her cry out with pain. She began to writhe against him, astonished by her own hunger.

'Please, master,' she begged, barely aware of her own words, 'please fuck me.'

'Oh, so keen already?' he said scornfully. 'Not yet, my beautiful little slave, not yet. We have a long night ahead of us.' He turned her away from him. 'Give me your hands.'

Maggie did as she was told, aware of the paradox of fear and desire, aware that only a short while earlier such a request would have had her screaming for help. She felt the cold bite of the handcuffs snapping shut around her wrists, and then the light receding as Max tied a blindfold over her eyes.

'You look magnificent,' he said, hands on her shoulders, pushing her down to her knees. She heard the sound of his trouser zip being lowered, felt his hand as it cupped her chin, holding her head still, and then the feel of his smooth helmet demanding entry to her mouth. Maggie opened for him, at that moment wanting nothing more than to give her master total pleasure. Kneeling in an act of worship, relishing the feel, the smell and the taste of his cock as it slid over her lips, she sighed with pure pleasure.

'Suck me,' he ordered, and then held himself still. She obeyed, moving her head and using her lips and tongue to please him.

'That's it... that's very good,' he panted softly. 'Good girl, that feels very good.'

Maggie moaned her reply as the taste of his growing excitement filled her mouth.

'You know what you are, don't you?' he went on. 'You're my dirty little whore, my little slave... my slut. What other kind of a girl would abandon her boyfriend at my call, and hurry across town to let her body be used by another man?' He began to thrust deeper into her mouth. 'Mmmmm, yes... only a slut would let herself be used like this, on her knees, hands tied behind her back. Mmmmm, that's it, suck harder you dirty little cunt. What sort of girl are you, Maggie? Letting her mouth be fucked... and *wanting* it. You do want it, don't you, Maggie? Hmmm?' Max paused, pulling his cock almost out of her mouth.

She groaned, feeling robbed, and then eased forward to draw his cock back deep into her mouth as the riding-crop licked at the cheeks of her backside.

'Oh yes, that's it... that's it you dirty little slut. Suck harder, harder now.'

Max's crude words and Maggie's helplessness threatened to consume her. She pressed her thighs tight together, trying desperately to find a way to her own orgasm. Behind them she could hear Kay begging to be released, begging to be allowed to orgasm too. Max's fingers tightened in Maggie's hair, holding her head still as he began to fuck her mouth in earnest.

'Have you any idea how you look?' he grunted thickly as his pleasure grew. It was almost too much for him. Maggie Howard kneeling in front of him, the excitement of Kay's beating fresh in his mind. He gasped, struggling to hold on, struggling to hold back. He knew that both Maggie and Kay were desperate for release. Maggie was trembling, aching to touch herself as she sucked him. She looked every inch the perfect slut, her pretty tits available to be fondled and used, her short skirt bunching up around her waist, her cunt wet, almost totally exposed, waiting for a cock... any cock. He threw back his head and cried out with pleasure as the spunk pulsed up and out of his body and into Maggie's sucking mouth. Behind them on the bed Kay wailed in fury and frustration because she couldn't bring on her own orgasm. Jet after jet spewed from his cock, filling Maggie's mouth as she tried valiantly to swallow it all. When almost totally spent he held her head still and thrust into her welcoming mouth, using her purely for his pleasure, prolonging his ejaculation and the last of the bliss.

As the final tremor dissipated his wilting cock plopped from Maggie's mouth. She didn't move, waiting like a good slave for whatever was to follow. Max bent down and cupped her wet sex.

'Please, master,' she whimpered, 'please make me come.'

Max smiled. It was far too soon for that. From the cabinet by the bed he took out a small vibrator and eased it into her sex. She almost fell forward against him as he slid it into her, and set it vibrating at a slow throb. Maggie pushed down onto the carpet, shamelessly struggling to fuck herself on the plastic column.

'There you are, my little whore, that should keep you happy for a while,' he mused. 'Although you have a lot more work to do before you are allowed to orgasm tonight.'

The doorbell rang and Max left the bedroom. Maggie felt a little rush of panic. She could hear the sounds of Max welcoming someone and then strained to pick out individual voices. No, there was more than one other voice, more than two, but how many? She could hear them climbing the stairs, drawing nearer, and then they fell silent.

Maggie blushed furiously under the blindfold, knowing that whomever Max had invited to join him in the bedroom was taking in the extraordinary sight of her and Kay.

Nothing was said, but she sensed people crowding around, and picked out the distinctive sounds of clothes being shed. She could also sense the growing excitement and anticipation.

She felt someone move close to her face and then heard Max's distinctive Irish lilt. 'Now, my little slut, do you remember why I told you I wanted you here tonight?'

'Yes, to help you with Kay, master,' she answered clearly.

Max's fingers nipped her nipples, just hard enough for there to be a little pain, making her wince beneath the blindfold. 'No, I told you what was going to happen to Kay, didn't I?'

'You said you wanted my help with the training of another slave.'

'Good, and you'll start helping right now.' Maggie felt his hand on the back of her head, pressing her forward, and then her cheek was brushed by another stiff cock. 'Open your mouth, my little slut,' he whispered. 'That's what you're here for tonight. I want you to make all these cocks hard. Make them ready to fuck Kay.'

Maggie's futile response was instantly muffled as the cock moved across her cheek and thrust deep into her mouth. It felt different to Max's, and a tremor of

200

excitement rippled through her body as she realised what was happening, reduced to a sexual aid for men who cared nothing about who she was, only what she represented: pure pleasure without a name or a face. The idea of being reduced to nothing more than a sexual toy made her shiver. The man standing over her pushed deeper, making her work to please him, and Maggie let go, abandoning herself to the pleasure, to the sensation of each new cock as the men took turns in her mouth, and along with it was the knowledge that each of the cocks would soon be thrust into Kay's prone body. She shivered, imagining her lodger being used over and over again.

Each man took his turn in her mouth, using it, enjoying it, panting huskily as she sucked until they were rigid. But each one pulled away before they ejaculated.

'I want you to get up now,' Max eventually said, removing the dildo, Maggie shuddering as it slipped out of her pulsating cunt. He pulled her to her feet, guiding her forward, unfastening the cuffs. Then with him holding her hand she was led across the room and cringed with shock as her fingertips were lowered to Kay's smooth calves.

'Here,' said Max, pressing a tube of something into her palm. 'My friends have come to play, Maggie. They're all going to fuck Kay now, one right after the other, some in her arse, some in her cunt, some in her mouth. You've made their cocks nice and hard for her, and now I think you'd better make her ready for them, don't you?'

Maggie felt Kay tremble under her fingers as she heard the instructions. 'I can't, I don't know how...' she said. The only female she'd ever been intimate with was Freya, and on that occasion Freya had taken the lead. And worse still, Kay was her friend, someone she shared her house with.

'Maggie,' Max warned, his tone threatening, and she knew that disobeying him was a bad idea. So slowly, fearfully, she slipped forward onto the bed and ran her hands up the backs of Kay's bound and parted legs, seeking the girl's sex.

'Please,' Maggie begged, 'please may I see what I'm doing?'

'Not yet, Maggie,' he denied her. 'I just want you to touch her, to feel her body. Now do as you're told or I'll take the crop to you and to her. Hold out your hand.'

Max squeezed a greasy cream onto her raised fingers, and she obediently and blindly lubricated between Kay's beaten buttocks, surprised when the girl lifted her hips to her tentative touch, actually twisting beneath her fingers, the lubricant coating her tight anus. Instinctively Maggie slipped a single finger inside, and then ventured another, and Kay began to moan and thrust against her, trying to work the fingers deeper still.

Maggie imagined the men gathered around the bed, watching the two of them together, lining up to use Kay's trussed body. Maggie's fingers slid deeper, fucking Kay while her other hand fumbled between her own legs, gasping as her fingers touched her throbbing pleasure bud. The men were urging her on, and she could feel her orgasm drawing closer and closer...

'Stop!' Max's voice cut through the air as the riding-crop swiped viciously across Maggie's buttocks. Panting, groaning, no more than seconds away from her orgasm, she fell still, trembling, denied the closeness of release. He guided her down off the bed to kneel on the floor at the foot of it, and then he handcuffed her to the metal frame.

She felt his warm breath on her neck as he bent over to whisper in her ear. 'Do you know what my friends are going to do now, Maggie?'

She could say nothing.

'Do you know?' he pressed, and she nodded. 'Then tell me, little one, what do you think they are going to do now?'

'They're going to fuck her, master,' she said.

'And where are they going to fuck her, Maggie?'

'In her cunt, in her arse, in her mouth,' she whispered, horrified by the crude words coming from her mouth and lurid images forming in her head.

'Yes, they're going to fuck her, Maggie,' he confirmed. 'They're going to fuck her until she screams with pleasure.' Max ran a finger down her spine, and she shivered. 'And then, my dear, they are going to fuck you.'

Before she could fully absorb the implications of what he said she felt the bed move under her hands and realised that more than anything else she wanted to be able to see what was happening. The mattress strained and suddenly Kay was begging.

'Oh yes, yes, please fuck me, please, please fuck me...' the words breaking into a deluge of incoherent sobs as the bed began to move rhythmically. Maggie strained against the cuffs, hungry to see, desperate to watch.

It was more than she could bear - the sounds, the movements, all contriving to drive her crazy with anticipation and desire. Some part of her, she was horrified to realise, was desperate to see Kay being fucked and used.

She was aware of hands on her hips, and knew Max was behind her, watching Kay being fucked. 'Tell me, master, please,' she begged. 'Tell me what you see.'

He sniggered, stroked her bottom with the crop, and then administered a stinging blow across it. 'Listen, my dear, listen to them, and imagine her being fucked by my friends!'

Maggie sighed with frustration, and heard the man fucking Kay begin to pant and gasp. He was close to the brink, ready to explode inside her body, and then Maggie knew he was there. She heard him groan, heard him grunt, and in her mind she saw him thrusting stiffly into Kay's helpless body, saw his whole frame tensing as he emptied his balls in the girl's available sex.

But it was far from over. There was movement again, the bed rocking, another man clambering onto it, thrusting deep into Kay. She moaned again, moaning as he stretched her, used her, flesh slapping flesh, faster and faster. Behind the blindfold Maggie closed her eyes tight shut. Kay began to come too, making the mattress buck as the man riding her giggled victoriously and ejaculated inside her.

Then Maggie felt Max thrusting into her, deep into her soaking sex. She sighed, relishing the penetration, his hands gripping her hips, pulling her back onto him, straining against the cuffs that held her to the gyrating bed.

Her mind was alight with sounds and smells; Kay's insistent cries as she came over and over again; a man telling the trussed girl how he was going to fuck her, then his triumphant expletives as he came too; the bed-frame shaking under her hands; Max's stout cock thrusting deep into her body; her own pleasure so intense she thought she might faint.

At that moment Max pulled the blindfold off, and the salacious images on the bed did drive Maggie over the edge into a shuddering orgasm.

Max leant forward and withdrew his unspent erection, whispering in her ear, 'I can't keep you all to myself, that would be selfish. What sort of a host would that make me?'

He rose and stepped away, and Maggie felt an anonymous hand rummaging between her thighs, groping her vacant cunt, a rampant cock brushing her buttocks, and she closed her eyes.

Chapter Nine

When they got back to Maggie's house Guido opened the car door for her. She was too tired to speak, other than to wish him a perfunctory goodnight. Her mind and her body were totally exhausted as she fumbled for her front door key.

'Well, well, well, just look who's here,' said a familiar voice as she slipped the key into the lock. Slightly bemused she looked around and was astonished to see Simon standing there in the shadows.

'What are you doing here at this time of night?' she asked, unable to keep the surprise out of her voice.

'Now, there's a nice thing to say to someone who was concerned about your welfare,' he said sarcastically. 'I thought the very least I could do was make sure you got home safe and sound after you deserted me like that. You could invite me in, for being so considerate. How did your interview go? What did they do, ask you to stay on for the after-show party or something?'

Maggie tried to gather her thoughts and her alibi. 'Something like that,' she said hastily. 'It was okay. It was fine.'

'So, was that their driver?' he probed. 'You must have made a good impression to wangle yourself a ride home.' Simon nodded towards the road, although Guido had long since gone.

Maggie gave a noncommittal shrug and opened the front door.

'You look tired; are you sure you're all right?' he asked.

'Look, I'm fine, Simon,' she said frostily. 'I'm touched that you came to check up on me, but to be perfectly honest all I want to do now is fall into bed.' She looked at him, and he looked crestfallen. 'Okay, tell you what, why don't you come in and have a quick coffee,' she relented against her better judgement, his expression instantly brightening.

'Great!' he beamed, following her inside. 'Thanks, Maggie.'

'Actually, Simon, maybe this isn't such a good idea, I really need a shower,' she said, once they were in the hall.

'Don't let me stop you. I'm quite domesticated you know. You go and have your shower and leave the coffee to me.'

Upstairs Maggie dropped the ruins of her new clothes into the bin and looked at her body in the mirror.

Her nipples were red and sore from bite marks and far too much attention. Her bottom was striped from the crop and her sex was sore. She closed her eyes, remembering the frenzied animal heat of the men as they took her again and again. She shivered. Until meeting Max she would never have believed herself capable of such behaviour.

Feeling increasingly tired she set the shower to hot and stepped gratefully beneath the refreshing torrent. The more she thought about it, the more she felt it had been a mistake to let Simon in. There was no way she wanted to be sociable with him; all she wanted was to crawl into the warmth and comfort of her bed...

Maggie shrieked as Simon, naked, squeezed into the shower with her. 'What do you think you're playing at?' she snapped furiously, incredulously, trying to cover herself with her arms. 'Get out of here this instant!'

But Simon just grinned at her. 'Oh come on, Maggie, stop playing hard to get,' he said infuriatingly. 'You know I've fancied you for ages. And all that crap about not fancying me? I'm not fooled by that for an instant.'

Was he drunk? 'Simon,' she said, trying to control her outrage, 'get out of my shower, my bathroom, and my house, now. Please, before you do something we both regret. Go now and I'll never say anything more about it.'

Simon giggled inanely, and then cupping her face he kissed her aggressively, one hand straying down to maul her breasts while a knee pressed determinedly between her thighs.

'Come on, Maggie, don't be so coy,' he growled, breaking away from the kiss. 'I know you really fancy me, and besides, you're all on your own. I know you're gagging for it, a girl in your position, no one to snuggle up to at night. Come on, you know you want to. I thought maybe you'd like a little bit of rough.'

He kissed her again, trying to force his tongue into her mouth, making her squirm back against the wet tiles in horror. 'I'll scream and wake Kay!' she spluttered, managing to push him away.

Simon's eyes darkened menacingly. 'Nice try, Maggie, but I've already looked in her room and she's not home,' he said ominously. 'There's just you and me, and this...' His face rubbed against hers as he kissed her forehead, almost paternally, while with one hand he brushed his engorged cock against her belly.

'Simon, get out,' she implored weakly, physically and mentally drained from the night's exertions. 'Please, just get out and let's forget this ever happened...'

Before she could stop him he pressed her back against the tiles, sneering at her words as he forced her legs wider apart with his knee, his breath laden with alcohol. She started to struggle, knowing there was no reasoning with him, but he merely tutted sarcastically and grabbed her hair, pulling her face within inches of his.

'Come on, darling,' he gloated, 'we both know you'll love it. Just relax, take it easy and enjoy a real man. I'm not going to hurt you, just give you the fucking you need to loosen you up a little.'

Maggie felt her anger flare, but he was too strong and easily quelled her resistance. She tried to push him away again, pressing her clenched fists to his chest, but he was unrelenting.

'Simon, stop,' she begged. 'You're drunk, and I know when you sober up you'll regret this... Simon, please...'

As she tried to knee him he dragged her out of the shower cubicle and threw her to the bathroom floor. Instantly he was upon her, giving her no respite, pinning her to the tiles with one hand while guiding his cock into her with the other.

'There we are, sweetheart,' he grunted. 'You know you love it really. Now just relax while I give you the best screw you've ever had.'

Maggie mumbled wearily for him to stop, but far from stopping Simon seemed to be further inflamed by her pleas.

'Shit, that feels fantastic,' he groaned, throwing his head back. 'Oh yes, that feels bloody great. I knew you'd feel this good, Maggie. I've always known it, and now I'm really fucking you.' Snorting and grunting he began to buck and twist inside her, driving deeper and deeper, moving increasingly raggedly, and quickly he ejaculated - too quickly for his liking - while Maggie felt tears of shame running down her face as he pressed fully into her and held himself there, his groin tight between her parted thighs, his penis throbbing rhythmically as it discharged his seed deep into her body. He snorted through clenched teeth, sinewy veins standing proud in his throat, his eyes shut as he luxuriated in the triumph of at last fucking Maggie.

He collapsed onto her, feverishly raining kisses on her face and her throat in some loathsome parody of love or affection.

'Phew!' he gasped in her ear. 'Wasn't that something? I knew you wanted me all along. I knew you'd be good, too. But not that fucking good!'

Maggie stared up at the ceiling in disbelieving horror.

'Shall I go and make us that coffee now?' he asked, sliding out of her, his cock leaving a sticky trail across her trembling tummy.

'Coffee?' Maggie said quietly, unable to believe what she was hearing. 'You bastard, Simon; how could you do this to me? Get out of my house now and leave me alone.'

Simon got to his feet, his expression smug. 'Don't be silly, Maggie. You invited me in for coffee; I didn't twist your arm. You wanted me to fuck you. That's why you came up here on the pretext of wanting a shower, rather conveniently leaving the bathroom door unlocked. You wanted me to follow you up and fuck you. You just won't admit it to me, or to yourself. It's about time you did, Maggie. It's about time you did.'

For long uncomfortable seconds Simon stared down at her, gloating, then turned and left the bathroom.

She waited until she heard the front door open and close, and then crawled back into the shower and washed away any traces of his touch. The water had gone cold when she finally got out of the shower, towelled herself dry and slipped gratefully into bed.

It was almost light when Maggie heard her bedroom door open. She woke from sleep with a start and instantly tensed, terrified it might be Simon back for more.

She heard light footsteps padding across the bedroom, felt the duvet pull back, and was about to react when a familiar voice said, 'Don't worry, it's only me. I thought you might need a cuddle.'

Maggie sighed with relief and surprise. She couldn't have put it better herself. The body snuggled to her was warm and soft and belonged to her lodger. Kay was the very last person she would have expected to climb into her bed at any time, least of all tonight.

'Are you okay?' Kay whispered.

'Sort of,' said Maggie, her voice trembling with unexpected emotion. It wasn't the after-effects of the evening spent with Max and his friends that unsettled her, but Simon's unsophisticated attentions. Kay's unexpected tenderness brought tears to her eyes.

Not that Kay was to know that, and she very gently kissed Maggie, who began to respond, and eased her tongue into Maggie mouth, holding her close while her hands stroked and caressed her trembling body. As she began to relax Kay cupped Maggie's breasts, murmuring soft words of encouragement while caressing her.

Maggie shivered as Kay worked her lips over her throat and shoulders, and then lower to her breasts, her soft kisses and fingers eagerly teasing her stirring nipples. Maggie let out a long sigh, moaning with a heady mixture of uncertainty and delight. Despite her fears Kay's touch was sure and persuasive, each caress lighting a thousand tiny flares in Maggie's sleepy mind.

'Oh,' Maggie moaned as she felt trembling flutters of arousal. 'We... we can't do this,' she stammered.

'Shhhhh, it's all right,' Kay soothed, the words humming on Maggie's flesh as she sucked one of her nipples into her mouth. 'Max told me to come home and make love to you,' she confided. 'He told me to make you sing with pure pleasure. Here, touch me, Maggie. I'm here for you. I've wanted you for some time. Let me show you.' Finding Maggie's hands she guided them to her own full breasts.

The girl's skin was as soft as spun silk and warm and fluid under Maggie's fingertips, her lithe form a stunning contrast to the masculine brawn of the others. Maggie gasped at just how beautiful Kay felt, and almost without thinking she lowered her head and drew Kay's erect nipple into her mouth. The blonde moaned appreciatively and lifted herself up, pressing towards Maggie in both invitation and acceptance of her tentative caresses.

With Freya, Maggie had felt very much the slave, dominated and taken by a cruelly dominant mistress. But curled up in Kay's arms there was just intimate pleasure, two girls making love to each other in a way she had never dreamt she would find so deliciously consuming.

Kay's fingers brushed Maggie's sex, making the breath catch in her throat.

'Trust me, it'll be beautiful,' Kay murmured, taking one of Maggie's hands and gently guiding it between her own legs. Maggie made no effort to resist, but was surprised at just how wet Kay was, her sex hot and seeping creamy silk. She knew this was a present from Max Jordan, a present to them both.

Kay gently guided Maggie's kisses down over her breasts and belly to the shaven mound of her sex. As she pressed kisses to the girl's flesh, Maggie could smell Kay's excitement and feel the ripples of pleasure sifting through her body.

For a moment, lying alongside Kay, her face and lips a fraction away from Kay's fragrant quim, Maggie hesitated, nervous and unsure. She had never been attracted to her own sex, but thanks to Max Jordan all that, and much more, had changed.

'Please,' Kay whispered, lifting her hips towards Maggie's waiting mouth. 'Please kiss me.'

How could she possibly refuse? Tentatively she pressed her lips to the fleshy lips, imaging what the kiss would feel like. Beneath her the girl gasped in delight and lifted her hips to give Maggie greater access, her fingers joining Maggie's tongue, holding her sex open for Maggie's caresses. Slowly, trying hard to still her own fears and doubts as much as anything else, Maggie slipped her tongue into Kay's open sex and licked like an inquisitive kitten, her taste buds suffused by the richly oceanic flavour of Kay's excitement. She let the tip of her tongue ease across the engorged ridge of Kay's clitoris, knowing instinctively that it wouldn't take much to push her over the edge. She nibbled and lapped at the engorged bud, sucking it eagerly.

'Oh...' Kay gasped, and pulled Maggie up to straddle her face. Groaning, the lithe blonde pulled her hips down, so that Maggie had no choice but to settle her own throbbing sex onto the waiting mouth. She immediately felt herself respond to Kay's intense caresses, felt her body accepting them.

When her orgasm came an engulfing wave swept through the two of them, and Maggie trembled uncontrollably with pure pleasure. She fell into a deep and contented sleep, curled up in the other girl's arms.

When she woke in the morning Maggie was alone, fresh sunlight streaming in through the bedroom window. She lay for a few minutes letting all manner of thoughts roll through her head, trying to work out what was real and what was a dream. One by one as the events and memories of the previous evening and night unfolded, she realised that of all of them she was far more embarrassed and confused by what had happened with Simon Faraday than anything else.

Over breakfast Kay didn't mention anything. In fact, she acted as if nothing had happened between them at all.

Fortunately Maggie and Simon's paths didn't cross until the end of the week.

'I really need to talk to you,' he said as she parked in the office car park and hurried across the tarmac to reception. It was first thing in the morning and Maggie had no intention of lingering.

'I've got nothing I want to say to you, Simon, and if you come anywhere near me I'll call security,' she threatened, with considerably more confidence than she felt.

'Oh come on, Maggie, stop playing games with me,' he countered, and she swung round, outraged by the condescending tone of his voice.

'Playing games?' she said. 'What do you mean by that, Simon?'

He shook his head in disbelief. 'Maggie, I know you've been on your own for quite a while, and I know what you like. You've wanted what I gave you for some time now. Don't you deny it,' he said quickly as she opened her mouth to object. 'Girls like you don't know how to ask for what they want, so you need a real man to show you. You've been giving me the come on for months, you know you have.'

She stared at him in total astonishment. Where on earth was all this patronising rubbish coming from? 'Simon, all I've ever done is be friendly towards you,' she stated, trying very hard not to lose her temper completely. 'I've never given you any encouragement whatsoever.' Why on earth was she even talking to the creep?

'What if I said I was sorry?' he said.

Maggie shook her head. 'It would mean considerably more if I thought for an instant that you meant it,' she said.

He glowered her. 'Have you ever considered that you've got some kind of sexual problem, Maggie?'

They were walking through reception, Simon scuttling along just behind her. She was beginning to get really angry, but fighting to maintain her dignity. She didn't want him to see he was getting to her. 'I don't have a *sexual* problem, Simon. The only problem I have is with you; now get out of my face.'

'I was wondering if maybe you're frigid,' he went on regardless, infuriating her, 'only most women find me very attractive?'

Maggie shook her head at the nerve and the arrogance of the man. If only he knew. She didn't bother gracing his incredible, conceited remarks with a reply, and instead stepped into a waiting lift and closed the doors in his face, shaking with rage as it smoothly started to ascend. What a bastard!

When she got to her floor and the metal doors slid aside, she was stunned to see Simon standing there in the corridor, red-faced and out of breath.

'Look, Maggie,' he wheezed, hands on hips, struggling to recover from the exertion of running up four flights of stairs, 'stop fighting me, will you. I wondered if you might be interested in spending a weekend with me in the country, that's all. A friend of mine has a lovely little cottage that we could borrow. It would be great if we could spend some time together.'

She shook her head in amazement. 'Simon, I'm only going to say this once more and then I'm going to lose my patience with you. I'm not interested in you. I've never been interested in you. I'm sorry if you think I've given you the wrong signals at any stage, but trust me, this is not some elaborate game of chase me, chase me. I genuinely don't want to go out with you. Not now, not ever. Is that perfectly clear?'

She couldn't have been more frank, but to her horror he smiled, still utterly undeterred. 'Whatever you say, Maggie.' And then he actually winked! She wanted to slap him. How could he possibly believe this was another round of her playing hard to get?

'Simon, I want you to know that I've found someone,' she said, trying a different tack, but he just shrugged.

'Funny you've only just thought to mention it, Maggie,' he said dismissively. 'But don't worry, I'm a patient man. I can wait.'

As she watched him walk away she wondered if it would ever be possible to have an ordinary relationship again, not with Simon but with any normal man. She suspected there was no way back from the place that Max Jordan had taken her, or the things he had shown and taught her so far.

Part of her was aware that this was only the beginning of her education.

The rest of the day was full and busy. Maggie opened her email, cleared her post, working quietly and effectively through the things on her desk and on the computer without being disturbed again by Simon. But as the day wore on she found it harder and harder to concentrate, wondering if and when she would hear from Max, after all it was Friday, wasn't he supposed to ring her?

Just before five she got a call from reception. 'Courier for you, Ms Howard, with a parcel. Shall we send him up or will you come down and collect it?'

Intrigued, Maggie headed downstairs to pick up what turned out to be a large flat black box tied around with an enormous silver ribbon. The security guy on reception grinned and winked. 'Looks like you're in for a good weekend, miss,' he said.

'Probably just a cake from my mother,' she joked.

The man laughed and handed her the box. On the form attached to it was the name Max Jordan in heavy typeface.

Back upstairs, safely installed behind her desk, Maggie pulled off the ribbons and then had second thoughts.

Although it was quite quiet - those who could had already left for home - maybe it wasn't such a good idea to open Max's present there. Glancing around to see if anyone was watching, she headed down to the women's cloakroom.

Once safely inside a cubicle she pulled off the wrappings. In the box was a black PVC miniskirt, a matching camisole top and high-heeled black boots - and a card that read, *Guido will pick you up at 18:00. The Master.*

It was Friday evening and the main offices were more or less empty. She could get changed and then slip out the back way down the fire escape to the car park without anyone seeing her.

Ten minutes later she stared at her reflection in the cloakroom mirror and smiled; no one who saw her in the PVC outfit would recognise the refined Maggie Howard who wrote magazine home and style articles. The vixen who looked back from the mirror had style all right, but not of the publishable kind. The hem of the tight skirt came to just below the cheeks of her bottom, and the little black top pushed her breasts together and forward, the plunging neckline barely covering her nipples, offering her breasts like ripe fruits. And the boots? Maggie giggled; the boots were wonderful. They emphasised her slim legs and she could only walk by swaying her hips.

Dressed in her play-clothes, Maggie pouted and touched up her mascara and rich red lipstick. Her reflection offered the promise of pure sex. With her eyes still firmly fixed on the wanton image in the mirror she slipped her hand down between her thighs and stroked the moist folds of her sex; she was getting wetter with every passing second. She glanced at her watch, wondering if there was time enough to bring this to its natural conclusion. Meanwhile busy fingers worked over her pleasure bud and she moaned softly as the pressure increased low in her belly. The whore in the mirror copied her move for move, writhing and pressing forward, legs apart, revealing the deep pink of her sex beneath the hem of the skirt. Maggie watched herself, watched her nipples harden within the shiny black top.

Then without warning she gasped for breath as an orgasm overtook her, making her convulse with delight and cry out with pure pleasure, and then she was still, slumped against the basins, trembling with sweet aftershocks.

It was nearly six, time to go and find Guido. Maggie glanced down at the boots and then slipped them off and put on the shoes she'd been wearing for work. At least this way she could hide the rest of her outfit under her coat.

Out in the corridor she hurried towards the fire exit.

'So there you are,' someone called, halting her in her tracks. 'I wondered where you'd got to.'

Maggie groaned inwardly. This was not happening to her. How had Simon Faraday tracked her down this time? He must have her on radar.

As if he was reading her mind, he said, 'I asked the guys on the front desk if you'd already gone home, and they told me you hadn't. What's this then,' he went on, admiring her make-up, 'out on a heavy date with your imaginary boyfriend?'

Up until now Maggie hadn't looked up; she knew exactly what she looked like and had no desire at all to see Simon's lecherous expression.

Simon caught hold of her arm. 'What's the matter?' he demanded. 'A little too near the mark, am I?' He pulled her towards him with a degree of unexpected aggression and her coat fell open.

Simon gasped, his eyes drinking in her mouth-watering appearance. 'What the...?' he began and stepping closer, tipped her face up to his and drooled at the breathtaking look of her.

'Well, well, well, what's going on here?' he said.

Maggie was speechless; what on earth could she say?

Simon grabbed her arms and pulled her closer. 'Well?' he demanded. 'Does your new man like you to dress up like a slut? Is that where you're going now? Maybe you like it a little rough, eh? Maybe our little bit of fun in the shower was just the thing that gets you off? Was it? Tell me, because trust me, I can play that game any time if that's what you want.'

Breathing heavily he pressed her back against the wall, forced his fingers between her thighs and with the other hand he molested her breasts.

'Stop it,' she warned, wriggling away from him, her mind racing. 'Don't you dare touch me. I have some say in this, you know. What I do is my business, not yours. As it is you've got it all wrong. I'm off to do a piece on a fetish club, and I can hardly go dressed in a flowery skirt and blouse, can I? This just arrived and I wanted to try it on, that's all.'

The lie sounded barely plausible, even to her. For a moment Simon froze and his eyes darkened; it seemed she'd hit a raw nerve, but she wasn't sure how or why.

'Are those the kinds of games you like to play then, Maggie?' he challenged. 'Fetish clubs, and things like that.'

'I'm not playing any games,' she snapped. She'd really had enough of obnoxious Simon. 'I've already told you, it's research. Now get out of my way. I'm meeting someone and I don't want to be late.' And remarkably, for once, he did as he was told.

Maggie made her way briskly towards the fire exit, and at no point did she look back to see Simon watching her go, his expression indicating the thoughts forming in his head.

Guido was waiting for Maggie in the car park, and touched his cap as he opened the rear car door, looking at her inquisitively.

'You okay?' he asked, taking her bag as she slipped off her shoes and pulled on the boots.

She nodded, a little bemused that Guido of all people should sound so concerned about her well-being. Looking back at the office block she saw Simon in a window watching the car draw away, and couldn't help wondering just what he was thinking, and perhaps more to the point, what it was he thought he'd discovered.

Chapter Ten

Once well out of town Guido pulled over into a quiet lay-by, got out of the car and opened the rear door.

Maggie looked out at him in surprise. 'What are we stopping for?' she asked.

'You forget the rules so quickly, don't you, Maggie?' he said. 'You're the slave here, remember? You do as you're told, you don't ask questions. Open your coat and get in the front.'

Maggie did as she was told, and Guido pulled a black leather blindfold out of his pocket and slipped it around Maggie's head, snugly over her eyes.

'There, now isn't that better?' he murmured. 'All wrapped up and ready to go. Max's pretty little toy.' He ran a hand over her face and then down to cup her breast, fingers teasing a nipple through the PVC and squeezing it hard until she gasped with pain. With his free hand he pulled the seatbelt across and buckled her in tight.

'You look a real treat, Maggie,' he said, pulling her hands together in her lap and cuffing her. 'Comfortable, are we?'

Maggie winced at the loss of freedom. 'No, of course not,' she said. 'Why are you doing this, Guido? There's no need; you know I'll do whatever Max tells me.'

'Come, come, you must understand that sometimes obeying isn't enough, Maggie. You have to realise that in our world obedience implies you have a free will, that you can choose - where as in fact, Maggie, you can be used, abused, discarded on a whim. The mistake you make is in thinking you have any choice or any power.'

He squeezed a hand between her thighs. 'You don't need to know why you're being bound, just that you are and if you make too much noise or ask too many questions, I'll gag you as well.'

Maggie took a deep breath, trying to settle herself; it didn't do to let her imagination run amok. Guido's hand squeezed towards her sex, and she shuddered as a finger grazed across her sex lips.

'Mmmm, you feel so good.' The finger parted the moist flesh, and Maggie's instinctive reaction was to try and close her knees against him.

'I wouldn't try to resist if I were you,' he threatened menacingly. 'That would be unwise.

'Mmm, you're so tight and so wet, you dirty little bitch,' he went on as her thighs relaxed a little and gave him freer access to her. 'You're lucky Max is waiting for us, or I'd fuck you here and now,' he stated confidently, pressing kisses to her face and throat. 'Maybe I'll fuck you on the back, when he's done with you. What do you think?'

She shook her head, afraid to answer, and from behind the mask she felt him move away, felt his fingers leave her body, then the engine hummed into life and they pulled away.

It was a longer journey than she'd expected, but eventually the car drew to a halt, one of the doors opened, and Maggie immediately heard Max's voice.

'Good evening, Guido,' he said. 'Any problems?'

'None at all, sir,' the driver reported.

'Excellent. I've parked the other car over by the trees.'

Maggie heard some keys exchanging hands and then was aware of Max swapping places with Guido. 'Good evening, Maggie,' he said in a low tone.

She turned unseeing towards him. 'Good evening, master.'

Maggie felt him moving closer, felt his breath on her throat, felt him taking in the details of her appearance. She shivered, aware that every part of her, body and soul, longed for his approval and that in that moment she was totally his.

'You look magnificent, Maggie,' he said, stroking her arm.

'Master, please can you tell me where we're going?' she ventured.

He stroked her cheek and very gently kissed her lips. 'Maggie, you know better than that. You will learn only to speak when spoken to.' He stroked a finger across her lips, and then pushed something firm and hard between them into her mouth.

'Open wider,' he commanded, and Maggie didn't dare do otherwise. 'Did you talk to Guido on the way here?' he asked, and she shook her head.

'Do you know what this is, Maggie?'

She shook her head again.

'It's a leather gag, and unless you learn to be quiet I will make you wear it all weekend. Do you understand?'

Maggie nodded, struggling to swallow.

'Good. Just one more thing.'

She felt the soft leather collar slip around her throat, marking her as his property, although oddly enough far from being intimidated, it gave her a strange sense of comfort.

'There,' said Max, then turned the key in the ignition and the car slowly drew away.

Showered and comfortable in a white towelling robe, her tarty clothing discarded on the floor of the pretty cottage's bathroom, Maggie brushed her hair in the mirror, feeling happy and relaxed.

She went downstairs, where Max sat waiting for her in the quaint lounge, the table set with linen and crystal, champagne chilling in an ice bucket, Guido dressed in livery waiting to serve them.

She looked at Max, aware of how vulnerable she must look.

He smiled at her and extended a hand. 'Come over here, Maggie,' he beckoned. She did as she was told and stood in front of him. He slid a hand up her thigh, beneath the towelling. 'Undo your robe,' he ordered, and she did without a second's hesitation. 'Now take it off.'

Again she obeyed, aware of her nakedness, but aware that above everything else that doing as she was ordered pleased Max. Was this the true nature of slavery?

'Bend over the table,' he instructed, 'and spread your legs.'

Slowly she did, settling herself on the crisp linen, amongst the fine crockery, and even before Max touched her she felt a great wave of desire roll over her. She wanted him, and whatever that wanting brought.

Max ran his hands over her naked back, slid them between her legs, adjusting her position slightly so she was easier to explore. Maggie knew she was wet; she knew she was ready.

Max stepped back to admire his possession. Spread out on the table she looked an absolute feast. He beckoned to Guido, who handed him the crop. He didn't need a reason to punish her. He would punish her because he could. He would punish her because she wanted to.

Maggie was trembling as she waited for whatever was to follow. She didn't look round, but waited patiently. At last she was learning. He studied her, eyes moving appreciatively over the ripe curves of her buttocks, the wetness of her sex, engorged with pure desire. He knew Maggie was expecting him to fuck her - but first there was the matter of a punishment to dispense.

Max drew the crop back and relished the gasp of shock and horror as it found its mark across her bottom. On the table she convulsed as the pain coursed through her, her fists clenching on the fine white linen of the tablecloth.

'One,' she gasped after a few seconds.

'Very good, my dear,' said Max. 'I thought for a moment that you had forgotten the most basic of rules.'

The crop cracked down across the tops of her thighs. 'Two!' she sobbed.

Three and four were slightly less painful, striping the fleshy orbs of her backside. Her skin flushed scarlet under his attentions. Five and six were lower again, making her squeal as they caught the tender flesh. He could hear the tears in her voice as she called out the number of strokes.

He ran a hand over her glowing skin. 'Good girl... only another nine to go.' He felt her shudder as the realisation that there was much more to come hit home, and with it came stroke seven. This time Maggie screamed, giving in to the acute pain.

Eight. Nine. Ten; knowing the end was some distance away, lost deep in the pain. The crop rose and fell, each stroke counted out after the gasp or whimper or shriek in response to the hurt.

'All done,' he announced, having delivered number fifteen with added intensity. He placed the crop beside her on the table, where she could see the implement that had caused her so much discomfort and humiliation. His hands kneaded her raw and angry welts, and Maggie instinctively lifted her hips to absorb his touch. She was grateful for his punishment and even more so for the rewards it brought. Max smiled thinly and without any prelude unzipped his trousers and sank his throbbing cock deep into her cunt.

Maggie gasped and pressed back to encourage him deeper still. Max sighed appreciatively; she was as wet and hot as he had ever known her.

He slid a hand under her belly to seek out her clit, and then pulled her hand down to join his. Maggie writhed as his fingers found the engorged ridge, meeting him stroke for stroke, their bodies working in sexual harmony.

Max felt his orgasm building, coming closer and closer. He felt her sex pulsate around his cock, felt her shiver and writhe beneath him. He grabbed her hair and pulled her up off the table. She cried out his name, her back arching as he clenched his jaw, stabbed with his groin, pinning her hips to the table, and filled her with his seed.

Her sobs of pleasure filled the room, and then she slumped forward again as if fainting.

Chapter Eleven

Maggie woke the following morning, safe in her bedroom back at Max's elegant townhouse; her body marked by the crop, her mind indelibly marked by Max's power over her.

She showered and made her way downstairs, naked except for her collar, for that was all that had been left out for her on the dresser.

Mrs Griffin served breakfast in the dining room overlooking the park, and Max invited her to join him at the table and not, as she suspected he might, on her knees at his feet.

'I'm very pleased with your progress, my dear,' he said, as they sat in the sitting room a little later, drinking coffee and relaxing in each other's company. 'You've come a long way in a remarkably short time, Maggie.'

She smiled at him, basking in his approval. Her body was at his disposable. Her marks were his marks. He sat on the sofa with her legs over his lap, reading the morning newspaper and stroking her thighs, as one might a much-loved cat.

'Your basic training will very soon be coming to an end,' he said casually, not lifting his attention or his gaze from the paper.

Maggie stiffened and felt the colour drain from her face, the sense of well-being evaporating instantly. Surely he couldn't mean what she thought he meant; it was too soon. Max looked at her, his features softening as if he could read her mind.

'My dear Maggie, I explained to you when we first met that my role as a training master is to help find the submissive, the slave within you,' he said. 'I bring it to the fore and then find the way to harness it sexually and emotionally, and I truly believe in your case that has already been accomplished. Look at you, look how far you've come. Am I not right?'

Maggie nodded, although at the same time she could feel her eyes filling with tears. This was not what she expected at all.

'Another couple of weeks and you will be ready to be sold to a permanent master,' he went on. 'A master who will train you as he wants, to his way of doing things. Trust me, my dear, the longer you stay with me the harder it will be for you to make that transition. I have shown you what is possible, what is in your heart, the nature of submission and obedience and the most basic rules, now you need to apply all you have learnt to a more permanent arrangement.' He sipped his coffee, eyes moving very slowly up over her body. 'Some girls take months to get to this point, but you're a fast leaner, a natural, but I knew that the day I first saw you. It is very nearly time for you to move on.'

Maggie knew that what sounded like a compliment was in fact the hastening of the end of their arrangement. She felt an ache in her chest and struggled to hold back the tears. How could she possibly bear to lose what she had only so recently found? 'I... I don't want to go,' she whispered.

Max smiled, stroking her thigh. 'There is no need to worry, you won't just be sold to any old undesirable, I can assure you of that. Our slave auctions are by invitation only, and those who attend are already part of an inner circle of connoisseurs. It's a unique club of carefully chosen members. The auction will take place over a weekend at one of my fellow member's country estate. It will be fine, trust me.'

She looked at him anxiously, and Max leant close and very gently stroked the hair back off her brow. 'Don't look so worried, we have time enough yet, my little one. And you knew this would happen sooner or later.'

Maggie nodded. 'But I thought it wouldn't be for a long time yet,' she began, aware of how vulnerable and needy she sounded. How could she explain to Max that she believed, hoped that their journey together had only just begun, that in some way even though he was her master he was also her guide into a foreign world.

'I have learnt to follow my instinct in these things,' he said. 'But enough of this, tonight I have arranged for us to go to the theatre.'

The theatre? She looked at him in surprise. There were so many things she wanted to ask him, so many things she wanted to say, how on earth could he possibly think of such a thing now?

Max's smile broadened. 'It will be your first formal introduction to some of the most influential members of our club, Maggie. These social events are very important to us - and I know you will not let me down.'

Maggie nodded, trying hard to hide her anxieties.

'Smile,' he said. 'It will be all right. Besides, surely you must know by now that I will always be here for you.'

She stared at him in astonishment, for it was by far the most intimate thing he had ever said to her, but any sense of comfort was short-lived. 'I'm always here for my slaves, Maggie, that is part of my role,' he continued. 'You are the latest in a long line of slaves, but trust me; very few come back for my help. Your fears will pass.

'Now, I have business in town this afternoon, so while I'm away I suggest you rest. It's going to be a long night. When you've rested Mrs Griffin will wake you and help you get ready for your night out.'

'So, all ready to meet the rest of the club, are you?'

Maggie started from her doze to find Guido leaning over the bed. As she tried to move he pinned her arms down and held her tight. Maggie looked round, trying to shake the sleep from her brain and at the same time work out exactly what was going on. The bedroom curtains were drawn but outside it was still daylight, and she sensed she hadn't been asleep for long.

'I'll scream,' she warned, trying to prise him off her.

Guido laughed. 'Really? And what good do you think that would do? Haven't

I already told you that as a slave you're always available for whoever wants to use you for whatever purpose? And besides,' he grinned, eyes alight with mischief, 'your master has gone to pick something up from town, or maybe he's gone to pick up someone. And Mrs Griffin? Well, she's down in the basement doing I don't know what, but trust me, whatever it is she isn't going to hear anything from up here, and that includes you screaming like a spoiled brat.'

'What are you doing here?' Maggie demanded, trying to gain some initiative from him. 'Why aren't you driving Max?'

He shrugged. 'Max doesn't want me with him all the time.' He moved her wrists and held them above her head with one hand, while with the other he pulled down the duvet. She was naked except for her collar.

'Very nice,' he leered, eyeing her body hungrily. 'Now, are you going to do as I tell you or are you going to try my patience?'

Maggie strained against his grip but he held her fast.

Guido's expression hardened. 'Another thing you should bear in mind,' he went on unmoved, 'is that you don't fool me for a second. I know you enjoy being treated like this. I see in you what Max sees: a natural submissive, someone who likes to be dominated, to be vulnerable in the control of others. You might struggle but we both know that you like what's on offer. And when you're up for auction? Word gets around about who is worth bidding for. I don't know what Max told you, but there are some real bastards in that club of his. It wouldn't do for me to put a word in with them about you, now would it?'

Maggie looked up at him. 'You're a bastard too, Guido,' she stated defiantly.

He nodded. 'Oh yes, you could be right. But Max and I both, don't forget that. Don't be fooled by him, Maggie. Max and I are two faces of the same animal.'

She shivered, wondering if it was true, and before she could react Guido pulled a loop of rope from his jacket pocket and slipped it over both her wrists, jerking it tight, wrapping it round and round on itself until she was secured. Not that she resisted him any more; there was little point. Guido's power, like Max's, extended beyond the physical.

Once her arms were tied to the bed-head Guido took his time looking her over again. 'Open your legs,' he ordered. 'We won't do anything too rough for now, after all, Max's friends will have the use of you tonight, so we can't have you too sore, now can we?' As he spoke he secured each ankle to the corners of the bed, opening her legs wide, then pushing a pillow under her hips he stood back to admire his handiwork.

Open, tied down, totally humiliated and ready for him, Maggie closed her eyes; she wasn't even safe asleep in her bed.

'It's such a shame you won't be here too much longer,' he said. 'Just when I was developing a taste for you.' And then Guido shocked her by crouching and lapping at her sex, burying his face tight between her thighs, working his tongue and nose into her, drinking her in. Maggie gasped and tried to wriggle away from him, but where was there to go? Her wrists dragged on the rope as

Guido pulled her onto his tongue, stiff to enter her like a tiny wet penis.

His eyes alight with lust he looked up at her from between her parted thighs, his tongue delving inside her. 'Does Max ever tell you how good you taste?' he mumbled, withdrawing his mouth for a moment. 'How good you smell?' He breathed deep, savouring her fragrance.

Maggie closed her eyes as Guido's fingers joined his tongue, fingers that not only breached her sex but also breached her anus, exploring the most secret parts of her body. He began to slide them in and out, stretching, making her writhe at the intense sensations despite her shame.

'Oh yes, Maggie, I'm going to miss you,' Guido whispered into the soft flesh of her sex, the words dark and resonant, Maggie feeling them as much as hearing them. 'Mind you, knowing Max it won't be too long before he finds a lovely replacement for me to enjoy.'

Maggie shuddered, trying to block out the cruel words, and despite the feelings of shame the passion was beginning to stir, each movement of Guido's tongue and fingers fanning the flames. She cringed, knowing Guido was as aware of her body's response as she was. He mumbled encouragement as she began to move instinctively against his mouth, her sex flooding with traitorous juices of excitement.

Even though tied to the bed her body sought his caresses, lifting as high as the bonds would permit, then she heard Guido snigger hurtfully as he pulled away and she strained to find his tongue.

'You really are a little whore,' he snorted, wiping his chin with the back of his hand.

'I know,' she said, her voice thick with desire. 'Why don't you fuck me, Guido, please?'

'You think I wouldn't?' he said.

Maggie felt his cock pressing at the lips of her sex, felt him trying to find his way into her body, and she, without conscious thought, lifted her hips a fraction to ease his entry. She gasped, still shocked by the way her body demanded satisfaction and pleasure. He stabbed his pelvis forward and sank his cock into her, stretching and filling her. Maggie loved the moment of penetration, the sensation making her shiver with delight, and then she heard a moan of acceptance and knew it was hers.

Guido sat back from her, fingers working over her clit, his shaft moving slow and deep inside her pulsating cunt, relishing the sensation of her body closing around him, while his other hand nipped and pulled at her breasts and nipples. Maggie tried to hold back the growing wave of gratification, tried to fight the heat building between her thighs, but knew it was a pointless exercise, merely delaying the inevitable.

Guido was driving them both relentlessly towards release. Maggie knew it wouldn't be long before both of them reached the point of no return. Above her he threw back his head, forcing himself deep, deep into her, his face contorted with the effort of struggling to withhold his climax, and just when she thought Guido was losing control she felt the waves of orgasm break over her, felt her sex sucking her tormentor dry.

Guido collapsed onto her, gasping for breath, sweat dripping from his face onto the pillow.

'Maybe I should leave you tied up,' he rambled. 'Maybe I should let Mrs Griffin find you like this. Maybe you'd like that... and maybe she would too.'

'No, please,' she whispered wearily, 'please just untie me.'

Guido pinched her nipple.

'So you know about Mrs Griffin then?'

Maggie was confused, just wanting to be left alone now. 'What about Mrs Griffin?'

'Didn't you know she was Max's first ever slave?' he goaded her, grinning broadly. 'I've seen the photographs of when he was training her. He had her pierced here... and here... to mark her as his.' He stroked Maggie's nipples to demonstrate, and then her clit. 'He was younger then, of course, so he thought it better if she went to an older master who could continue her training appropriately. And then a couple of years ago when her master died she came home to her roots. And I just know she'd be delighted to find you all nicely tied up for her. She likes women as much as men; I know that for a fact. Perhaps she likes them even more than she likes men. Would you like me to call her up, so she can demonstrate?'

Maggie pulled on the ropes that held her wrists. 'No, please Guido, please untie me.'

'Why should I?'

Maggie froze. What reason was there? What was there that she could offer him he hadn't already had or could take? Under Max's roof she was a slave, there for the benefit of others. Not Guido's slave, true, but a slave nonetheless, a thing to be used and fucked on the whim of masters and mistresses. And he was right; if Mrs Griffin came in now she was as likely to fuck her as anyone else.

Guido pulled out of her, his flaccid cock wet against her inner thigh. 'Don't worry, Maggie, I won't leave you tied up. We can't have Max's pride and joy getting cramp or rope burns on those pretty wrists or ankles. At least not tonight, not when you're going to be on show.'

With relief she lay back and let Guido untie her, longing for him to leave so she could curl up into a ball and go back to sleep and pretend his visit was no more than a bad dream.

Behind the false mirror Max watched avidly. He didn't like to admit it, even to himself, but seeing Guido fucking Maggie had ignited a little flicker of jealously in his gut. He shook his head. Maybe the sooner she went the better.

In the small bedroom Maggie whimpered as Guido ran his hands over her naked flesh, his exploration demeaning and perfunctory, a parting gesture. Maggie tried to turn away but Guido caught her hair. 'Aren't slaves supposed to do something else?' he asked darkly, jerking her head up towards him.

Maggie stared at him, apparently uncomprehending, so Guido knelt on the side of the bed and ran his limp cock over her cheek, leaving a trail of moisture in its wake. Comprehension dawned on her face, then Guido jerked her head and she drew his cock into her mouth as Max had taught her to do.

'That's better,' Guido sighed as she licked his cock and balls, then he pulled away and let go of her. 'Sweet dreams,' he said, and then left the room.

Guido was close to the end of his training too, and Max would be glad to see the back of him.

It was several hours later that Max watched Maggie walking downstairs towards him in the evening dress he had chosen for her. Boned and cut in a soft velvet, the colour of red wine, it complemented her creamy complexion and emphasised her narrow waist and full hips, the skirt falling like heavy curtain to the floor. She looked almost regal, not a glimmer of the encounter with Guido showing on her face or in her demeanour.

Mrs Griffin had helped her with her make-up, and to dress her hair into a soft bun with tendrils that fell around her face to soften her features. Standing at the bottom of the stairs, caught in the lamplight, she looked exquisite, a possession truly worthy of a man of his status.

Her eyes glittered with delight; she knew she looked good. Max nodded his approval and indicated that she should turn around so he could assess her fully.

'Very nice, but I have a few final touches to add before we leave, my dear,' he said, and produced a small jewellery box from the pocket of his dinner jacket. Inside was a fine black ribbon with a tiny M picked out in diamonds, and matching drop earrings.

'There we are, your dress collar,' he said, as she turned to let him fasten it around her slender throat.

Beneath the dress Max knew she was totally naked, because he had watched her being prepared for him in the false mirror. Watching Mrs Griffin neatly trim her sex, watching Maggie submit to the woman's ministrations, delighted him in ways he could not explain and was the perfect antidote to witnessing her with Guido.

Mrs Griffin knew all about the mirror and had carefully guided her charge to stand in front of it so that when she massaged Maggie's back and breasts with perfumed oils it was as much for Max's benefit as for Maggie's.

Opening the girl's thighs to trim her pubic curls, drawing kohl around her eyes and rich red lipstick around her full lips had all been done with an eye on their unseen audience too, and Max appreciated every second.

As Maggie turned towards him now, eyes demurely downcast he felt a great wave of pride and affection toward her. By now he knew every inch of her body and her mind. For an instant he felt a tinge of regret that she would be leaving so soon, but his instinct told him it was time to move on before she became too attached or perhaps, he thought, worse still, before he did.

'Very good,' he said. 'Now lift up your skirt, there is something else I have for you.'

Maggie blushed and then looked up at him.

Max met her eyes. 'You have something to say, little one?' he pressed, but Maggie shook her head, knowing better than to question his instructions, whatever her thoughts, and did as she was ordered, pulling her skirt up above her waist.

Max nodded and admired what was on show. High-heeled shoes emphasised her shapely legs, and above smooth thighs the ridge of her pubis was oiled and soft and smooth as a silk.

Max took a second box from another pocket, and inside were two lengths of silver chain, fixed together in the middle of one so that they formed a T shape. The length of the T wrapped tight around Maggie's waist, while the other pulled up between her legs, fixed at the front of her belly by a small padlock, with Max's initials embossed on it.

The chain sat snugly between the lips of her sex and between the cheeks of her bottom, fastened to press tight into her flesh.

Max smiled as he tested the tautness by slipping his fingers under the links. It looked exquisite nestled deep in her sex, and he knew it would rub and nip at the delicate flesh every time she moved so that all evening there wouldn't be a moment when she wasn't aware of her subjugation and slavery. He stroked down to the rise of her mons, pressing the chain onto the ridge of her clit. The silver links rubbing gently against her would also make her very wet.

He scrutinised her closely. 'Comfortable?' he asked, and she nodded nervously. 'Good, then drop your skirt back into place; it's time to leave.'

Mrs Griffin picked up a black velvet cape from the hall stand, the lining chosen to match Maggie's dress exactly, and wrapped it around the girl's shoulders. With the hood up she looked enigmatic and mysterious and Max was struck - as he often had been over the years - of the delightful paradox of having a girl as both slave and companion who to the eyes of the world was beautiful and demure, and yet knowing that beneath the sophisticated exterior lurked a slave who would do anything he commanded, whose body and soul were his to possess, to take or to give away as he chose. It was heady stuff.

Maggie settled in the back of the car as they made their way across town, the chain nipping her sex like eager fingers. Max started up a conversation and Guido watched her every move in the rear-view mirror. What would her life be like after the auction? It seemed so cruel to be sold when she had only just acclimatised to Max's way of life.

The light was beginning to fade as they drew up outside the theatre. Guido got out to open the car door for them, touching his cap in a gesture of respect and subservience that Maggie suspected was little more than an act. He caught her eye and winked, and she coloured as Max glanced at her.

'He is nothing,' he stated as they walked to the theatre entrance. 'He may use your body occasionally, but you must understand that's all it is. He has no power over you that you do not give him.'

Maggie stared at him in amazement. 'You know about Guido?' she gasped.

Max nodded. 'Of course I do,' he said. 'I know about everything that does on under my roof. Besides, he is still one of my pupils, just as you are.'

The idea horrified Maggie. 'So will he be a master one day too?' she asked.

Max shrugged. 'Who can say? While Guido is in my service he will receive the training, he will go through the motions, but my experience is that masters are born, not made. I'm not sure he has the right balance of care and control.'

As he finished speaking a man in a dinner suit approached them and smiled. 'Good evening, Mr Jordan,' he said politely, 'how very nice to see you again. Your box is ready.'

'And my friends?' Max asked.

'Most are already seated,' the man informed him.

Maggie looked at the man curiously. Did everyone know about Max, or was this man another member of the club? An usher showed them upstairs to a luxury box where two other men and two women were already waiting for the performance to begin. Maggie didn't need to be told that the women were slaves; their whole demeanour gave them away. Like her they were beautifully dressed in evening gowns, and both had little black ribbons around their throats and sat in silence with eyes downcast.

She shivered, aware that she was glimpsing again the magical doorway into another world. Max indicated that she should sit alongside him, so she did so and sat with her gaze fixed on the floor like her fellow slaves. Max nodded greetings to his fellow theatregoers, and then the orchestra began the overture, making the prospect of any conversation unlikely.

The musical was a lavish production of Hamlet, with a full orchestra adding to the already rich story. As the tragedy began to unfold Maggie looked around at the other people in the box. Both men where in their late forties or early fifties, distinguished and worldly. One of the females was around Maggie's age, whilst the other, a tiny blonde with big blue eyes, looked younger and was quite obviously overawed by their surroundings.

Her master rested a hand on her thigh, and slowly but surely lifted her dress so he could stroke her exposed cunt.

In the boxes opposite Maggie saw that other members of the audience appeared to be slaves and masters too, each of the women wearing the same black band around their throats. Were all these people a part of Max's exclusive club?

In the box alongside theirs was a woman Maggie recognised, dressed in black velvet. It was Freya, and beside her was Beau, wearing a black tie that performed much the same function as the chokers the female slaves wore.

During the interval Max and Maggie made their way to a luxurious anteroom on the same floor, where uniformed staff served champagne cocktails to the twenty or so masters and mistresses and their charges. It appeared that only the masters engaged in conversation with each other.

'So, is this your latest?' said a large man sipping champagne from a glass dwarfed by his huge hand. On his arm was a diminutive brunette, who stood no taller than his chest.

Max nodded. 'Indeed it is, Cedric,' he said.

'And is this the girl you'll be putting up for auction?'

'Yes, but have no fear, you'll get a chance to put her through her paces before the sale.'

The tall man laughed. 'I was sorry to have missed your last house party. I hear Mike's new filly is quite a find, too.'

Max nodded in acknowledgement. 'Indeed she is,' he confirmed, and Maggie blushed as she realised they were talking about the night she had helped Max with Kay. She glanced around the room from the corner of her eye, trying to pick out familiar faces, trying to see if her lodger and her master were there too.

'There will always be another time, Cedric,' Max added.

'Yes, but not necessarily with this one,' he looked her up and down. 'What did you say her name was?'

'Maggie.'

'Maggie...' The tall man tried the name out on his tongue, as if tasting some unusual food. 'How about tonight?' he then suggested. 'I will lend you Bella, if you like. I know you've always had a soft spot for her.'

Max's expression didn't falter. 'Later perhaps,' he declined the offer tactfully. 'We've hardly time during the interval.'

'I suppose not,' the man conceded. 'But I'd like a look at what's on offer.'

Max clapped Cedric on the shoulder. 'You are always so eager, my dear chap,' he chuckled. 'There will be plenty of time before the auction. Now come along and have another glass of champagne.'

Beside him the little brunette's eyes darkened, and Maggie could almost taste her jealousy.

Max guided Maggie towards one of the waiters, but Cedric waved him away. 'Not for me at the moment, I'll catch up with you later,' he said.

Max snorted. 'The man is a pig,' he murmured under his breath. 'He and Bella have been together since she was sixteen. In essence she is his slave and he is her master, but it's well known that she rules his little harem with a rod of iron. If she doesn't like the slave he buys then life as one of Cedric's stable can be a trial by fire. He should sell her; it would do her the world of good to feel the taste of the crop wielded with some purpose.'

Maggie shivered and turned to look at the couple's retreating backs. It hadn't occurred to her that the usual jealousies and insecurities had any place in this strange world. What if Cedric decided to buy her? What would life be like then?

The five-minute bell rang and everyone made their way back to the auditorium, where Maggie again looked around at the faces of the audience as they settled back into their seats. As the lights went down, across the heads of them Cedric smiled and lifted a hand in her direction, and quickly Maggie looked away, not wanting to encourage him. As he caught the gesture Max's hand dropped onto her thigh possessively.

'Don't worry,' he whispered. 'I won't let Cedric have you.'

Maggie shivered, wondering what influence Max had to ensure Cedric was kept at bay, and as the curtain went up for the second half she couldn't help worrying about what the rest of the evening might hold for her.

As the final curtain call was taken and the applause gradually died away Max rose effortlessly. 'Now for dinner, my dear,' he said to her. 'I don't know about you, but I'm absolutely ravenous.'

She had assumed they would be taken on somewhere by Guido; a private house or a restaurant, perhaps, but in fact a uniformed usher directed them back to the anteroom where double doors had been opened onto a luxurious dining room set with candles and linen and cut crystal that glittered magically in the flickering light.

Tables had been set around the room, the centre dominated by a larger table on a raised dais. It was here that Max, Maggie and the two couples who'd shared their box were led. Maggie blushed, feeling uncomfortable as the focus of attention, for all the other diners had taken their seats before she and Max were shown to theirs.

The food was exquisite, the service immaculate, but all the time they were eating, above the buzz of conversation and laughter, Maggie could sense the electricity of expectation in the air. As coffee was served one of the waiters went from table to table with an ice bucket, and each master drew a folded piece of paper from inside. Maggie noticed that when they reached the top table, while the other masters took a piece of paper Max politely declined and the waiter moved on.

Eventually, once all the tables were clear except for coffee cups and liqueur glasses, Max turned to her. 'Maggie,' he said.

She looked at him anxiously. 'Yes, master?' she whispered.

'Get up and take off your dress.'

She cringed inwardly, and for a few seconds stared at him in dismay and horror. Surely he couldn't possibly mean it? Of all the things she'd been expecting this wasn't one of them. There had to be at least forty people gathered in the dining room, not counting the waiting staff. She bit her lip, feeling her colour rise.

Max's expression hardened. 'Well, Maggie?' he pressed. 'Would you prefer that I rip it off you and whip your disobedient little arse until you scream for mercy?'

Slowly, her pulse roaring in her ears, she rose and the hubbub of conversation dropped to a low murmur, and then fell silent completely.

Slowly she reached back and unfastened the zip of the evening gown, feeling the heat of humiliation and embarrassment coursed through her veins as she caught Cedric's eyes. His ruddy face was full of undisguised lust. Slowly she slipped the straps down off one shoulder and then the next, and slid the dress down to reveal her full breasts. Her hands were trembling and it took every shred of courage and self-control not to pull the fabric back up and cover herself.

The dress lowered to her waist and she eased it down over her hips to reveal the chain around her waist and between her legs. There was an appreciative murmur as the dress finally dropped to the floor, and she looked at Max, her complexion flushed crimson.

He took her hand. 'Get on the table,' he commanded.

Maggie let out a tiny whimper, audible only to those around them. Even so, she did as she was told and lay down on her back amongst the remaining silverware and crockery.

'Very good,' he said. 'Now open your legs wide and touch yourself.'

Maggie froze for a moment, but his eyes were broody and she knew there was no going back. 'Stroke yourself, my little one,' he ordered. 'Don't let me down, now.'

Maggie closed her eyes against the shame engulfing her, and sliding a finger beneath the chain began to circle her clitoris. Her sex was embarrassingly wet, her clit already sensitised by the constant rubbing of the chain links.

'Give my friends a little more,' he urge, and with her other hand Maggie began to stroke her breasts, teasing her nipples into rigid peaks. She could feel the eyes of the all people in the room upon her, terrified and mortified and yet in the same instant breathlessly excited by the feeling it ignited in her, the sense of power rippling though her. She began to finger herself more urgently, her thumb working her pleasure bud, and she started moving against the caress, lifting her hips, opening her legs wider still. And against all the odds she felt the pleasure begin to build in the pit of her belly.

'Ask me,' Max reminded her, drawing her out of the dreamy state into which she was falling.

Ask him, her mind urged; ask him now before it's too late. 'Please, master,' she murmured, 'may I come?'

He chuckled approvingly. 'Yes, little one,' he said, and eased a finger deep into her sex. She cried out in pleasure, lifting herself to give him greater access. As she did the first wave of orgasm rolled through her body, and she could feel her sex closing around him and surrendered.

She fucked his fingers like a whore, driving herself on and on to greater and greater heights until finally she could take no more and fell back, all tension gone, lying still, aware again of the eyes on her and the press of the table against her back.

Max stood and stepped away, took an envelope from his pocket and opened it.

Maggie closed her eyes again, unable to imagine what might follow. 'Number seventeen,' he announced to the room, and Maggie stiffened; what did that mean?

There was a general murmur amongst the diners, and then a guffaw of delight from someone on the far side of the room, and then Maggie realised with repulsion that not only was she the cabaret, she was also first prize in the raffle!

With her eyes still closed in a futile attempt to block out what was happening to her, Max handed an unseen master the key to the padlock and cold hands

225

slipped under the chain to unfasten her. 'You're so wet,' drooled a gruff voice. 'Your cunt looks so succulent... good enough to eat...'

Maggie was almost afraid to open her eyes, but she had to, and was confronted by a craggy, elderly man looming over her. Not that his age or appearance mattered, of course; she had no say in the matter; he'd won her and that was his only concern.

'Get up on all fours,' he ordered, and Maggie did as she was told and felt the man struggle up onto the table behind her, heard him unfasten his fly, and felt him push her head down onto the tabletop so that her bottom and sex where presented for him.

'That's better,' he wheezed, his fingers pushing deep inside her, and then she was aware of his cock nuzzling and demanding entry at the engorged entrance of her sex, and of a murmur of approval rippling through the onlookers as he eased his cock into her vulnerable body.

Grunting like an animal he stabbed with his hips and embedded his erection fully inside Maggie, one hand on her hip, the other seeking her swaying breasts to roll and pinch her throbbing nipples. Maggie whimpered against the discomfort, so very shamefully close to an orgasm. Behind her the old man pushed more aggressively and she guessed it wouldn't take much to draw him over the edge. Then just as she began to find his rhythm, accepting her fate and wanting to conclude it promptly, the man slapped her buttocks sharply with a rigid leather paddle. She bucked instinctively and he snorted with delight.

'Ride me, you lovely little bitch!' he guffawed triumphantly, like a jockey driving his mount on to greater efforts. He beat her again, harder this time, and it was obvious to Maggie that her pain excited him. She cried out as he struck a third time, the slaps in time with his ever-quickening thrusts, and then they were both there at the pinnacle and Maggie felt him come, felt his cock throbbing deep, deep inside her, and cried out as the waves of pleasure swamped over her.

Chapter Twelve

'Maggie?'

She looked up from her desk, her mind a million miles away from the bustling offices of the magazine. It was the first day in almost two weeks that Maggie had been back in to work, preferring the peace and quiet and thinking space of working from home. Her prolonged absence meant that there were a huge pile of notes and post in the in-tray for her to sort through, and innumerable messages on the answer machine. Not that Maggie was unduly worried, she had already emailed in the stories and articles she'd been working on, well inside the deadline, so the day had been spent mostly on administration and sorting out ideas for future features and articles with the editor.

Across the desk Simon grinned at her. 'Well, well, well, nice to see you back at long last, Maggie,' he said. 'So how did your research go the other week? Recovered, have you? I've been wondering where you've been hiding. I was going to give you a ring to see how you are. I have to say, your outfit - the one you had on when I last saw you? - it took me by complete surprise. I didn't have you down as the kind of girl who likes fetish gear. Mind you, we live and learn; they always say it's the quiet ones you've got to watch. And I must say,' his voice dropped to a conspiratorial whisper, 'you looked fucking gorgeous in that gear. I could have screwed you there and then.'

Maggie felt her hackles beginning to rise. This was getting ridiculous. 'Please go away, Simon,' she said bluntly. 'I'm really busy, and I don't want to talk to you.'

He blew a lurid kiss at her. 'Oh come on, baby,' he went on, totally undeterred. 'You and I have got unfinished business together.'

Maggie sighed. 'I don't think so, Simon,' she disagreed. This was getting way beyond a joke, and as she spoke she surreptitiously turned the computer screen away from him and clicked the mouse so that the email she had just been reading disappeared behind other pages. It was the thing she feared most - the email from Max Jordan with details of the forthcoming slave auction. It seemed that every time she had any dealings with Max at work they coincided with running in to Simon.

'Look,' he said, his voice still lowered so no one else could hear their conversation. 'We just got off on the wrong foot, that's all. I'm very attracted to you; you must know that. I only want to know you better, that's all. Why not give it a chance, Mags? Let's start over, shall we? What have you got to lose? You looked bloody fantastic in that PVC outfit, and I'd have sold my soul to have taken you out that night.'

Deep down she was pleased to have made such an impression, it was just a shame that she had no other feelings for Simon other than immense dislike and pure annoyance. He was like a mosquito that kept buzzing around bugging her, but for the sake of good manners she made every effort to keep her expression and her tone as neutral as she could manage. 'Simon, I keep telling you I'm not interested,' she reiterated. 'But you just don't seem to get it, do you? So I'm going to lay it on the line one more time. I'm not interested in you, and I've already told you that I'm already seeing someone else, and if you persist in harassing me I'm going to make a complaint. Now is *that* clear enough for you?'

It wasn't quite all true, but she was hoping it would deter him from harassing her.

'Really?' Simon said sceptically, ignoring the threat. 'That's all very convenient. So tell me again, where did you find him? In a lonely-hearts ad? Or did a friend take pity on you and fix you up with some no hoper.'

It was all Maggie could do not to slap his smug face. 'That's it; I don't want to talk to you, Simon,' she said, reaching the end of her tether. 'I've got a few more things to do here and then?'

'And then you're off home to see your imaginary boyfriend?' he said with an infuriating grin, and then sauntered back off across the office.

Maggie looked away, not trusting herself to say anything. Things were bad enough already. Max's instructions to her were explicit. Guido was to pick her up from her house the following day, Friday, at lunchtime. She was to ensure to keep the whole weekend and Monday free. There would be an exhibition on the first evening, when the various lots up for sale would be put on view for the masters, mistresses, and any guests to examine, and then they would be put through their paces for anyone who requested it. On Saturday morning the viewing would continue and then after lunch the sale would begin in earnest.

Maggie stared at the computer screen, a great wave of grief and nervousness rising in her chest. She had come so far over the last few weeks since meeting Max, without him the journey undertaken would have been impossible. He had become such an important part of her life and she feared losing him almost more than she feared the unknown.

Maggie glanced up at the office clock; by this time tomorrow she would be well on her way to the mysterious location, just a lot in a slave auction, numbered, catalogued and ready to be sold to the highest bidder. She shivered and tried to still her panic by turning her attention back to the practicalities. The email said she was to wear a long coat, black stockings and her collar - nothing else. Guido would have the rest of her outfit when he collected her. If she was honest with herself, Simon Faraday and his unwanted attentions were the last of her worries.

'How on earth do I get into this?' she asked, looking at Guido, who had arrived promptly with a black cardboard box tied around with a huge red ribbon.

In her hand was a black rubber corset with attached suspenders, cut to support her breasts but not quite cover them, and it was open at the crotch to reveal her sex lips. Guido handed her a container of talcum powder.

'Dust plenty on yourself and in the corset, and then roll it up and pull it on,' he instructed her. 'When you're done I'll polish you.'

They were standing in the hallway of her house, with an overnight bag at her feet, and it occurred to Maggie that Guido fully expected her to dress in front of him. It was strange how things had changed. She slipped off her raincoat under his watchful gaze, praying he didn't want to fuck her before they left. Knowing that Max wanted her to make him proud she had carefully oiled her body and meticulously trimmed her pubic hair, just as Mrs Griffin would have prepared her had they been at his house. Make-up and perfume carefully applied, she was aware of the paradox of wanting to please Max and yet at the same time knowing that each passing minute drew her closer and closer to losing her place with him.

Guido watched with icy amusement as she wriggled into the tight rubber corset, helping her pull it up over her hips and ribs and then breasts, easing the straps up over her shoulders and then with a soft cloth and a little spray canister buffing the latex to high shine. Maggie looked at herself in the hall mirror, the stretchy material seemed to hold her in and push her out in all the right places, making her breasts appear full and ripe above a narrow waist and rounded hips.

Guido's hands moved appreciatively over her tightly encased frame, and stopped buffing long enough to slip a hand between her thighs. 'It suits you,' he said, dropping to his knees to help her fasten the suspenders to the tops of her stockings.

His close attention caused her to blush. 'Who is going to be at this auction, Guido?' she asked anxiously. 'Will Kay and Mike be there, and all those people from the theatre?'

He looked up at her. 'Probably, and a lot of the others besides,' he confirmed. 'And the old guard as well, members who only come out of the woodwork to take a long hard look at the new blood.'

'And where is this place we're going to?'

'My, my, but we really are nervous, aren't we?' he mocked. 'It's a place up north, a country estate owned by Sir Hugh. He and Max are old friends, they go back a long way. He's a good man, and if you're lucky maybe he'll buy you. Or maybe you could persuade Max to give you to him as an early Christmas present.'

Maggie felt her eyes filling up with tears. How could she possibly tell Guido that she had barely slept the night before worrying about what might happen to her, wondering where she might end up and with whom. She had no idea what the rules of the game were. Then to her total surprise Guido straightened up and put his arm around her. 'Don't worry,' he said comfortingly, pulling her close. 'It'll be all right.'

'I don't know if it will, Guido,' she said openly. 'Where's Max? Why isn't he here too?'

'He's gone on ahead to help with the arrangements. But really, you shouldn't get upset. This is the way it goes. Max will make sure it works out all right for Maggie. He's got a knack with this sort of thing. All his girls have ended up okay. Honestly, his slaves command a high price, and you're one of his all time favourites. You'll be just fine. Max will see to it.'

Maggie was grateful for his kindness, even if she suspected it would be short-lived. Guido looked at his watch. 'Come on, you better get your coat on, we've a way to go yet.'

He was right. The drive to Sir Hugh's country estate seemed to take hours. Maggie's skin felt hot and damp under the rubber corset and her coat. As cityscapes gave way to rolling countryside and lush green hills, she watched fascinated, lulled into a waking doze by the constant movement of the car as the miles unfolded. On one occasion as the car swung out to overtake a lorry Maggie, disturbed awake by the manoeuvre, shifted position and realised how hot and uncomfortable she was in the corset.

Guido smiled at her in the rear-view mirror. 'Why don't you take your coat off?' he suggested.

For once she agreed with him, and oblivious to what sort of image she presented in the back of the car she slipped it off, curled up on the backseat with the coat under her head and let sleep claim her.

Eventually the car slowed and Maggie opened her eyes just as they drew up to a huge pair of wrought-iron gates. Guido slowed to a crawl while a camera on the wall scanned them thoughtfully, its single critical eye watching them closely. Slowly, haltingly the gates creaked into life, and once moving swung open silently, allowing them to drive on to the estate.

The avenue that led to the house swept in through a copse of trees, finally opening out onto a dramatic vista - an old country house surrounded by a moat and acres of rolling parkland, with a herd of red deer grazing under some distant oaks. Maggie gasped. It was far, far grander than anything she had anticipated.

It was built on a great square. Outbuildings and walls with turrets and castellations led the eye to the main house where ornate formal gardens flanked each side of the main entrance, which was reached over a drawbridge.

'Impressive, huh?' said Guido, as they drove slowly along the sweeping avenue to the house.

It was quite an understatement.

'We're staying here?' gasped Maggie, dragging her coat on; there was no way she wanted to arrive wearing nothing but the exotic rubber corset.

'No, don't cover yourself up,' Guido stopped her. 'That's the whole point of you wearing it; Max will want to show you off.'

They rolled in under the main gates, which were topped with the family crest, under the heavy wooden portcullis and across the gravelled quad to the entrance where Maggie could see Max waiting. Guido opened the rear door of the car and told her to wait, although it was all she could do to stop herself from running up the stone steps and into her master's arms.

Standing to one side of Max was a very distinguished man who Maggie guessed was their host. Guido took a fine leather lead out of his jacket pocket, snapped it to Maggie's collar and then led her, wearing only the black rubber corset, stockings and high heels up the steps of the house, where he handed the lead to Max.

For the moment Maggie was oblivious to her appearance. She could see the pride on Max's face, and wanted nothing more than to please him, even though it struck her that his was not the look of a lover but of a collector, delighted by the impression his possession would make on others.

Their host smiled. 'Well, damn me, Max, if you haven't done it again, although I suppose after all these years I should expect nothing less.'

'Thank you, Hugh, would you care to inspect her?'

'A little preview?' the man mused appreciatively, eyeing Maggie up and down, and a good slave to her master, she kept her eyes respectfully downcast. 'Yes, of course, that would be most agreeable.'

Max tucked the looped end of the lead between her teeth and she stood as she'd been taught, very still with her hands behind her back, feet apart so that Sir Hugh could examine here.

'What very nice breasts,' he said, cupping first one and then the other in his palms, brushing the nipples with his thumbs, the treacherous little buds hardening instantly under his touch. 'Very nice indeed.' He nodded appreciatively and dropped a hand to her flat tummy, and then lower to the mound of her sex, a single finger parting the wet lips of her quim, working lower to enter her.

'Hmm... nice and tight here,' he considered. 'And what about her delightful bottom?'

'You'll find it's in a similar condition,' Max assured him. 'She might need a little stretching yet if one would want to use her regularly, but she is very willing, very eager to please, and very nicely spirited, too. She's actually good company, unlike some I've trained. What more could a devoted master want?'

Sir Hugh nodded sagely, his eyes narrowing as he considered and concurred with Max's words. Then he withdrew his finger and touched it to his lips, then sucked it, appearing to savour the taste and fragrance like a connoisseur considering a fine wine or a Cuban cigar.

'But is she presentable?' he asked, his eyes holding hers as he addressed Max.

'That goes without saying, Hugh.' Max took Maggie's lead again. 'Now would you object if I took her upstairs and got her settled?'

'Good God, not at all man!' Sir Hugh bellowed good-naturedly. 'Thank you for letting me have first view of your latest acquisition. I'll see you later - I promised Monty that I'll try out his new pony team.'

As he left Max stroked her cheek. 'Well done,' he said. 'I know Sir Hugh, and I know you made a good impression on him.' The compliment made Maggie feel warm inside and surprisingly secure, considering where they were and why they were there. 'Now, we have a suite in the west wing. I suggest we go upstairs, unpack, have a little something to eat and then explore the house. There are things here that will be very new to you. The whole house, in fact the whole estate, is a hedonist's paradise. The auction always generates a lot of interest and even those who aren't buying or selling like to come along and, well, exhibit, meet old friends, catch up, show off a little. But before we put you on the block there are some things I'd like you to see.'

Maggie looked at him questioningly, knowing her expression betrayed her apprehension.

Max pulled her close to him. 'Don't be afraid, my little one,' he comforted. 'I won't let anything happen to you that you're not ready for.'

Maggie held her tongue; despite wanting to tell him that she wasn't sure if she was ready for anything the rambling house may have in store for her.

Inside the main door the hall opened up into a huge galleried space. Even though it was summer a log fire burned in a large fireplace. The area was lined with panelling and hung with ancestral portraits, and she could see the family resemblance between the faces depicted in the oil paintings and Sir Hugh. It was a magnificent reception area that implied permanence and a sense of unbroken husbandry.

In stark contrast to the gravitas of the surroundings, on stone plinths either side of the fire stood two iron cages, like oversized bird cages, and in each was standing a naked man, hooded, wrists manacled together behind their backs. Their cocks and balls were encased in a series of leather and metal hoops that held them in a state of semi-erection. Beside one cage a tall bald man dressed in a white ball gown and silver high heels was feeding one of the caged slaves grapes on the end of a long stick.

In open-mouthed awe Maggie followed Max towards the sweeping staircase, finding it impossible not to glance to one side through open double doors into what looked like a ballroom. It was full with people, some naked, some dressed, the general hubbub drifting out to meet them. That gave her some idea of how big an event the auction was. The hall seemed to be full of people mingling, talking - masters, mistresses and their slaves, dressed in all manner of costumes or naked except for collars and chains.

Max, following her gaze, smiled. 'All in good time, my dear,' he said. 'All in good time. Let's go upstairs and get settled first.'

Maggie hadn't realised how hungry she was until she got to the room. In a handsome suite that overlooked the deer park someone had laid out a cold buffet on one of the side tables. She must have looked at the delicious spread with hungry eyes, for Max, taking a crop from the desk, said, 'First things first, my dear. First things first...'

He approached her. 'I am delighted to see you're correctly dressed,' he said. 'I want you well marked before you go on the block tomorrow.' He indicated the sofa. 'Now bend over.'

Maggie hesitated; she had a love-hate relationship with the crop, and other implements Max used on her. She hated being beaten and yet at the same time she loved it. It was a shock to know that it turned her on in a way like nothing else did. She realised with a terrible sense of surety that anticipating her punishment, enduring it, and revelling in the memory of it afterwards was one of the most exciting parts of her relationship with Max. It was a symbol quite unlike any other of just how much she was prepared to give to him. Combined with the sexual pleasure and sense of total submission and humiliation this subtle game was quite unlike anything she had ever experienced.

She took a deep breath, turning her thoughts inward, gathering herself in some secret place that allowed her to relish and ride the pain. She heard the crop cut through the still air and gasped as the leather cracked raw and angry across her buttocks. 'One!' she snorted. He hit her harder than she'd anticipated and the first stroke brought tears to her eyes.

'There is no need to count, my dear,' he informed her, and she wondered if that meant he would go on until she could take no more?

The crop found its mark again. This time Maggie shrieked, but before she could recover he hit her again. After six his fingers massaged the glowing flesh, a mixed blessing for although she was delighted by his touch, at the same time rubbing made the blood flow all the faster through the welts.

At twelve he stopped again and Maggie whimpered, rubbing her head against his steadying arm.

'I'm going to miss you so much, Maggie,' he stated, and held the crop out for her to kiss.

Stunned, she murmured her thanks, her heart aching.

Max helped her to her feet. 'Now go and tidy yourself up and eat, we have a long night ahead of us.'

He smiled indulgently while she ate a very late lunch. As she gazed out of the window a small cart trundled by on the gravel path below, and then another. Maggie watched them, and then realised with a start that they were being pulled by women - heavily built naked women, with plumed headdresses, harnesses and bells, trotting in step, whipped on by a liveried driver. They were matched pairs and fours, some blinkered, all turned out as smartly as any show ponies she had ever seen.

Max stood behind her and handed her a glass of champagne. 'Pony girls,' he said, in answer to her unspoken question. 'They are Sir Hugh's particular passion... those two in the front are identical Swedish twins. All trained, bred, beaten, treated as close to the real thing as he can manage. He likes more sophisticated creatures for the house, although in other most households pony girls double as house slaves or bed mates.'

'Will I end up as a pony girl?' she asked uneasily.

Max shook his head. 'Unlikely,' he said. 'Possible, but unlikely. You'll be sold as a companion body slave. A decorative creature to share a discerning man's bed and maybe his life.'

Max adjusted the rubber corset so that her buttocks were shown off to their best advantage, the marks of the crop still red and fierce, and then he rolled down the bra cups so that her breasts were fully exposed.

Maggie stared at him as he picked up the crop again. He smiled thinly and she cringed. 'Put your hands behind your neck,' he ordered, and Maggie felt an icy chill grip her, guessing what was to follow.

He stroked the loop of the crop under her chin and then said, as if to still the anxiety and fear in her eyes, 'Six quick strikes, they will hurt and then they'll be done. Do you understand?'

Maggie nodded and closed her eyes in readiness. He was right, they were quick, they did hurt and she screamed as the crop cut across her delicate flesh.

'That looks better,' he said as she squirmed into his arms for comfort. 'Now finish your lunch.'

Half an hour later Max clipped on Maggie's lead and led her back downstairs. Nervous and extremely apprehensive, she felt quite overawed by her surroundings.

On low dais and plinths in the ballroom were all manner of things to bemuse and amuse and electrify the senses. On one was an oiled, naked man, manacled to a great cross. Behind him a muscular coloured master dressed in leather shorts and a full facemask applied a whip with force, raising great welts on the slave's golden skin.

On another dais a small muscular man was hog-tied and suspended from an ornate metal frame. On yet another stood a petite Eurasian girl entirely covered in tattoos, her expression icy cold and empty.

'Are these people all for sale?' Maggie whispered in amazement.

Max's eyes narrowed venomously and Maggie knew she had broken one of the fundamental rules and spoken without permission, but even so she was still horribly curious.

'No,' he snapped, 'some are here for their masters and mistresses to show them off. To put them through their paces, to let us all enjoy their special tricks and skills.'

He pointed across the room to where two beautiful blonde girls in plumes stood strapped into the little cart Maggie had spotted earlier. On either side of the magnificent hearth, in wicker baskets, were two redheaded youths, sitting to attention like two well trained and perfectly matched dogs.

In one corner a large man dressed in no more than leather cuffs and a thong was juggling melons, while alongside him a naked female contortionist, collared and at the end of a fine silver chain, had the undivided attention of at least a couple of dozen men. On a stage three male slaves had weights attached to their balls and a man was taking bets on who would last the longest before calling enough.

They walked slowly along rows of human exhibits, until they finally got to an area that Maggie began to realise was for sale lots.

Eventually it seemed they had reached their destination, where stood a row of women chained to blocks, dressed much as she was in some nominal garment that barely covered their bodies. They were of all sizes and ages, the only common denominator that they all wore collars and were chained to the little dais upon which they stood.

Max led Maggie to an empty dais at the end of the row, and she began to tremble as several of the browsing masters, each with a catalogue in hand, turned their attentions to her.

Max snapped her lead into a ring on the surface of the low dais. 'Don't panic,' he told her. 'I won't leave you and I'll be here tonight if you need me.' Maggie suddenly felt sick and faint. Although she wanted more than anything to please him and show him she was a good slave, this was almost more than she could bear. Her loyalty was to him, and she couldn't imagine being with any of the others who approached the dais and looked her over like prime horseflesh. Would one of these men be her eventual keeper?

'Very nice,' said one of them to Max. 'May I?'

Max lifted a hand in a gesture of invitation. 'You know the rules, Rupert,' he said warmly. 'You may touch but no more. If you would like more then you must register your request with the auctioneer.'

Maggie watched the men come and go from lowered eyes. It seemed they were allowed to inspect her, ask her to turn this way and that, look and carry out a perfunctory inspection, but no more. Max answered what questions they asked, although she guessed that as soon as he felt she was settled he would leave her to her own devices to go and look at what else was on offer.

And she was right, for eventually he nodded and made his way back into the crowd.

Alone and unguarded Maggie kept her eyes demurely downcast, trying hard not to attract attention to herself. She heard one of the men explaining to his companion that if a would-be purchaser wished for more access to any of the lots then their name was added to a list under the lot number. Then the auctioneer decided who got what for the night and whether such an encounter was public or private.

Maggie had finally begun to settle a little when a group of men came in through the double door. They made a noisy entrance, at odds with the polite hum and murmur of conversation that filled the hall. The noise made everyone look up, and instantly Maggie realised with horror that amongst the new arrivals was none other than Simon Faraday!

She immediately dropped her gaze again as she saw him scanning the room, wishing she could make herself invisible. This couldn't be happening. There had to be a mistake. Maybe it was someone who closely resembled him.

She peeped again and then quickly down. No, there was no mistake. It was most definitely Simon Faraday. How on earth could he be there? How was it possible? Simon Faraday showing up was the most unbelievable and worst thing that could possibly happen.

To her horror he caught sight of her, his eyes widening momentarily, and then he smiled triumphantly and sauntered over. He didn't speak, not a word, but instead he arrogantly looked her up and down.

Casually he cast his eye down at the list of bids, marked something on the sheet and then moved away without so much as a word or a backward glance. Maggie shuddered, instinctively aware that there was no way this would be the end of it.

A little while later a man dressed in dark green livery came up to the block. He had a chain fastened to his waist on which hung a large key ring, weighed down with dozens of keys, one of which Maggie assumed would open the lock that attached her lead to the plinth.

'You've been selected by one of our patrons to keep him company for the night,' he said as he bent to unlock her, then straightened up, his eyes greedily devouring her vulnerable beauty.

Maggie suspected that he had his fair share of the goods on show when the masters and mistresses weren't looking. She bit her lip anxiously and glanced around the room, searching for Max, trying to guess who'd had enough influence to secure her already. She had assumed the decisions were made at the end of the day.

He jerked the leash and pulled her down to his level. 'Maybe I'll try you out myself,' he hissed, 'when the master has done with you.'

Maggie shuddered as he slid a cold hand over her thigh and cupped her sex. 'Nice tight arse, nice tight cunt, that's what it says in your auction notes,' he leered, licking his lips. 'Wouldn't mind trying you out for myself...'

Before she could react he clipped a pair of handcuffs on her, then against a backdrop of appreciative looks and comments he led her through the crowd. She reddened, trying hard to block out the crude comments and avaricious stares. It seemed that everyone knew where she was destined, if not with whom. As they reached the doorway she looked around again, frantically trying to spot Max amongst the sea of faces. Did he know she was being taken away? Had he given his permission? Her stomach tightened into a tangled knot of disquiet.

The man led her upstairs, keeping ahead of her so that the lead stayed taut between them. On one of the landings he knocked on an ornate door, and waited for permission to enter.

'Come in,' called a muffled voice, and Maggie took a deep breath to try and steady her nerves. Oddly enough, in some ways it reminded her of her first encounter with Max. Maybe it wouldn't be so bad after all...

'Well, well, just look who we have here,' gloated a familiar voice, and Maggie froze in horror, her worst fears - the ones she'd been trying hard to suppress - confirmed. 'Fancy meeting you here.'

Simon Faraday was lounging on a leather sofa, a glass of wine in his hand. Another man stood by the fireplace leering at her, both of them looking the worse for drink.

Simon beckoned her closer. 'I genuinely had no idea until I saw you up on the dais that you were involved in our little club,' he said. 'I must be slipping. I knew Max had a new slave in his stable, but I had no idea it could be you. Small world, isn't it, eh Maggie?'

Maggie kept her eyes firmly fixed to the floor as the man who'd delivered her to the suite unlocked her wrists and tucked the lead between her lips.

'Nothing to say for yourself?' Simon taunted. 'My, my, my, isn't that something? I think this is the quietest I've ever known you. Now strip, I want to see again what's on offer. One fumbled fuck on the bathroom floor hardly counts as a fair appraisal.'

Maggie was quite unable to move, and then she heard another familiar voice. 'You know better than to behave like this, young lady,' said Max Jordan, and she glanced round in astonishment to see him sitting in the window seat sipping a glass of champagne. She almost cried with relief, even though his expression was stern. 'Don't keep my associate waiting.'

Reluctantly, feeling somewhat betrayed, she unfastened the suspenders from the stockings and peeled down the corset. Simon nodded his approval, indicated she should turn around, and Maggie did so, aware of his eyes crawling over her flesh.

Putting down his wine, rising and stepping closer, he smiled. Maggie waited, and then without warning he reached out and snagged his fingers in her hair, pulling her close, kissing her aggressively. 'I'm going to make you wish you'd been more cooperative with me,' he threatened ominously. 'We all know that Max spends a long time getting the best out of his girls, a mixture of cruelty and kindness pushing the limits. Let's see just how far you've come, shall we? And if you're really lucky, well, who knows what tomorrow might bring? I could do with a new slave.'

He sniggered and dragged her through into the adjoining bedroom, where he threw her on the bed, slightly knocking the wind out of her. His silent companion followed them in and closed the bedroom door, separating her from Max.

She gasped for breath. 'Don't hurt me, Simon,' she pleaded miserably. 'I'll do whatever you want, I promise.'

'Oh, I know you will, it's just a shame you didn't think of that earlier.' He grabbed her breasts, squeezing them tight until she gasped with pain. A part of her believed that any moment now Max would come in and rescue, but realistically she knew he wouldn't. But nevertheless his presence meant that Simon wouldn't go too far, she was sure of that, and retribution would be milder than he might inflict if left to his own devices.

'Get on the bed and lie on your front,' he ordered. 'I'm going to show you just who is the real master around here.'

She did as she was told, trembling as Simon and his unknown friend bound her hand and foot, tying her down spread-eagled on the brocade quilt. Then Maggie heard something cut the air and screamed in shock as a cat-o'-nine tails exploded across her buttocks.

'Shall I gag her?' asked his companion, his tone sinister.

'No, no,' Simon stopped him. 'I like to hear her scream.'

Maggie's body convulsed as he struck again, the spiteful leather fronds wrapping around the soft flesh of her thighs and flanks. There was no mercy and she cried out again and again as the cat found its mark. At last he was done and untied her, pulled her up onto all fours and without ceremony fed his throbbing cock deep into her cunt; an act of glorious conquest.

Maggie was too tired and too shocked to resist him. He pulled her back against his groin, thrusting deeper and deeper, and then he bucked twice and filled her with his seed. Then rolling to the side onto his back pulled her down to him, smiling as he stroked her hair away from her tearstained face.

'I think my friend has need of you now,' he said. 'And then I'm going to roll you over and lick your little cunt until you scream for me to stop. You need to get used to my friend and the things we both like. I intend to bid for you at the auction, so just think, by this time tomorrow you could be all mine.'

As Maggie tried to absorb the enormity of what she'd been fearful of hearing, she felt the other man clamber onto the bed behind her. He slipped his fingers into her wet sex, and then smeared Simon's sperm and her juices up over the tightly puckered closure of her bottom, and she gasped as he probed with his cock and eased it into her tight rear passage.

Beneath her Simon smiled victoriously, and then got up onto his knees, and

237

holding the back of her head he pressed his flaccid cock to her mouth. 'I want you to clean me up now, bitch,' he ordered. 'Just like Max taught you. Suck me, and who knows, by the time my friend here is finished with you I might be ready to fuck you again myself.'

Chapter Thirteen

When Simon and his quiet friend were done with Maggie, Max Jordan clipped her lead on and took her back to his suite. Although she was sore and tired, as soon as the doors were closed behind them she felt the tension easing, but it seemed her ordeal was not quite over.

Max slid his belt from the loops of his trousers. 'I'm very disappointed with you, Maggie,' he said, folding the belt in two.

She was about to protest, but knew it was pointless and would make things worse, not better.

'I thought you understood the first rule a good slave learns is total obedience?'

She nodded, but he grabbed her hair and pulled her head back so that he was looking deep into her eyes. 'It's not good enough, my dear. You know better than to nod. What is the first rule a good slave learns?'

'Obedience, master,' she said, gasping as he jerked her head back further still.

'And trust? Haven't I told you that I will always look after you?'

'But what if Simon buys me at auction tomorrow?' she protested, oblivious now of the punishment she might incur for speaking without permission.

Max snorted and shook his head. 'Relax, Maggie, Simon isn't the only one with friends in high places.'

'But he managed to get me taken to his room tonight.'

Max smiled knowingly. 'Indeed he did, my dear. And how do you think he did that?'

Her eyes widened in terrible comprehension. 'You?' she gasped. 'You arranged for Simon to have me?' If this had been a test then Maggie knew she had failed miserably. 'I'm so sorry,' she whispered meekly.

'You know that slaves aren't allowed to be sorry; it implies they have self-will. So now you have to beg forgiveness, young lady.'

She looked up at him, eyes brimming with tears. 'Please, master,' she whispered, 'forgive me, please.'

Max stroked her face. 'You are very special to me, Maggie, but you know the rules. Get on your hands and knees.'

She did, trembling furiously, but even so she had a sense of relief; with Max she did understand the rules, she knew exactly what was expected and against all the odds she did trust him implicitly - it was the rest of the world she doubted.

Max ran a hand over her bottom as if to settle her. Then Maggie heard the belt cutting through the still air, heard the gasp, felt the red-hot glow of pain as it spread through her body, fused with the sense of well-being, of coming home, of being safe.

The belt found the mark again, this time she shrieked and as she did Max hit her harder and then harder still, on and on until she was lost in the overpowering sensations.

When he was done Maggie heard the belt drop to the floor, heard the sound of his zipper and an instant later the drive of his raging cock sinking into her sex, and then she cried out in a mixture of discomfort and pleasure as he pressed fully into her. She threw back her head and cried out his name, sobbing with pure delight as he drove into her again and again.

While Max fucked her, cruelly forcing his cock deeper and deeper into her cunt, Maggie moved with him, hungrily desperately. For all the world it felt to her as if he was claiming back what, at least until tomorrow, was his.

Hours later Maggie woke in Max's bed, curled up in his arms, his hand cupping her breast, his breath warm and reassuring on the back of her neck. For a moment or two she felt at perfect peace, until her mind cleared and she realised that today was the day of the auction.

What if Max was wrong? What if Simon somehow managed to buy her after all? What if some unknown buyer stepped in? What would her life become without Max Jordan?

She closed her eyes, praying for sleep to reclaim her but her stirring had disturbed Max. For the last time she turned slowly in his arms and wriggled down the bed, he turned sleepily to allow her to move and then gently she drew his flaccid cock into her mouth.

It was bliss, he was soft and warm, the skin of his sleeping cock like silk against her tongue and yet still with the promise of more. Slowly, very slowly he began to harden at the same time as stirring into wakefulness. Max moaned with pleasure as she stoked his balls, paying special attention to the sensitive area between them and his anus. He murmured, opening his legs to give her greater access.

Eagerly she licked up over his shaft, and when he was powerfully rigid she eased onto her side, pulled one leg up, and still warm from sleep and barely conscious he guided his cock into her from behind, her body opening to him like a blossoming flower.

He thrust deeper, groaning softly as her body welcomed him. 'That feels good,' he whispered, voice still thick with sleep. 'I'm going to miss you, Maggie,' he mumbled, and inched deeper still. Maggie shivered as he pulled her hips back to him, his desire increasing with consciousness. As he began to find his rhythm she struggled to hold back the tears. After a few moments he rolled onto his back, bringing her with him, still joined, so that she was on her back, lying on him. 'Touch yourself, Maggie,' he whispered, moving her fingers over her clit while still easing in and out of her.

Her body hummed as her fingers echoed in time with the rhythm of his thrusts. She began to gasp for breath, feeling her sex tighten around his thick shaft, driving them both forward into oblivion.

A while later, showered and perfumed and exquisitely made-up, Maggie followed Max down into to the ballroom, dressed in a black silk basque, seamed black silk stockings and high heels. The basque, a final present from Max, emphasised her narrow waist and rounded hips, the suspenders framing her naked sex. She knew it was a look he favoured.

Max walked slowly down the stairs and into the melee in the large room, letting the gathered purchasers take a long hard look at his prize possession. Maggie kept her eyes down at the floor as they made their way amongst them, three paces behind him wearing her collar and leash. He led her backstage where a line of girls was already waiting in silence, their eyes wide with trepidation and nerves.

Max smiled and stroked her cheek. 'If ever you need me,' he said, 'simply give me a ring. You still have the mobile I gave you?'

Maggie nodded, unable to find the words she longed to say.

'Good,' he said. 'Well, in that case I have to leave you now.'

'Leave?' she echoed timorously, and as she spoke the man who'd delivered her to Simon the day before pulled her into line, unfastened her collar and handed it back to Max. 'W-what do you mean, leave?' she stammered as the man slipped another plain leather band around her throat. 'You didn't say anything about leaving.'

'You really must learn to be quiet, Maggie, it's going to get you into so much trouble,' Max said, taking the collar the old man offered him. 'I've business to see to back in town. But don't worry, Guido will be here to keep an eye on you.'

Guido? Maggie felt faint. 'But...' she began, and then stopped. What was there left to say? He kissed her cheek, the kiss as chaste as one given by an ageing uncle to a favourite niece. 'Good luck, my little one,' he said. 'Ring me if you need to.'

At least he didn't say goodbye, but Max Jordan turned and was gone. Maggie felt terribly alone, but immediately the man handcuffed her hands behind her back, and before she could protest he dragged her across the stage and added her to the line of girls waiting to be led to the block. At the head of the queue were two tall blonde women, dressed in black studded leather bra and shorts, and who led each lot out onto the stage to the auction proper. As the curtain rose and fell Maggie caught a glimpse of the buyers standing in the main hall.

As an Asian girl made her way up onto the block, Maggie caught sight of Mike and Kay standing amongst the onlookers, and behind them Simon Faraday, programme in hand.

Slowly, inexorably, the queue of lots shuffled forward, the air heavy with perfume. Maggie's stomach began to churn and she wished for the all the world there was somewhere to hide, somewhere to run to. Simon, she knew, was just as dogged as Max but without his worldly sophistication might play dirtier. And what about Guido? Although Max had said he was merely there to keep an eye on her, hadn't he said he might try and buy her too? The first slave in a new master's stable. Guido hadn't any of Max's surety and was cruel by contrast.

After what seemed like an eternity the two leather-clad women took charge of Maggie. She could feel her heart beating in her chest and felt sick and faint as the curtains parted. She could see Mike looking her up and down and studying the catalogue, and momentarily she caught Simon's eye. He grinned with all the warmth of a basking shark.

'Lot twenty-five,' announced the auctioneer. 'Slave Maggie trained by Max Jordan. Good breasts.' One of the women cupped her soft tits in her hands and tweaked the nipple erect while her twin sucked the other, Maggie blushing furiously. 'Good and tight...' he reported, and one of the women slipped a leather-clad finger deep into her sex, Maggie gasping as the woman's thumb brushed her clitoris. 'Very responsive,' the auctioneer continued. 'Who wouldn't be delighted to find a nice little bitch like this tied to the end of their bed every morning?' There was ripple of laugher as the man picked up his gavel 'Turn around,' he said to Maggie, indicating the required movement with his hand.

Blushing furiously she turned slowly under the watchful gaze of countless pairs of eyes, and when her back was to them the auctioneer said, 'Bend over and hold the frame.' She did as she was told, at which point one of the leather-clad women spread her legs and pulled apart her buttocks to reveal both her sex and the tight puckering of her anus. The woman then slipped a finger back into her sex to murmurs of approval from the audience.

'And so, what am I bid for lot twenty-five?' asked the auctioneer, tapping his gavel on the desk. 'Who will start the bidding? You sir?'

Maggie, glancing back over her shoulder, saw Simon raise a hand and heard him make an opening bid. Slowly she closed her eyes, praying for a miracle.

Max picked up his mobile to take the call.

'She's just gone up onto the block,' Guido reported.

'Good,' said Max, and glanced out of the window at the rolling countryside. 'It shouldn't be long now then. I take it there's much interest in her.'

'Like bees round a honeypot,' the disembodied voice confirmed. 'I'll ring you when the sale is over, shall I, sir?'

'Yes, fine,' Max said thoughtfully, and then before he could hang up he added, 'just wait a minute, Guido.'

Up on the block Maggie tried hard to blank out the stream of rising numbers, tried hard to blank out the sounds of the voices calling their bids. It was all too much. She felt dizzy and sick, the room was hot and noisy, the bidders, although not boisterous or crude, where hungry and excited. From the corner of her eye she could see Guido watching her with avid interest.

Meanwhile the last man left bidding against Simon pulled out. 'So, going once... going twice...' called the auctioneer, lifting the gavel. Maggie froze... and then above the murmur of the onlookers she heard Guido add another two hundred pounds to the previous bid.

Maggie relaxed a little, but still had mixed feelings; a relief that at least Simon Faraday had some competition, but anxiety too. Did she want to be owned by Max's driver? Would he be any better than Faraday? Surely he wouldn't really buy her? She had no idea what he did when not in Max's service, but could he afford her? What would her life be like with Guido?

Simon upped the price again, a glint in his eyes and determination giving his voice a real edge.

Guido added another two hundred, at which point Simon looked round in total disgust. A hush fell in the room as the onlookers began to realise that there was a real battle of wills going on.

'The bid is against you, sir,' the auctioneer said to Simon.

'I know that,' Simon snapped angrily, and added another two hundred.

The auctioneer raised his eyebrows at Guido, inviting another bid, and Guido nodded and added two hundred more, and this time Simon threw up his hands in disappointment.

'No slave is worth that,' he growled, and turning his back on the stage stalked furiously out of the auction room.

Maggie didn't know whether to laugh of cry. Had Guido really bought her? The price was ridiculous. One of the ushers helped her down from the stage and then led her away to a backroom to await collection. A few minutes later Guido walked in, then passed a docket to the man keeping watch over the newly bought lots.

'You had better be worth the money, that's all I can say,' grumbled Guido, snapping the lead taut and taking her back out into the entrance hall.

'Where are we going?' asked Maggie, anxiously hurrying along behind him as he led her through the old house. Her mind was racing.

Guido looked back over his shoulder and snapped the leash tight 'Quiet!' he ordered. 'You know the rules.'

Maggie shuddered; hadn't Max told her that her mouth would get her into trouble? But there was still something she needed to know, however much it cost her.

'Are you my new master?' she dared to ask.

Guido swung round and pulled her too him, kissing her hard as he cupped her sex. Maggie closed her eyes, submitting totally to his touch. After all, what was the point in resisting, wasn't this exactly what Max had prepared her for, and surely better to be owned by Guido than Simon?

Guido pulled back and smiled at her, almost as if he could sense her finally conceding the fight and giving in. Maggie realised just how much she was going to miss Max. Had Guido finished his training now, too? And if he hadn't and continued to work for Max... she tried to imagine being owned by the servant of the man who trained her. Although at the very least she would perhaps see Max, it would be sweet torture to be with Guido and to watch her true master training another slave.

'Where to now?' she asked, unable to keep the sense of resignation out of her voice.

'Home, slave.'

'Home?' Maggie asked in surprise. 'What do you mean, home?'

'Your new master is waiting for you.'

Maggie frowned. 'But I don't understand,' she said, puzzled. 'What do you mean, my new master? I thought you'd bought me.'

Guido snorted. 'For that price?' he scoffed. 'Don't flatter yourself, Maggie. I'd want half a dozen slaves for what he's just paid.'

'Who then?' she pressed desperately. 'I don't understand.'

Guido pulled open the front door, and there outside on the gravel drive was a familiar car. Maggie felt her heart tighten in her chest, for Max Jordan was at the wheel, the passenger door open, and in his hand he held her collar. Maggie's eyes filled with tears of relief and joy. It seemed she had found her true master after all.

Maggie lay back on the couch staring up at the ceiling. She was naked, with her arms up behind her head, her legs spread wide.

Max smiled down at her. 'I want you marked as mine forever, Maggie,' he said. 'You understand that, don't you?'

She nodded; there was nothing she wanted more, however afraid she was. She bit her lip, only too aware of the balding man working quietly beside the couch preparing his equipment. He looked at Max, who nodded, and with that the man clamped one nipple tight and pulled.

The sensation of the needle passing through the base of the teat took Maggie's breath way and made her cry out in shock and pain, and seconds later he pressed the ring home which made her gasp and then swallow down another cry.

The ring felt cold and alien in her flesh.

'All right?' asked the man, and Maggie nodded bravely, although she wasn't sure whether he was talking to her or to Max. She looked up at her master and saw the delight in his eyes at the sight of the first nipple ring in place. The rings he'd chosen for her were the twins of those worn by his housekeeper, Mrs Griffin, ornate silver hoops around which was a stylised version of his initials. His first slave and his last both marked in the same way, that was what Max had told her the night before as he handed her the tiny jewellery box as a present to mark their first anniversary.

Maggie smiled, unsure that she would be his last slave, it seemed unlikely, his hunger for female flesh was legendary. But even so she was deeply touched, and more than that, the rings marked her as his.

Above her the man clamped and then pulled the second nipple taut, Maggie closed her eyes and this time, knowing what to expect, let the pain pass through her along with the needle and the jewellery. But what was to follow next was the piercing she was really afraid of.

243

Max took hold of her hand. 'I love you, you know that don't you, little one?' he said. Maggie nodded; through all he had done to her and the men and women he had given her to, she still knew it was true. Max loved in a unique and terrifying way.

Between her legs the man clamped the lips of her quim apart and taped them back so that she was totally exposed. With a gloved hand he sterilised the area, clamped and then pulled the hood of her clit. Maggie swallowed hard, trying not to panic, trying not to cry out, and then there was searing pain as the needle passed through the delicate flesh. Maggie grimaced and writhed, desperately clutching Max's hand.

'All done,' said the man, placing the equipment back on the bench.

Maggie opened her eyes and took the mirror the man offered her. She looked amazing; the rings in her nipples looked wonderful, the one in her clitoral hood sensational. Max smiled, and as if he could read her mind, told her, 'It looks magnificent, slave.'